OLYMPUS

D1714505

OLYMPUS

K A WILLIAMS

ISBN: 978-0-578-57699-2 (Softcover)

First Edition

Any references to historical events, real people, or real places are used fictitiously. Names, characters, and places are products of the author's imagination.

Front cover images by Kristen Williams.

Book design by Kristen Williams.

Printed by IngramSpark™

kawilliams.sales@gmail.com

k-a-williams.com

For my parents.

You convinced me
that I could be anyone
and I could do anything.

I love you.

ALSO BY K.A. WILLIAMS

Firebird

1

POISON

"Be discreet," they told us.

It's the opposite of what we did. And in many ways, that's all that saved us. There was fire, but when the devil comes knocking, there usually is. Of the destruction, we were directly responsible for the smallest part.

Of course, we were blamed for it all.

I stood in the long grass, under a purple sky, and watched Phobos rise. It was a small moon, but that wasn't strange to me. The grass was yellow, it was healthy, and that's what I'd come to expect. Things that were green were things that were dying, and that's just how the world worked.

This world, at any rate. My world now, I suppose.

You can see Earth from Mars, but I never have. I didn't want to see it. Something deep inside of me squirmed at the very thought of home. *Home.* This was my home now. It had to be.

Because on Earth, I'm one of the most wanted women in the world.

I drew a deep breath, putting the ship to my back and starting up a gentle rise. My mind wandered back to the Pigeon, to the message it had carried before it self-destructed. I thought of the look on Firebird's face when it finally arrived.

Fear turned deep within me, cold and hungry. This mission was different. *We* were different. There had been a shift, the difference between working for money and working toward a goal.

As I crested the hill, I closed my eyes. I could feel the grass as it swayed gently with a Martian breeze. It tickled the tips of my fingers. It wasn't a hot day, and that was blessing enough. The summer humidity had been slowly cooking us in our own bodies. I was almost fully Adapted to the Martian air, so it didn't bother my lungs the way it used to, but that somehow made it worse.

I didn't miss Earth. It had never truly been a home, more a house that I was on the verge of selling. And I don't miss *her*, the woman who brought me into that world.

But in the quiet places, when my mind had time to wander, I heard again the gun's *crack* and I saw the *red* as it blossomed from her chest. I saw the surprise in her unnatural blue eyes, and the way her dark face paled under the unforgiving light.

A year ago I watched my mother die, and the part of me that was grateful squirmed like a creature in pain.

I opened my eyes. Unlike Earth, Mars was fresh. Humans hadn't evolved here, hadn't spent thousands of years plundering the soil. On Earth, the only trees were in the designated O2 centers, and those tortured plants existed solely for a purpose. You couldn't walk between them, nor sit in their branches and watch the sunset. On Earth, a thing's usefulness defined its existence.

But here, on Mars, there were wild places, fresh and new as a baby just born.

The breeze picked up, stirring my unruly halo of black hair. Ori kept asking to cut it, but after watching her shave her own head, my original *no* proved well founded. Besides, I was growing fond of my mane. It encompassed my newfound freedom.

Shading my eyes against the afternoon sun, I scanned the savanna. The stalks of yellow grass had spiny heads, but the softer foliage near the ground was dark blue. There were short, strangely flat trees dotting the rolling hills, reminding me more of Earth than any other Martian biome. The air was thick with the sound of insects and the deep, subtle *hum* from our home and salvation, the spaceship *Redwing.*

Finally, I spotted her. Or, rather, I spotted the top of her wide-brimmed hat. She sat in the grass on the next rise, her back to me. I glanced over my shoulder, marking *Redwing*'s position. The last thing I needed was to get lost in the Martian long grass. You wouldn't think that I could misplace a spaceship, but I didn't want to meet the creature that would eat me out here if I did.

I started down the hill. Vegetation snatched at my clothes, and I gave wide berth to anything that looked a shade too dark. Dr. Ravin had pointed out what she called a *Venus Briar*, but Ori said it was *Devil's Snatch* and that it could shoot thorns a few centimeters into my leg. Dr. Ravin hadn't disagreed with her.

We'd been here for two weeks, waiting for our client to contact us. I could feel the restlessness in the ship, and it was only a matter of time before Ori started stabbing people. She'd already shaved her own head, after all—the rest of us couldn't be far behind.

I considered calling out, but something in Laurensen's posture made me hesitate. If I knew her at all, she'd known the instant I stepped off of *Redwing*. Besides, after the constant close quarters and chaos of the ship, being in the open air—hearing my own breath, rather than those around me—was a blessing too sweet.

As I reached her, she raised a gloved hand. Not in greeting, but in warning, the closed fist of a command. I froze mid-step, every cell in my body electrifying. I remembered the first time I'd ignored a similar gesture from her. I'd almost been eaten by a spider the size of a dinner table.

Slowly, her fingers beckoned me forward, but I got the message. Move slowly. Keep quiet. Preferably don't bother her at all.

But I had a mission. So, I crept forward, mindful of where I placed my boots, hyper-aware of how the grass dragged against my pants, like fingers grazing over paper. My eyes darted across the savanna, searching.

I came alongside Laurensen and dropped into a crouch. She sat cross-legged, her rifle—*Widow, powder-based*—across her lap. Her elbows rested on the weapon and she was leaning slightly forward, her mismatched green and blue eyes fixed straight ahead. She wore a bandana around her neck—one she was prone to pulling over the lower half of her face. Her leather duster laid by her side, and her tan shirt was soaked in sweat.

In front of us, there was a lake. Reflecting the purple sky, it was encrusted by bright blue, fleshy plants that grew in the churned, red mud. It wasn't a particularly large body of water, but it was more than enough to sustain the small herd of—I'd guess hippopotamuses—that currently wallowed along the western shore.

They were roughly the same size as their Earth cousins, but darker and with bigger ears. Much bigger. I cocked my head, grinning. Their ears were probably a meter long, and framed their faces like a basset hound's. When one turned to look at me, their width doubled, revealing white hairs that trembled. The creature snorted, and a fine mist erupted from round nostrils.

"He's so—" I started.

Laurensen's hand flashed toward my face and I flinched back, biting my tongue. As she lowered her hand, she pointed with two fingers at something in front of her. I squinted into the sun, scanning the lake. I saw the hippos, but I didn't feel like they were an immediate threat. They looked so bulky, a part of me refused to believe that they could manage to charge that distance in anything less than a minute.

I glanced at Laurensen, searching her gaze more closely. A small part of me gave a tremulous flutter when I saw that her pupils had widened, nearly obscuring her mismatched irises.

Rawn Laurensen was a Bestial BioMage, a fact that I had stumbled across a year ago when she saved me from being trampled to death by a herd of migrating Nightmares. Like all BioMages, her pupils dilated when she focused her Will, her *magic*. I looked again at the lake. The hippo that had been watching me shook its bulky head and returned to the water, blowing bubbles.

That was when I heard it, a rumble so low, I could feel it in my chest. I frowned, searching the grass between us and the lake. Something shifted. I blinked, my eyes refocusing.

"Oh," I involuntarily said, my blood chilling.

The *lion* was halfway between Laurensen and the lake, maybe five meters. He was crouched low in the grass, glassy eyes fixed to her. The low rumble came again, his lips peeling back. Though much smaller than Earth-born lions, his canines were as long as my hand, thin and sharp. His mane seemed to shift color with the grass beneath him, changing from blue to yellow as he stalked closer. I could see the muscles under his skin shifting. Like most Martian creatures, instead of fur, his skin was thick and rubbery. The mane reminded me of a Nightmare's, and the tips of it flexed like the grass he moved beneath.

"Laurensen," I breathed, one of my hands straying to the knife at my belt.

I don't know why I bothered saying anything. The most I'd achieve would be breaking her focus, in which case the beast would likely eat us both. But there are moments in your life where you simply have to say something and being stalked by a Martian lion—well, I guess that's one of them.

She kept her hand out to him. The lion prowled closer, his shoulder blades sliding back and forth, sharp points on his back. I could feel my heart crawling up into my throat. He was close enough for me to see that his pupils were slits like a cat's, instead of Earth-born lion's pupils. They widened and contracted as he moved his head, his focus shifting from Laurensen to me.

Silence gathered around us, collecting between the blades of grass. The air stilled, the sun sank, and the hippos faded from my mind. Slowly, I turned my gaze to Laurensen. Her pupils pulsed, contracting and expanding. It was like I could see the animal's thoughts in her eyes, the changing temperament. Then they suddenly flexed and nearly her entire iris went black.

The lion pounced.

I'm not proud of it, but if I hadn't just peed a few minutes before, I would have wet myself right then. I jerked back as the creature landed in front of Laurensen, rising up to his full height. I saw his long, black claws flexing, their needle-like tips sinking into the ground. His fangs, too thin for their length, gleamed. They were coated with something shinier than saliva. He drew a deep breath, his chest expanding, and pressed his wide nose into Laurensen's waiting palm.

I realized my mouth was hanging open, and I closed it slowly. There was a pause. Then, both Laurensen and the lion sighed.

Her pupils contracted back to their normal size, once again revealing the green and blue irises. And the lion's dilated as he gently snuffled her hand, then her arm. At last, he put his nose against her ear and snorted, hard enough to knock her hat askew.

Laurensen chuckled and the lion took a step back, sparing me a dismissive glance. I swallowed, my tensed muscles relaxing. The lion rubbed his face along Laurensen's shoulder, and she ran her hand down his side to a place behind his right foreleg. She began to scratch, and he flopped to the ground, sending a flock of dry seeds to swirl into the air.

"Is this what you do," I asked, watching as the lion rolled onto his back, letting Laurensen scratch his chest and belly, "when you're bored?"

The sniper was smiling, and that in itself was an oddity. She glanced at me and shrugged.

"Ori has knives," she said, leaning forward so that she could use both hands. "I have lions."

The lion in question was squirming on his back, his face sagging into what looked like a smile as gravity pulled his lips back. I watched as the long fangs retracted into his gums, not unlike a house cat's claws. I cocked my head.

"He's smaller than what I would have expected," I said.

"Martian lions are venomous," Laurensen said, running her hands down his sides. "They sacrifice size for potency."

"Venomous?" I repeated, watching as the beast began to kick with its back legs, catching Laurensen's arm several times. "Just their teeth?"

"Claws too. Martian-born lions lick their claws to coat them with the saliva. They have venom sacks just here," she worked her way up to the base of his jaw, and began to massage him.

"Cute," I sighed, pushing my hair back from my face.

Laurensen's smile slowly faded. The lion's ears perked toward the lake, then he rolled onto his stomach, his back arching as he raised his head and drew short breaths, testing the air. His tail was long and slender, and tipped with barbs. I assumed that they were venomous as well, and eased back.

"How does it work?" I asked, watching him pant. "Being a Bestial BioMage? Do you tell him what to do? Can you give him commands?"

Laurensen snorted, grazing me with the same dismissive glance that the lion had.

"You can't *command* anything."

"Then what?"

She quirked her mouth like she needed to spit, her hands going to the gun in her lap. She picked up an oiled cloth from her side and began to polish the weapon with the air of someone resuming a project.

"If you can't understand it, I can't explain it."

"That's not how teaching works," I grumbled.

I saw the corner of her mouth twitch, but that was the closest thing to an answer I was going to get. I looked again at the hippos. A younger one was prancing through the water, sending great geysers out with every bounce. His ears were ridiculously big, and when he shook his head, they pummeled him.

"Do these lions move in packs?" I asked, considering attempting to scratch him.

"Prides. And yes, they do," she said, turning the rifle and squinting down the sights toward the setting sun. It bathed her tanned face, making her glow while the gun drank in the light, like the blackness of outer space.

"Are there many around us right now?" I asked.

"What if there are?"

"Would you know?"

"Would you?"

I scowled at her.

"No, I wouldn't. I'm not a Bestial BioMage, *Rawn.*"

I'd noticed that our crew was very particular about their names. In the first article I'd written about Harry I'd called her "Harriot", and she hadn't talked to me for a week. But Laurensen merely snorted and checked her rifle's chamber.

"Well, if we don't both get eaten before I can get you back to *Redwing*," I grumbled, "then Firebird wants us. The Pigeon finally came. We've got our mission."

If I hadn't spent the last year studying Laurensen and the rest of our crew, I wouldn't have noticed the slight tensing of her shoulders, nor the way her pupils contracted. I wouldn't have seen her hands shift on the rifle.

"What is it?" I asked, though I could already make a good guess.

Laurensen looked away, and I followed her gaze. Something behind my heart tightened.

"Doesn't have a good feel to it, is all," she murmured.

Far to the north, we could make out the hazy outline of a mountain.

2

REDWING

When we terraformed Mars, we destroyed Earth. That's what they like to tell us, anyway. The truth is, Earth was already destroyed. Mars just gave us an alternative.

The three Martian Overlords rose to power in the decades that followed colonization. Humanity fled from the dying Earth in droves, the promise of open sky and fresh air proving temptation enough. Of course, Unified Earth had attempted to control Martians. Of course, as history is so prone to telling us, it didn't work.

Long distance relationships so very rarely do.

* * *

"Where is Eerie?" I asked Laurensen as we approached the ship.

She had her rifle propped over her shoulder and her hat brim was pulled low, even though the setting sun was at our backs. She shrugged, shrinking deeper into her leather duster.

"He comes and goes, on the savanna."

I glanced at the sky. Eerie and I had made our peace, but there was an instinct deeper than trust when it came to creatures who live in the sky. Particularly when they're the size of horses and bear the unstable temperament of a vengeful god.

My concern for Eerie shifted to the back of my mind as Laurensen hopped onto *Redwing's* ramp, her duster swirling. The assassin was right—there *was* something strange about this mission. The amount of credits, the anonymity of our client, the continued secrecy: if we weren't in such dire need for funds, I doubted Firebird would have accepted the contract at all.

Redwing was a beautiful ship. The rust-colored wings angled gracefully down to the ground, resting low and humming with the perfect engines that bespoke Brute's fine touch. It was graceful without being delicate, large without being bulky. It had the inky black cockpit of a Unity vessel—Earth Tech boasted unbreakable glass—with the slightly glossy sides of Martian Tech. Brute said that the shine was from *Diamond*, a network of hair-thin shields capable of collecting and distributing kinetic energy. Ori had said that she wanted some for her lip balm.

As I pushed my way through the airlock, I felt the familiar tightening around my lungs. I'd learned to close my eyes, but that did little to help the uncomfortable warmth from the strange membrane of...I suppose I could call it *air*, but that might bring to mind invisible, life-giving gas. The Martian Tech airlock was like semi-solid darkness that squeezed every cell of my body and made my heartrate spike. I couldn't breathe in it—air*lock*—and if I tried, it was like a vacuum spawned in my lungs.

I'd like to say that I'd mastered the airlocks over the past year, but that wouldn't be a truth. The fact is, airlocks are just another Martian oddity that you *never* really get used to.

The discomfort passed and I opened my eyes, drawing a relieved breath as the reddish hallway of *Redwing*'s entry greeted me.

Instantly, I was doubled over, coughing and gagging. My eyes began to water, and it took every bit of my self-control not to vomit on my own feet.

If I said it was garlicky, you might think back to the last time you made spaghetti and dismiss my reaction. No, this was no mere *garlic* smell. The toxic stench infiltrated my very pores, like a thousand burrowing ants. It clawed at my throat and seared my eyeballs. I straightened, pressing my satchel to my face and trying to suck air through the coarse burlap. Laurensen's mouth was a flat line, her expression something in between murder and disgust.

"What," I gasped, resting my hands on my knees, "*is* that?"

She didn't bother answering. We stepped hesitantly forward, following a sudden peal of manic laughter toward the back of the ship. The hallway was plenty tall enough for us to walk upright, but I maintained a semi-crouch, seeking the fresher air near the floor.

Redwing had three more personal rooms than she did crew, and each occupied door was locked fast—an oddity, but not when I factored in the stench. The little red lights blinked along the doors as we passed them. There was another blast of laughter— it was coming from the kitchen, I realized— followed by a sharp curse and the unmistakable sound of someone being struck with a frying pan.

Laurensen stepped boldly through the door to the kitchen, something like vengeance in her stride, but I peeked around with more trepidation. I'd come to recognize Ori's many laughs, and this one bordered on the crazy that usually led to gunfire. I blinked, squinting into the haze of noxious gas.

The first thing that I saw—the first thing that any sane person would see—was Regina. The big woman wielded a frying pan in an overhead arc, not unlike how someone might swing an axe, and brought it down an inch from Ori's hand. Ori, quick as a snake, twisted sideways and jabbed at Regina with a spatula, catching the larger woman in the right breast.

There is a moment in any battle where you can *feel* the change in the air, the sudden freeze of energy before a charge. It's the moment when the soldiers fully accept that they're about to kill someone, that there's no going back, that they *need* to kill.

If I had to describe the atmosphere in the kitchen at that moment, that seems apropos.

Regina snarled something and flung her frying pan to the side—narrowly missing Laurensen—and hurled herself at Ori.

There were never two more physically different women. Regina was tall and thick-bodied, with white-blonde hair and the palest complexion I'd ever seen. Her biceps were the same circumference as my thighs, and her stocky legs and short neck made her look like she was all arms.

Ori, on the other hand, was whip-thin and as black as the dark side of Phobos. She had a wide grin that flashed like lightning, and it seemed even brighter now that she'd shaved her head. Although also tall, most of her height came from her legs, and I'd seen her trip over nearly every part of the ship. But when she ran, she was like a bolting deer. And when she fought, she brought to mind a viper.

Regina managed one punch to Ori's ribs, but that was all she landed before the serpentine woman had her legs tangled around her and they both went flying to the floor. Laurensen watched with the detached interest of a woman who had placed a small bet on the outcome, one hand resting on the rifle over her shoulder.

As Ori and Regina brawled on the floor of our destroyed kitchen, I finally spotted the source of the garlic-fume. We had a small stove with a single, black-glass burner. And, currently sending up clouds of black smoke, there was a melting bottle of *Easy Herb*. My stomach turned as I saw the milky substance bubble from within— reminding me of nothing so much as puss— oozing and blackening on the burner.

The thing about *Easy Herb* is that it's designed for space travel, so the company condenses their spices and pumps them into the smallest possible container. The garlic currently terrorizing *Redwing* was the next best thing to tear gas.

There was a high, mechanical giggle from farther around the corner. I edged cautiously into the kitchen, spotting Brute hovering toward the back. She saw me and clapped her hands, whirring along the wall to my side.

Brute was our engineer. Sometimes, she moonlighted as a mad scientist, but on a ship like this one, no one could really blame her. She was a tiny woman with long, black pigtails that coiled in her lap. She sat on fat, red velvet pillows within the safety of a glowing, robotic orb that she had lovingly dubbed Jiggy. Her delicate fingers rested over twin holograms near her knees.

Brute was Earth-born, the daughter of a wealthy of-then Japanese family. To hear her tell it, her parents chafed under the steep taxes Unity placed on their wealthier citizens and so when she was old enough, they decided to make the voyage to Mars. Sometimes, she talked about the cherry trees, and how she remembered their petals dancing on clear water. It was the only story I could get from her about her family.

Like all Earthlings, Brute had needed to be Adapted to live on Mars. Her parents, so far as I knew, had taken to it easily enough. Brute, however, should have died.

Sometimes, Adaptation doesn't work. Sometimes, it simply kills Earthlings, as surely as poison in their veins. I'd asked Dr. Ravin about it, but the leading scientist in Martian Adaptation and Evolution didn't have any more of an idea than the rest of us. Sometimes, people just die.

And if her family hadn't been so wealthy, Brute would have. Instead, they hired an engineer to design some sort of facility to maintain Brute. She'd been constrained to living in a single room, unable to take so much as a step outdoors.

At least, that was what she'd told me during our interview. She said that was why she had become an engineer, why she had designed Jiggy. And when I asked her if her parents had been proud, the telltale lights around Jiggy's circumference had gone as dark a red as I'd ever seen.

I learned after that, we didn't ask Brute about home.

Now, my friend bumped into me in her customary greeting. Jiggy was what I liked to think of as an oversized volleyball hovercraft. Brute gave me a wide grin from within, and I smiled despite the stench and the mess and the brawling warriors at our feet.

"I see you found her!" Brute said, nudging toward Laurensen. "You missed a lot, though!"

Something about the way Brute talked made it seem like every sentence ended with an exclamation point.

"I can see that," I said, still breathing through my satchel. "How can you stand the smell?"

She winked conspiratorially at me, tapping at the black glass dome around the top half of Jiggy.

"Finest air filtration system in the known Worlds," she boasted, the lights around the center of Jiggy glowing a rich yellow—a color I'd come to associate with pride. "They could set off a gas bomb and I wouldn't know! Well, minus air quality results," she added, squinting at a little screen toward her left knee. "Jiggy lets me know everything about the world around us."

I smiled at her, though my eyes were watering.

"Don't suppose you have something like that for me?"

She grinned.

"Of course I do! We could use the masks I designed for space walks. Naturally, they are a self-contained oxygen reserve. Or we could use the filtration suits that I designed for harsh atmospheres—like the inside of active volcanoes or the marshes to the south. You know, the ones we used on our last assignment!"

Brute trailed off, her dark gaze shifting to something behind me. I turned to find Harry standing in the doorway, an expression of supreme disgust on her tanned face. She looked from the brawling couple to me, her hazel eyes sharpening accusatorially.

"I suppose that I should have let them know about the Pigeon before I went to find Laurensen," I said, my voice muffled through my satchel.

Our pilot was a middle-aged woman of average height with dirty-blonde hair that she kept in a low ponytail. She wore baggy pants belted high at her waist and a button-down shirt with the sleeves ripped off. She wasn't as athletic as Ori, but she kept a trim figure and the muscles in her arms rolled under the tattoo of a phoenix on her right bicep.

Maintaining eye contact with me, Harry slapped a small, red data pad next to the kitchen's entryway. Instantly, the lights in the room turned magenta and a warning siren blasted through the ship. Brute squawked indignantly, but she wasn't fast enough to escape through the door.

Being a spaceship, *Redwing* was equipped with innumerable safety devices. One of them, in the instance of a fire, was set to jettison the air in a room into outer space while simultaneously dropping a sheet of white fire-suppressant foam from several nozzles in the ceiling.

In seconds, the room was covered, the white substance turning pink in the magenta lighting. A small splatter had found its way onto Harry's face, and it somehow made her look even more intimidating. She continued to glower at me as I slowly lowered my satchel—I imagined it was the only part of my face that was clean. I felt a dollop of the gunk roll down my back from the top of my head.

Harry dropped her hand from the panel and the lighting returned to normal. Ori and Regina slipped in the foam as they clambered to their feet, Ori with her front covered, and Regina with her back. Laurensen, on the other hand, sniffed, her hat having protected her face from the gunk. She looked at her freshly cleaned rifle, then seemed to consider levelling it at Harry. The stove—automatically shut down—hissed fitfully with the residual heat, small bubbles finding their way up through the coating of suppressant.

"What," Harry said, deadpan, "in the rusting hell."

"Look at the mess you made," Ori said, shaking her arms and sending a shower of suppressant across the room. She blinked at us, her dark eyes wide in the mask of white. When she grinned, she looked like a maniac.

Harry stared at her, her jaw muscles working. Then, she said:

"Meeting, in the cockpit."

The pilot took one last glance around the room, then cocked a finger at me and turned away. Brute, now a ball of hovering goo, shouted something rude after her. There was a pulse of energy, then Jiggy shed the suppressant like some kind of fuzzy coat, the goo turning to liquid and dropping to the floor. It reminded me of the way Jiggy repelled rain. I gave her a hapless shrug before following Harry, slipping a little on the floor.

In the wake of the chaos, our footsteps seemed much too loud in the hallway. As I wiped gunk from my arms, the globs hit the floor and immediately turned to liquid. In fact, by the time I'd followed Harry to the cockpit, most of the suppressant had dissolved from me. I was soaked to the bone and I brushed fitfully at my satchel, hoping that the data pad within could withstand a thorough soaking.

Harry threw herself into her pilot's chair, still scowling at me. I returned the expression, intentionally ringing my hair out on her floor.

Because *Redwing*'s cockpit was entirely made from Earth Tech glass, it offered us an unobstructed view of the world surrounding the ship. Harry's chair had a multitude of levers and buttons on the arms, and it was a well-known fact that anyone who sat in it without her permission was poking at death.

"I don't see why *I* am the one you're mad at," I complained, finishing with my hair and beginning to ring my shirt out. "I'm not the one burning garlic and brawling in the kitchen."

"I *told* you to tell Ori and Regina. You know how they get." Harry drew a deep breath. "If they go a day without shooting someone, they're edgy. It's been two weeks."

"And all that Ori did was shave her head," I said, giving her an exasperated shrug. "I figured that they'd manage to contain themselves for another hour. I needed to get some fresh air."

"Yes, we *all* need that now."

"What's your problem?" I snapped, dropping to the floor, crossing my legs. "And why didn't you stop them earlier? You can't tell me that you didn't *smell* that."

Harry stared at me for a moment before she sighed, sinking back. There were dark circles under her eyes and despite two weeks of rest, she seemed exhausted. I felt a nagging pang of guilt.

"I had the door sealed. Trying to get some peace and quiet," she said, offering me half of a smile. "I'm sorry. I suppose we all need to blow off a little steam."

"Yeah, well, some of us could probably manage to do that without setting the ship on fire," I said, glancing accusatorily at the doorway as Regina and Ori ducked through.

"There was literally nothing on fire," Ori said, dropping down to sit next to me.

Regina grunted, crossing her massive arms and leaning against the other wall. Jiggy came whirring through the door a minute later, her lights a muddy shade of green. Brute glowered at Harry from within, coming to a halt next to Regina.

"Do you have any idea how much power it takes to clean and dry this place after something like that?" she asked. Then, without waiting for an answer, she finished, "We'll need to refuel before our next mission, thanks to you and, frankly, if we don't get another deposit soon, I don't think we can afford it."

"If we *ever* get to start our next mission." Ori grumbled, pulling a knife from the back of her belt and picking at her already nonexistent nails.

"That's what I was going to tell you," I mumbled, shooting a glance at Harry. "We got the Pigeon. It's being decrypted."

Ori shrugged.

"We've gotten three Pigeons so far," she said, flicking something off of the knife. "Each one is the same. *Stand by.*"

"But this one is *still* being decrypted," Harry said, pausing as Laurensen entered the cockpit.

The assassin seemed surprisingly calm, though when she sat on the edge of a console, she threw down a large black sack at her feet that reminded me uncomfortably of a body bag. Rifle across her lap, she leaned forward and unzipped the bag in one smooth motion. I peeked in to find a wide assortment of attachments for her gun. Scopes, clips, vacuum seals, and something that looked surprisingly like a bayonet—she sifted through them, eventually extracting a stiff-looking cloth. With methodical slowness, she began taking her rifle apart, drying it in silence.

"The ship's environmental system would take care of that," Brute mumbled, still sounding plenty peeved.

Laurensen snorted, turning the gun and squinting down the barrel. I wasn't surprised to find her incidentally aiming at Harry's head. The pilot scowled at her.

"Where's Ravin?" Regina eventually asked, more of a grunt than a question.

The little green intercom light next to Harry's elbow suddenly turned green, and the doctor's Russian accent filled the little room:

"*Dr.* Ravin. I'm in my office. And until the stench of your hooligan pastime is completely eradicated, that is where I shall remain."

"Why didn't I think of that?" Ori said, stabbing her knife back into her belt and beginning to rise.

"Because you're the reason we've got this mess," Regina said, putting her big hand on Ori's head and shoving her back down.

"*I'm* the reason?" the woman started to spin, and I expected she was going to take out Regina's knees, but mercifully that was when we heard the sound of someone opening one of the locked quarters.

As a unit, we stilled. The atmosphere of the room shifted, an invisible weight settling around us, and we listened to the footsteps come down the hallway. By the time she appeared in the doorway, we were solemn as the grave.

There are certain forces in the world that carry an indefinable pull. Most of them are forces of nature, knowledge that rests in our most hidden minds. But a select few reside in living matter, and their very presence is like a gravitational pull. They are irrefutable, leaders and monsters alike. They are a force unto themselves.

This one, we called Firebird.

3

ILENA

She wore her black hair short on one side and swept over to chin-length on the other, emphasizing a ragged scar along her right jawbone. Her skin was dark tan and marred by countless pockmarks. Her hawkish nose and wide eyes gave her a predatory look, as did the fluid, purposeful way she moved. It was like watching the muscle glide under a lion's skin, bones and flesh sliding into place.

She would have once been described as Native American, until the cultures of Earth had been bleached into a single entity. And while Unity had fallen, their legacy remained—a legacy that had more than changed people's minds. It had rewritten them.

I had never asked her, but even if Unity hadn't eradicated the societies on Earth, I couldn't see Firebird identifying with any culture. She was a woman unto herself, a power undefined, and it was all that I could do to meet her gaze.

She paused in the doorway, eyes sweeping the room. Her irises were dark and her pupils slightly too large, making me wonder if she was constantly flexing her Will.

However, unlike every other BioMage I'd met, she didn't press it against us.

For years, I'd identified as Mute— someone who could not be influenced by BioMages. I could still feel their Will, however. It was like a pressure against my third eye, something between discomfort and pain, and I felt it even when the BioMage wasn't actively trying to force her Will upon me.

Firebird maintained such strict control, I could barely tell she had power at all.

"Brute," she said, stepping into the room, her hands behind her back, "can the ship's systems do anything about the smell?"

I cringed. Although I had— somehow—gotten used to the stench, and the actual haze had been blown from the ship, we all still reeked of burned garlic. I turned, and I could smell it in my hair.

"I really don't know," Brute said, her joviality squelched. "She's trying, and," a data pad hologram whirled to life in front of her eyes, "she *is* using energy to do something, but I can't tell that it's getting better." Another flurry of motion with her fingers, and the data pads shifted. "Looks like it's about the same."

"Pity," Firebird said, glancing at Ori.

"Hey," she said, a knife appearing from up her sleeve. She used it to gesture at the cockpit as a whole, "We're all bored. If you think about it, this is one of the least offensive things I could have done."

"How could that *possibly* be true?" Regina snapped, rolling her eyes down to her companion. "All that I wanted was dinner."

"It's midday," Ori said in return, pointing at Regina with the knife. "If you're going to try to eat dinner for lunch, I don't understand why *I* am the problem."

Firebird sighed, staring flatly at her two best fighters for a moment more. Then, she turned to Brute, pulling something small and glowing from her pocket.

"The transmission is ready," she said, holding it out to her.

Jiggy's lights flared bright yellow.

"Oh, praise be!" she whirred to Firebird, the item in the commander's palm suddenly flying toward her with the gravitational field. "Just let me plug in."

The data chip looked different from what I'd become accustomed to. While Brute was an excellent engineer and a brilliant inventor, she wasn't always working with the best equipment. And so, much of what she created looked like something I'd find in a garage's dump.

Our client was different.

The data chip was roughly the size of my pen's cap. The soft glow it emanated was from the script scrolling around its edges, marking it as Martian Tech. There was a small red light toward one end.

"Looks like a tampon," Ori said, craning to see it as Brute returned to the center of the room.

Brute hesitated, staring at Ori with the expression of someone who knows what's about to happen. She sighed, and then inserted it into a small slot near Jiggy's base.

Ori burst out laughing—much too loudly for the confines of the room—and Regina rolled her eyes again. Laurensen glanced at the exchange before continuing to clean her rifle, heaving a heavy sigh.

"It's not that funny," Brute grumbled. "Alright, give me a second. This is a massive file."

"Maybe you're just too sensitive?" Ori offered, her white grin massive.

Firebird gave her a look, and she quieted.

"Did this one blow itself up like the rest?" Regina asked.

After being approached by a nameless operative and given instructions to go to a set of coordinates and await our client's contact, we had received three transactions. But each one had arrived in a Pigeon, a small robot similar to Jiggy, and after we removed the data chip, it had self-destructed. Ori had tried to skip the middle man and shoot it out of the sky herself a couple of days ago, but she'd been drunk and had mercifully missed.

"Indeed," Firebird said, watching as Jiggy's lights turned a murky brown. Brute was frowning at the holograms flying across her glass.

"Strangest quest I've ever been on," Ori muttered, stabbing the tip of her knife into the sole of her boot.

"Our client values discretion," I said, instantly regretting it as Ori turned to me.

"Our *client*," she mocked in a surprisingly good impersonation of my Unity accent, "is either a bloody coward or a real bastard. Who else would pay us five-thousand credits up front?"

"With a promise of fifty more," Regina added.

"I still have the sneaky suspicion that the *client*," Ori gave me another look, "is just trying to keep us out of the way for a couple of weeks. I mean, why else would we be in the middle of rusting nowhere?"

"Sneaking," I corrected.

"What?"

"Sneak*ing* suspicion."

"You have one too?" Ori arched a brow and I sighed.

"Alright," Brute cut in. "Here we go."

The cockpit dimmed. Lights around Jiggy's circumference made her glow in the darkened room, Brute's small face tinted brown. Her thin fingers flew across a series of commands, and then tendrils of blue light fountained from the bottom of Jiggy toward the floor. They touched the black glass, then curved upwards, making a blue dome around the robot.

"Oh," Brute said, and the tendrils in front of her twisted, forming a trapezoid. "The orders are in text. Right. Oh," and this time, the word was drawn out and left to hang in the air.

"What is it?" Harry asked, frowning at the trapezoid.

The hologram lurched forward, zooming in on the shape, and I made a small, involuntary sound. There were tiny lights rotating around the trapezoid, twisting in and out of its edges. They looked like flies. But then, the hologram gained detail as it magnified. Soon, the image filled most of the room, enfolding Brute within its girth, and I realized that the flies circling the shape were *ships*. And not just any ships, either.

"Are those *transport* vessels?" Harry asked, leaning forward, her nose an inch from one of the little lights.

"Some of them," Firebird murmured, walking slowly around the image, her hands still clasped behind her back. "I see cargo ships, too."

"Rusting hells," Regina muttered, her pale face glowing. "Do you see those," and she jabbed a finger at the side of the trapezoid.

There were a few hundred lumps on the outer sides of the shape. Each had a small, red light blinking on its top, and they seemed to be swiveling, following the little ships as they came and went from the sides of the shape.

"Are those weapon stations?" Ori asked, sounding unpleasantly cheerful.

"Laser bases," Brute corrected, completely obscured by the hologram. "Defensive. They could easily bring down an entire fleet."

"Bloody hells," Harry breathed. "Do you *know* what this is?"

"The fuel station *Ilena*," Brute said, sounding like she was reading a script. "This footage was taken yesterday, and is as accurate as possible."

"Is that like a space station?" I asked, squinting at the tiny ships moving around it. I wasn't an expert, but I knew that both transport and carrier vessels were massive. Probably ten times the size of *Redwing*. And they looked like *flies* in comparison to the *Ilena*.

"Same idea," Harry murmured, leaning forward and resting her elbows on her knees. "But legally, there is only one Martian Space Station. It's neutral ground for the three Overlords. They built it on Phobos." She paused. "It's almost as big as the *Ilena*."

"I don't understand," I said slowly.

"Space Stations mean power," Firebird said, still pacing the circumference of the hologram. "Incoming ships go through their customs. No one passes from Earth to Mars without going through the Space

Station. Not legally. So, any one Overlord can't control it. *Fuel* stations have no such restrictions. And the *Ilena* is the largest Martian fuel station."

"So, while all ships have to pass through the Space Station," Harry continued, "most of them then have to pass through the *Ilena,* too. She has the largest fuel reserve of any space craft."

"Rocket fuel," Ori corrected, sounding pleased with herself.

I was no scientist, but I understood the manufacturing process for rocket fuel took years. Something about breaking down hydrogen molecules. And I wasn't sure, but I thought the water reserves on Phobos were the first real source of fuel for Earth-Mars transit. That was before we learned how to terraform Mars itself, of course.

"Someone has been stockpiling fuel for years, then?" I asked.

"Decades," Harry said.

"And unlike the Space Station," Firebird gestured at the hologram, "fuel stations can be privately owned. The *Ilena* belongs to Overlord Andronicus."

"Hence why we're here," Ori said, pursing her lips and waggling her finger in the air, her Martian accent shifting to something pompous. I'd come to recognize it as her *wealthy bastard* imitation. "Sticking it to the rapscallion!"

Regina swore under her breath.

"This is what we've been waiting for," Firebird murmured. "This is what we were made for. Finally, an assignment that furthers our cause. Brute?"

"Our mission," Brute nodded. There was a pause, and then she began to read:

"*The* Ilena *is a fortress designed to overpower large forces. This is her weakness. A small unit, moving quickly, could slip through her defensive net and infiltrate the base. Your mission is simple. Infiltrate the* Ilena, *extract data, and exit without being detected.*

"*I require the files for fuel consumption from the years 2999-3001 as well as the molecular formula that was adapted during those years. You will upload the data onto a supplied data chip, then bring it to the original contact point. An associate will be waiting to receive, as well as forward the remaining 50,000 credits to an account of your choice. Be prompt. Be discreet.*"

Brute stopped, and we watched the ship slowly turn in the center of Harry's cockpit. Eventually, she finished:

"Then it just repeats the message."

"Not too heavy with the intel, are they?" Regina grunted.

"Well, actually," Brute did something, and the hologram abruptly magnified, taking us so close to one of its laser depots, we could see in the little window to where the operative was maintaining the console. "It's *extremely* detailed. From the size of the file, I'd assume that this hologram will play in an endless loop, and it has over three hours of raw footage. With a little study, I'll know almost every route, technical flaw, and defense orbit this station has. I'll also be able to get a pretty good idea of what kind of tech we're looking at. I mean, check this out."

She maximized the hologram. We now could see through the walls to the wires within, the elaborate matrix laid bare before our eyes.

"Not only that, but I can strip the image," another twitch, and the outer shell faded away, leaving only the wiring, and the heat signatures of the workers. "See? We even know the guards' routes. And, with a quick calculation," I heard a gentle hum, recognizing the sound of Jiggy cooling itself, "I know that there are around 2,400 employees working on board the *Ilena* at the time of this footage."

"Cute," Ori said, picking her teeth with the knife. "So, I definitely heard the word *discreet*. Is that some kind of joke?"

"Discretion would be advised," Brute muttered. "The *Ilena* has the fire power to blow *Redwing* out of this universe. I mean, she could literally *disintegrate* us."

"That, and since she's owned by Andronicus," Harry sat back in her chair, folding her arms, "you can bet that the security will be tight. Best weapons, highest tech, all the shiny bells and whistles."

"But, also because this is Andronicus," Firebird finally stopped circling the hologram, coming to a rest beside the pilot, "we're taking this job. I'll never pass up an opportunity to put a hole in his power. He's hoping to be the Emperor of the Worlds—I don't intend to let that happen." Firebird paused, drawing a slow breath before she continued. "He won't be expecting a unit as small as ours to infiltrate the *Ilena*. Arrogance and wealth make for an easy target. Our client is correct. Discretion and speed are optimal."

"I've always wondered how he managed to keep up his fuel reserves," Harry said. "With his demand, supply should have run low years ago. He provides for over half of the outgoing vessels, as well as local units. There must be something to his production."

"That molecular structure should be worth a heap of credits, then," Ori sat suddenly upright, her knife jabbing toward the hologram. "If we got our hands on it, there could be one hell of a bidding war."

"We didn't get our reputation by betraying our clients," Firebird said, and her words were like distant thunder. When she looked at Ori, her irises darkened. Ori flinched.

"I didn't mean we *should*. I'm just saying, it's a good idea."

Firebird stared at Ori for another long minute. Then, she turned to the hologram.

"How long do you need?" she asked Brute.

A few more hums from Jiggy.

"A few hours. The security net is surprisingly straightforward. I'll be able to get *Redwing* in pretty easily. Just a matter of overlaying another ship's signature. Routing to a central computer system will be a little tougher, and we will have to manually upload the data. Don't want a trace back to us."

"That's why our client kept sending us Pigeons, instead of wireless transmissions?" Harry asked.

"Exactly. Whoever our client is, she or he doesn't want any association with Firebird. Just in case." Brute seemed to shrug, and the hologram sucked back into Jiggy, leaving me blinking into the semi-dark room. "Give me three hours."

"And where is the *Ilena*?" Regina asked.

Harry hesitated. Then, smiling, she raised one finger and pointed toward the sky.

4

BLACK

There had been war, after my mother died.
But it had not been a war as Earth wars had
been before. There were no generals, no
medics, no soldiers, and certainly no heroes.
There had been only Martians, and the people
they slaughtered.

In fact, Earth had posed so little
threat, in the year following my mother's
death, Overlord Andronicus ruled the larger
continents. I hesitate to name them. It has,
after all, been decades since cities, countries,
and continents went by anything other than
sectors. Unity had preached that peace can
only be obtained through a complete melding
of societies.

Of course, that meant they had to be
melted down first.

When Unity had first risen, Earth had
fought against it. And, once, they had almost
won. But that was before the BioMage. That
was before Unity rewrote history, and thereby
a world.

My mother, a Lord Commander of
Unity's Thirteen, had been a BioMage. And
her death had crippled Unity's power. More
than that, Overlords Andronicus, Mariana,
and Shay had already infiltrated the

42

Command at the highest levels. The loss of my mother merely gave them the opportunity they'd been waiting for.

When the bombs fell, they fell on confusion and despair. For without the Thirteen BioMages, the leaders of a society literally lost their minds. And so, Unity had burned.

The problem was, so had Earth.

* * *

My armor was bright red, and it wasn't mine.

I'd gotten pretty good at putting it on, all the same. The segments were crafted from the finest Martian Tech. So fine, in fact, that as with wines that were a step above my usual swill, I understood my armor as something that got the job done, and did it in ways that made me feel important.

Its previous owner's name was Maya, and she'd apparently been one for flowers. Roses, as a matter of fact. As I slipped on the lightweight helm, I took a moment to breathe deeply. It wasn't an overpowering scent. Rather, it reminded me of a garden path after a gentle rain, rocks still warm from the sun. It was a wonderful smell, and when I opened my eyes, part of me was disappointed to find that I was still in my quarters on *Redwing*.

Martian armor served several purposes, not the least of which being bullet resistance. Not bullet *proof*, as Ori was fond of pointing out, but bullet resistant. Brute said that bullet-proof armor was too heavy for our usual missions, and as someone who does quite a lot of running during said missions, I was inclined to agree. So, the bright red bullet-resistant armor that was not mine made me feel—if not invincible—then at least powerful.

My quarters on *Redwing* were the same size as everyone else's. But, I was yet to decorate. In fact, the only real change that I'd made during my year on board was to buy a real bed, not a hammock. The swaying made me nauseous.

I kept my quarters gray. Unity was a toxin that had shaped my crippled life, but we become familiar to even the evil things in our childhoods. Unity may have been evil, but it had been *my* evil. And so, I slept best in the muted gray of a Unity base.

The security panel by my door turned white and, a moment later, someone knocked. I turned, snapping the last closure of my helm into place. The floor under my feet was gently humming, but that was the only evidence of a hard burn. *Redwing* truly was magnificent.

My door whirred open and Firebird smiled at me. There was something about her, in the past few months. Something even I, a journalist with an eidetic memory and a knack for finding trouble, couldn't quite put my finger on. I'd say she was happy, but I knew better.

"You're ready?" she asked, taking a single step into my room. The door remained open behind her.

"I am," I said, my voice mechanical from the helmet's relay.

"Good," her smile made me uncomfortable in ways a frown never had.

"Is there something wrong?" I asked.

"It's unsettling," and she came the rest of the way in, far enough for the proximity sensors to allow the door to close. "My people are uncomfortable with the mission."

"Doesn't happen often," I said, remembering our last mission. "Ori didn't mind blowing up that treatment plant."

Firebird's smile sharpened.

"Ori never has a problem blowing things up. I think that you wrote something along the same lines."

I nodded, pulling my utility belt from my bed. Since carrying a satchel in armor usually led to me ripping it, getting shot, or dropping my data pad, I'd taken to wearing the utility belt during missions. The holster was gravity-based, and it held a single powder-based weapon, one with a heavy barrel and the capacity to stop a charging Martian rhino. It only held six rounds, but as Ori was fond of saying, if a gun takes more than that, then *what's the rusting point*?

"Anything in particular you want me to keep an eye on?" I asked as I buckled the belt into place. It fit snugly around my hips, and the Grav-Holster *clacked* against my thigh.

"Actually," and Firebird took a step closer, her dark eyes like puddles of ink, "I'd prefer if you focused on yourself."

"Myself?" I asked, barking an incredulous laugh. "What in the world for?"

"Well, over the past year, you've humanized my crew. You've made them out to be people with a dream, not just renegades with an objective. And it's changed the way we operate. I couldn't be more pleased, but you're forgetting about yourself. You are as valuable and unique as any other member of the crew."

"Last time," and I made a face like I'd just bitten a lemon, "I tripped over a powerline and nearly blew us up *with* the treatment plant."

She almost laughed, a small cluck in the back of her throat.

"Yes, but you were there. I don't know if you realize this, Jezi, but the Worlds look at us through *your* eyes. They want to know who you are."

"I don't want them to," and darkness blossomed behind my heart. "I don't want anyone to know."

Her smile faded. She put a hand on my shoulder.

"I understand. But I don't need you to give your biography. I need you to be a human, a member of our crew. You're more than the collection of our voices."

I shook my head.

"That's what you pay me for. To collect your voices."

"As you say," she winked at me. "We're coming up on the *Ilena*. I'll have you on the ground."

"As always," I flashed a grin. "Where would you be without your number one operative?"

My sarcasm was lost on her. She nodded, and I got the distinct impression that she was agreeing with me.

I followed Firebird out of my room and into the cockpit, feeling more than a little confused. It's sad, I know, that her cheerfulness confused me. But still. I'd gotten used to her grim disposition, the morose face she showed the public. Having her wink at me and make jokes made me uncomfortable in ways I can't describe.

Ori was already there, dressed in her sleek, black armor. She turned to me, white grin and white eyes the only visible parts of her face within the helm. It was disconcerting. She wore a thick, short knife on one hip and a pistol on the other, an oversized silencer bespeaking a powder-base shot. She nodded at my own gun, one I had dubbed Mule because of the way it kicked.

"Too loud," she said through the helmets' relay, her voice metallic against my ear.

"I don't plan on needing to use it," I said, stopping beside her. "That's what you're there for."

"Because that always works out so well," her laughter was much too loud within the confines of my helmet, and I scowled at her.

The cockpit was dimly lit, the glass around us black. I looked above Harry's consoles, to where the rearview was displayed, and saw the Martian atmosphere pulling away. On ancient Earth, Mars had been called the red planet. But post-terraforming had left the world a cacophony of color. The yellow savanna stained the continent where we had been camped, dark blue rain forest dominating the world toward the equator. And the ocean, which covered most of the southern hemisphere, reflected a purple sky.

My eyes traveled to Olympus Mons, the highest Martian peak. It was now almost directly under us, and even as Mars shrank and I could see the contours of a globe, I still could make out its white dome. I drew a slow breath, gaze moving to what laid ahead.

The *Ilena* dominated Harry's viewscreen. As the hologram had suggested, it was a trapezoid, with the bulky shape of a vessel intended solely for the vacuum of space. Something chilled in my feet, like waking from a nightmare and finding the darkness a little too close.

"Woah," I breathed.

"The white whale," Ori said, grin flashing.

"That's not really how Moby-Dick works," I mumbled, though I knew Ori wasn't listening. I'd referenced the book once, and now anytime we saw something larger than she was, Ori called it the white whale. Regina had almost killed her for it, once.

As we neared the fuel station, I began to feel cool sweat running down my arm. The armor absorbed it quickly, but not so quickly that I didn't recognize the dampness in my pits. I always got nervous before missions. But the ship that steadily grew in front of us was more than a mission: it felt like suicide.

"Isn't she a beauty?" Brute whirred into the room, Jiggy's lights a soft shade of yellow. "Completely constructed in space, of course."

"Gorgeous," Harry muttered, more than a little sarcastically. "You've got my signature in place, don't you?"

"Overlaid with precision, ma'am," the yellow turned to gold as Brute's voice gained a note of pride, "They'd have to be bloody rocket scientists to see us as anything other than the Asteroid-class *Regent* in route to Earth, pending refueling." She giggled. "That's the best part. We're going to refuel while we're there."

"Hence the Asteroid-class," Harry nodded, sounding mollified. She paused. "Brute, they probably *are* rocket scientists."

"What about an Asteroid-class?" I asked, still watching the *Ilena* creep across Harry's screen. It nearly filled the view, and we still had a long way to go.

"They're fancy-man private ships," Brute explained, her accent turning to a mocking lilt. "Delicate little things intended for speed rather than endurance. They can't take the fuel lines of a passenger or cargo vessel, so they actually have to dock within the *Ilena* to refuel with the smaller lines. Takes bloody forever. *But*," and she drew the word out, her lights even brighter, "that's how we're going to get in. Better still, the signature is one of Andronicus's ships, so they're not going to delay entrance. In and out, my dears!"

"Who else is on ground?" Ori asked, slapping a hand against her holster. "I'm the muscle, Jezi's the Fool, where's our brain?"

Ori had taken to calling me the Fool, something she'd picked up from an old-style play we'd seen while in the Chryse. And, granted, I often found a way to bungle their missions. But still. I shot her a dirty look.

"Actually, given the delicate nature of our mission," Brute swiveled toward us. "A smaller unit would have a better chance of getting in and out undetected. Every person we let off of *Redwing* compromises our signature overlay."

"So, what are you saying? It's just Ori and I?" I turned to stare at Firebird, like I would stare at someone who just told me that I'd have to drown a puppy. "Are you insane?"

Firebird's smile still haunted the corners of her mouth, and I finally got the joke.

"You *are* insane," I said.

"No worries," Brute said, whirring closer to me. "I'll be your brain. That is, I'll be in communication at all times. I've analyzed the *Ilena*'s security, and if we match our frequency to the ship's automated relays, they'll read our transmission as one of their own. Besides, the *Ilena* is the kind of ship that takes her security for granted. I mean," and Jiggy swiveled in a way that brought to mind someone gesturing at the ship that now completely obliterated our viewscreen, "*look* at her."

My eyes darted across the fuel station, marking each laser depot. We were one of a hundred ships approaching her, and easily another hundred were already in orbit, thick fuel lines trailing back to the station like veins. I glanced down, and saw the globe of Mars, Olympus Mons still directly under us.

"Why me," I asked, more to myself than anyone.

"Because you've gone on every mission since Unity," Firebird said, resting a hand on my shoulder. She and I stared at the *Ilena*. "And because Ori can't do it alone."

"Don't worry, Fool," Ori said, punching me lightly. "I've got your back."

My anxiety had turned to something with teeth, and as Harry's com flared bright red with warning that someone was scanning us, I felt my bladder weaken.

A blast of static, then:

"*Fuel Station* Ilena *requesting identification*," a man's voice infiltrated the cockpit, his tone disinterested.

"Asteroid-class *Regent* requesting docking and refueling, access ID *7alpha8omega3*," Harry read back to him. "Routing to Earth, passcode *Alpha-stroke-776.*"

There was a pause. My heart thundered in my ears.

"Identification confirmed. Proceed to docking bay *Alpha-niner-niner.*"

"More like *neener-neener*," Ori whispered, chuckling.

I made a small noise, shrinking inside my armor.

A network of lines appeared on our screen a moment later, routing instructions to our docking bay. Harry followed them, her hands moving gently across her console. We circled the *Ilena*, her bulk turning slowly beneath us, and the overlay on the viewscreen maintained a greenish hue. I knew from the last time we'd used automated docking that if they turned red, the dock's gravitational field would seize the ship and take helm control. Harry, of course, had intentionally given over *Redwing* last time, as it was the only way to get past security. This time, she maintained such unwavering command, the automated docking never even shifted to yellow.

Docking bay A-99 was smaller than the surrounding bays, where maintenance crews were working on the larger *Venus* and *Tiran*-class starships. I could see Brute's face illuminated within Jiggy, her eyes glinting in the soft blue light of her hologram monitors. Her brow furrowed slightly.

"What is it?" I asked her.

"We're being tracked," she said slowly. "But not by the *Ilena*. It's a different signature. Hold on."

A few quick waves of her fingers, and her monitors shifted across Jiggy's glass. She nodded.

"It's the same as our client's."

"So, the bugger doesn't trust us to do the mission on our own," Ori scoffed. "Can we do something to tell it to piss off?"

Brute shook her head, still frowning.

"It's distorted. Must be coming through a cloaking field."

"When they took the hologram, there must have been a cloaked ship,"

Firebird's voice was soft. "Otherwise, the *Ilena* would have investigated."

"True," Brute nodded, shrugging. "Makes sense that they would monitor our mission."

"So, what's the problem?" Ori asked as Harry maneuvered *Redwing* around, nosing her toward the docking bay.

"It's just that the cloaking distortion is…" Brute trailed off, Jiggy's lights going dark brown as she considered. "Well, it's *different*. I barely recognized it."

"Different in what way?" Firebird pressed.

There was a long pause. I watched the docking bay doors slide apart, the *A-99* paint breaking down the middle. As *Redwing* glided inside the *Ilena*, Brute whispered:

"It seems *big*."

There was a gentle bump as Harry set us down inside the hanger. Brute gave her head a brisk shake then, with a few quick dashes of her fingers, she shifted her holograms.

"Right, on to the dangerous part. I've got the *Diamond* shields reflecting the *Regent*'s ID. So long as no one here knows what the ship actually looks like, we're effectively disguised. Jezi," Jiggy swiveled to me, its lights brightening. "I'm going to walk you through this. I've got the relay on a constant feed," a hologram appeared at the bottom of Harry's monitors, displaying Jiggy.

I turned my head, and the hologram's display shifted, relaying my point of view.

"Ori," Brute continued, "you're going to hear my feed to Jezi. I'll also be monitoring the heat signatures within the *Ilena* so I'll let you know if anyone is getting too close. Your route should be unhindered. I'm going to guide you into the ventilation shaft, then work you up the *Ilena* and into a maintenance room. There, you should be able to find a computer. Then it's a simple matter of getting through the firewall. Shouldn't be too hard, with this data. Jezi," and a small data chip hovered out of Jiggy and toward me, "you'll need this. I should be able to help you find the correct file. But if not, I wiped the chip. It's *huge*, so we'll just," and she cleared her throat daintily, "shotgun it."

Ori snorted.

"I don't think that means what you think it does," I said slowly.

"Like shooting something with a shotgun?" she asked.

"The ole spray and pray," Ori said, checking her gun's magazine.

Brute paused, frowning at her.

"I mean that we'll download everything the chip can hold from the requested years."

"Not to crash your party," Regina had appeared in the doorway, her big arms crossed, "but shouldn't you get moving?"

"You're just jealous that I get to escort our Fool," Ori said, winking at her.

"Still don't see why it has to be me," I mumbled.

Regina snorted, but Firebird quieted them with a small wave of her hand. She was staring at the view screen, watching as the fuel lines began to automatically extend from the sides of the big gray room.

"Are those going to fit *Redwing*," I asked, glancing toward the front of the ship, where a wall of dark glass stared condemningly at us.

"We're technically an *A*-class ship," Harry answered softly, not looking happy. "But just the same, I'd appreciate it if you got moving. When she finishes refueling, we're going to have to get out of here."

"Right," Ori slapped a hand on my shoulder, wheeling me out of the cockpit.

"I still don't get why it has to be me," I said, allowing Ori to shepherd me down the corridor toward the airlock.

"Comic relief?" Ori suggested.

"*Because you've got to earn your keep*," Regina's voice appeared in my helmet, and I winced.

"Am I on relay to the entire crew?"

There was a horrifying chorus toward the affirmative within my helmet. Ears ringing, I shook my head. Ori and I stopped before the airlock.

"*Right,*" Brute's voice. "*I'm engaging the cloaking shield. Required a bit of flexing, so don't dally. There's a vent directly across from you. Get to it, and I'll override the security net.*"

"Huzzah," Ori said, before she shoved me out of the airlock.

I swore as darkness sucked me in. Within the suit, I couldn't feel the telltale vacuum of the airlock. But still, it was disorienting. And when I came out of the other side, there was a three-meter drop to the floor of the docking bay. Luckily, the gravity was low. I landed in a crouch, more gracefully than my usual exit, and I glanced quickly around. There was no one in the bay. The automatic fuel lines were just now engaging.

Then Ori landed on top of me, and we both went down in a tangle of armor.

"*Rusting skies,*" Harry swore at us. "*Discreet.*"

"I literally don't know what that means," Ori said, righting herself and then hauling me to my feet.

"*You're right, Ori was definitely the better choice for this,*" Regina grumbled.

"*Hush,*" Brute's voice. "*You guys see the vent?*"

We turned away from the ship. There was a square grid roughly a meter high in the far wall. I could see the warmer air waves emerging from it as the bay was slowly pressurized.

"Aye," Ori said, shoving me forward.

The air around us was distorted, and I knew that Brute's cloak was engaged. As we ran, it was like the ground was rippling. It made me nauseous—it always did—and I closed my eyes as much as I dared, squinting through my lashes to the vent.

When we reached it, Brute told me to place my hand on its edge. I complied, and the metal of my fingertips slowly began to heat. The holographic monitors around the edge of my screen turned red with warning lights, though there were no sound alarms. Brute must have disabled them. Quickly, the metal under my hand began to shimmer.

"*Right*," Brute said. "*Now slide your fingers around the perimeter.*" I did so, the metal at the edge of the vent beginning to glow. Heat radiated from my gauntlet in waves. "*And now Ori, see if you can rip it off.*"

"With pleasure," she said, nudging me out of her way.

She laced her fingers within the grid, braced her feet against the wall, and gave a tremendous heave. The grid popped off of the opening easily, and Ori stumbled a step back, nearly dropping it. She grinned, nodded at me, and then went to toss the grid to the side.

I grabbed her arm before she could, starting to repeat the word *discreet*, but Ori hissed at me and wrenched free of my grasp.

The metal of her armor where I'd grabbed it shimmered with the heat.

"*Would you two quit dinking and get into that hole?*" Regina snarled into our helmets.

Ori shrugged, dropped the grate, and ushered me into the vent. It was a horizontal shaft, and I had to crawl. I heard the cooling units in my armor engage, and the heat waves from my gauntlet slowly subsided. Lights around the edges of my helmet flicked on.

"*You're going to be coming up on a vertical shaft shortly,*" Brute said, her voice eerie in the dark confines of the tunnel.

"It's been so long, I wouldn't even know what to do with it," Ori cackled.

I ignored her, thinking back to the last time we'd refueled.

"We've got, what? Twenty minutes?" I asked, anxiety once again needling its way back into my chest.

"*Approximately.*"

I crawled faster. Ori continued to chuckle behind me.

"You look like a crab," she said.

Thirty seconds later, we found the vertical vent. It was the same size as the one we'd been crawling through, but as I stared up it into darkness, I couldn't help but think that it was shrinking. Ori tapped the back of my hand.

"Remember how to use the Grav?"

"How could I forget," I mumbled. I hadn't known the armor contained magnetic locks until Ori had engaged them and left me stuck to the outside of *Redwing* for an hour.

I prodded a series of holo-buttons on my forearm. Instantly, my hands and feet engaged and I was stuck to the floor of the vent.

"I'd set it a little higher, if I were you," Ori said, grinning at me. "Wouldn't want to go sliding back down the shaft."

I shot her a dirty look, but did as she said. When I lifted my foot, I was pulling against the magnetized boot. With a deep breath, I stuck myself to the vent and pulled my body up, the enhanced strength of the armor assisting me.

"*Right on schedule*," Brute encouraged us as we climbed. "*You've got about ten meters to go, then there will be a horizontal tube.*"

"You know, I've been wondering," Ori said after a while. "Could you do this without your armor? With your Metalness, I mean?"

I'd been wondering the same thing.

"I don't know," I answered slowly, sweat beading along my hairline as I climbed.

"For the first of your kind," Ori scoffed, "you'd think you'd be a bit wiser."

"That's not how that works," I muttered. "I don't have a mentor. How could I ever be a superhero?"

The truth was, I was afraid of my own power. When Unity had first discovered that I was a MetalMage—able to influence metal objects—they had sent me through a rigorous set of tests. Most often, I shoved metal violently away from my person. But other times, it would come rocketing toward me. Both useful. Rarely interchangeable.

"Well, we should try training you," Ori said, not sounding the least bit winded, whereas I was beginning to pant. "Seems like a rusting waste."

Although I cringed at the thought, she had a point. And so, I grunted with something that could have been acquiescence and continued to climb. A short time later, I found the horizontal tube.

"I'm here," I told Brute, crawling far enough into the vent that I could safely disengage the Grav.

"*Brilliant. Follow that until you come to a grid. And Ori, be quiet. There's someone ahead of you.*"

Ori snickered. With a deep breath, I began to creep along the tunnel. Just a few meters in, I came to a door of solid metal, red lights blinking over a data pad where the handle would be.

"Er, Brute?" I asked.

"*Hold on. That's a seal. You didn't think they pressurized the docking bays with their life systems, did you?*" she chuckled. "*Just give me a minute. Jezi, in your belt, you'll find a disk about the size of your palm.*"

I fished through my pockets until I found it. It was dark metal, and when I held it, a series of Martian Tech lights flickered to life around its circumference.

"*I had it set to automatically detonate when it reads the signature of your gauntlet,*" Brute said, sounding pleased with herself.

"Detona—" I started, about to fling it away.

Instead, the disc abruptly dropped to the tunnel floor. It landed with a too-loud *clang* and the lights around its circumference flared red. A second later, Ori and I were in darkness.

"*Don't panic,*" Brute said, cheerful. "*It's a portable airlock. Quite the bit of tech, if I do say so myself. If you move forward, you'll be able to find the seal.*"

Swearing under my breath, I inched forward. Sound was nonexistent within an airlock, a fact for which I was grateful as I bumped into the seal, then ran my metal fingers along the metal door to the telltale give of a data pad.

"*One second,*" Brute muttered. Through the com, I could hear Jiggy's cooling fans beginning to hum.

A moment later, then the door shot upward, making me fall halfway through, disoriented and tangled in my own armor. Muttering curses, I crawled forward, fully expecting the door to come crashing back down onto me. Instead, I emerged from the portable airlock and light seared into my eyes.

"You good?" Ori asked, tapping the side of my helmet.

I nodded slowly, squinting at her. She was, of course, grinning.

"We've got another grate," she said, looking at the end of the tunnel.

It was similar to the docking bay's, though this one seemed thinner. Indeed, when Ori rested her hands on it, the entire thing bowed outward.

"*Hold up,*" Brute hissed. "*Remember? There's someone here.*"

I crawled up beside Ori, squinting through the slats of the grate. It looked like a storage room, crates and metal beams stacked in its center. Movement caught my eye, and even though my suit contained the sound, I held my breath.

"We've got one...I'd guess, *nerd?*" Ori said.

The man was short and thin, and his back was to us. He had a white lab coat on, and was working at a computer on the far side of the room. There was music playing softly, some kind of jazzy mix, and he was humming. I felt a pang of guilt when I saw the hungry look on Ori's face.

"*Ori,*" Firebird's voice, "*nonlethal.*"

"But," she whined. "It's been such a long time."

"*Ori!*" Harry snapped. "*We're on the clock.*"

With a gentle push, she popped the grate free. It was a small sound, and Ori held the metal rungs with her finger tips, so that it didn't go flying out. She exited with the fluidity of a spider, gently setting down the grate and then pressing herself against the stack of equipment. I followed, picking my way out of the vent.

"*That's the computer we're going to use,*" Brute said. "*So, get rid of the...nerd?*"

"On it," Ori said.

She disappeared from my side, slinking across the floor. She still reminded me of a spider, black and skulking. I eased around the equipment, keeping her in my line of sight.

The technician finished his typing, still humming, and glanced at the monitor over his head. I followed his glance and saw a scrolling series of numbers. Putting a hand on a crate, I leaned farther out of hiding.

Here's the thing with Martian Tech armor. While it is 'lightweight' in comparison with bullet-proof Earth Tech, it still isn't by any means *light*. The armor powers itself, and thereby makes me feel like it weighs nothing. However, if I were to take a guess, I'd say that it more than quadrupled my body weight.

So when I leaned on the crate, I did so with much more force than I'd intended.

The pile shifted, and the metal bars that had been propped up against it went clattering to the floor.

The technician jumped straight into the air, like a cat, and when he spun around and saw me—an idiot in a bright red suit—he froze, his mouth popping open. We stared at each other for a second, unsure of who was the predator and who the prey, and then he whirled back to his computer and slapped his hand down on what probably was an intercom.

Ori was a viper. She sprang to her feet and seized his wrist, wrenching his hand away from the button. Her other arm darted around his throat and heaved him back from the computers, cutting blood and oxygen off from his brain. He started to scream, but she clamped her free hand over his mouth and nose, black gauntlet obliterating his face. He struggled weakly for a moment, then slowly went limp in her arms.

She dropped him unceremoniously and brought two fingers to her helmet, like a hat tip.

"Say this for Jezi," she said, "it's always more interesting when she's along."

"I'm sorry," I muttered, standing from the crates. "What is all this garbage, anyway?"

"*You're in waste management*," Brute said, voice a little too high. She cleared her throat. "*Right, disaster averted. Jezi, get to the monitor.*"

I obeyed, glancing at the man's unconscious form. His face was scattered with acne, and his thick glasses had cracked. I winced, glancing at Ori, who had taken up a station next to the exit, a surprisingly thick metal door.

"I'm here," I said, sitting in the technician's chair and pulling myself forward.

"*Sweet. Now, Jezi,*" Brute's tone turned condescending, "*take a moment to look to your left.*"

I obliged. At the back of the pile of junk, I saw a massive door like that on a docking bay.

"*You see that?*" She asked. "*That's a jettison into outer space. You're in the garbage dump on section 99. Do you understand that you don't want to push any buttons?*"

"Well that's just dumb," I said, irritated. "Why would they put the computer that jettisons garbage into outer space *in* the garbage dump?"

"*Because you wouldn't want anyone on the outside of the room doing it,*" Harry answered, more quickly than I'd expected. "*That's how people get accidently jettisoned. There's a countdown after the doors are activated, time for everyone to clear the area.*"

"*She's right!*" Brute agreed. "*Great! Now, look at the monitors for me. I'm going to assume control.*"

"You're going to wha—?"

My question was answered as my armor suddenly came to life around me. The fingers began to twitch on their own, typing on the data pad, and I squawked indignantly, my head turning on its own.

"I finally get why Jezi had to come," Ori giggled, slapping a hand against the top of my helm. "Maya's armor is the only one with Automation."

"*Technically,*" Brute murmured, sounding distracted, "*I didn't even need Jezi to be in it. But Firebird likes for her to get the hands-on experience.*"

"You all suck," I grumbled, my arm twitching to the side and typing into a second data pad.

Ori, still chuckling, came away from the door to look over my shoulder.

"How's it going?" she asked.

"*As promised,*" Brute answered. "*I'm hacking into the main data storage now. Surprisingly little security. That's why I picked waste management. They already have access to storage, so I just have to get past the firewall for the main system.*"

"How long?" I asked, my body jerking suddenly to the right.

"*Sorry, sometimes the Automation shorts out,*" Brute didn't sound sorry in the least. "*Just a couple more minutes. They're going to detect us once I'm in, so I've got to shut down some security so that they can't pinpoint us. Overriding all defense systems,"* she giggled. *"They'll think we're coming from literally everywhere."*

I sighed.

"Huzzah," Ori said, punching my shoulder. "This is rusting hilarious. You're a little crippled girl's puppet."

"Bite me," I growled, my right leg suddenly kicking out.

"Brute," Ori said, "could you make her start dancing?"

"Maybe later," she said, giggling. *"We're in!"*

Instantly, the lights in the room turned red. Sirens went off through the ship. I felt the solid lump of fear I'd been trying to swallow suddenly plummet into my gut.

"Brute?" I asked. "I thought you had the defensive systems deactivated."

"I do. The important ones, anyway. It's alright that they know we're here—it's going to take them forever to figure out where I'm hacking from. Right. Why don't you take your arm back and get that data chip. I'm worried I might crush it."

My arms both suddenly dropped as Brute disappeared, and the little monitors under my gauntlets cracked. Brute swore at me, and I swore at her as I dug into my belt's pouches, fumbling around until I came up with the data chip.

68

"*You see the little slot near the bottom right-hand side of the computer screen?*" She asked, sounding less amused.

"Yeah?"

"*Put it in there,*" she said.

"You sure you trust me with that?" I asked sarcastically, shoving the data chip in.

She giggled, resuming control of my arms.

"Hey!" I snapped, my fingers dancing across the keyboard.

"*What? We're on a tight schedule.*" A pause. "*Right, I've got the files.*"

"*That easily?*" Firebird's voice.

"*They're pretty well marked. Now, I just need to access their science base. The fuel formula should be...hold up...right.*" And she tapped the keyboard with one last definitive twitch. "*I implanted a homing device on the data chip. It's doing the work for me. It's seeking out formulas with—*"

"Nerd," Ori said.

A pause.

"*And there we have it,*" Brute said. "*Grab the chip and let's get out of here.*"

"*We're nearly done fueling,*" Harry warned. "*We've got maybe five minutes before systems are go.*"

Another flare of anxiety. I grabbed the chip and yanked it out.

Suddenly, the little white lights around its perimeter turned bright red.

I hesitated, the chip in my hand.

"*Hold up,*" Brute said slowly. She assumed control of my armor again, hoisting the chip closer to my view. "*It's sending some kind of transmission.*"

"*Transmission?*" Firebird's voice darkened.

"*Yeah,*" Brute mused, turning my hand this way and that as she studied the chip. Readouts began to scroll across my viewscreen. "*It's simple enough. Basically just a signal.*"

"*Where's it going?*" Harry asked.

Brute paused.

"*It's the same as the origin. Where we were being monitored from.*"

"*You think that our—*" Harry started.

"*Get out of there,*" Firebird interrupted, fury flaring behind her words. "NOW!"

"*I don't—*" Brute started.

Suddenly, the *Ilena* vibrated, a rolling *thud* rumbling through the corridors. Brute's presence vanished. The abrupt absence made my armor short out, and I collapsed, the data chip spinning from my hand and across the floor.

"What in the rusting world is—" Ori started, reaching to help me up.

Ilena shuddered again. The sirens—which had been wailing since Brute hacked into the system—went silent. Then, I heard the distant sound of an explosion.

Pause.

Ori and I looked at each other, her hand frozen in front of me. A wail built toward the back of the ship. Another shudder. The wail gained power, sending the deep, anguished siren of a hull breach resonating through the ship.

5

MORTAL

Of course, the Martian Overlords had never worked as a unit. Since the first three rose to power and overthrew Unity's control of Mars, they had subtly shifted in strength, warring quietly, undermining one another with the convoluted strategy of a three-player game of chess. And, when Earth fell, Overlord Andronicus's sudden seizure of the major continents seemed like the winning move. Overlords Shay and Mariana were trapped, their kings encircled.

I heard more than a few people say that there was no way for them to win.

Here's the thing with chess. There are rules. It's a game. And, no matter how many times it's compared to life, chess isn't life.

They flipped the board. Let the pieces fall where they may.

* * *

"Get up!" Ori shouted, heaving me to my feet.

"The data!" I screamed, even though our helmet relays didn't need me to. I searched frantically, trying to ignore the sirens. The ship vibrated again, and I caught a glimpse of red light under one of the crates.

Scrambling, I snatched the data chip and slipped it into one of my belt's pockets. Ori was already in the vent, waving me toward her. I paused. The technician still laid unconscious on the floor, his broken glasses askew. I looked from Ori, to him, and back again. Then, throwing my arms up in a *WHAT DO YOU WANT ME TO DO* fashion, I grabbed him by his wrists and dragged him toward the vent.

"Seriously?" Ori snarled at me, not offering to help as I heaved the unconscious boy into the vent.

"I can't just leave him here! If there's a hull breach, he'll be helpless! It's our fault that he—"

"Save it," Ori shoved herself into the temporary airlock.

Grinding my teeth, I grabbed the boy under his arms and inched my way backwards. Even with the suit's enhanced strength, pulling him in the tight confines was difficult. I'd almost reached the airlock when something shoved me forcefully to the side.

"What?!" I gasped, whirling to find Ori scowling an inch from my face.

"The seal is locked down. Breach protocol. Move!"

Heart flying, I pushed the technician back out of the vent and scuttled after. Ori exploded free, her black armor glinting in the red light. She came to the unnaturally thick door, tried the handle. It didn't budge.

"Breach protocol," I whispered.

There was a small window about eye-level with Ori, and she pressed her helmet close to it. Then, taking a step away, she drew back her fist.

"You're going to punch your way through the door?" I asked, cradling the technician in my lap.

When Ori brought her fist forward, she hit the fracture-resistant glass with the weight of a small shuttlecraft. Whereas my armor had all of the fancy Martian smarts, hers was the Martian equivalent of a tank. Three punches and the glass essentially dissolved.

She slipped her arms through, then her head, and with a mighty bound, she sprang through the window like a tendril of smoke slipping through a cracked chimney. There was a moment's silence. Someone screamed.

"Ori?" I whispered, struggling to my feet, technician still in my arms.

"*Stand back*," Ori's voice crackled through my helm. Something must have been blocking long-distance transmissions.

I heard the unmistakable whine of an acid-based weapon being primed. A second later, the handle on the door *exploded*, bits of molten metal vomiting into the room. I swore, turning my back to the door a second before Ori kicked it open. She stood there, a massive gun braced on her shoulder, green nozzle still glowing red from the over-charged shot. At her feet, a guard in a white uniform laid twisted in the broken glass, his neck bent at an unnatural angle.

"So much for nonlethal," I murmured, hoisting the technician over my shoulder and hurrying to Ori.

"I think we're past protocol," Ori said, turning.

We were at the junction of two hallways. The one in front of us seemed to travel unhindered into darkness, whereas the one on my right took a slow bend.

"Well, Lurk?" Ori asked, shifting the gun from her shoulder to her other hand, arching a dark eyebrow at me. "Which way?"

I stared at her blankly for a second. Then, my brain finally kicking in, I drew a sharp breath and closed my eyes.

Having an eidetic memory is both a blessing and a curse. As I pictured the diagram of the *Ilena*, I had to work my way back through it. Brute had briefly gone over where we needed to enter and why, but that tangled with my first memory of the ship, and the snarky remarks Ori had made, and the way Regina had looked at me when Firebird told me—not her—to suit up. Which reminded me of *why* I had gone, and how Brute had used me like a puppet, and—

Ori slammed her hand against the side of my helmet hard enough to make the warning lights flare. My eyes snapped open and I glowered at her.

"Enough dallying!" She didn't need to shout, and she made my ears ring. "We're sitting ducks here."

"This way," I said, not at all certain. I was still tracing the route in my mind. More than that, I was trying to think of where the escape pods were.

We started down the curving hallway at a jog. The technician's head bumped miserably against my back, and twice I almost dropped him, his lab coat slippery against my armor. As we jogged around the corner, Ori picked up her pace, edging in front of me, massive gun raised.

The wall on my right became glass. The perimeter of the outer shell was an observatory, along with several suites for visiting dignitaries. Yes, it was a fuel station. But Overlord Andronicus—from what I'd come to understand—was one for entertaining.

The first thing that I saw was the red flare of laser fire. The second, the orange glow of an incoming rocket. And third, the green flash as Ori fired her gun.

I shouted, stumbling back from Ori, blinking the blinding light from my eyes. Beyond her, I saw the bodies of at least five white-clothed guards melting on the floor. Distant shouts marked more to come.

"Wrong rusting way," Ori said, turning to me. "Back we go."

I straightened, my gaze going to the window. The rocket was almost to us, a glowing asteroid in the black sky. My gaze went past it, to the *wall* of ships. There were over two-hundred of them, at the very least, *Viper*-class starships, designed for close-orbit combat. Their red lasers fountained at us, searing thin holes in *Ilena*'s sides.

A second later, the rocket collided, not ten meters under us. Orange fire belched past our window, along with scraps of metal and soft, spinning bodies. Ori shouted, shoving me back the way we had come, but I held my hand out to her, my mouth slowly opening.

"Rusting *what*?" Ori snarled, again making my ears ring.

"Look," I said, staring out the window.

"Yes, I rusting see them. It's a bloody fleet come to blow us out of orbit, and I don't want to be standing here when they do!"

"No, *look*," and I pointed to *Ilena*'s side, where the smoking remains of her innards continued to dribble into space. "She has no shields."

Ori's eyes flashed. She bent, picked up a piece of twisted metal, and heaved it at the glass. It didn't so much as scratch it.

"See? Not our rusting problem."

"And the laser stations," I leaned forward, bumping my helm against the glass.

"They're not firing. Ori," I turned to her, my heart numb. "*We* did this."

"We didn't do rusting anything!"

"Brute said that she disabled the defensive net to get past the firewall," the ship shivered, sirens screaming. "*We* did this."

"Listen to me, Jezi," she grabbed the seam of my helmet, where the glass met metal, and yanked me forward, until I could see the veins in her eyes. "We have to *go*, or we are going to *die*."

I blinked, nodded. Ori slapped the side of my head and started back the way we had come, pushing toward a full sprint. I followed her, wrapping my arms around the little technician. A second later, I heard the glass behind us fracture under the weight of another rocket. I glanced over my shoulder. The black glass had transformed into a network of white lines, like a thousand overlaying cobwebs.

As I watched, they slowly began to turn orange.

Ori rounded the sharp corner, but I slowed. When I came to the original doorway, I looked into the waste room. I stopped. A violent shiver came from the belly of the ship. We lost gravity.

"Rusting hell, Jezi! What are you doing?" Ori asked, tapping her forearm and engaging her Grav-Boots.

I followed her example, nearly losing the technician. He floated up and away from me, like a fat balloon. When I hit the floor, I didn't follow her. Instead, I shouted:

"I've got an idea!"

"You don't have to yell!" Ori screamed back at me, following me into the room.

I shoved the man into Ori's arms—making her drop her gun, which incidentally floated lazily toward the ceiling—and turned to the monitors I had just hacked.

"What's your rusting idea?" Ori asked, holding the technician by his collar, letting him turn in the air. Her dark eyes were wide as she glanced through the open door and down the hallway. We both heard the screams.

"Remember what Brute said?" I asked, looming over the computer and scanning the security keys.

The ship was in breach protocol, but I had just hacked my way into the main computer. I closed my eyes, remembering. Then, with a quick series of numbers, I was in.

"I don't rusting remember her saying that we should get ourselves blown up dinking on a computer."

"This room—it's waste management. The garbage," I jabbed a finger at the heap of crates, currently turning drunkenly in the air, "gets jettisoned into space."

"That doesn't help—oh, hell." Ori stepped closer to me, the technician's head bumbling against the monitor. "You want to jettison *us*?"

I looked at her, my fingers hovering over the command.

"*Redwing* wouldn't leave without us," I said. "But Harry would sooner cut off her hand than let her ship get stuck in this death trap. They're probably just outside. Besides," and I looked down the hallway, to where orange fire began to roar around the corner, "I don't see how we have a choice."

Ori stared at me for a second. Then a manic grin spread across her face.

"I like it. Let's boogie."

"Right. So if I bypass the countdown," I tried a different passcode, working my way into the program, "all that we will have to do is hit this button and..."

I looked at the technician.

"They must have emergency masks here," I said, springing from the computer and running the perimeter of the room.

"Jezi!" Ori snarled at me, her voice turning to static as I got farther away. "Bloody forget him!"

I rounded the corner of the crates, frantically searching for the oxygen masks. *Redwing* had ten, and that was a flea of a ship in comparison to *Ilena*. I'd just made it around the back of the room, where I could see Ori on the far side, when the ship *screamed.*

It wasn't the sirens. And I'd swear, it wasn't the 2,400 people who called this ship home. I'll go to my grave believing that when the center of the ship gave way, *Ilena* was the one who wailed.

Something in the air intensified. Ori looked at me. I saw the mask then, near the door we'd entered through, a little emergency light blinking above it. My gaze fell back to Ori. There was something there, something like an apology.

And she brought her hand down on the console.

I shouted at her, but it was too late. The door behind me groaned, the latches disengaged, and the pressure blasted them wide open. A hurricane hit me. I tried to right myself, my Grav-Boots sliding as I was pushed toward outer space. The technician's limp body came flying at me. I leaned forward, hoping to grab him.

That's when the first crate hit me, square in the chest.

My armor's monitors flared red, warning lights scrolling across my vision. One second I was on the floor. The next, I was spinning. My chest throbbed. The world that wasn't a world whirled beyond my helm, blackness and fire. My arms flailed. Something cracked against my hand and I was spinning with it. My Grav-Boots connected with a rod of metal. I took it with me.

The *Ilena* bled chaos into space.

That was when the panic set in. Raw and primal, it had me gasping, panting, hyperventilating. The open space was ink. But I was spinning, and every now and then, the open atmosphere of purple Mars whirled past my vision. I saw the *Ilena*, cut clean in half, fractured holding tanks spewing fuel.

I vomited in my helmet. It went up my nose. Tears flowed freely from my eyes. I was choking.

I was going to *die.*

Something grabbed me. The spinning slowed. Then, as the universe came to a standstill, I turned and found Ori, her hand wrapped around my wrist. She had one Grav-Hand working, and she was adhered to a massive crate, its slow rotation giving her a grounding. She looked past me, to where the *Ilena* was dying.

When I looked, it wasn't the ship that caught my attention. It was the broken, white-robed body.

"*No!*" I shouted, wrenching free of Ori's grasp and disengaging my Grav-Boots before kicking off of the crate.

Focused, my aim was true. I caught the technician in my arms, pulling him tight against my chest. I fumbled with my armor, trying to find something—some lever or a secret compartment—that would carry an emergency oxygen mask. I looked at his face.

His broken glasses were gone, of course. His face was twisted, terrifying shades of black and red. He looked like he was screaming, but you can't scream in space.

I clutched him, cradled him, pulled my knees tight behind his back and buried my face in his too-clean lab coat.

We floated in silence, somewhere in between the broken body of *Ilena* and the purple skies of Mars.

6

FAILURE

"What do you stand for?"

That's what they asked my mother, at a conference some ten years ago. Her unnatural blue eyes had surveyed the room. She had a way of making everyone feel like they were the center of attention, even though that attention was only a reflection.

"Equality," she had said.

People didn't cheer in Unity. It was one of those things that simply wasn't done. But that one, simple word from my mother's dark lips had sent a stir through the crowd like wind on the water.

"Equality," I had mouthed after her, hearing the lie.

We all have to stand for something. That's what she taught me. What she didn't say was that it doesn't make us right.

* * *

"Jezi," someone said my name. Someone touched my face.

"Jezi," someone else? I didn't know. I didn't open my eyes.

Part of me wished I never would again.

I was on *Redwing*. I could tell from the gentle hum under my shoulders, the warm air against my skin. I could hear the people, gentle murmurs and unpleasant scrapes. I thought I heard a gun. I thought it was being cleaned.

The technician's face floated through my inner eye. Bloated and purple. I groaned.

"Jezi," and Firebird caught me.

I was gasping, sitting bolt upright in a bed, and Firebird had her arms around me, anchoring me. I was crying. I was screaming. I didn't know why I was doing either.

"Easy," she whispered, her mouth close to my ear, her breath warm.

Grounding.

It's what lets electricity flow. It's what keeps you from spinning in space.

"It was *us*," I whimpered, my words bestial.

"Easy," she whispered again, softer this time.

The world was dark. I was falling. I was grounded.

* * *

All told, Ori was unconscious for five days after *Ilena*. I was for six. We had floated in space for hours, and our oxygen reserves had been low. In the debris, it was a miracle that Harry found us at all.

When I woke the second time, I didn't cry. I remember looking to the right, my head loose on my neck, and seeing Firebird at my bedside, her chin dipped to her chest, a data pad displaying bright numbers in her lap. Her eyes were hardly open, dark pools barely reflecting the scrolling numbers. I stared at her, and I wondered why I was here. Why *any* of us were here.

"Hey," was all I said.

Firebird looked up. Dark circles ringed her eyes. She smiled at me, but it was a haunted thing, and it haunts me still. She rested a hand on my arm.

"How are you feeling?"

"Like I just got blown out of an exploding spaceship," I answered, because that seemed like the easiest thing to say.

She sighed. We stared at each other.

"I'm sorry that happened to you," she said.

"Could have happened to any of us," I replied.

Her mouth thinned.

"But it happened to *you.*" She paused. She had other things to say. I could see it behind her eyes.

Silence filled the quiet places in the room.

"All part of the job," I eventually said. "How's Ori?"

Firebird's thick mouth quirked.

"Same as ever."

"We were betrayed," I said, sitting up and propping the lonely pillow against the flimsy headrest. "The data chip sent a transmission and five seconds later, there was a flotilla blowing us out of the universe."

Firebird nodded slowly.

"I know."

"What happened to you?"

Her fingers tapped restlessly against the data pad.

"When *Ilena* first was attacked, it didn't take long to realize why. Brute...well, Brute is struggling with this. But at the time, she thought that you wouldn't be able to get out the way you went in. So, we pulled out of the docking bay, cloaked, and...watched. Waited," she sighed again. "It took a while to find you. To run sensors, we had to decloak. And at the time..."

I nodded.

"You couldn't, without an armada—"

"Plowing us, yes," Harry stepped into the room, tossing an apple at my head.

I caught it—barely—and she winked at me.

"Wouldn't have left you, though," she continued, throwing herself down on the end of my bed. "Just didn't want to endanger my baby."

"*Redwing* is ship," came a thick of-then Russian accent. "Not baby."

I jumped, realizing for the first time that Dr. Ravin was also in the room. She was a tall woman with an outrageously long neck, and she was currently leaning over a table behind me, scribbling half-heartedly on a sheet of paper. Her dark hair was piled haphazardly on her head, and when she turned to glance at me, her pale face made her look like—and I wasn't the first one to say it—a stork.

"So," Harry continued, slapping a hand on my shin. "How's our journalist? We've kept you alive for over a year now," she took another bite from her apple. "Beginning to get attached."

I smiled, taking a bite myself. It wasn't good, the mushy kind people used for pies, but in my dry, stinky mouth, it was better than sugar.

"I'm alright. I—"

"Heyo!" and Ori stepped into the room, followed by Regina. "Look at what didn't die in a vacuum. How's the body?"

"I'm fine," though now, weariness hung on me like a soggy towel.

"Good," and Laurensen was the last in the doorway, though she didn't come all of the way into the room. "Then maybe we can start talking about who to kill."

That brought the room to a standstill, though truth be told, I was a little relieved to no longer have to talk about myself. Firebird nodded.

"If you're up to it, Jezi?" she asked.

"Killing people is what I do best," I said. Ori laughed. And laughed. And eventually, I threw my apple core at her.

I was up, sponged off, and dressed within the hour. By the time I made my way to the dining table, the rest of the crew was already there, filling all the chairs. Regina stood and offered me hers. I protested, but she grunted and shoved me toward it. Let me tell you this. When Regina shoves you at anything, there isn't much protesting left to do.

"Where are we?" I asked, glancing at the view screen that inhabited the ceiling of our dining and common area. Trees towered over us, the narrow gap in their twining branches barely large enough for *Redwing* to drop through. They filtered the sunlight, bathing us in purple, and Brute must have dropped the filtration system, because when I breathed deep, I could smell the rain.

"Chryse," Harry said, and she didn't sound happy about it.

"We're still going to the rendezvous point, then?" I asked, my mouth thinning as I looked to Firebird. "Even though they tried to kill us? And murdered 2,400 people."

"Got a debt to be paid," Ori said, tossing her knife into the air. We watched it spin. She caught it in nimble fingers, twirling the flat of the blade. "Sum of 50,000 creds. And then, I'm going to take...what's the saying? A liter of flesh?"

"Pound," Regina said.

"Yeah, I mean, I was planning on cutting, too. You're more of the pounder. But what—"

"For Worlds' sakes," Dr. Ravin sprang to her feet, her thin mouth pulled toward a constant grimace. "Why are you speaking?"

Ori stuck her tongue out at her. Firebird sighed.

"It is fairly obvious who our client is," she said, pulling the attention of the room, like a magnet gathers flakes of metal.

"It is?" Ori blinked at her.

"Idiot," Dr. Ravin muttered.

"Hey," and the twirling knife came to a standstill, pointing at the doctor.

"There are only three people on Mars capable of commanding a fleet of Viper-class starships," Firebird continued, eyes flicking toward Ori.

"And I'd put creds on it not being Andronicus," Regina muttered, hooking a thumb in her pocket.

"So," I swallowed, "it's either Shay or Mariana?"

"It wasn't Shay," Harry muttered. She had her hands clasped together, her elbows on her knees, and she stared at the place between her boots as though meaning to burn through the floor. A wedding ring dangled from a chain around her neck, catching purple light.

"It wasn't," Firebird agreed. "Even if Shay did have access to that many *Vipers*, she'd never risk her Country going to war with Andronicus."

"Overlord Mariana," I said, and the words were ash on my tongue. I gave my head a brisk shake. "If it was her, then why would we even consider going to the rendezvous? She tried to kill us once already."

"Did she?" Firebird looked at me. "If she wanted us dead, she wouldn't have let us escape so easily. She wants that data chip."

"Doesn't necessarily mean she didn't want us dead," I reasoned. "It just means that she wanted the data."

"Either way, it wasn't doing our health any favors," Ori's knife was spinning again. "I say we go, and we gut this contact. Then we have Laurensen blow Biggie's head off, just like she did that Overlord back in Madtown."

"To what end?" Firebird's voice hardened. "Killing Mariana would only strengthen Andronicus further, and he already rules most of Earth. What do you think he's going to do with those soldiers, the resources and reserves? What do you think he's going to do with the BioMages?"

"Rule the Worlds?" Ori offered, cocking her head.

"More or less," I muttered, thinking of Earth.

"If what you're saying is that we need Mariana," and Harry's voice was a poisoned thing, "then you're all fools."

Firebird sat at the head of the table. Her hands were clasped in front of her and when Harry spoke, her twirling thumbs stilled. She stared at Harry for a moment, and the pilot met her unwavering gaze with one of resolve.

"Mariana is toxic," Harry said. "And siding with her is no better than siding with Andronicus. She'll use us. And if we're successful, *she*'ll rule the Worlds."

"Highly preferable to Andronicus," Dr. Ravin said, and I blinked at her. Her voice had gained a note of—if not fear—then distaste.

"We all have our histories," Firebird eventually said. "But if it comes down to Andronicus or Mariana, Mariana at least has something like honor."

Harry snorted.

"I really like calling her Biggie, instead of Mariana," Ori threw in. "Like the rest of rusting Mars. You sound like nerds."

"Andronicus rules from Olympus Mons?" I asked, ignoring her.

"Aye," Ori said, absentmindedly stabbing the edge of her boot.

"And he's using Thirteen to maintain discipline, right?" I continued, barely waiting for Firebird's nod. "Then he's no different from Unity. Worse, even, because he doesn't have their regulations. If we let him rise, then we've accomplished nothing. My mother's death accomplished *nothing*."

The air in the room turned heavy.

"And if you let Mariana take over," Harry said, softer than ever, "then Maya's death meant nothing."

Firebird closed her eyes. Her fingers whitened as she clenched them.

"The data chip is a homing device," Firebird said, a note of resolve ringing through the room. "Brute thinks that she managed to block its signal before we landed here, but she's uncertain. We could destroy it, and not get paid. But we need credits. We could let them come to us, and ambush them. But we lose our reputation. We could meet at the rendezvous. But there's no guarantee that they won't kill us after they have the data."

"And there's the small fact that we just played a key role in murdering 2,400 people," I said. "If we don't show at the rendezvous, I'll bet our *discretion* won't mean a damned thing when Biggie pins this on us."

"And Andronicus is not forgiving man," Dr. Ravin said.

"I still think that I'd like to have a little chat with the bloke who comes to pick up the data," Ori said, flipping her knife again.

There was another pause. Firebird straightened.

"We're here. They know we're here. Enough. Ori and I will take the data to the rendezvous. Harry, I want you to move the ship to Zone 2. After that, take a shuttle and drop Laurensen near the rendezvous, where I want her to take position somewhere above us, just in case."

Harry's eyes sharpened.

"What then?" she asked, her voice like broken glass.

"Then? We'll make the drop, and have a discussion with our employer," Firebird's eyes challenged her, but Harry didn't drop her gaze.

"I should go," she said. "I know Biggie better than any of you."

"You're too involved," and when our commander said it, it was a fact. "And we don't need to provoke her, not when we're walking this line already. We'll be safe enough, with Laurensen in the sky."

The assassin, quiet up till now, nodded from her place beside Harry. She liked to lurk during meetings, a trait that I honestly could have learned to live without. Sometimes, it was like she actually was a shadow. Right up until the point that she shot someone.

"You sure about this?" Harry growled.

"No," Firebird said, meeting her eye. "But this is what is going to happen. We have two days to kill before the rendezvous—I suggest we prepare."

We stared at her for a moment, equally uncertain. Then, Firebird stood.

"I don't know what you're waiting for. Jezi," and I felt something inside my chest cringe when she turned to me, "walk with me."

The rest of the crew left to prep, and Firebird led me from *Redwing*. I followed her, wondering what she was going to say, wondering if she was going to tell me I should stay in the Chryse. I wondered—though it didn't seem like a strong enough term—if she was going to *fire* me.

The air outside was thick with humidity, the familiar heat making my curls tighten. When I jumped down from *Redwing*, my boots sank into the soil. Firebird turned to me.

"Catch," she said.

And she threw a bullet at my head. I flinched, trying to bat it away, but she'd thrown it hard and had me thoroughly off guard. It bounced off of my forehead.

"What?" I asked stupidly, looking from her to the bullet now at my feet.

"You're the Worlds' first MetalMage," Firebird said, her eyes flat. "And you just let a bullet bounce off your face."

My look of bafflement quickly shifted to one of irritation.

"I don't know how to work it," I said, for what felt like the thousandth time. "I've got no direction. Everything that you've told me doesn't work, and Laurensen pretty much told me to go bugger myself. Just because I'm the first doesn't mean that I'm good at it."

"Good at it?" Firebird asked, arching a thick brow. "I watched you on your mission. You never even considered it."

"That's because I'm as likely to do what I want as I am to make our ship implode!" And, for absolutely no reason, tears burned my eyes. It wasn't fair.

Firebird stared at me. And I glowered back. I don't know how long we stood like that, but it was long enough for my temper to flare. I reached out, my hand over the bullet, and—still glowering at Firebird—I commanded it to fly into my hand.

Nothing happened, of course.

"You haven't successfully used your MetalMage in a year. Is that accurate?" Firebird asked, ignoring my efforts.

"Yeah. And I don't know that I'm ever going to again. Unity tried to beat it out of me," my hand trembled, remembering the needles. "Are you going to try that, next? Is that really what sending me on all of these missions is about? Because if you're trying to stress me, you've succeeded. But there's something...*missing*. It's like I'm trying to drink from an empty glass. Or from a bottle that still has the cork in it. I don't know what I'm doing."

I paused, then finished:

"I don't know what I'm even doing here."

"I thought I'd made that clear," Firebird bent down, picking the bullet up from the ground. "You're here to document our—"

"Yes, yes," I snapped. "I'm here to document your missions. To make you into people with a dream, not rebels with an objective. I'm here to sway the public and to keep records for the histories that you someday want to write. And, *oh yeah*, I'm here because you think you can use me for my MetalMage. Well here's a twist, Firebird," and I threw my hands out, exasperated, "I suck at it."

Expressionless, she tossed the bullet again at my face. It bounced off of my cheek, this time. We stared at each other. Maintaining eye contact, she squatted down, picked the bullet up, and threw it again. Right off my nose.

"What the hell," I said, watching as she retrieved it.

"When we found you," she said, tossing it at my chest this time. "You were holding a dead man. Did you know him?"

"I was still holding him?" I asked, my voice breaking. The bullet hit above my right eyebrow. "*Firebird!*"

"Did you know him?"

"No. And stop that!" It almost went into my mouth. I tried to snatch it out of the air, but she was faster. The next time, she threw it harder.

"You know what, I don't have to deal with this," I started to turn, and the bullet hit the side of my head, hard enough this time to hurt.

"If you didn't know him, why were you trying to save him?"

"Because I'm a bloody human being!" I twisted to the side, avoiding the bullet this time, putting *Redwing* at my back.

Firebird calmly fished through her pockets and came up with another one. She rolled it across her fingers, watching me, her lips pursed.

"You helped kill over 2,000 people, and you were worried about one man who you don't know?" she tossed the bullet into the air, making me flinch. She caught it, one eyebrow arched.

"I didn't know that they were all going to die, at the time," I said, narrowing my eyes.

"When, exactly, did you realize that it was going to happen?"

"I don't know. Maybe when Ori and I saw the flotilla. Why does this matter?"

"It matters because I'm not sure you're cut out for this line of work. Regina doesn't think you're tough enough. Ori doesn't think you're a good enough fighter," the bullet spun, bright in the purple light, before disappearing again into her hand. "Ravin, she thinks that you need to be in a lab, where Adaptrists can run tests on you, try to figure out how your lineage allowed for MetalMage."

"Then to hell with all of them," I snarled. "I'm here because I chose to be, because you *asked* me to be. And if you don't like the way I do my job—if you don't like that I try to protect defenseless civilians—then to hell with you too."

Firebird froze, though it was something a shade too close to a smile that haunted her lips.

"To hell with me, then?" she asked. "What if I told you that I thought you were capable of more? What if you believed me?"

"I am who I am," I said, growing more irritated by the second.

"That's all any of us are," her eyes flashed. "Even when we change, we are who we are. It's the potential that keeps us up at night, and the burning need to see it fulfilled."

And the bullet was flying at my head. I don't know what was different. Maybe some hidden desire to impress Firebird. Or maybe it was simpler than that. Maybe it was as easy as falling down.

Regardless, a part of me bared its fangs, and power flooded my mind. I could sense the metal around me, the bullet in the grass, the one flying at my head, the ones in Firebird's pockets. *Redwing*, the ship something beyond simple *metal*. I felt them all.

And I snarled.

The bullet rebounded away from my face, never touching me, and shot past Firebird's ear at an alarming rate. There was a *crack*, and the bullet buried itself into a nearby tree, making the young growth tremble.

Mouth agape, I peeked around Firebird and realized that I could see clean through the tree I'd 'shot'.

"Just something to keep in mind," Firebird said, clapping her hand on my shoulder.

7

PRACTICE

"Waiting," I muttered, tapping my pen against the blank sheet of paper. "Who wants to read about waiting?"

It had never occurred to me just how much of a wild, purposeful rebel's life would involve *waiting*. I remembered waiting for my newest assignment, back before I'd joined the crew. I remembered sitting in a *waiting room* last year, *waiting* to meet Firebird for the first time. It seemed like we were always waiting for something, no matter how important, and I was beginning to chafe within the stagnant air.

And now, as we *waited* for the date of the rendezvous, I felt close to screaming.

Since writing wasn't doing anything for me, I sighed, dropping my pen and stretching. My spine gave several audible *pops*. Laurensen, standing a few meters to my right, suddenly pivoted, a gun appearing in her hand.

"What are you doing?" I asked, not nearly as startled as I should have been.

"Practicing," Laurensen muttered, cocking her head as she aimed down her pistol.

"But you're not shooting at anything," I shifted carefully in my collapsible chair, leery of the way it creaked.

"Don't have anything that needs killing," she answered, twisting and aiming at a stump instead.

Zone 1 was our favored camp, as it had a large grassy field just south of *Redwing*'s landing pad. It allowed for some much-needed open sky—as the jungle around the Chryse was dense and filled with creatures intent on dissolving and devouring our persons. The yellow grass was soft and short, unlike the savanna that we had been waiting in for weeks, and I wiggled my bare toes appreciatively into the plush turf.

Eerie snorted behind us and I twisted around, smiling at the creature. He was a Nightmare, best described as a Martian Pegasus, and his dark hide glinted in the full sunlight. He was laying down, his legs tucked under his chest, and his black wings were folded back against his sides. He had a pair of horns curling back from his forehead and when he looked at me, I saw an inky reflection of my own dark face in his intelligent eyes.

"It amazes me that he can find us, after our missions," I said, digging into my pocket and procuring a treat.

Laurensen glanced back at Eerie, her eyes softening.

"We've been together for a long time," she said. "I know where he is, even when we're nowhere near each other."

"So, it has something to do with being a Bestial BioMage," I mused, smiling as Eerie's hot tongue lapped at my palm, licking up the berries.

"I suppose so," she muttered, returning to shooting the things she *wasn't* shooting at.

Laurensen had her duster on, her hat pulled low, and the revolver in her hand was an old-style powder-base weapon. When I thought about it, I wasn't sure I'd ever seen her use anything except the powder-bases. Ori, for comparison, only ever used elemental guns—such as acid and fire—although I suspected that was less for efficiency and more for the way it made things explode.

"How did you meet him?" I asked, twisting my pen back and forth.

"Back in the Country," she said, putting an emphasis on *country* that made me think it was something more.

"But *how*," I pressed.

Laurensen's jaw tightened, aiming across the field. She held the gun in one hand, her body positioned at an angle, and her back to me. I could see the glint of one of her mismatched eyes.

Eventually, it became clear that she wasn't going to answer me. I sighed, shifting again in the chair—which protested with a squeak of metal and strained fabric—and staring at the blank piece of paper. It felt like it was silently mocking me, pale, dead, and empty on my lap.

There are times when I wondered why I ever wanted to be a writer. My brain felt like it was well and truly empty, my words dry in my pen. When I thought about writing about the *Ilena*, something dark curled up in protest inside my chest. And when I thought about writing about yet another *wait*...

Movement caught my eye and— relieved for another excuse not to work—I looked up and spotted Regina on the side of the field. She must have come from the jungle, as her hair was damp and plastered to her skull, and there were several red scratches on her pale arms. She hesitated when she saw Laurensen and I, but eventually continued into the field. She wore her blue athletic wear, sleeveless and tight, and she was twisting something on her right forearm.

When she reached the middle of the field, she turned her back to us and held her arms out from her sides, slowly moving onto one foot. I had seen her exercise once or twice before, and it always surprised me that someone as bulky as Regina could be so delicate, so graceful. I sighed, resting my hands on the paper in my lap, and watched as she slowly went through the motions of what she called *dancing*.

"It's a form of combat training," Laurensen said.

I blinked up at her, surprised to find her watching me.

"What?"

"What she's doing," she nodded toward Regina. "It's a combat-centered bodyweight training. Like yoga."

"Oh," I blinked. "Is it for her sword?"

I had been surprised when Regina first procured a silvery sword on our mission a few months back. It was some kind of BioTech that had been laid into the meat of her forearm, some kind of compound laser with a set base.

"I suppose," Laurensen shrugged, pointing her pistol at the ground, deftly flicking the chamber open and closed. "Works well for hand-to-hand, too."

"I've never seen you or Ori do anything like that."

Laurensen snorted.

"And you've rarely seen Regina do it, either, but here we are. We don't always need you sticking your nose into our business."

I blushed, looking quickly away. The truth was, I *did* feel bad, always following the crew around, digging for nuggets from their pasts. But it was my job, so I put my head down and bulled ahead. That had been easier a year ago, before I started to consider them my friends.

"How's your shooting?" Laurensen asked.

I laughed.

"About the same as it was last year. Frankly, I don't think I *want* to kill anyone. Maybe that's why I can't hit anything."

"And maybe it's because instead of practicing, you're sitting there staring at a piece of paper."

I made a face at her.

"Well, are you volunteering?"

In answer, Laurensen flipped the gun around in her hand so that she was offering the grip to me. I blinked at her, more than a little surprised. When she frowned at me, I hesitantly set my work aside and stood from the chair, accepting the gun.

It was heavier than I anticipated, its grip warm from Laurensen's hand. The barrel was slightly longer than an Earth Tech revolver, with delicate inlays worked down its dark sides. I turned it over in my hands, admiring the craftmanship.

"You know how to load it?" she asked.

"Sort of," I glanced at her. "If it's anything like Mule."

"Similar base, different weapon." Laurensen reached into a pouch at her back, brushing the duster out of the way and extracting a handful of heavy-looking bullets. "This is a chamber revolver, so you load each bullet as opposed to snapping a magazine in."

"I see," I accepted the bullets and then fumbled with the weapon, trying to get the chamber to open. I could feel Laurensen watching me, my cheeks reddening as I dropped one of the bullets in my struggle.

She leaned over and plucked it from the grass, taking the gun back from me and showing me how to flick it open, her wrist giving a practiced twist. Silently, she loaded the weapon and handed it back to me.

"Thanks," I muttered, raising the gun and aiming down the barrel at the stump she had been using. "Why didn't you use bullets?"

"I know what I'm aiming at," she answered, moving to stand behind me, her rough fingers wrapping around my wrist as she adjusted my arm. "I know where my bullets would go without needing to waste them."

"Oh, me too," I said sarcastically.

Laurensen ignored me, releasing my wrist and taking a step back.

"Keep your elbow locked, you don't need it kicking back and breaking your nose. Stand up straight, slouching allows for too much movement. Steady your breathing, stop shaking, and don't take so long. When you decide you're going to shoot something, you shoot it. Don't waste your time worrying about it. Aim, fire. That's all there is to it."

"All there is to it," I repeated.

That wasn't all there was to it, I knew. But worried that I'd already taken too long and feeling the weight of her judgment, I squeezed the trigger.

The gun kicked, though not as hard as Mule, and all I could do was wonder where my bullet had gone, as it had decidedly *not* hit the stump. I lowered the gun, my palm tingling, and glanced bashfully at Laurensen.

She snorted.

"What are you looking at me for?"

"Waiting for some ridicule or advice, maybe both," I answered, glancing back down at the gun.

"Don't waste time being embarrassed, not if you're working to be better. Anyone who judges you for that isn't worth your embarrassment. If you were still sitting in the grass doing nothing, *that's* when you need to be ashamed. Try again. Use both hands, you're not in a rusting movie. And make sure you're using the sights."

"I don't have to aim this much with Mule," I said, taking the weapon in both hands and raising it.

"Mule is a cannon. And any time I've seen you use it, the person you're shooting at is already on top of you. Don't let them get that close."

I shot at the stump and saw a small puff of dirt fly up beside it. Licking my lips, I wiggled my feet back into the dirt and shot again, this time clipping the stump's edge.

"Seems like this would be a good deterrent," I said.

"It is, if the person you're shooting at doesn't care too much about getting to you. Chances are, if you're shooting at her before she gets to you, she's going to shoot back."

"So I should practice moving," I said, springing comically to the side, shooting the last round. It went wide of the stump and thumped into a tree at the edge of the field instead.

"Maybe, if moving doesn't point you toward camp," she said, putting a finger on the gun's barrel and pushing it toward the ground.

"Oh, sorry," I cringed, glancing at Laurensen. She sniffed.

"When I said *don't worry*, I didn't mean *don't think*. You've got a gun. You're going to kill someone. Make sure it's the someone you want to kill, first."

Laurensen took her pistol back and holstered it. Eerie seemed to take that as a command. The Nightmare pushed himself upright, giving his horse-like body a brisk shake before nudging the small of Laurensen's back with his nose. Standing, Eerie seemed to have a more delicate build than Earth horses, his bones thinner and his neck slightly longer. He spread his wings, stretching them, and nearly bowled me over.

The sniper moved to her companion, running her hands down his neck to the joint of his left wing, scratching just under the muscle there. The Nightmare tucked his head and nudged at her, leaning into her hands and settling more weight than I would have been comfortable pressing against. Laurensen didn't seem to mind, her smile calm and reserved solely for Eerie.

"What country did you meet him in?" I asked. "Did other people there ride Nightmares? Or is that just your thing?"

Laurensen was quiet for a moment, and I assumed that she would just ignore my question, as that seemed to be the set standard for her whenever I went picking at her past. But, as she moved her hands under Eerie's chin, she said:

"Originally, he only let me near him because I am a Bestial BioMage. I don't have to touch his mind now, though—haven't for years. That I know of, no one else in the Country ever rode one."

"*The* Country?"

"Shay's Country, now," she glanced at me. "But the Country belongs to no one."

"Oh," I frowned at her. "You're from Overlord Shay's, then? Did you grow up there?"

"I did."

I chewed at the meat of my inner cheek, considering Laurensen. She was in as good a mood as Laurensen could be. I drew a deep breath, bracing myself.

"But you assassinated the last Overlord, right? In Madtown? Isn't that also Shay's Country? You're not even really able to show your face there, are you?"

To my surprise, Laurensen laughed.

"I'm not allowed to show my face in more places on Mars than there are on Earth," she said, pulling her duster off and tossing it across my vacant chair. It immediately collapsed under the weight.

"Then why do it?"

"Same reason you go digging around in my business," she said, throwing one leg up and over Eerie.

"Why's that?"

"I'm good at it," she said, nudging Eerie with her heels.

The Nightmare shot forward, his wings spreading and his hooves thundering against the soft grass. I watched as he propelled them upwards, kicking hard and beating the air. Eerie taking off was an explosion of energy, especially when he carried Laurensen. Once in the air, he could soar for hours. But getting there was obviously a strain, something that had hardened him into the fierce creature I knew.

They circled the field, each turn taking them higher. My gaze fell to Regina, but she was keen on ignoring me, her motions smooth and focused. She was on one leg now, the other drawn up across her thigh, and she was making a slow rotating movement in her torso, twisting as far as I'd think was possible. It made my spine hurt, just watching her.

Heaving a sigh, I turned and dug around under Laurensen's duster, finding my paper and pen crumpled under it. Then I grabbed my collapsible chair and tried to fold it back into the tidy bundle I'd found it in. Instead, I pinched one of my fingers in the three twisted legs. Swearing softly, I tucked the mess under my arm and started back up the path, toward the trees.

During the night, the Martian jungle was alive with color. The bioluminescence inherent in many of the trees and shrubs, moss and fungi, allowed for a wide spectrum of color—red, magenta, deep purple, shimmering gold. When I would walk this same path in the dark, the shifting colors reminded me of a kaleidoscope, slowly turning around me.

However, in the daylight, the Martian jungle was sullen. Fat leaves, dark blue with dirty, yellow veins curled up around me. Small white flowers in the near-black trunks of trees shrank back into their protective casings at my passing. It smelled of heavy soil and decay, with the occasional whiff of something sweet like honey. Birds nested high overhead, small creatures scuttled quickly underfoot, and I had learned after my first month of living in the jungle— one did not simply walk barefoot in the Martian jungle.

Halfway to the ship, I slowed. The birdsong, usually a cacophony, had faded around me, leaving a hungry kind of quiet. I wet my lips, glancing over my shoulder. Laurensen usually worked to keep the native predators back from our camp. But, in my experience, no one was perfect. I considered going back to the field, since that was the safer route. But then, I heard something.

I cocked my head, narrowing my eyes at the dense vegetation on my right. It was brushy, with giant thick-leaved ferns stretching well over my head. The sound was soft, a hoarse, empty kind of cry. It made me think of someone weeping, but it was a note off, a breath too thick to be called a sob.

The sound slowly died away, turning instead to a rattling kind of breathing.

I set my things by the base of a tree, crouching lower, looking for tracks in the soft dirt. There were none. But when I straightened, I saw that several of the thick ferns had been bruised, their leaves turning slowly red instead of the near-black purple. I didn't know much about tracking, but Laurensen had dropped a few helpful hints during the past year. Glancing back toward the field, I drew a quiet breath and stepped onto the path.

Instantly, my boots sank into the moss. It grew in a blanket under the ferns, which I had to duck and weave around as I followed the sound. It was growing softer the closer I got, and I paused, worried that I was about to be eaten by something more clever than I was. I remembered Ori telling a story about a Martian jaguar that mimicked the sound of a dying animal to attract curious prey. I'd thought she'd been trying to scare me, at the time. But right now, with the Martian jungle wrapped around me, her story seemed a touch too on point.

Resting my hand on my belt, where I had a small knife tucked in a sheath, I continued hesitantly forward, crouching lower to the ground, trying to avoid the ferns. I came around the base of a tree and saw a small clearing.

My blood ran cold.

With a cry, I darted forward, tripping over the tangled roots under me. There was a bed of thick moss, the dark green cushion turning black where I touched it. And, in its center, with the blackened vegetation curling around her tiny body, was Brute.

Jiggy was on the ground just out of her reach, the glass dome open. I could see the black footprints where Brute had walked on the moss. She'd gotten maybe five meters before collapsing. I grabbed her shoulders, pulling her up, shouting her name.

I had only seen Brute outside of Jiggy once before, when I had broken the little robot with my Magic. She had seemed like a flightless bird, thin-boned and twisted. Now, however, there was something empty about her.

Brute kept her ebony hair in thick pigtails, and they trembled over the ground as I scooped her up, dragging her back toward Jiggy. She had some kind of device in her mouth, maybe a filter, and it was embedded into her cheeks. A metal smile. Her eyes were closed and her lungs were spasming. The sound I had heard was the air as it was forced through the device, a thick whining sound. Brute's olive-colored skin was turning blue.

I fumbled with her tiny body, dragging her back to Jiggy, folding her arms and legs and tucking her into the red, velvet pillows. My hands were shaking as I tried to pull the dark glass dome closed. When it wouldn't budge, I started slapping my hands down on the different monitors by where Brute's knees usually were. I cried out, twisting back toward the trail, trying to get someone to help. But we were alone.

Jiggy's controls were in Brute's native of-then Japanese. As a child of one of the Thirteen, I had never learned anything except the Unified language. They had eradicated all cultures, rewritten all texts, and done away with anything that could give a group of people "individuality in common". It was a contradiction in terms, I knew, but the driving force that had powered Unity.

Now, I felt my eyes begin to burn with tears of frustration. I tried the last panel, prodding each character, and something in Jiggy's door activated. With a puff of air, it flipped down, very nearly catching my hands inside of it. I saw the free hair around the edge of Brute's scalp stir as Jiggy's filtration system worked to give her artificial Earth-air. It was dark within the little robot—I'd apparently turned down the lights in my wild fumble—but I could see her eyelids as they fluttered, her thin chest pulling at the artificial air.

I let free a cry of relief, falling back in the moss. It was damp, instantly soaking through the seat of my pants, but I barely noticed. As I watched, Brute's eyes opened and she dragged in a ragged breath, the wheezing filter still in her mouth. She clawed at it, ripped it angrily out, and choked in her protected dome. For a long time, she crouched and clutched at her throat, leaning over her consoles, her head bumping against Jiggy's glass.

Finally, Brute's coughing subsided. She rested there for a long time, breathing quietly, and I had the distinct feeling that she was avoiding looking at me, either embarrassed or afraid. I touched Jiggy's side: its filters whirred softly.

"Are you alright?" I asked, gently as I could.

Brute's shoulders slumped within the robot, shaking as she wept. She rocked her head back and forth against the glass, and it was the most broken *no* I had ever seen. Biting my lip, I patted the robot's side.

"What happened? Did you fall out? Is there anything I can do?"

Suddenly, Brute snarled, shoving herself back from the glass, scrubbing her sleeve against her eyes. She threw the little filter she had put in her mouth and it bounced harmlessly off of the glass, falling down between monitors and pillows. When Brute lowered her arm, letting me see her face, instead of sorrow, I saw fury.

"I *hate* this place," she snarled.

"Brute..." I trailed off, drawing a slow breath. "I'm sorry. I wish I could help."

"I thought that I had figured it out," she said, her voice tight from crying. "I thought that I could make a portable filter, something that would let me walk and move freely, like the rest of you. But no matter what I try, this world is *toxic* to me."

I chewed my lip, not knowing what I could say, *knowing* that nothing I said would help her.

"Brute..."

She shook her head, drawing a sharp breath. Straightening within Jiggy, Brute tapped at the different screens, procuring the holograms over her knees. Jiggy lifted from the ground, the lights around its circumference turning the deepest of blues.

"Don't worry about it. I'm used to this. It's just that sometimes," she hesitated, her eyes flashing when she glanced at me. "Sometimes, I think I'd do anything to be able to walk again."

"No one could blame you for that."

"Couldn't they?"

"Not if they cared about you the way we do," I stood, dusting moss from my backside. "We'd do anything to help you out of there. Are you going to be alright?"

"Yes. And no." She hesitated. "And Jezi, you can't say that. What I would have to do to get out of here, I think would be a price no one here can willingly pay. I'm still not even convinced it's possible."

"You mean like the filter you just tried? If there's something we can do to help you, all that you have to do is say it. We'd do anything."

"Not anything. Think about the *Ilena*. Think about what I did to her."

"That wasn't just you, Brute. Firebird, all of us, we *all* accepted the mission. It wasn't your fault." It was the wrong thing to say.

Jiggy's lights flashed red and Brute twisted away from me, darting back.

"What do you mean, *wasn't my fault*?"

"I just mean that the *Ilena*...you couldn't have known what disabling the firewall would do. It wasn't your fault."

"Sure, and it wasn't your fault either. But how does that help you sleep at night?" Brute's voice suddenly filled the little clearing, startling several birds overhead. I shrank back, raising my hands.

"I'm sorry, Brute. I didn't mean anything. I just don't want you to be—"

"Be *what*? I'm a crippled little girl who can't even figure out the sub-written commands on a memory chip. I wiped the data from it. I should have seen that there was still a hidden message, one that was encrypted. But Firebird wanted it done *right now* and I didn't run a second check after wiping it. So, yes, Jezi! It *is* my fault. And I *hate* Mariana for it. I've never hated anyone so much. Not in my entire life!"

"Brute..."

"And now, I can't even take a step outside of this robot. I can't breathe. I can't talk. I can't even call out for help," her sobs were amplified by Jiggy, and they made the sensitive ferns around us turn a dark, bruising red. "How exactly am I going to exact my revenge on Mariana? What can I do about *anything* in this life?"

"If you just give it some time, Brute, I think—"

But she was gone, whirring back into the jungle along the path to *Redwing*. I stared after her, my mouth slightly open, my heart heavy in my chest.

8

ELEGANCE

"Are you angry?" I asked Harry, watching as she closed the shuttle's dome.

"About?" she asked, checking her nav display.

"Not making the rendezvous," I settled down in the back of *Galaxy 2*, nestled into the dark red pillows.

Regina snorted from her place beside me, and I shot her a dirty look.

"Does it matter?" the larger woman said, rolling her eyes to me. "Firebird made it plenty clear. Biggie's a client, and we keep our word to our clients."

"And you're not at all worried that she only took Ori? A year ago, Biggie tried to blow us out of the sky just for entering the Chryse. If she tried to kill us once already, what's stopping her from doing it again after she has the data?"

"An assassin," Regina nodded toward Laurensen, who once again was lurking. "And, frankly, if Biggie wanted to kill us, we would be dead."

"That's not entirely true," Harry muttered. "She's wanted me dead for years."

Galaxy 2 was the shuttlecraft Firebird used for short transits from our base camp in the Chryse to the city. It was a *Globe*-class craft, with a white bottom and a black dome of glass for the top. Perfectly circular, it comfortably fit three people in the back, while Harry sat cross-legged in its center, holograms and displays filling the dark globe with muted, blue light. As the engines kicked in and we lifted off of the ground, lights around its inner circumference brightened slightly.

"You're family," Regina said, and there was something nasty about her smile. "She wouldn't kill family."

Harry sighed heavily, though she didn't seem as disturbed by Regina's comment as I might have been.

"That was never really true, even when Maya and I were married," Harry eventually said. "The good news is that as long as I'm not with Firebird, she's probably safe."

We were rising straight up, *Galaxy 2* humming gently. The Martian rainforest spread out beneath us, the soft purple glow of bioluminescence giving shape to an otherwise dark world. It was cloudy, and a murky haze to the west marked Biggie's Chryse.

"Maya was her daughter, right?" I asked, though I already knew the answer.

There was a ticking kind of silence. Laurensen shifted on the other side of Regina, her heavy duster pulled tight, nearly obscuring the rifle that she held in her lap.

She had the collar tugged up, so that all I could see under the brim of her hat was the wicked gleam of her mismatched eyes.

"She was," Harry murmured.

"Probably be best if Laurensen didn't show her face, then," Regina didn't look at the assassin.

"Obviously," Harry snapped.

"Why?" I blinked, looking from Laurensen to Regina.

Harry shoved her hands forward and the shuttlecraft suddenly took off, speeding toward Biggie's Chryse with the kind of reckless determination that only comes from fragile resolve. Despite the excellent Grav-Compensators Brute had installed, I felt my stomach flatten itself against my spine. I giggled.

"Oh, for rust's sake," Regina growled at me. "How old are you?"

"Too old to care," I said.

The journey from our Zone 2 base to Biggie's Chryse was about half an hour, and we made the rest of it in silence. I caught a glimpse of Harry's face as she navigated her way past the auto-lane, and the grim set of her jaw made me think of the way Ori looked when she needed to do something grotesque. Like her laundry.

Martian Skyways have four lanes, incoming and outgoing, auto and manual. Harry, being Harry, never used the auto lane, and so we zipped along at twice the average speed. I was pretty sure that there were no regulations when it came to flying in the manual lane—if you were crazy enough to go in there, it seemed Martian law gave you your right to suicide.

Biggie's Chryse was a party, as always. The skyscrapers were like mountains, and we dove along the river of Skyway between them. Massive advertisements danced on the sides of the buildings. Near the top, glassy archways marked the transports between upper floors. And, even through the soundproofing, I could feel the bass.

Biggie loved ancient-style swing music, but with new, Martian beats. And she had the music playing within the city at night, like one massive dance floor. Beneath us, blurring together in a monstrosity of colors, I saw the people in the street. Some actually were dancing, some were just on their way somewhere more important, but all of them had Biggie's signature style: bright colors, wild hats, big voices.

Harry dropped out of the manual lane, zipping onto a narrower Skyway in between two dreary buildings. As she sat us down, I felt the darkness creeping in, like we were in a bubble watching the bright world spin beyond our reach. Regina muttered a curse.

"I'm not going to fly to the drop, bold as you like," Harry said, glancing at Regina.

Galaxy 2's engines began to cool, filling our dome with the *hum*, and it set for a poor counterpoint to Regina's scowl.

"If I wanted to be dropped in a dumpster, I would have taken the rusting public transit," she said.

"Bite me," and Harry made a rude gesture, her middle finger prodding the button near the ceiling with the same motion. The front of the dome crept back and allowed us exit.

I was the first out of *Galaxy 2*. I had my satchel, and it felt good to have its reassuring weight on my shoulder again. Within was my tablet, and a small '90 powder-base pistol that Regina had given me. It wouldn't do anything against armor, but if I aimed at "the mushy parts" I might slow someone down. Mule was too loud and too bulky for Biggie's Chryse. Or so I'd been told.

Regina was next out, and she needed to bend almost in half to duck through the opening. She straightened outside, clasping her hands behind her back and arching to the chorus of several loud *pops*.

"You look..." I started, staring at her.

"I look?" she asked, rolling her massive shoulders forward and cocking a brow.

"...Nice," I finished lamely.

Nice wasn't the word. *Elegant* was the word, but I didn't dare call her that. In all the time I'd known Regina, she wore simple shirts and loose pants made for walking. Her pale hair usually stood up on her head in the unruliest of fashions, and the closest thing I'd ever seen to her wearing makeup was the time she'd passed out on *Redwing* and Ori had drawn glasses on her.

Now, she wore a white silk shirt with a starched collar, buttoned down and hanging loosely around a pair of black dress pants. Her coat was tailored, and it cradled her muscular figure in a way that made me realize that not all her curves were muscles. She had her hair spiked on the top and swept smoothly back on the sides, a pair of blue sapphire earrings in the shape of teardrops trembling just over her shoulders.

"She's just shocked to realize you have breasts," Harry said, jumping down from the shuttlecraft.

Harry looked like Harry always looked. Beige shirt with the sleeves ripped off, dark pants with suspenders, and a dark fedora over her low ponytail. She winked at me, but I could see the tension behind her eyes.

Laurensen was the last out. The shuttle's door crept closed behind her, and she didn't so much as glance at us. With a swirl of a duster, she was striding down the road, away from the busy, bright street. Harry stared after her for a moment. Then, with a pointed look at Regina, she said:

"I need a drink."

"With everything that's going on?" I asked, scurrying to keep up with the two women as they started toward the main street.

"Everything *is* why I need the drink," the pilot muttered.

"I'm not drinking anything in this part of town," Regina said, fidgeting with something on her finger. "Probably make their wine in a toilet bowl."

"You've got two good legs," Harry's voice was darker by the minute. "Won't kill you to walk for a bit."

We stepped onto the main street, and my senses were instantly overwhelmed. Light, sound, chaos: the world was a mad place, boiling with nearly too much life. The Skyway roared over our heads, the muted thrum of a thousand shuttles almost drowned out by the rolling beat of a strange, jazzy tune. There were no lonely souls playing music, not in Biggie's Chryse. She liked what she liked, and that's what she quelled her people under.

We were soon caught up in the current, folks walking and running and riding hover bikes. Harry let herself be shepherded along, her brim low and her eyes downcast. I'd noticed that I got better results when I copied her posture, fewer people shoved me out of their way if I was the one bulling ahead. Regina, on the other hand, stood tall and dared the folks around her with a single look of her strikingly blue eyes.

"Don't they ever get sick of the music?" I asked, noticing a skinny man wearing a pair of oversized headphones.

"The higher-end apartments are soundproofed," Harry said, her hands in her pockets, her shoulders nudging toward her ears in a shrug. "But you get used to it."

"I don't see how that's possible," I muttered, though neither of the women would be able to hear me.

Noise aside, color was another assault on the senses in Biggie's Chryse. The skyscrapers' sides were walls for advertisements, bright ships and greasy food rolling up the great spires. The dizzying illumination dazzled the pavement, as did the flickers of light that marked the different lanes.

Technically, everything on the ground in Biggie's Chryse would be defined—by Earthly standards—as a sidewalk. There were hover bikes and skates, plus the occasional carriage-like shuttle, but all high-speed modes of transportation were restricted to the Skyway. My eyes followed one of the more muted advertisements up a skyscraper, and I saw the clear-floored landing pad at its peak.

Glassy structures with soft, yellow lights laced between the skyscrapers like spider silk. They were bridges, landing pads, and elevators, allowing people access to higher rooms without the need to go inside. Most office workers made their entire commute without ever needing to come to ground-level.

Harry followed the main street, occasionally glancing down the alleys. I wasn't sure if she was looking for someone, something, or simply on the hunt for danger, but she had me on edge. Every now and then, I'd feel that uncomfortable prickling at the back of my neck, and I'd throw a glance over my shoulder, fully expecting to be looking down the barrel of someone's gun.

Such was my life.

Eventually, we came to a city square with a fountain in its center. The street wrapped around it, many people pausing to take in the view. The advertisements were toned down here, to where some buildings only had twinkling lights drifting down their facades, like snow. Smaller buildings rimmed the square, and many had outdoor dining arrangements, with bright red awnings and the occasional blue fireplace.

"Dolphin Square," I said. It was one of Harry's favorite places, and whenever we managed to slink into the city under Biggie's radar, we spent our down-time at Clarence's Pub.

"Backward way of getting here," Regina grumbled.

I glanced at the big woman, surprised to see that her usual look of contempt had been replaced by one of...anxiety? No, that wasn't quite it. She noticed me staring, and offered me a frown instead.

"Problem?" She asked.

"You're...different," I said, instantly regretting my choice in words. "What I mean is, you're not acting like...Is something wrong?"

"Mind your own business." She turned to Harry. "How long?"

"Maybe an hour before they rendezvous. Are you going to—"

"My com is on," she said. "I'll be nearby, if you need me."

And just like that, the big woman turned and started off toward a different building, with a golden façade and gentle, swirling lights. There was a resoluteness to her stride, a boldness in the way she straightened her back, and just a hint of sensuality to the way her hips shifted. I realized my mouth was hanging open, and I closed it slowly.

"Where's she going?" I asked as Harry started toward Clarence's.

"Meeting someone, I'd suspect," the pilot answered.

"But who? Is she...*dating* someone?" The notion was so absurd, I nearly tripped over the entryway into the pub. "Not to be rude, but she doesn't strike me as the dating type. I've never seen her so much as flirt with anyone," whereas Ori essentially ambushed men and women, pouncing with fangs bared. "And now she's got a date?"

"Best be asking her," and that was all that Harry was going to say on the subject. "Close the door behind you."

I obeyed, heaving my shoulder into it. It was a heavy, beast of a door, with rough wood and thick iron banding. I avoided touching the metal. Something about iron bothered me in ways that titanium and other higher-end metals did not. As the entryway was sealed, the din outside subsided.

Clarence himself was a portly man with a red beard and a shining, bald head. He wore a white apron, and the bar he worked behind was elevated, so that patrons had to climb a couple of dark steps to even sit on the bar stools. The lighting was dark, and he used real lamps, their golden flames lending a trickling kind of glow to the mahogany bar.

"Clarence," Harry said, trotting up the stairs and throwing herself onto the stool. She tipped her hat back with a knuckle, something like a smile touching her lips.

"Harry," he nodded, sliding a glass coaster in front of her. "The usual?"

She nodded, watching as I clambered into the stool next to her. There were only a few other people at the bar, and they sat at the far end. One round table was at the front of the room, near a small window that looked onto the street. The rest were toward the back, seven in all, and three had lonely-looking customers at them.

It was one of the busier times I'd seen at Clarence's. I watched him climb a library ladder up the wall of shelves, his short-fingered hand plucking a dark bottle from the top. A few of the shelves, built in smaller nooks, had actual books in them, their leather bindings displaying gilded words. Earth books. I felt a pang somewhere behind my heart.

"I can't decide if I love or hate this place," I said.

"I figured you'd like it for the soundproofing, if nothing else," Harry said. Soft, gentle, Ancient-style jazz floated through the room, soothing my temper. It was big band, truly classic stuff.

"Oh, I love everything about it. It reminds me of Earth, of my favorite pub in of-then Oxford." I paused as Clarence sat a tumbler in front of Harry. "That's what bothers me."

He pulled the cork—an actual cork, not the synthetic "garbage" that Martian distilleries used—and the bottle gave a throaty *thwop.* When he poured, the whiskey that swirled into the glass was rich gold. Harry breathed deeply, her fingers turning the drink like a jeweler would a gem.

"Alright, Jezi?" he asked, turning to me. I smiled.

"Think you could make a martini for me? Gin, of course."

"Of course," he had a rough face, like someone of the Ancient North American West. "Dirty, yeah?"

"You know it," I watched him limp off, his one mechanical leg leaving the stench of metal near my nose.

Harry closed her eyes, taking a slow sip of the whiskey. Say this for her, she knew how to enjoy a drink.

"I'm not totally convinced we should be drinking on this job," I said.

"This is the only job I *would* drink on," Harry answered, eyes still closed, lips still close to the glass's rim. "And I'm not technically *on* any job."

"Is it because of your history with Biggie? There didn't seem to be a problem when our client approached us. Why would she make trouble now?"

"Not my problem, since I'm not there," Harry touched the glass to her lower lip.

I snorted.

"I can't believe that Biggie doesn't know where you are. What's keeping someone from coming in and taking us? I don't see how you're this calm. They just killed…" I lowered my voice as Clarence returned with my martini "…a lot of people."

Harry stared at her whiskey. Worried that I'd spill, I leaned forward and sipped at my drink without picking it up. Salt and gin, cold as ice in a classic martini glass. I closed my eyes, letting go of a breath. Maybe this wasn't such a bad idea after all.

"I know Biggie," Harry eventually said. "She won't kill us. She wants something."

"Yeah, the data," I took another sip.

"More than the data. If it was just data, she'd have us use a Pigeon. She wants Firebird. And when Biggie wants something," she smirked, "nothing short of murder will keep her from it."

"We're killing her now?" I took another sip.

"No, we're not killing her. Firebird's right," Harry shrugged. "Between Olympus Mons and the Chryse, this is the lesser of two evils. But what do I know," and she winked at me, "I'm just the pilot."

The pilot who stole Overlord Mariana's only daughter from her. I leaned back in my stool, coming as close to lounging as I dared, and eyed the ancient books. There was something safe about Clarence's, even with everything going on around us. It was hard to be on edge.

"How did you and Maya meet?" I asked, my usual caution dulled by the martini.

Harry smiled, which surprised me. She cast me a look with the side of her eye.

"This is the first time you've asked me about her."

"Seemed like an opportune moment."

She paused, twisting her glass this way and that. She was taking it slow, which was a bit of a relief. Biggie might want us alive, but I wasn't keen on the idea of being attacked with only drunk-Harry at my side.

"She was wearing white," Harry's words were as smooth as her whiskey. "A gown, I suppose. Her hair was long and black, and she kept it tied up on the sides. She had an elegance about her," she shook her head. "Something I've never seen the like of since. Charming, I suppose. Bold, in her own way. She knew how to make a statement, knew how to walk a line I couldn't see. I saw her by that fountain," a small nod toward the Square. "She was dancing."

"Dancing?"

Harry's lips quirked. She took another, deeper drink.

"It was her wedding day," she said.

I frowned at Harry, my mouth still a little open for a question I'd now forgotten. The door to the pub opened, and the pilot glanced toward the entryway, a half-thought gesture. She paused, then her eyes widened.

"Wha—" she started.

A heartbeat later, someone slammed her hand down next to me so hard, it sounded like a gunshot. I squeaked, nearly flying into Harry's lap as I leapt from my stool. Regina stared past me, her sapphire earrings swinging madly from her lobes.

When I met her gaze, the fear within me came to a crystalline halt.

"This," said the big woman, as she raised her palm, "was sent to me, in Zander's name."

From her thick fingers, a golden ring dangled from a silver chain.

9

WEBS

I *remember the day Jerry asked me to marry him. I remember the way my guts twisted up, the way my heart had skipped a beat. It was raining, of course. His red hair was clumped on his forehead, his shaggy beard dripping. He stared up at me in a way that stabbed my heart, his eyes blue and beautiful.*

The ring hadn't been fancy, but it had been old. His grandmother's. I remember that it was cold, when he slipped it on my finger. It shouldn't have fit, but it did. I remember wondering how he'd known my size.

When we kissed, I felt a spark. I called it love.

I still don't think I know what love is.

I think about him, sometimes. I wonder what he did with his life, after I left him. I know that I miss him, in the lonely hours of the night. But after my brother died, after I went to my mother and asked to join Unity, I'd known there was no room for a husband in this new, cruel world.

I'm not sure there'd ever been room. Not in my heart. Not in my mind. And certainly not in the sterile, tired thing I'd once thought of as a soul.

* * *

"Regina," Harry started, reaching around me for the ring.

"*In* Zander's *name*," Regina hissed, her fingers tightening on the chain. She shook it, and the ring spun crazily.

"Who's Zander?" I asked, staring open-mouthed at Regina.

The silence between them twisted, like an animal in pain. Regina's jaw tightened, and the muscles in the sides of her face bulged. I thought that she was going to spit at us. Then, she let the chain slide off of her fingers. It hit the bar in front of me, a miserable puddle of metal. I could see tiny indents in her skin.

Harry hesitated, her gaze moving to the ring as though it might snap at her. I frowned at it.

"Isn't that the same as..." My eyes flicked to Harry's neck. "Was that Maya's?"

The pilot reached out, resting her fingers on the ring and sliding it toward her. Her hand trembled. She drew a slow breath. Then, almost reverently, she scooped the ring and chain into her palm, pocketing it without looking at it.

"How could she know?" Harry whispered, staring through her drink on the bar.

"I don't rusting know," Regina talked as though her teeth were hinged together, a growl deep in her mouth. "But she has him. And I'm going to rusting kill every last one of them."

A furrow appeared between Harry's brows.

"Why would she take Zander? Unless Firebird didn't make the rendezvous, and we know that she intended to. She likely has her data and she destroyed the *Ilena*."

"And she wants more," Regina leaned in, too close to me, snarling at Harry: "Now what are we going to do to get him back? You know her. You know the base. Get me in there."

"We charge in guns blazing, and you'll get Zander's head on a pike," Harry's eyes snapped toward Regina, and there was something darker about them. "Was there anything else?"

"Does there *need* to be?" Regina hissed.

"*Who*," I interjected, "is Zander?"

Regina's scowl slid toward me, but I kept my chin up.

"He's her husband," Harry said.

My mouth popped open, almost as quickly as Regina's did.

"I told you to keep that to yourself," she was just short of punching Harry.

"Like it matters now," Harry shot back. "The most powerful woman on Mars knows, and she's got him bottled up somewhere in her palace. Do you really think

Jezi knowing that Zander exists is going to somehow compromise his security?"

Regina fumed, her teeth grinding. Then, her thumb jerked toward me, her gaze snagging mine.

"You write anything about this, and I'll rip your fingers off," she promised. Then, to Harry, "You still haven't told me how we're getting him back. I will break down her door, if I have to."

"Just take a breath," and Harry slid stiffly from her stool, like a woman twenty years her elder. "And remember who we are. The first thing we do is contact Firebird. She should have made the drop by now. Clarence," and the bartender glanced at her, glass in his hands, "Just charge it."

He gave a shallow nod, eyes returning to his polishing. If he had heard what Regina said, he showed no sign of it. I followed the women from the pub, feeling a warmth blossoming somewhere in my chest.

Because being intoxicated right now was obviously just what I needed.

When we were once again in Dolphin Square, Harry pulled a data pad from her back pocket. The display opened blue, but when she tapped the communications icon, the screen flashed red. She frowned, trying again. Then, with a wary glance at Regina, she said:

"We'll try the shuttle."

"Someone's blocking our coms?" I asked, heartrate increasing.

Neither woman answered. Not that I expected them to, really. My questions often hung in the air, like miserable pieces of bait.

The journey back to the shuttle was a forced march, with Regina's long stride devouring ground. I scrambled to keep up. I wasn't out of shape, per say. But when it came to pacing Firebird's crew, even Dr. Ravin left me scrambling.

Several times, I caught a glimpse of someone in the crowd watching us, dark eyes and stilled forms. But by the time I caught Harry's sleeve to point them out, the people had shifted and the person disappeared. She said it was my imagination. I wanted to agree with her.

But, I knew better.

By the time we reached the shuttle, I was panting for breath. It sat in the abandoned alleyway, white and gleaming. Harry reached it a beat before Regina did, slapping her palm down on the entry pad. It flared green, then immediately turned red. Both women stilled. Harry pulled her hand back, hesitated, then stepped away.

"You try," she said softly.

Regina raised her hand slowly, and I thought I heard a muttered oath, before she placed it gingerly on the pad. A pause. Then, red.

"Bloody—" Regina started.

Something cold pressed into the small of my back.

Now, I've had guns pressed against me before. It's a hazard of the trade. But I was wearing two shirts and a leather jacket, and while the thing pressed into my back was the size of a gun's muzzle, I definitely should not have felt *cold*.

"Easy," a deep, rasping voice at my ear, a hand on my shoulder. "Let's not do anything rash."

The blood in my ankles turned to ice, which then shot straight up my legs. Fear clung to me, like spider silk, and when I drew a breath, it was in sharp, silent response. The cold thing pressed harder, and I felt it…*wrap* around the base of my spine. Not like it broke the skin, there was no pain: only a sensation of solidity, a tendril of winter.

Regina and Harry spun. My eyes widened as weapons appeared in their hands. Harry held a small pistol, its blue muzzle bespeaking an electric-based shot, and she gripped her wrist with her free hand, aiming down the length of her arm at the person behind me. Her hazel eyes flicked to my face, and I saw something in her harden.

Regina had angled sideways, and a long, slender blade appeared in her left hand. It was silver, and shadows pulled toward it like metal filings toward a magnet. It didn't glow. It *ate* darkness. I'd seen her use it before, to cut wires in the belly of a ship we looted. Where its fine edge had touched them, the wires had melted.

"Easy," my captor repeated, giving me a small shake, as though reminding the other two that I existed. Regina didn't so much as spare me a look. "We'll take this one step at a time."

"Spider," Harry said, her aim unwavering.

"McKinley," the person behind me answered, Harry's last name filling me with a new kind of dread. This man knew us. More than *us*, more than the Firebird's crew. He knew our *persons*.

His voice was edgy and hoarse, something rattling in his chest when he breathed. His hand on my shoulder tightened and the coldness at the base of my spine...*twisted*. My eyes watered, though whether from pain or fear, I wasn't sure. I started to raise my hands, not even sure what I intended to do with them.

"None of that," he said, the coldness twisting again, making white lights pop around the edges of my vision. "I don't need to hurt you."

"That's a crock," Regina said. She took a sideways step toward us, a fencer's pose, and she raised the tip of her sword. Her suit jacket reflected an *absence* of light.

"Pardon?" He asked, pushing me slightly forward, making me take a small step. He came with me.

"You've always *needed* to hurt people," Regina said. "Come out from behind her and fight me like a human being, you sniveling dog."

"Ah, Gina. How I've missed you."

Regina's eyes narrowed, her nostrils flaring as she sucked oxygen. I'd seen her in fights before. I knew what came next. Something small inside of me whimpered, the coldness tightening. Blisters of pain raced up my spine, electrifying my nerves, chilling the base of my skull. Something hot ran from a nostril, tickling the small hairs on my upper lip.

"Careful," Harry warned, glancing at her companion.

"Only Zander calls me Gina," her knuckles popped as she twisted her blade sideways, like she meant to carve me in half to get at the man called Spider.

"And he's been calling it out repeatedly," he said, chuckling. "Particularly when I was with him."

Regina paled, making a ghost of herself.

"If he is hurt," she started, her voice draining into darkness.

"Nothing permanent. But we did have a few questions, and he's something of a tight-lipped bastard."

"Regina!" Harry snapped as the woman lunged forward, sword raised.

I don't know what happened. I don't even know enough to describe it. I saw Regina's sword angling sideways, like to slice off the hand on my shoulder, and then...*pain*. The alley went white, my ears popped. There was something screaming inside my head. My extremities went numb. My spine, every vertebra in it, lit up like the sun. I felt agony collect along the base of my skull, like roots cracking stone. I thought I was flying, I thought—in a very real way—I was dead.

And then, as quickly as it came, it was gone. The alley darkened as my vision returned, my ears ringing. I could still feel the coldness at my back, and my throat felt raw. I wondered if I'd screamed.

Regina stood a pace away, her sword's edge hovering a hair's breadth from my neck. I was twisted slightly sideways, like a human shield, and I could feel the man at my back, could feel his grip turn. There was something crazy in Regina's blue eyes. Harry stood behind her, the tip of her gun steady. She was glowering at Regina's back.

"Incapacitators," Spider announced, supremely satisfied. "Delightful, aren't they? Physically, I can turn her into a puppet. And mentally? No BioMagic whatsoever. It would appear that it works on MetalMages, as well. Isn't that nice?"

Sweat trembled in droplets on Regina's brow. At long last, she looked at me. Her mouth thinned.

"Now, Gina," and the man behind me twisted, pushing my throat closer to her blade, "you haven't even asked why I'm here."

"You have my husband," she whispered, and something like fear slipped into her voice.

"*I* don't have him. But *my* Lady, *she* very much does. And she'd like a...tête-à-tête, if you would. It's been such a long time, after all."

"And if we refuse?" Harry said, her voice an icy, dead thing.

"My dear," and the mouth was closer to my neck, his breath tickling my hair, "I think we both know the answer to that."

Regina's blade trembled, like it actually *hungered* for blood. Then, with a sharp breath, she flicked it away. The blade seemed to dissipate, lights swirling out from it until it had dissolved back into the air. Spider straightened, pulling me up with him. He gave me a brisk shake.

"Good as new, love. The rest goes simply enough. I'm going to open this shuttle, and McKinley, if you'd be good enough to pilot us home? My Lady has been *dying* to see you. When was the last time? When you delivered her daughter's corpse?"

Harry blinked. She still hadn't lowered her gun. Regina looked at her.

"They have my husband," she said.

The pilot was still for a moment longer. Then, releasing a breath, she lowered her pistol. Spider kissed the side of my neck.

"Lovely, darling. And now," he tugged, pulling me along as he sidled down the alley, past Harry. He stopped by the shuttle, one hand remaining on my shoulder while the other slapped against the panel. A flash of green light, a cheerful *chirrup* from the machine, and the dome swiveled backwards.

He backed in first, dragging me after. I was pulled to the back of the shuttle. It was a rounded ceiling, of course, and lower where we were. As Harry stepped inside, something jabbed me in the meat of my thigh. The nerves electrified in my legs as my muscles suddenly went lax, dropping me to my knees so quickly, I felt my kneecaps *crack* against the shuttle's floor.

"Come now, dear," Spider purred toward Harry, as the pilot hesitated. "You've got a shuttle to fly. And Gina, darling, if you'd be so kind as to sit facing me, just there," he nodded toward one of the cushions. "I like to keep an eye on people's faces, just to be sure. You understand."

Regina was silent as she took her place. Something behind my eyes ached, and a fresh dribble emerged from my nostrils, trickling around the corner of my mouth. I licked instinctively, and blood laced across my tongue.

"I'm sorry," I said, my voice empty in the little cockpit.

146

"Now, now," Spider purred, mouth again by my ear. "Nothing to be sorry for, love. Just one of those things. McKinley, I've got a constant feed through to the Lady. Should we stray off course…"

"You don't need to threaten me," she said, taking her place, the holograms brightening as the shuttle closed.

"And I trust you remember where you're going?" Spider asked.

The engines within the shuttle hummed to life. I glanced at Regina, the woman staring at Spider with such intensity, it was a wonder the man hadn't simply melted. Her eye caught mine, and she winced.

Not bothering to answer, Harry maneuvered us out of the alley and into the Skyway. We followed it deeper into the city, gathering speed like a charge gathering momentum. The coldness twisted, and my lungs betrayed a whimper, the cockpit brightening.

"You just can't let someone be?" Regina asked, her voice tight.

"I really just can't," he admitted, his fingers drumming along my shoulder. "It is my greatest weakness."

"Leave her alone," Harry said, not turning. "You've got what you wanted."

"That's the thing, dear," and his mouth brushed my neck again, teeth sliding on skin. "Like my darling Gina pointed out, it's not *want*. It's *need*. And control has just never been my strong suit."

Harry didn't speak again. But I felt the shuttle quiver as she pushed the thrusters, forcing even more than her usual break-neck speed. And for once, I was grateful.

"The whore didn't mention what she wanted us for, I suppose?" Regina said.

"*Tisk-tisk*," Spider purred. "Is that any way to talk about your Overlord?"

"When I'm done with her, she won't be Lord of anything."

"Now why would you want to go and do a thing like that?" I felt Spider's smile. "After all, she's a fair and clever ruler. Just look at our flourishing Mars. Just look at the happy people."

Regina paused. Then, her mouth sharpened into a smile.

"It's not what I *want*," she said. "It's what I need."

"I suppose we'll see if your control fairs any better than mine, then."

And this time, when the lights brightened and my spine turned into a lightning rod, I knew that I screamed. I screamed like a babe dying in winter. I screamed like a cat, a tiger, a *lioness*. And when the pain dialed back, turning to a dull throb at its origin, I whimpered like a puppy.

So much for bravery. So much for honor, dignity, and all the rest. I would have done anything at that moment, if it meant I'd never hurt again. *Anything.*

Spider gave me a brisk shake.

"Why don't we just keep to ourselves, hmm?" His fingers tapped at my collar bone. "Prolonged exposure has rendered...*unfortunate* results."

"Wouldn't think you'd be bothered by death," Regina muttered, eyes skimming mine.

"Oh, dear me," he laughed, and I shivered. "I am appalled by it, by the very nature of mortality. You see, if something *dies*," he sighed, "it'll never scream again. Just rotting meat. Disgusting, a body is, once robbed of soul. Positively foul."

Regina looked like she wanted to say something, but with one last glance at me, she clenched her jaw and kept silent. Spider began to hum, toying with the device at my back. He didn't turn it on, but rather twisted it, like a cat toying with a flightless bird.

It wasn't until I couldn't see that I realized I was crying.

10

ORACLE

———————————

"You'll be invincible," my mother told me. "You will wield a power like the Worlds have never seen."

* * *

"Strength without Will," I whispered.

I opened my eyes to darkness. The floor was stone, and it was cool against my cheek. I blinked, dragging air into my lungs. I didn't remember passing out. I suppose that people rarely do.

I sat up, and my muscles responded shakily, like I hadn't eaten in days. The air around me felt...empty, like a cave's deep, deep breath. The floor beneath my body was smooth, polished marble, perhaps. I stretched my legs out, and my flesh felt strangely damp. I shifted, realizing that I was naked.

"Harry?" I whispered to the room. My voice didn't carry, as it would in a chamber. Instead, I felt like it was pressed back against me—an unwanted intruder in a lonely world.

Getting to my feet was a slow, painful process. The small of my back throbbed and when I brushed my fingers against the base of my spine, it felt like the flesh there had been scorched. I pushed my hair back from my face, a matted tangle like sheep's wool, and squinted into the darkness.

A cool, blue light emanated in front of me, seeming to have no origin. There were pillars, twisted and tall. They wandered into the inky black of the ceiling. I blinked. No, not a ceiling. Above me, there were stars. I focused on them, and they seemed to brighten, though I recognized no constellations.

My eyes returned to the light. With a shaky breath, I began moving forward, my bare feet padding across the smooth floor.

"Hello?" I tried again. Again, quiet pressed back against me. It reminded me of an empty church, of something hallowed and unbroken. It felt somehow wrong to puncture the silence.

There was water on the floor. I stopped, blinking at the edge, the place between the stone I stood on, and the pool I couldn't quite see. Or rather, couldn't quite understand. Beneath my feet, it was dry. But a hand's breadth from my toes, a pool of water waited, its surface smooth and clear. The blue light emanated from somewhere in its depths.

Something began to bother me. Not because of the place or even how I'd come to be here, but rather something deep, deep inside of me. Like when I walked in the forest alone at night, and my instincts would suddenly flare for no obvious reason.

"Hello?" I whispered again, glancing at the empty, echoless room.

Wetting my lips, I slowly knelt at the pool's edge. I had no reflection, even when I leaned over it, putting my nose close to the water. I couldn't see any particular light, nor any reason for the water to be glowing, but the blue room suddenly brightened. And something about it reminded me of music.

When I looked up, I was not alone.

Midway through the pool, a person had appeared. No, not a person. A person's *head*.

There was a small base, like that on a delicate statue, and a rod angled up from it, a black piece of metal no bigger than a pencil. The rod connected to the base of a woman's head.

She was stony, but something different than *stone*. Her features were angular, and her sculpted hair was rigid and smooth. But when I saw her eyes, when I looked at the slit pupils, I knew that I was not looking at a *thing*. There was soul there, and in the same way I knew the world was alive and the universe unfathomable, I knew that it was ancient.

"Two Worlds," when she spoke, her lips did not move. Her voice rumbled through the chamber as mine had not, as

152

though she bore wing upon the stillness and never knew the tightness of suppression.

"What?" I whispered. The wrongness, the sense of something not quite right, twisted inside of me. I clenched my fists, confused.

"Two Worlds wake, and nine turn together," the woman's face moved toward me. The base slid across the surface of the water, not disturbing it, leaving no trace of ripple. The way she moved, it made me think that there was only a skim of water on the floor, and she was sliding on the stone. But when I looked into it, it was as deep as a soul.

"Who are you?" I asked.

"A universe awaits," her voice had no particular accent, nothing quite recognizable, and when I realized I was trying to fit her to a nation, to a place, I felt a trembling sense that I was doing something *unfair*.

"A universe awaits?"

"And still, only the nine turn," she said.

"I don't understand." I leaned closer to the face, searching her stony features, looking into her fathomless eyes. "What are you?"

"Zander," someone said from behind me.

I whirled, scrambling to my feet and nearly slipping on the edge of the pool, and found myself facing Regina. Except that she wasn't Regina, or at least not the Regina I'd come to know. Her hair was longer, tied half back and silky, pale blonde. She wore gray, Unity gray, and there were the gleaming badges of an Enforcer over her heart. Her face was younger, her eyes brighter, and when she looked at me, I saw terror.

"Regina?" I asked, my own voice brittle in the stagnant air.

"They took him," she said, and her voice broke as she lunged forward, her hands seizing my shoulders. "Zander, they took our boy."

"Zander? What boy? Regina," and I squirmed out of her grip, "what's happening? Where are we?"

She snatched my hand, and I was surprised by how smooth her fingers were, completely devoid of the calluses and scars I knew she had. I glanced down and saw a wedding band.

"Who?" I asked, raising my eyes slowly to meet hers.

"They have him," she repeated, sobbing.

She sank slowly to the floor, hugging herself, trembling.

"Have who?" I prodded, glancing toward the pool. The water was shivering, like something deep in its basin was vibrating, and the woman's head stared emptily back at me.

"I don't know how they found him," Regina continued, ignoring my question. "You said we would be safe, you said that no one could break through the security net. But they did. And they took him. Zander, they took our son. Our sweet, sweet boy."

And she began to scream, and suddenly the pool was red, churning like blood in veins. I felt the world around me go cold, felt—for only an instant—the sheer *will* of the woman at my feet. And then, she was gone, and the room was quiet, and the water was water again.

"It's ridiculous," an of-then Irish accent said. I turned, finding a different woman standing across the pool from me. "How they don't get it."

I opened my mouth, but didn't speak. Instead, I frowned. The woman began to walk slowly around the pool, watching me as though we had been having a conversation, shaking her head slowly, like she didn't like what I was saying. I blinked. Her hair was long and matted, and her face had the hollow shadows of someone who'd never gotten enough to eat. But when I saw her eyes, one green, one blue, there was no mistaking her.

"Laurensen?" I asked hesitantly, edging back.

"Running was the best thing I could do," she said, her voice rising.

She wore some kind of blue uniform, dirty and torn, padded as though for winter. Her hands were red with dirt, and when she looked at me, I was slammed by a wave of pity. She had been crying, and the red dust on her face was streaked across her cheeks. She raised a pistol, pointed it at my head. And while it wasn't the first time Laurensen had made such a gesture toward me, this time it was different. There was a resolve behind her eyes that sent a deep flutter of fear straight to my core. I knew, with sudden certainty, that I was about to die.

"You taught me what family was," she said, hatred haunting the hollow corners of her eyes. "You told me what it meant. How could you be surprised? How is this anything but," and she pulled the trigger, "ridiculous?"

I stumbled back, falling, but even though she'd been aiming at my head, there was no bullet, no flare of pain. Laurensen was gone, vanished before I hit the floor. I stared at the place she had been, my vision still showing the ghost of light that had appeared at the end of her pistol.

"You said that I would be okay."

I twisted, and found Brute laying beside me, her tiny face drained of color. Her black hair was tangled with sweat, and it lay around her in twists and snarls. She smelled of vomit, and her white hospital gown was stained.

"You said you would take care of me."

"I don't understand," I whispered, reaching for her.

"Father," her voice broke. "You *promised*."

She began to convulse, violent spasms that raked her tiny body. Her eyes rolled back in her head, a scream froze in her throat.

And she was gone, leaving a sour odor hanging in the air. My head was spinning, and I felt sweat rolling down my sides from my underarms. I looked again at the pool, and it suddenly darkened, making the woman's head an empty silhouette.

"Is she dead?"

Harry was beside me, on her knees. She looked most like herself, maybe only a year or two younger, but there was something fresh about the pain in her eyes, something shocked about her pallor. She looked slowly up at me.

"You killed her?" and it was less of a condemnation than a question, like she was waiting for a magic trick.

"Killed who?" I begged, terrified and confused and very much alone.

Harry stared at me for a moment, searching my eyes. Hers suddenly hardened. She stood in a single, enraged motion, hands fumbling at the back of her belt. She gave a sudden jerk, and there was a pistol in her trembling hands. She was pointing it at me, and I could see the tears beginning to run down her face.

"You *didn't have to*," she screamed at me. "She was fighting! She would never have done it! She would have overcome it! Firebird meant *everything* to her!"

"Everything?" I asked, though I didn't truly understand why.

Harry was gone, and instead, Dr. Ravin was there, her eyes wide and her mouth open in a silent scream. I screamed, too, and flung myself away from her. Her face was streaked with blood, her dark hair wild around her fragile-looking bones, and her eyes were rolling back in her head, every muscle in her dark-suited body taught and strained. She was horrifying. She was horrified.

And, just as suddenly, she was gone. I was panting, still on my back. I saw something move in the shadows of the pillars. I wanted to cry, then. Fear had wrapped itself so firmly around my heart, it was all I could do not to close my eyes and sob. But then the thing stepped closer, emerging from the deeper shadows, and I was staring at Firebird.

She, unlike the others, was quiet. Her dark eyes roamed over me, taking in the details of a person I didn't know. None of them had seen me, not *me*. But the way Firebird looked at me was not the way the others had, like I had stolen their last thread of hope. Firebird looked at me in the same way a woman would look at a dog that had just, for no reason, bitten her.

She was younger, but her face was still pock-marked and the deep scar still ran along the edge of her jaw, though now it was pinkish. Her hair was cut shorter, nearly a buzz, and she wore a heavy, leather duster over a sandy-colored uniform. The duster's mantle was dripping.

She knelt slowly beside me, looking into my eyes, almost like she was searching for something that wasn't there. Darkness began to turn within her. She reached slowly out, touched my face, and her fingers were like iron, rough and hard-earned.

"Jaimie," she whispered, the name framed on her chapped lips.

"And so it begins."

The voice filled the now empty room. Firebird had vanished, though I could still feel her touch. I rolled slowly to my knees, once again facing the head. Its eyes were darker, its pupils deeper, and when the voice came again, it chilled something in my mind.

"And so it shall end."

The pool went suddenly still. Not like water on a calm day, but like ice, just now taking the chance to form. I looked down, and I saw something in its depths, something red and orange and *twisted*. It looked like fire, if fire was alive.

I looked again at the face, but my gaze slid off of it to the figure standing across the pool. She was tall and in a black trench coat, half her head shaved and the other died a brilliant green. She was pale, and illuminated by the orange fire beneath the pool's surface. It glinted in black eyes.

The black eyes of a BioMage.

Heat began to slowly radiate from the pool's surface, and I shakily stood. One step back, then another. The floor beneath my bare feet was almost too hot to stand on, and it was gradually getting worse. The woman stared at me. I stared at her.

"Stop," I whispered.

The room was getting brighter, the fire under the water growing in intensity, and the flickering shadows around us caught shadows of demons, hellish creatures flitting through the pillars.

"Please," I begged, tears welling in my eyes and smoke curling slowly up from my feet. I began to stumble backwards, but the heat was coming from everywhere at once. The ground began to tremble. Dust fell from the ceiling.

"Burn," whispered the woman.

And then, she screamed. She *howled*. It was power and fury and terror. It was the crystalizing dawn, the burning blood of a fever. It was everything and it was nothing and it poured out of her all at once.

And the world was engulfed in flame.

* * *

I was dead. And that was the only thing that I was sure of. The world was dark, neither hot nor cold, and the air around me was the stagnant empty of places deep, deep underground. In an absent way, I wondered if I'd been buried.

But then I opened my eyes.

"Welcome," a voice rasped, all too familiar.

I jerked instinctively away from it. My brain was programed to expect pain with that voice. I felt shackles catch against my wrists and ankles. Slowly, as though rising from a coma, I became aware of the hood over my head. Pinpricks of light winked through the material. A fluorescent bulb, an empty room, a gap-toothed grin.

"What are you doing to me?" I whimpered, twisting my wrists, feeling the metal scrape against my flesh. It made me sick, filled my nostrils with its iron stench. "Please, what do you want?"

"Answers," he said, as though it was the most obvious thing in the world. "Just words."

He ripped my hood off, and I was blinking at a cold, unforgiving world. The room was stark white, brighter than Unity gray. I was sitting in what could have been mistaken for a dentist's chair, except for the shackles, and I was in the same clothes as when we were captured.

Dangling over me like his namesake, was the man called Spider.

When he grinned at me, I saw that his upper canines had been removed, giving his speech a distinctive *wetness*. His face was oddly smooth, his eyes a strange shade of hazel, and his long, hooked nose was much too close to mine. A mop of sandy hair completed the picture, curls looping around his ears.

"You haven't asked me any questions," I said, pressing my head back against the chair, trying to get as far from him as possible.

"So true," his grin widened as he lurched back from me, clapping his hands together enthusiastically. "You're so bright, like a little pop of sunshine."

He wore a white technician's coat and his hands were pasty, smooth and cold, like raw chicken. He grabbed my wrist with one of them, and I cringed.

"So let's talk, yes? A simple conversation between two friends, wherein one gets to do all of the answering. It's a good thing, yes? What real understanding is about. Tell me, sunshine, what did you see?"

"The inside of your hood," I said.

His mouth thinned, his eyes chilled, and the transition was so abrupt, it sent a shiver down my aching spine. Without meaning to, I glanced to the side, to a metal table overburdened with metal instruments. I thought of the thing he'd pressed into the small of my back. I thought of the pain, of the absence of *Will*.

"You should know," he said, pale fingers sliding away from my wrist, "I have no sense of humor. Do you want to try again?"

"I don't understand the question."

He paused. I couldn't help it—I was overly aware of his hands, of what his slender fingers were doing. Right now, he tapped them in rapid succession against his wrists.

"You know, people come from all over both Worlds, just for the chance of seeing what you just did. Some say that she is a god. The Greeks of ancient Earth worshiped her as an Oracle. Did you know that? They thought she spoke directly to Apollo. Of course, they were all insane. But still. A few goat offerings aside, they weren't far off."

"Apollo?" I paused, inadvertently sifting through my memories. "Are you trying to tell me that that *thing*…that statue…that was the Pythia?"

"Pythia. Now there's a name I haven't heard in a while. Most prefer Delphi. But why not? Did she introduce herself to you? Did she change form?"

"You're talking about that statue of a head? Of course she didn't. It's a statue. Of a head."

"I can't tell if you're trying to be funny again," and his hand went to the metal table, not even looking, and his fingers wrapped around something with a hook at one end. "Do you want me to find out?"

"I thought I was dreaming," I said. "And I never remember my dreams. It's a blessing, really. Because I remember literally everything else. Eidetic memory. You understand."

"I trust that is not true," and he brought the hooked instrument around, placed its sharp tip under the fingernail of my right index finger. "It would be so unfortunate for you, if it were. You see, I will not believe that you don't remember anything. And so, if you truly don't, you're about to experience worlds of pain with no chance of relief."

He slid the instrument gently back and forth, so that I could feel its sharp edge just tickling the meat under my nail, like I was about to trim it too short and see the line of blood. I was sweating. My heart was fluttering frantically, as though it fully intended to beat itself free of my chest. I looked at him. He looked at me.

"I was confused. And scared," I wet my lips. "I'm not sure what I saw. There was a pool of water," Harry's sobs, "there was the woman's head," Regina's wedding ring, "and I think, now that you mention it, there might have been a goat."

All the while, a rational part of my brain was wondering how much I could tell him before it was damaging to Firebird. Because I knew from my mother, people always talked. No matter how big, no matter how brave, no matter how precious their cargo: there are limits, and good torturers always know how to find them.

And, as an Empathic BioMage, my mother had been the best of them.

He pressed his cool thumb against the base of my last knuckle, forcing it against the chair's arm. I felt the first tingle of resistance, as the hooked instrument forced my fingernail upwards. Sweat ran down my hairline, nausea built in my stomach. I don't know how to describe the kind of terror that comes from true helplessness, from knowing that the person next to you *wants* to bring you harm. It's a different kind of fear, one that builds slowly at the base of your skull. It's primitive, it's wicked, and it's the only thing you can think about.

"I don't know what else to tell you," I whispered.

There was nothing dramatic about it. A simple, smooth, *gentle* twist of his fingers, and my nail popped up. There as no pain. Not at first. Blood bubbled up, where the instrument had cut me, the meat under the fingernail red and soft. I stared at it, something in the pit of my stomach squirming.

"Simple, isn't it?" he asked, placing the tip of the instrument against the tender meat. "Say something I like."

As the metal touched me, I felt the pain. It was a chilling pain, not overwhelming but deeply *wrong*. It was the kind of pain that made me clench my fingers and toes, made me press my head against the back of the chair. It made every nerve in my body tangle into a little ball of lightning and the air in my lungs tighten to a whimper.

He arched a brow, twisting the instrument, and I thought I might vomit.

"There are rules," a woman said.

The metal flicked, and the instrument was removed, Spider's eyes shifting to someone behind me. My heart was hammering, and I twisted in the chair, trying to see who it was. Her accent was soft, her voice like honey, and it was coming from too close to the floor, making me wonder if she was sitting.

"There are rules," she repeated, "to the Pythia. One is that she never tells you of someone you don't know. Another, she never tells you of yourself. It's troubling, that. I do so want to know what she thinks of me. Which is why I introduce all of my friends to her, at one point or another."

The woman walked around the back of my chair, and I felt her hand brush across my hair. I twisted, widening my eyes, trying to see her.

"But my enemies," and the woman stopped, just outside of my view. "I make sure that they meet her straight away, preferably before they know me—should they survive, I wouldn't want them retaining anything of Pythia's about *me*. You never know what she might say. And, since enemies they are, Spider helps me find the truth of their stories. Girl, I want you to know that you are the last of your friends to meet her. It's nothing personal, but I'm sure that you understand that their stories were more interesting to me than yours likely will be. Regina, for instance, told me of a place I'd been so longing to see. And Harry?" she paused, like the name left a bad taste in her mouth. "There are moments when she seems to believe that she can breathe life back into my daughter."

"Daughter?" I whispered.

"And, you should know, they both had interesting things to say about *you*."

The woman continued around me. She was short. More than short, she was a dwarf. Her round face was tanned and beautiful, with oval eyes the color of rich chocolate. Her hair was silky and black, braided so that it looped around her neck like a scarf. She wore red, bright red, and the silks trailed airily behind her.

The small hand she placed on my arm was encrusted with gold rings, fat and cumbersome. She was warm. Or maybe, I was just so cold, even the distant touch of a Martian Overlord felt kind.

"You're Biggie?" I asked, the irony sharp in the hateful little room.

The woman laughed.

"Oh, the unmasking. So disconcerting. But never fear. I gave myself the nickname, when I was just a girl. It stuck. It always has, as I always knew it would. People like it and they don't even remember why. You see, they think it's funny or they think it's cruel, but the truth is that I took that power from them the day I accepted who I was. And look at me now," she smiled, and her lips were painted to match her dress. "Overlord Mariana, ruler of the Chryse and all that it touches."

"That wasn't what surprised me," I lied.

She cocked a brow.

"If you're an Overlord, you can't tell me that you believe in Ancient Greek myths,"

I said. "Pythia isn't even in history books, anymore. The only reason I've heard of her is because I went to an ancient school."

"Straight to the heart of it, aren't you?" she patted my hand, nodding at Spider. "Pythia is more ancient than you know, and she has been granting wisdom to our tiny Worlds for longer than even that. And dearie, I take her very seriously. She has saved my life countless times, given me the ambition and the direction to conquer a third of a World. I have listened to the dreams she told me, and I have unraveled the mysteries she blessed upon others. Friends and enemies alike. So, love, do not think for a single minute that you will be leaving this room without telling me *everything* she said."

I swallowed, glancing at Spider, then at my ruined finger. Blood dribbled around the nail, which had sunk back down, like the lid of an opened can.

"You said that Regina and Harry have already been here," I said, forcing my eyes to her. "Are they alright?"

"Right as rain. Better, even, than you," she smiled sympathetically. "Regina's weakness is her husband: Zander, I believe. He's seen better days, at this point. And Harry? Harry knows, knows the things I'm willing to do to people, to hear the Oracle's words. Sweet, I didn't even have to touch her."

"I didn't know that Regina was married," I said. "If I didn't know that, what could I possibly have to say that would interest you? These people don't let me into their lives, barely let me in on their missions. I'm useless to you."

"Perhaps, once. But now," and her voice gained a thread of irritation, making Spider move into action, the hooked instrument touching the nail of my middle finger, "now you've spoken to the Oracle. And you're the most interesting person in the world to me."

"I didn't see you," I said. "Why would it even matter?"

"I already told you, girl, you don't see people you don't know—it's the rule. Who *did* you see?"

"Harry," I answered. "Regina, Brute, Ravin, Firebird, Laurensen. The crew. But you could have guessed that much."

"Were they younger?" she asked, cocking her head, seeming surprised.

"They were."

"And what did they have to say?"

"Nothing. They were silent, like ghosts. I thought that they weren't real," I shrugged. "I was terrified. Maybe if you would have told me what was happening to me before locking me in that dungeon with a woman's head, I would have retained more information."

Overlord Mariana snorted.

"Quaint. At least this one is funny, Spider. Let me tell you something the crew told me about *you*. Harry said that she saw you, and you were standing next to a coffin, watching water bead up and roll off of the wood. You were holding someone's hand, but that someone turned to ash before her eyes."

The coffin. I felt a pang, like a bullet against my heart. Tears welled behind my eyes. Not for the loss, but for the betrayal. How could Harry tell this woman anything?

"Regina, she was firmer in her stance. Had to make poor Zander scream. In the end, she saw you and you were the same, but ever shifting. She said that sometimes, you looked like your mother. She said you carried your mother's crown," Biggie paused, searching my eyes. "A curious thing to carry, wouldn't you say?"

"It wasn't a crown," I whispered, tears breaking. I remembered the marks the Amplifier left in her black forehead.

"Yes, well, perhaps I'll make that point to Regina. Now, darling, I'm going to leave you to Spider. I'm not going to have him ask you any questions. And even if you started screaming answers, no one will be here to care. He will remove each of your nails, and he will do with your tender flesh whatever he pleases. And when I return tomorrow, whatever's left of you will tell me everything the Oracle said. And I will let you die a clean, quick death. This is the offer left to you. I'd say I was sorry," and she started for the door, "but frankly, I don't think anyone is going to miss you."

I looked at Spider and he smiled at me, lips sucking back from the places his canines should have been.

"Wait," I was trembling, and it made the instrument Spider still held under my fingernail begin to scrape at flesh. "Wait, please, I—I saw someone."

"We all do," she said, opening the door, not turning.

"No! I saw someone, someone I didn't know. You said there are rules? Well she broke them."

Overlord Mariana paused. And when she twisted back toward me, the corner of her mouth was hooked into a smile.

"Tell me," she said, eyes darkening. "Did it involve fire?"

11

WICKED

"When victory comes, it's rarely the victory sought," he said, adjusting the collar of his uniform, Unity badges glinting in the cold light.

"What are you?" I asked, shooting my brother a dirty look. "Some kind of bloody philosopher?"

"No," his snapped, turning to me. "I'm a bloody Commander."

"Is there any other kind?" my husband asked, sitting at his desk behind me, pen scratching on paper.

"Jerry, don't," though when I looked at him, I smiled.

There was a pang of affection, something very close to my heart. When he looked at me, the world was a little warmer. It wasn't much, but it was what I called love.

And so, in that moment, it was everything.

* * *

They put me in a cell. It was a nice enough place, with clean white sheets and a carpet on the floor. There was a glowing orb in one of the corners, not quite enough to read by but more than enough to make out which was the toilet and which was the chair.

It's the little things, in the end.

I sat, alone, on the floor, as far from the door as I could get, and cradled my hand to my chest. Lined with blood, it throbbed like a toothache. The nail itself looked fine. I knew that if I touched it, it would lift off of my finger again. It made my stomach turn.

I didn't sleep, though exhaustion clung to my very bones. I had told Biggie about the woman with the fire, told her every detail. And when I had finished, she'd told Spider to release me. He'd seemed reluctant, like a spoiled child being told he couldn't have the newest toy. But thinking like that made me nauseous, so instead, I made it my one goal to think about nothing at all.

I don't know how long I sat there. There were no windows, save a small barred one in the door. I was somewhat surprised to find it made of wood, and the walls of stone. It reminded me of an old castle, if an old castle also had a glowing data pad near the door's lock. I wondered absently if I could hack it.

It was a fleeting wonder.

When I heard someone outside, I pulled my knees tight to my chest and resisted closing my eyes. Terror ran in a steady current through my veins, like electricity. There was a short shuffling outside. And then, the lock disengaged with a heavy *thud* and the door opened to reveal Ori.

She was wearing her black armor, but her helm wasn't in sight and she carried no weapons. The man behind her was in a white uniform, and his assault rifle had the green glow of a fully charged automatic.

"Ori?" I asked, my voice tight and dry, like someone recently found in the desert.

"Rusting hells," she snarled, striding into the room, her heavy boots pounding across the carpet. "What have they done to you?"

She grabbed me by my arm and hauled me to my feet, none too gently. I gaped at her. Instead of her usual smile and reckless demeanor, the Ori who held me had a grim twist to her mouth. Her eyes were hard.

"Well?" She asked, giving me a brisk shake. "What've they done to you?"

"Nothing," I said, reflexively clutching my hand to my chest. "I'm alright."

"You don't look alright," she said.

"Where are Harry and Regina?" I asked. "What are you doing here, so...without resistance?" I glanced at the guard.

Ori's mouth turned into an even harder line and, releasing me, she turned and stormed back out of the cell.

"Think you could manage walking and talking?" she asked over her shoulder. "I don't want to spend a single extra second in this piss pot."

With one last glance for the guard, I scrambled after Ori. There was a distinctive hunch to my shoulders and, yes, I did fully expect to be shot in the back. But he seemed content to follow us in silence, rifle still held to the side, and I scurried to keep up with Ori.

Biggie's castle, for I couldn't think of any other thing to call it, had red carpet on the floor and black ceilings. The walls were dark stone, and the sconces were set just a little too far apart, making long shadows in the hallways. There were servants, moving quietly, dusting and cleaning and doing whatever Martian servants do, and I could hear the muted sound of the Chryse moving through the walls.

Ori walked in silence and I was content, for the moment, to let her. She seemed on edge. Which, while understandable considering the circumstances for most people, was more than a little disconcerting for her. In fact, I was fairly certain that if she'd come in guns-a-blazing, she'd be in a much better mood.

We came to an elevator, with golden bars across its entrance. Everything about the place seemed rustic, everything with a flair of history. There was a manservant to the side of the elevator and he slid it effortlessly open. Ori shouldered past him with a grunt, and I followed. Our guard remained stationed outside, face invisible behind a black visor.

The servant slid the door closed and we were moving, Ori swaying in her armor. She glanced at me.

"What?" She grunted.

"What are you doing here?" I gestured at her. "Like this? I'd figure you'd have shot up the entirety of the Chryse, at this point."

She snorted.

"Would have, if Firebird wasn't so rusting clever."

"How do you mean?"

"You'll see," she growled, glancing at me. "What'd they do?"

"Not much," I admitted. "And I didn't tell them much, either. I swear."

Ori looked at the elevator door as it crawled open.

"Doesn't really matter at this point."

I frowned at her, but followed in silence. We were in a large room, with a wall of windows on the righthand side. They were casting bluish light into the warm room, and I realized I was looking at the inside of a massive aquarium. Something huge and squid-like turned within it, dark tentacles twisting against the glass.

Biggie was by the far wall, seated on a throne built to size. It was carved from black stone, with red orbs hanging around its edges. The reddish light mixed with that of the blue water, making the air a deep, deep purple.

In front of Biggie, standing at an angle to her, was Firebird.

Our commander glanced at us as we entered the throne room, her dark hair shading darker eyes. She took us in with a slow, soaking look, her mouth thinning. She was armed, her pistol hanging at her hip and a long rifle across her back.

Near the aquarium, I saw Harry. She didn't look at us, staring instead at the tentacles as they swayed in front of the glass. Regina was nowhere to be seen.

"And we have a deal," Biggie said, clapping her bejeweled fingers together.

Firebird was still for a long moment, her eyes moving to my hand. I tucked it self-consciously behind my back. Her eyes flicked to mine. There was something there that I had not seen before, not really, not like *this*. Behind the layers of control and discipline, there was *fury*.

She turned back to Biggie, one of her hands resting on the pistol.

"You said they were unharmed."

"And truly, I did not misspeak," Biggie gestured at me, hand glinting. "It's but a scratch, a little memento of her time among us. Believe me. It could have been much worse. Lucky for her, you arrived when you did. Another hour, and dear," she shuddered.

"And Regina?" Firebird whispered.

"Safely locked away. It's for her own good, you understand. She was quite...troubled."

"We get Zander, too," Ori snarled, stepping closer to Firebird, momentarily blocking my view. I edged sideways, closer to the aquarium.

"Ah," Biggie raised a finger. "You see, if I let *everyone* go, what insurance do I have? I need to know that you're not going to turn around and kill me in my sleep. He's quite safe, I promise you. And should you complete my mission in a timely and successful manner, I'll be releasing him back to you."

"We had a deal," Firebird's words were a low growl, a warning.

"And I've fulfilled it," she gestured at the room. "You have your crew back. Last I checked, Mr. Lamont was not *part* of your crew. And even if he were, like I said, I need my insurance."

"If you're keeping him to protect yourself," Ori countered, striding to stand beside Firebird, her hands balling into fists. "Then why would you ever *stop* needing him. This isn't going to end with the mission. We're not idiots."

"If you were, I wouldn't be hiring you." Biggie drew a slow, pained breath, as though hurting us was the hardest decision she'd ever made. "You understand, Firebird?"

The room filled with silence. It was crystalizing ice. Firebird slowly looked at Biggie, and the small woman actually shrank, cringing back from her gaze. There were guards on either side of the throne, and they stepped forward. The gesture made Ori take a violent motion toward them. Firebird caught her elbow at the last second.

Despite Ori's armor and Firebird's bare hand, she managed to pull her back. Her eyes never left Biggie.

"My word is enough. And your mission will be completed. There is incentive enough for both of us."

"And my safety?" Biggie arched a brow. "Surely retribution is at hand," she nodded toward Ori without looking at her. "Your dogs are not chained."

Firebird's grip tightened on her arm.

"If you keep Zander, Regina will not be fully with us. And if we are to be successful, I need my *entire* crew. First, you're going to bring her here. Second, you're going to bring Zander. And third, I will guarantee that for what you have done, you shall not be harmed. But hear this," and Firebird pointed at the Overlord with her free hand, a gesture so threatening, it might as well have been her pistol. "The next time you touch my people, I will tear your still-beating heart from your chest and *feed it to my dogs.*"

The Overlord paused. And then, she began to laugh, slowly clapping her hands together. I heard a door open behind me, and I turned to see Regina ushered through. The big woman didn't seem to be harmed, but a sheen of sweat covered her face and darkened her shirt, one of the sleeves ripped. Her jaw was clenched and there was murder in her eyes.

"You see, Firebird? I am a woman of my word. And, if the stories are to be believed, so are you. However, somewhere in the course of our conversation, you seem to have gotten the impression that we were negotiating. Dear, this is a job. And I have given you your orders. Let this not end with us as enemies, but be the first job of many. You're an asset, dear, and I'm a frugal woman."

Regina stopped beside me, breathing heavily. She staggered, and I caught her under her arm, surprised when I found myself supporting most of her weight. She swayed against me, groaning.

"The hell?" Ori snapped, grabbing Regina's other arm before I could buckle. "What's wrong with her?"

"Had to drug her, I'm afraid," Biggie spread her hands wide. "What was I to do? This dog is rabid."

"Zander," Firebird whispered, looking at us with the side of her eye.

"I keep the husband. There is no middle ground here. If my mission is completed in a timely fashion, and meets with all my demands, he will be released back to you."

"I'm...not...leaving him," Regina wheezed, trying to pull away from Ori, murder in her eyes as she stared down Biggie.

"Regina," Firebird caught her shoulders, a warning in her voice. "We'll get him."

The big woman snarled, but her eyes were unfocused. I don't think she even saw the room. Firebird looked at Biggie.

"You'll have word in seven days," she said.

"I'd expect nothing less," the Overlord answered, smiling at us over her steepled fingers. "Luck."

Harry, quiet until now, pushed herself away from the aquarium and strode to us. She looked the least disheveled, low ponytail still tidily under her fedora, and when she reached to take Regina's arm, the big woman jerked away from her, snarling something unintelligible.

"Come," Firebird muttered, leading the way from the throne room.

Harry walked at my side, too quiet, and Regina continued muttering under her breath, one foot dragging. Sweat began to tickle my back. I leaned closer to her, trying to understand. Finally, I made out a single word:

"*Traitor.*"

12

KINGS

———————————————

"They call Andronicus the Mountain King," Dr. Ravin said. "And it's because of Olympus Mons."

"Imagine that," Ori muttered.

"He controls a third of Mars," the Doctor continued, ignoring her. "And most of Earth. He has the armies, the credits, and the ambition. At the moment, nothing Shay nor Mariana can throw at him would be enough to take back control."

Redwing was quiet, tonight. Around me, the crew had fallen still. Ori's hands were empty, and she leaned in the corner with murder in her eyes. Laurensen was absent— I hadn't seen her since Biggie's Chryse. Regina, still recovering from the drugs, was sitting on the floor, back slumped against the gunner-station of the cockpit.

Harry, of course, sat in her pilot's chair. When I looked at her, she avoided my gaze.

"Nothing," Firebird said, standing with her back to us, looking out the front windows, "except us."

"So it would seem," Dr. Ravin sounded far from convinced. "Or, at least, that's what she wants you to believe."

"You sure that bitch isn't sending us into another *Ilena*?" Ori asked. "I'm not in the rusting mood to get blown out of orbit again."

"No," Firebird snapped, making me flinch. "I'm not sure. How could I be?"

"You're the most powerful rusting BioMage *the Worlds have ever seen*," Ori said, and I'm pretty sure she was loosely quoting something I'd written. "You're the only one who *would* know."

"She's Inceptive, not Empathic. She forces ideas into people's heads; she can't read them," Dr. Ravin explained, unnecessarily.

Ori screwed her face up like she was about to go on a rampage, but Firebird cut her off:

"The fact of the matter is, we've taken her mission. Our only objective for the time being is to complete it."

"We've bedded the devil, then," Harry muttered.

"I'm sorry," Ori snarled, her sarcasm cutting the somber air. "I couldn't make that out. Is there someone else you'd like to betray?"

Harry's eyes snapped to her, but there was more than anger there. As I searched, I felt a nagging sickness rise. She looked…guilty.

"There's no proof that anyone betrayed anyone," Dr. Ravin glanced between the two of them. "Is there?"

"Of course not," Firebird murmured, still not turning.

"And yet the fact remains," Ori gestured at the room, and I cringed when her finger stopped at me. "Our people have been *tortured*. Our coms were hacked, our shuttle reprogramed, and I'm sorry, but no one has the tech to do that without an inside *rat*. And from what Regina's been muttering about for the past ten hours, I'd say that the *rat*," and she spat the word at Harry, "is probably the same *rat* who spilled her guts without so much as a how-do-you-do?"

"I know what Biggie is capable of," Harry said, almost too softly for me to hear. "She would have found out what the Oracle told me, one way or the other. I wasn't going to give her the satisfaction of watching me bleed."

"Well thank the Worlds for that," Ori threw her hands in the air. "She may have just helped that pompous toad, but at least she didn't give her the *satisfaction of watching her bleed.*"

"You don't understand." Harry lowered her gaze, fedora hiding her face.

"You're right, I *don't* understand. I don't understand how you told her everything, without so much as a hangnail— no offense, Jezi."

I clenched my fist, and the nail radiated pain. I smiled anyway.

"None taken."

"Spider would have gotten the information from me. All that I bought us was bargaining room. Biggie lives for that witch's proverbs. You tell her what she wants to hear, and you are rewarded. All of our lives were hanging in the mix. I did what I thought was best for the crew."

"Don't you *dare*," Ori hissed, leaning toward her. "Don't you *dare* act like what you did wasn't to save your own hide."

"I told her, too," Regina said, voice flat and stale as day-old beer. "I told her everything."

"At least you put up a fight, from what I hear," Ori jerked her thumb toward the big woman. "But don't think for a minute that I'm not coming after you. You should have let her kill Zander before you let go of one iota—"

"Don't," and when Regina's eyes flashed to meet Ori's, I'd swear that actual sparks flew. "Just don't."

Ori paused, chewing her lip with a ferocity that made me actually taste blood. After a hateful moment, she turned to me.

"Well I never would have guessed it, but our little journalist is the only woman here with a proper set of guts."

"I told her things, too," I muttered, shuffling in my lonely corner.

"Yeah, about a rusty fire witch."

"That witch," Firebird broke in, finally turning to us, "is the reason we're here."

When I looked at Firebird, I saw a younger woman. She looked no different, acted no different. But, like with a childhood friend grown older, I knew that she *was* different. The scar on her jaw, I remembered it being fresh. And her eyes, so *full* and dark, I remembered when they were as fragile as the first breath of ice on a black lake.

I hadn't told them, not everything. I cringed to think what Laurensen would say, if I told her the Oracle had shown her crying. I'd said what I thought was important, which was mainly what I told Biggie, plus a few more details involving the fire witch. But certain truths...they were too precious to share.

"So Overlord AndroniButts," Ori said, rolling her eyes, "is obsessed with fire. Why is that so important? Why is that enough to make Biggie herself capture, torture, and shoot us off into Olympus Mons?"

Firebird nodded to Dr. Ravin, who cleared her throat.

"Overlord Andronicus is a scientist," she began, dark hair trembling around sharp cheekbones. "Everyone knows that. What most people *don't* know is that he's quite," and she paused, taking a sharp breath, "mad."

"Still don't see why—" Ori started.

"Then shut your mouth and listen," Dr. Ravin snarled, her of-then Russian accent thickening. The room stilled for a moment while she breathed. Then, at last, she said:

"He conducts experiments, with an emphasis on the evolution of Martian adaptations. He accelerates the process. So far as I know, he's the reason most Martian creatures appear as they do now. Lions were introduced less than a decade ago, and yet already they have adapted into the smaller, armored, venomous versions you see today. What would usually take centuries, he's accelerated to only a few years."

"You sure do know an awful lot about this mad Mountain King," Ori flashed a white smile, not at all friendly. "Could it be that you're *another* traitor?"

The doctor, if it was possible, paled.

"Ori," Firebird warned, exhaustion breathing around the name.

Ori's grin tightened, but she didn't say anything more. Merely leaned back in her corner and watched Dr. Ravin in the same way a predator would watch its wary prey.

"Well, yes, I suppose," the doctor continued after another pause. "I was once employed by Overlord Andronicus. So, it could be said that I'm betraying him. But in my defense, there has never been a man born who deserved it more."

"Continue, Doctor," Firebird prompted, folding her arms. "Please."

"As I was saying, Andronicus is a scientist—"

"Mad scientist," Ori muttered.

"—and as a scientist," the Doctor forged ahead, "he understands the importance of the sciences when it comes to warfare. Not excluding his advancements in the medical and mechanical fields—as well as a great deal of innovation with hydrogen-based fuel sources—he led the charge into the field of BioMagic. The first Bestial BioMage was created within Olympus Mons, as were the first Amplifiers. While Unity developed the mechanics behind amplifying thirteen BioMages, Andronicus invented the *concept*. You could say that Unity's final rise to power was due to his intervention in Earthling affairs."

Thanks for that, I thought, remembering my mother's 'crown'.

"And so," Dr. Ravin finished, "if Overlord Mariana is to take him down, she's going to need to steal that which he holds most dear. His innovation."

"How in the rusting World is she going to do that?" Regina snapped from her place on the floor, turning the room even more sour.

"Well," the Doctor looked at her with skepticism. "She's already done it. Part of it, at least. By destroying the *Ilena* and hijacking the data for his fuel production, she'll already be able to spearhead that industry. We're talking *trillions* of credits. Not to mention the power that comes hand-in-hand with operating the largest, most efficient fueling station on Mars. All that remains," and she glanced at Firebird, "is his work in the biological field."

"The fire witch?" I asked.

"PyroMage," Firebird corrected.

"PyroMage?" Harry asked, shifting so that she could look at her.

"It's honestly not a surprise," Dr. Ravin said, pulling a data pad from her suit pocket. A few quick taps from her long fingers, and a hologram appeared in the air.

It hovered in the room, consisting of a single, pale globe with three small points on its surface. They were labeled *Bestial, Inceptive,* and *Empathic.*

"There are three types of BioMages, or *BioMagic,* if you will," she pointed to each label. "And that was all we knew of for a while, so that's what the general populous accepted as truth."

"Bloody general idiots," Ori said pompously.

Dr. Ravin shot her a sharp look.

"But Andronicus was never satisfied. After the first BioMage, he became obsessed. He began to experiment, first on BioMages, then on—as we know them—Pawns...people who can be influenced by BioMagic, but contain no power of their own. Then, finally, he experimented on Mutes. Being a Mute himself, if a test showed positive results, he ran it on himself. He was convinced that Mutes were undiscovered BioMages, a fact that he pleaded with Unity to accept for ages."

"The more I hear," I said, almost too softly to be heard, "the more I realize that most of the pain I've experienced in my life was because of this man."

"Most of the pain the Worlds' have experienced, Jezi," Dr. Ravin said, as though I hadn't noticed that part.

I frowned at her, but she continued robotically on.

"When I left his service, he was just beginning to toy with the idea of elemental Magic. Since none of the tests on Mutes were met with positive biological results, and assuming that his theory about Mutes was true, then the only remaining solution was a different kind of Magic.

"And then," she nodded at me, "*you* came along. The Worlds' first MetalMage. Or GeoMage. I haven't decided. Really, Jezi, if you just let me conduct a few experiments, I feel that I could unlock your true potential."

I stared at her, something like fury gurgling in my extremities, but before I could say anything, she threw her hands into the air.

"Of course, of course, it's your choice. Humanities, I'm not a monster. The point is, Andronicus caught wind of what you were capable of, of your past—since his Unity contacts included your mother and her experiments with you—and he realized where he had been going wrong. A year later and," she grinned, gesturing at Firebird, "we have our first PyroMage."

Ori frowned.

"Firebird is the PyroMage?"

"What, no," the Doctor grimaced, waving her hand, still gesturing at Firebird. "She is an Inceptive BioMage." Again, she indicated the hologram originating from her data pad. "So far as I know, a human can only wield a single form of Magic. Otherwise, that contradicts Andronicus's theory of singularity, and if that isn't true, then there really is no way to explain BioMagic at its—"

"Rust me," Ori dismissed her sharply, "just get to the point."

"The point," and Firebird straightened, pointing at the hologram. "Is this."

Dr. Ravin tapped a few buttons on her pad and the first globe winked out, making room for four new ones. They were roughly the size of softballs, and each had three smaller circles orbiting their perimeters, like tiny moons. The first was labeled BioMagic. The next, GeoMagic. The other two were blank. On the smaller, orbiting globes of the BioMagic sphere, I saw the same *Inceptive, Bestial,* and *Empathic* labels. On the GeoMagic hologram, one read

192

MetalMagic and the other two bore question marks.

"That diagram," Ori said, leaning toward it. "Is a hot mess."

"Well it's obviously not completed," Dr. Ravin said defensively. "And I'm only assuming that there are thirteen sets of Magic. And, yes, I do realize that my diagram only supports twelve kinds. But thirteen...well, it corresponds with the known laws, and if I'm going to make—"

"*Ravin*," and Ori threw herself against the wall, sliding down it with a dramatic sigh. "Just tell me what to blow up."

"We're not blowing anything up," the Doctor said, her gaze hardening. "Our objective is to infiltrate Olympus Mons, extract—"

"I swear, if you say data right now," Ori narrowed her eyes. "I'm going to lose my rusting mind."

"What's left of it," Dr. Ravin snapped.

"*Enough!*"

Regina's shout rattled through the room, making me jump and Dr. Ravin drop her data pad. It clattered to the floor like a dead thing. We all stared at the big woman, watching as she shoved herself to her feet. Circles framed her eyes like bruises, her short hair flat and greasy. When she looked at Firebird, I could *feel* the anger, like a fire crackling.

"She has *my* husband," she breathed. "And if I'm to understand this correctly, if we fail, she's going to kill him. So, there is no failing. Do you," and her gaze swept each of us in turn, "understand me? I swear, Firebird, if she hurts Zander, I'm going to kill her. I don't care what you told her. I don't care what we promised. He is all that is left to me, and we *will* get him back."

Firebird met her gaze. Ori shifted uncomfortably, ducking her head. Eventually, Firebird stooped, picking up the fallen data pad. While she tapped at the screen, she said:

"You are right. We have to succeed."

"So what, exactly, is our mission?" I asked.

"Infiltrate Olympus Mons," Firebird repeated. "And extract the PyroMage."

"She's being held there?" Harry asked. "Or is she working for him? How can we be sure?"

"How do we even know this witch exists?" Ori asked. "Beyond the ravings of a madwoman who preaches the gospel of a stone head?"

"She exists," Harry muttered. "The Oracle does not lie."

"I'm not saying she's lying," Ori said, shooting Harry a dirty look. "I'm saying that you're all stark-raving mad."

"I saw her too," I said, for what felt like the thousandth time. "And—"

"Again, not saying that you crazies didn't see her," Ori said.

"The PyroMage exists," Firebird interrupted, her voice rolling over us like thunder. "She is our objective." A final tap on the pad, and the hologram of a woman appeared before us, her green hair and half-shaved head glowing, as though backlit by fire.

Firebird finished: "And her name is Eve."

13

WITCHES

The flight from Biggie's Chryse to Olympus Mons was the longest of my life. Harry flew all night, alone in the cockpit, and when I offered to join her around midnight, she'd refused. I tried to sleep, since that seemed like as good a way as any to pass the time, but my hand was throbbing and when I closed my eyes, Spider's face floated in my dreams.

So, I spent the flight at my desk, writing what I could, using the pen and paper that Brute had found for me in a back-alley vendor somewhere in Madtown. Say what you will for technology, my paper has never been hacked. Though, once, Ori did break the lock on my safe and read my journal. In the end, there's only so much you can do.

We landed several clicks from the mountain, in a quiet valley Dr. Ravin called the Quilt. Looking out the window, I could guess how it had gotten its name. Snow laced the dark rock, making patch-work patterns across the desolate landscape.

Olympus Mons is Mars' highest peak. It's a sprawling beast, with foothills and a wandering base. The volcano itself, snow-capped and black against the pre-dawn sky, rose from the surrounding mountains like a dragon over snakes.

I had become accustomed to the flat, hot, humid, *dense* jungles to the south, around the Chryse. The most time I had spent in the outdoors had been a year ago, when Laurensen and I traveled by foot—and, later, by Nightmare—to Madtown. That had been a very different world from the one that waited for us now. The elevation combined with a northern climate allowed for the first Martian snow I'd seen. And, unlike everything else about Mars, it seemed very much the same as Earth's.

That made something lonely twist behind my heart.

When Harry at last relinquished the cockpit in favor of her bedchamber, I took her place. As the engines cooled down and the world waited for dawn, I sat in the pilot's chair and stared at a blank sheet of paper.

I had an eidetic memory. Remembering how things happen was never the problem. For me, the problem was making them something more than simple memories.

Of course, I was familiar with the term *writer's block*. I had never cared for it, personally. Not the thing, but the term. There's no such thing as a block, there are only hurtles.

And right now, I was stumbling over mine.

I don't know if it was the pain in my finger when I gripped my quill, or the way Harry looked at me when she passed me in the hallway, but something was hiding in the back of my mind. I'd write a word, maybe two, and I'd stop and wonder at what a *pain in the ass* it was. Why did I bother writing anything? Surely it was impossible to string more than a handful of words together. My journal, a simple string of facts, that was easy. But taking these memories and making them a story…

I looked again outside. I couldn't see Olympus Mons, not since we landed in the Quilt. Something about that, something about the soft patterns of snow outside my window, made me hungry, a gentle kind of urge that built belligerently in the back of my mind.

"You seem lonely," a soft voice came from behind me.

I didn't need to turn to know that it was Brute. I had seen precious little of her since the Chryse, and I smiled, relieved to hear my friend.

Jiggy's lights were a soft blue as she whirred up to hover beside me. I could barely make out Brute within the dark glass, her face all shadow and angle. It appeared she also was in poor spirits.

"It's hard to be lonely on a ship as small as this," I said.

"And yet we somehow manage."

"Something wrong, Brute?"

She sighed, and the image of her sobbing in a hospital gown flashed in my mind. I blinked it away, giving my head a brisk shake.

"I'm worried about the crew, I suppose," she said, twisting Jiggy just enough that she could face me. "Regina and Ori are fighting, and Harry won't talk to anyone. I just worry that our family is breaking."

"Regina and Ori are *always* fighting."

"But this is different. It's...*colder*. It scares me in a way I can't describe."

"I suppose you're right. But you know them—they always work through it, one way or the other. I'll bet you that Ori stabs her by the end of the week and they're laughing about it in another month. And so far as Harry goes," I paused, also worried. "Well, I think it's something she just needs to work out on her own."

"That's true," and a smile hid somewhere in her dark face. "You know what I wish, Jezi?"

"What do you wish?"

"I wish I could get out of Jiggy and *run*."

I fidgeted, suddenly uncomfortable. We hadn't talked since I'd found her in the jungle. Jiggy's lights dropped to an even darker blue.

"Do you know what I liked to do, back on Earth?" she continued.

"You mean before...Jiggy?"

"I used to go to the cherry trees, when the blossoms were falling. And I'd run through the shallow water of our estate's fountains and try to catch them out of the air. Each one I'd catch, I'd bring back to my father. He pressed them in an ancient leather-bound book."

"That sounds beautiful," I said, because what else could I say? How could I put that soft, lingering *ache* behind my heart into words?

"It was," she sighed, looking to the blank paper in my lap. "What are you doing?"

"Trying to write Firebird's story," I admitted, glancing guiltily at the nothing in my hands. "Can't say it's going well."

She paused. Then, Jiggy's lights suddenly brightened. Still blue, but a different blue. An inspired blue.

"Is there anything you liked to do, back on Earth? Something that you were good at? Something that put you in the wind and made your heart race?"

"Like catching cherry blossoms?" I asked, smiling.

"Exactly like that."

"Sort of," and there it was again, that twisting lonely. "My...Jerry and I had two homes, both in of-then North America. One was in a northern region, where my mother worked. And the other was in the mountains.

That one was his, and he taught me how to..." I trailed off.

"Taught you how to what?" She prodded, lights still brighter.

"Well, I got him his job, you know? For the Sector X Truth. We were friends in college," I shook my head. "That doesn't matter. The thing is, he taught me how to snowboard. And one day, I realized I was good at it. It was *my* thing, after that." I wrinkled my nose. "I don't know why I'm telling you this. I haven't thought about him in a long time."

"Or snowboarding," she giggled.

"Or snowboarding," I agreed, shooting her a look. "Don't you dare tell the others. I can hear Ori already."

"It's nothing to be ashamed of," she pressed. "I feel like I remember it being a...*cool* sport."

"Maybe once. And maybe for someone else. But I'm supposed to be the professional journalist, not some snow-nut adrenaline junkie."

"Adrenaline what?"

"It's an old Earth phrase."

"Ah," her lights darkened. "It's been a long time since I lived there. Hard to remember, sometimes."

"I get that," I said sympathetically. "Sometimes, I can't even remember what Earth felt like. You know, like when you first step outside and you smell the air and feel the sun and hear the birds and you *know* you're home? I don't remember what that was like, anymore."

"I don't remember what it was like to walk," she said, shrugging. "Count your blessings."

* * *

Dawn came and went. As the ship began to stir, I relinquished my place in the cockpit to Ori. She was her usual morning self, and I made sure to steer well clear. There are morning people, and then there are Oris.

I found myself wandering. Firebird was in her quarters with the door closed, so any hope at discussing the mission was out. No one was in the kitchen, which I had long since found to be the only place the crew went when feeling social. I arrived back in my quarters, but it was even more empty than the kitchen.

My eyes fell on a fresh set of winter clothing. I didn't know where they came from, though I suspected Brute would systematically steal from the other crewmember's closets when she felt I was in need of a new garment. She'd discovered upon my arrival that I was the same size as Maya, and since then had been pilfering Harry's closet.

Did I feel bad to be wearing a widower's dead wife's clothes in front of her? Yes, of course I did. Did I feel badly enough to go shopping?

Never.

And so, taking the hint, I donned a pair of long underwear, several synthetic layers, and a sleek, high-tech jacket that instantly warmed to my body's temperature. They were called YellowJackets (and yes, they were yellow). Patented Martian Tech, they maintained a constant core temperature. The only problem people had encountered was that if you put one on a hypothermic person, they maintained *that* core temperature.

Freshly geared up, I headed out of my chamber, down the hallway, and through the airlock.

The first thing I felt was the inside of my nose freezing. It startled me, and I barked a cough, stumbling forward on my insulated Grav-Boots. The second thing was the exhilarating sense of awareness that only comes from colder climates. I blinked, eyes watering, and just like that, I was *happy*.

Around me, the Quilt's mottled face twisted. I always loved the way light snow laid on the rock, like ribbons. Still early, the sky was a kind of blushing purple, and it made the snow's natural whiteness a strange tint of blue. I breathed.

I started walking, boots crunching softly against rock and ice and snow. Putting *Redwing* at my back and the rising sun to my fore, I simply went.

There was something freeing about being in the cold, about looking at a mountain. Jerry used to say that it was like flying, and certainly I agreed with him where snowboarding was concerned. But that was a separate thing, a *personal* thing. Mountains: they were a magic unto themselves.

When I came out of the valley, Olympus Mons was there to greet me. Still a long way out, the volcano nonetheless dominated the northeastern sky. It was impressive, certainly the loneliest mountain I had ever seen. And yet, thinking back to the white shoulders that loomed beyond of-then Denver, I couldn't help but think it was something *lacking*. Lacking what, I couldn't say.

I turned from the mountain, scanning the Quilt. My heart fluttered. Farther along the ridge that I stood upon, I saw a solitary figure dancing in the early light.

No, not dancing. The woman was twisting, turning, her footsteps equally paced. In her hands, a silver sword spun.

Regina stood alone, maybe a hundred meters from me, at the highest point of the ridge. Her sword, thin and quick as a whip, sliced the air. She was not fast, but what she was doing could never be called slow. It was *precise*, executed with such exactness, my mind hungered for the next motion.

She was beautiful in a way only true beauty can be. Her pale hair caught the morning light, like spider silk after the rain. The sword was a single beam of light, a trembling droplet that catches the sun just right. My mouth went dry.

Simple as that, I needed to write.

Pulling my journal from my satchel, I sat on a bald rock and took up a pen. My handwriting was sloppy, because of my finger, but that didn't matter now. Nothing mattered now. My mind was focused, and story ran though me like a river.

It had always been this way. I could force myself to write. But those were just words. When there was *story*, it was everything. And that…well, that just couldn't be forced. I wrote of our capture, of Firebird's eyes when Ori brought me to her, in Biggie's hall of stone. I wrote of Brute and the way her hands fluttered over her knees when she spoke of Earth, of the things she could no longer breathe.

And I wrote of myself, and the aching loneliness the mountains had found. The same aching loneliness that they had once—ironically—filled. There was impending doom, there was fear and loss. But there was also hope and beauty and something silver in the early morning light.

I didn't notice when the sound of Regina's exertions ceased, but three pages later, a shadow fell across my paper.

I looked up to see her, blonde hair plastered to her head with sweat, her blue eyes dark. I hadn't noticed before, but she had what my mother had once called 'honest eyes'. They shifted with her mood, reflecting the world around her in different shades. I'd always assumed that my mother had been cheating—she had been an Empathic BioMage, after all—but Regina proved her right.

"I'm sorry," I said, slipping my pen back into my satchel. "It is a beautiful spot— I didn't mean to intrude."

Though, in truth, I would have done anything to have the wash of relief that that bit of work had brought me. More than coming up with something for Firebird, a writer needs to *write*. Otherwise, we're just juggling empty words in our minds like some kind of circus clown.

She glanced at my satchel, then at my hands, and last at my face. Something had hardened in her—though I certainly would never have called her soft—since Biggie's Chryse. I glanced at her left hand before I could stop myself, but there was no ring there. Suddenly feeling guilty, I started to rise from my rock.

"I'll leave you be," I said.

Regina's hand on my shoulder was more than enough to put me back down. I cringed, not knowing what to expect. But when her words came, they were soft as they were cold.

"I am sorry," she said, "for talking to Mariana."

I hesitated, uncertain for a second what she was referring to. Then, cringing, I answered:

"Don't worry about it. I wouldn't want you—anyone—hurt just for something as simple as...what you told her." Though it wasn't simple. It was everything. It was why I sat here now, why my mother was dead, why I was on Mars and had given Firebird her name.

It was probably why I wasn't snowboarding in the of-then mountains with my of-then husband.

She shook her head.

"What I did is unforgivable." Regina sighed, her breath fogging in the sharp air. "I am ashamed."

Wetting my lips, I glanced up at her. She'd retracted her sword, but the band of metal around her forearm still radiated heat, the waves obvious in the cold. I sighed.

"*Yo* Ruse," I said, using my mother's honorific, "used to tell me that my lover was a handicap to me. She told me that he could be used against me. *I* am ashamed that I believed her. Honestly, Regina, I would be more upset if you would have guarded my secret rather than protecting your husband. Sometimes the choices you make—the really hard choices—shape *you*, not your future."

She looked at me then. And I felt like I saw Regina for the first time.

"Come with me," she said.

So, I went with her. It wasn't like with Firebird, where her request was a demand impossible to ignore. And it wasn't like with Brute, who I *wanted* to go with. Regina wanting me to walk with her felt something like an honor, and I was inclined to treat it as such.

We moved along the ridge to the place she had been practicing. The snow and ice were crushed in neat patterns, and I realized that each of her footprints exactly matched those before. In front of me, to the east, there was a sheer drop, maybe fifty meters, onto the belly of the Quilt. Though, if I'm being honest, from this angle, it didn't look soft at all.

"This," and Regina fell into one of the positions she had used earlier, "is Resting Stance."

She didn't draw her sword this time, but rather held her hands as though bearing an invisible one. If I squinted, I couldn't tell that she was unarmed, so perfect were her gestures. I shook my head.

"You don't have to do this," I said, feeling awkward. "You don't owe me anything. And if I'm being honest, a few more fingernails and I would have told him anything he wanted to hear."

Regina's stare went flat, and abruptly I was back on the outside. She straightened to her full height, letting her hands drop.

"You fight like a small boy," she said, clapping her hands in front of my nose. "All noise, no punch. If you are ever confronted by someone who can shoot straight, you're going to die. Every day you are still breathing is a miracle. This world is full of people who would bring you harm, who would kill the people you love. I am offering to teach you. Why are you being difficult?"

I shifted, drawing a slow breath. Then, raising my gaze to meet hers, I said:

"It's just that I don't want you to feel like you *have* to be my friend. You don't *owe* me anything."

Regina snorted, a flicker of her old self.

"I'm not offering to be your friend. This," and she fell back into the position, "is Resting Stance."

Wetting my lips, I unshouldered my satchel and tossed it to the side. Then, after a quick glance up and down Regina's frame, I closed my eyes and pictured it. Slowly, I settled my body lower, knees slightly bent, arms straight out, hands pointing. It was very close to the yoga pose for Warrior.

Suddenly, Regina slapped me.

Yelping in surprise, I sprang back from her, eyes flashing open to find her glowering in front of me.

"What was that for?" I snapped, touching my throbbing cheek. The cold added bite to the blow, and I felt the skin reddening as I spoke.

"How do you expect to fight me if your rusting eyes are closed?" she asked.

"I didn't know that I was fighting you," I said. "I thought we were...stretching. I remember the posture better when I close my eyes."

She slapped me again.

"WHAT?" I barked, grabbing my other cheek.

"You don't have to remember what's right in front of you," she said. "This," again she shifted into the position, "is Resting Stance."

Scowling at her, I unblinkingly assumed the posture. Regina held it for a heartbeat. Then, she moved ever so slightly, rotating her palms out.

"This is Bridge Stance."

I felt the tightening in my forearms, my tendons stretching and palms heating. And she was twisting, left arm crooking over her head and her fingers of her right hand pointing again.

"This is Viper Stance."

And so, we trained. In five minutes, I was sweating. In ten, my muscles were

210

trembling. When I lost track of time, every part of my mind was on what Regina was showing me. She didn't hit me again, and I didn't close my eyes. Every now and then, she would correct me, her hands surprisingly gentle.

"The base of great swordplay is in your body, not your sword," Regina said, taking us through the motions again. "The same is true for any weapon. You can't shoot between heartbeats if you don't know how to feel them. There is poise in fighting, otherwise it's just death. And death isn't the point."

"It isn't?" I asked, breathing hard.

"Of course not."

"Then what is?"

"If you don't know, I can't teach you," she said.

And again, through the motions.

"How long do you usually do this for?" I asked, shifting with her, anticipating the next posture.

"As long as I can. You're dropping your right arm."

"My right arm is heavy," I muttered, hoisting it back up.

"That's because it's fat."

"Hey!"

I shot Regina a look, and she smiled at me, a glint of mischief in her sapphire eyes.

We continued. I don't know for how long. The sun was fully in the sky by the time

I gave up. With a groan, my butt hit the ice and I flopped back, panting and staring at the purple dome above me. Regina's face appeared in my view and I narrowed my eyes at her.

"If I do that one more time," I said, "I honestly think I'll die."

"That wasn't bad," she admitted, sliding down to sit beside me. "Wasn't good, either. You still are like a small boy, all hands and effort and no thought. Still. It could be worse."

"In the same way rotten fish is worse than pickled herring?"

She gave me a sideways look.

"You're a strange girl."

I shrugged, wiggling into the snow, trying to cool off. I had long since shed the YellowJacket, and now I was down to my long underwear top. It was an obnoxious shade of purple.

"Thank you, Regina," I said. "I needed...something."

"With work, I think I can get you shaped into something resembling—if not a fighter—then at least a decent woman."

"There are other kinds of women besides fighters. You do realize that, don't you?"

Regina hesitated, staring toward Olympus Mons. When she answered, it was like each word carried a weight of its own.

"*All* women have to be fighters," she said. "They're the Worlds we live in, Jezibell."

"*That* is not my name."

"Jezidiah."

I sighed, quick and shallow.

"It's Jezriah," I said, sitting up. "Jezriah Lark Ruse."

"Lark?"

I shrugged.

"Lark, Lurk...I was a journalist. I felt like I spent an inordinate amount of time lurking. Just seemed to work."

Regina nodded.

"Jezriah. Wasn't she a prophet in Earth's Third World War?"

"She was indeed. My mother believed all women are fighters, too," I glanced at her. "Even—*especially*—the pacifists."

Regina and I were quiet for a long time. We stared across the Quilt to Olympus Mons. I saw ships coming and going, like little insects returning to the hive, and every now and then, the sun would catch a window's glass. Otherwise, I would never know that there was a city there, let alone a palace.

"Have you ever seen him? Andronicus?" I asked.

"I have not."

"Do you think we're going to be able to get into...*that*? It's a bloody mountain fortress ruled by a mad scientist, who's obsessed with war. I feel like he's going to have one hell of a security net."

"We have Brute," Regina shrugged, as thought that was all that mattered. "If anyone can get past him, it's her."

Something cried out behind me, and my very soul brightened. Twisting, I saw a lonely form in the sky, approaching from the southwest, wide wings spread on crystalline air. With a grin, I waved at Eerie and Laurensen.

"I feel like he's got a whole lot more than just Brute to worry about," I said, rising to greet them.

14

MONS

"Getting in is simple," Dr. Ravin said. "Andronicus brings people in constantly. He has made his fortune from the bodies of humans. The problem, as you can guess, is getting out again."

We were in the kitchen seated around the circular table, and Dr. Ravin paced in front of the counter. There are thin women, and then there are women like the Doctor. She was skeletal, wispy and fragile. Her eyes were dark, as were the circles under them, and her cheekbones made me think of glass. Long, black hair was pulled back in a strict bun and she wore—as she always wore—a black suit.

"After we have the witch," Ori said, hunched over her plate, mouth full, "why don't we just blast our way out? Riddle them with bullets. That kind of thing."

"If it really is a PyroMage, what's stopping us from *burning* our way out?" Regina added.

"We don't know for sure that this Mage exists," Dr. Ravin said. "And we certainly don't know what kind of power we're dealing with. Jezi, for instance, cannot control when or what she's pushing. The force varies, and she lacks any kind of discipline."

"Hey now," I frowned at her.

"Additionally, we don't know her state of health. We might need to carry her out, might need to fight our way as well," the Doctor pushed on, "we cannot rely on the unknown. Which is why," and she drew a deep breath, "I'm coming with you."

There was a pause around the table. And then, Ori started laughing, spraying half the table with a mouthful of cider. Regina swore at her and Firebird flinched back, avoiding the majority of the blast.

"I'm sorry," Ori said, wiping her mouth with the back of her hand. "But that's literally the first time I've ever heard you volunteer for *anything*."

"She's good at volunteering other people, though," Regina added, looking sulky.

"The Doctor," Firebird said, sighing, "has agreed to go, for a price. We've already agreed on the details."

The wraith-like woman paused, her bony hands clenched at her sides. The loose hair around her face was trembling, and I felt a sudden pang of sympathy for her. I remembered her scream, I remembered the horror in her eyes. Shifting uncomfortably, I cleared my throat.

"I'll go, too," I said, a little because I was tired of being forced into the missions, but also to get the spotlight off the Doctor.

"A smaller group will have a better chance at avoiding detection," Dr. Ravin began, glancing fretfully at Firebird.

Our commander was silent, rolling a spoon over her fingers, untouched bowl of rice turning gelatinous in front of her.

"I don't want my people unprotected," she eventually said. "Too often, we focus on discretion rather than protection. Regina and Ori, you're both on. Be well armed. Doctor," and she gave her a hard look, "I'm trusting you'll be able to handle it."

"I'll manage," she said, standing a little straighter.

"Then we're in accord. But I want you armed. No," and Firebird raised her hand as the Doctor began to protest, "I'm not arguing. Be armed. Jezi, I'm fine with you going so long as you keep in mind what we're doing there. I don't want you tripping up Regina and Ori. Stay in the back and help the Doctor when you can."

She paused, looking again at the spoon in her fingers. A name wandered through my mind: *Jaimie.*

"Where do you want me?" Laurensen asked, sitting beside me, still in her duster. She looked exhausted, hair windblown and face raw.

"With *Redwing.* You and Harry will guard her and be on call for extraction. As the Doctor said, getting out will be tricky. Brute needs to have our communicators up and working," Jiggy—floating behind Firebird—sank slightly back.

"I'm sorry," Brute whispered. "I don't know how they managed to hack us last time. It won't happen again."

Firebird nodded, not turning.

"What's done is done."

"So that's it then," Ori shoveled another spoonful of the gray mush into her mouth. "Me and Regina blow the place wide open, then our little weasels scuttle in and find the prize. Suits me fine."

"Not quite," and Firebird let her spoon drop to the table. "I'm going, too."

"What?" Dr. Ravin instantly paled—though how that was possible with her pallor, I don't know. "Absolutely not."

Firebird arched a brow at her, and I was surprised that the Doctor didn't shrink back. I certainly did, and her gaze wasn't directed anywhere near me.

"Andronicus *collects* Mages," the Doctor said, searching the table, looking for support. "Sending Firebird into his hall is like dropping a beef-steak in front of a wolf. He'll devour her. I can't think of anywhere in the Worlds she would be less safe."

"I think you'll find me more ominous than a beef-steak, Doctor," Firebird said, a smile crooking one side of her mouth. She seemed...*sharper*, a predator catching sight of prey.

"No. Firebird," and she shook her head, pleading. "You don't understand. He's obsessed and you're...well, you're the most powerful BioMage in the Worlds. *And* you're Inceptive. You're pure gold, straight heroin. He is—"

"Quite mad, yes," Firebird drew a deep breath, blowing it out through her mouth. "That changes nothing. This is my mission, Doctor, and I need to be there."

"Why? Why in the Worlds would you need to be there? Between Ori and Regina, we've got the firepower. And I'm the brain. Jezi, well I'm sure that Jezi will prove useful."

"Hey," I grumbled.

"Frankly, we don't need you," the Doctor straightened. "And I don't see why *this* is the mission you've decided to take interest in. You've let us go freely enough before. Why now?"

"Because of the one thing Mariana didn't explain," Firebird said, sitting back with an air of finality.

"What's that?"

"If the PyroMage *wants* to be extracted."

That made the table grow eerily still. I frowned, running my thumbs around each other in my lap. When I thought of the woman who could summon fire, I didn't have the impression that she was *content*.

"What would you change, even *if* that's the case?" The Doctor eventually argued. "BioMages are Mute to each other. That's basically the whole point."

Again, Firebird half smiled.

"Leave that to me," she said, and I felt a pang of uncertainty—Firebird was powerful, no one could doubt that, but had she found a way around a *law* of Magic? "And, it's beside the point. If we have trouble, I can get us out of Olympus. I might be the *only* person who can. And I'm tired of watching my people be put in between these Overlords. We have a purpose. We are here to keep the Worlds from falling under another tyranny—another *abomination*—like Unity. Our employers are under the impression that we can be manipulated into making that purpose their own."

She tapped her knuckles against the table.

"No more. We'll be in and out before they know we're there. And if not...well," she nodded toward Ori, "then we'll go with Plan B."

"These days, it's more like Plan A," Ori giggled, nudging Regina's side. "Am I right?"

Dr. Ravin sighed, looking resigned.

"If you're sure. But I would like to formally say that I do not approve of this. It's reckless and adds a danger to our mission that could otherwise be avoided."

Firebird merely stared at her.

"But, as you say, this is your crew," and the Doctor sighed. "All I have is my advice. So, here's what I know."

* * *

220

We waited for dusk.

Armored, I fidgeted with my pistol, checking and rechecking the chamber. While I'd named it Mule for the way it kicked, after firing it in close confines I'd realized it had something to do with the sound, as well. Powder-based, bright red, and bulky as a loaf of bread, Mule hung from my belt like a corpse.

Regina and Ori were suited up and ready for war. Each carried two rifles slung across their backs, a pair of side arms, and I knew that Regina had at least one sword connected to her forearm. Regina also had a large, heavy-looking backpack that we had an extra set of armor stored in. They had their helmets tucked under their arms and they leaned against the wall across the hallway from me, both—for a change—quiet. In fact, the entire ship had an air of unearthly stillness. It had me on edge.

Firebird was in her quarters and the Doctor paced back and forth between the two gunslingers and myself, nervous as a cat. It was the first time I'd seen her in anything but her black suit. Instead, she wore white armor, utilitarian and sleek. Her helmet dangled, forgotten, from one of her hands and when she shook her head, her ever-present bun lost a few more strands of shiny, black hair.

"I'm still thinking someone is going to recognize you," Regina said, eyeing the Doctor as she paced.

"It's been ten years since I was there," Dr. Ravin fiddled her belt's empty holster. "If anyone could recognize me, I'll see them first and avoid the situation. The benefits of having me along far outweigh the risks. Believe me, I've done the math."

"Didn't Firebird tell you to take a gun?" Ori asked, frowning at the holster.

Dr. Ravin froze, as though just now realizing that she was—in fact—moving. She stared hard at the floor.

"Firebird knows that I wouldn't be able to shoot anyone, even if I did have one," she said. "The mere thought of blood..."

"Here," and Ori tossed a small pistol at her, one that she kept at the small of her back. "No blood."

Dr. Ravin stumbled, catching it instinctively and then immediately letting it plummet to the floor. We each flinched, knowing that Ori had a tendency to leave the safety off. When nothing happened, Regina swore.

"Rusting skies," she said, bending over and scooping the pistol from the floor. "Be careful."

"You see?" the Doctor said, recoiling when Regina offered it to her. "It's safer for everyone involved if I don't have a weapon."

"Including the people who are shooting at you. Take it," this time, Regina shoved it at her and it wasn't an offering, it was a statement.

Dr. Ravin took the pistol in two fingers, eyeing it like I would a venomous snake.

"What is it?" she asked.

"I call it Pisser," Ori said proudly. "Acid-based. Basically a cute little acid-thrower. It'll melt the face off of anyone getting too close."

"Just put it in your holster," Regina muttered, returning to her slouch against the wall.

Dr. Ravin complied, and immediately adopted a hesitant lean away from that side. I glanced down the hallway, toward where I could see the afternoon light drifting in from the cockpit. Not long now.

"So, I'm curious," Ori said, still looking at the Doctor. "What *was* your price? And how did you get to name one while the rest of us Fools just have our allowance?"

"None of your business," the Doctor's eyes flashed.

"Has anyone seen Brute?" I asked, partially because I didn't like the way Ori narrowed her eyes at the Doctor.

"Not since the briefing," Ori said, making a knife appear in her hand. "Why?"

"She's just usually hovering around, at the beginning of a mission," and I felt her absence in my gut, twisting like something that was deeply wrong. "It isn't like her to be so reserved."

"She has seemed off," Regina agreed softly.

"Probably just pouting because Biggie hacked our coms. Someone out there is better at her job than she is," Ori snorted. "And if we're being honest, shouldn't she feel a little bad? I mean, she could have gotten us up and running again."

"Ori," I muttered, my admonishment making her stiffen.

"What? Say it like it is." She grinned at me. "She's dropped the *ball*. Get it? Because she *is* a ball."

"Brute isn't the ball. Jiggy is the ball," Dr. Ravin corrected.

"Oh, of course," Ori rolled her eyes excessively. "Thank the gods we've got you along, Ravin. We'd all be rusted without your clear and impactful insight."

The Doctor glowered at her. But, before any of us could further insult the other, Firebird's door opened.

I rarely saw Firebird in her armor. It was a muted, sooty kind of black, rather than Ori's shining obsidian. Her sides and inner thighs were rust-red, and her helmet was a wicked, sleek thing with a narrow band for her eyes. Used to my own wide glass view, I wondered how she could possibly see.

Firebird looked at her forearm, dimming the blue display until I could barely see it. She nodded, looking at us.

"Are we good?" she asked, her gaze landing on the Doctor.

224

"As well as can be expected," she answered, sweat visibly beading along her hairline, looking uncomfortable in her sleek, white armor.

"Don't know what party she's going to," Ori said, pushing herself off the wall and unshouldering one of her rifles, "but I'm pumped. Let's boogie."

Firebird nodded, glancing again at her forearm.

"We've got a narrow window," she said. "No detours."

"After you then, boss," Ori said, giving her a ridiculous bow and gesturing toward the airlock.

Firebird quietly complied, stepping through and disappearing. The rest of us followed suit, with me bringing up the rear. I didn't know how I felt about rear guard. It seemed like every time I was back there, something ended up trying to eat me.

In the Quilt, the sun had long since disappeared, only evident by the dark red sky to the west. The snow was mottled and dark around us and though I couldn't feel the cold within my suit, I could *taste* it. I glanced at Dr. Ravin as she donned her helmet, struggling to get it over her bun.

Firebird tapped her com and something on *Redwing*'s undercarriage gave away. With a hiss of hydraulics, a compartment opened in its side, revealing what looked to me like three surfboards. They were long and flat, but made from some kind of burnished metal. When Firebird pulled one down, red and gold lights flared down its narrow sides.

"Oh, *hell* yeah," Ori said, grabbing one of her own. "Now we're talking."

"Doctor, Jezi, have either of you flown a Wraith?"

"Ancient Gods," Dr. Ravin said, staring at the boards open-mouthed.

"I'll take that as a no," Firebird muttered, setting hers down and taking the third one. "Regina, you take Jezi. Ori, the Doctor."

"C'mon, Doc," Ori said, grinning her wicked grin within the dark helmet.

When she dropped the board, she kicked it in the side as it fell. Instead of shooting away from her, it absorbed the hit, the lights on its sides flashing brighter. And instead of hitting the ground, it pulsed about a foot above it, the air between it and the rock radiating heat waves. As I watched, the snow turned to water and ran in thick rivulets down the rock's face.

"I don't want to," the Doctor said, very seriously.

"How'd you rusting think we were going to get to the mountain? Walking? We'd be at it for days. C'mon!"

Ori reached down and jerked Dr. Ravin bodily onto the Wraith, pulling her tight. She stood on it like a surfboard and, despite the Doctor's fretful struggles, seemed as poised as she had been on solid ground. Beside me, Regina quietly activated our board and let it drop.

"It's simple," she told me, stepping onto it. "And its base has a Grav-Field. You won't slide off."

"Smart," I said, stepping up in front of her.

The truth was, I wasn't scared. I was *exhilarated*. For the first time since landing on Mars, I felt like I understood something. Really *understood* it.

"Tail me," Firebird said, stepping onto her own Wraith. "If there's trouble, split up and regroup here. Don't continue to Olympus alone. And Ori, be gentle. She's no good to us unconscious."

Ori laughed, as though the very thought of her misbehaving was ridiculous, and the Doctor let free a soft whimper. Or maybe it was a prayer. Sometimes, it was hard to tell the difference with Dr. Ravin.

Regina kicked back her boot and a bar sprang out of the side of the board, levered up on the nose and rising to be perpendicular with the board. A sail of iridescent gold shimmered after it, lights trailing back its edge. It looked like a sailboard, and as I gripped the bar in front of me, my heart was thunder in my ears.

"Pay attention to your coms," Firebird said, kicking her sail up. "And turn down those lights."

The gold and red lights along the edges of the boards instantly dimmed to muted purple. Regina reached around me, gripping the bar on either side of my hands, and our armor barely left enough room for us both to stand. Firebird edged to the lead, holding hers with one hand while she leaned back, scanning us.

"Let's move."

And she kicked forward, pulling her body in as her board shot up the Quilt's side. Ori was next, and the Doctor's shriek ricocheted through my helmet.

"That's going to get rusting old," Regina muttered.

She stomped her foot down and we were off, shooting after the other two boards with a fury. The sail glowed like the aurora borealis, shifting colors as we were propelled skyward by the ridgeline. I felt my stomach lurch. I'd become so accustomed to Brute's sophisticated Grav-Simulators, I'd almost forgotten what it felt like to *rush*.

I burst out laughing, leaning forward into the wind, one hand dropping from the sail's bar as I asked the Wraith for more. I don't know what made me do it, maybe an instinct from my time in the mountains. Somehow, I *knew* how to control this machine, knew what made it turn, what gave it speed, and I was *safe*. I kept my knees slightly bent, my breath slow and deep, and I narrowed my eyes as we crested the rise. We shot up like a geyser, then drifted down and forward with a fresh burst of speed.

Easy as that, we were rocketing toward Olympus Mons.

The volcano's peak was dipped in red by a sun I could no longer see. Powder snow was being kicked up by Firebird and Ori's Wraiths, swirling past us like tiny vortexes. Marbled black rock blurred under us to a sheet of gray.

I leaned forward and to the right, pushing the Wraith. It responded like a well-trained horse, adjusting to my posture and edging us away from the group. Regina countered, pulling us back behind Ori.

"What are you doing?" She asked, sounding grim.

"Racing," I answered, a laugh behind my teeth.

Regina snorted something that sounded like *crazy*, but I didn't care. Ignoring her subtle countering, I once again pulled away from Ori, then edged past her.

I've heard philosophers say that we're all just racing toward death, that it's an inevitability that taunts us with its unwavering resolve. I understood that in a way I'd never understood religion. I *wanted* to roar at my destination, wanted to challenge it. It was the same drive that had pushed me to be a writer, the same that had led me to challenge my mother. And, if I'm being honest, it was what drove me still. I had joined Firebird because if there was a destination, she knew the shortcut.

And so, Ori and I raced toward the snow-ribbed sides of Olympus Mons. I hit a rock, after a while. Rather, I *vaulted* a rock, the obstacle throwing us into the air like a ramp. I laughed and Regina joined me, howling at Ori. We shot in front of her and, quickly, I was pacing Firebird.

She'd ignored us thus far, like a patient mother tolerating her noisome children. But when I started to pass her, she very quietly and very purposely slid her foot forward and sprang back into the lead. And, despite all of my urging, I couldn't catch her again. Whereas I was all power and speed, Firebird was grace. She moved with the Wraith like the body of a bird shifts with its wings, riding every current, understanding every whorl in the earth.

Watching her was a thing of beauty, and I was content with my place at her flank. We shot toward Olympus Mons in a lopsided triangle, Dr. Ravin's soft whimpers the only punctuation to the roaring wind.

That was when we found the first piece of wreckage.

I had thought that it was another ridgeline, but the angle was too sharp. As we neared, I saw the glint of a window, the muzzle of a dead laser. The air smelled sharp, like fuel and smoke and destruction. The rock face around the fallen behemoth was a crater.

And it was one of thousands of pieces.

"The *Ilena*," I whispered.

"What's left of her," Regina said.

We wove through the wreckage, Firebird slowing. Of course, I could see no bodies. If there were any, they were inside the twisted metal. Any others had been burned to ash when the ship entered the atmosphere.

My anxiety returned, like a spiny monster twisting back into my guts. There were tracks in the snow, places where some attempt of rescue had been made. And, after that, I was sure there were even more scavengers, digging through the *Ilena*'s carcass. We passed a few small groups of people with black hovercrafts, but they were hardly bothered to look up from their work.

An hour passed. Olympus continued to rise, an ancient monster with sharpened teeth. I had read that this was not what Olympus Mons had looked like a thousand years ago. I had read that it had once been a plateau, a shield volcano. But the first Emperor of Mars had done something—some act of god or man—and built this into the looming giant I now raced toward. I did not understand the science, and I regretted not taking the time to study it. Something I could understand wouldn't fill me with the nameless dread of the unknown.

The sun set and, as the first stars began to twinkle into being, we came to what Dr. Ravin had called the Wires.

They were ribbons of black rock, crisscrossing the stony surface and catching pockets of loose snow. They were big enough to rock our Wraiths, a motion that was just a little too jarring, and it set my teeth on edge. Firebird angled toward the western edge of the volcano, moving parallel with the ridges, and I started to catch glimpses of life.

Not plant or animal life, of course. Merely suggestions of humanity. I could see ships on the northeastern side, coming and going from what Dr. Ravin had said was the landing pad. There were black windows in the mountain's sides, patches that were a shade too dark. Without light, they were almost indistinguishable from the terrain, but we were looking for them. And, through the com system, I could hear the Doctor quietly counting.

"It's coming up," she said, chilly in our helmets.

"Behind me," Firebird made a smooth gesture with her free hand, and Regina and I instantly fell to the back, letting Ori slide into her original position.

Dr. Ravin continued to count. We were most obvious now, darting beneath the glassy eyes of the Mountain King, and while small and cloaked in darkness, I still waited for the bullets. Surely, we couldn't just breeze into this fortress.

"Here," the Doctor whispered.

Firebird slowed. Her Wraith nosed down a gentle slope, one that seemed to drain into the foot of the mountain. Dr. Ravin's face, a haunted outline within the glossy helmet, was fixed to Olympus like a girl confronting the monster under her bed. As we came to a stop beside Firebird, the Doctor said:

"We should leave these here, for our escape."

She said it in a way that made me think we'd never be coming out of this place alive, her voice like a carcass. Nonetheless, Regina and I stepped off of the Wraith. Without thinking, I tapped the machine's side with the toe of my boot. The sail folded back into the board and the lights winked out, metal settling gently on the black stone.

"Fantastic," Ori said, twisting this way and that, the sound of her spine popping audible through the coms.

"On me," Firebird said, again checking the device in her forearm. "How's our window, Doctor?"

"Still on target," she answered, voice barely audible over the soft static of the coms.

"Are we going to lose communication when we get inside there?" Regina asked, moving to stand beside

Firebird. She planted herself there with the air of a woman making a point.

"We do, and I'm beating Brute bloody," Ori said, twisting the short assault rifle off of her back and slapping it down into her off-hand. "Boogie?"

"Soon," the Doctor started walking toward the mountain's base, where our small ravine met with the black rock.

As we approached, I saw that where the ravine met the mountain, there were metal slats worked into the stone. They were black, running horizontally, maybe four meters wide and half a meter tall. They reminded me of something...

"We're not going into another ventilation shaft?" I asked, groaning when the Doctor nodded.

"As I said, they regulate the volcano's core temperature. It's still active, it's how he powers his city, but he obviously doesn't want it erupting."

"So you're telling me that this is a vent for a rusting volcano?" Ori asked. "I feel like you should have mentioned that in your debriefing."

"It's one of many vents. And I did mention it. You just weren't paying attention."

"And we're going into it?" Ori shook her head. "Won't we be cooked?"

"Most of the heat goes to power. It'll be fine. Here, it's about to open."

We lined up behind Doctor Ravin, Firebird immediately behind her with me in the rear. I glanced over my shoulder at the Wraiths, and felt an empty pang somewhere behind my heart. I no longer let the crew know when I had a bad feeling about these things, since I usually had a bad feeling about these things, but this time, my bad feeling was less of a warning and more of a threat.

With a resigned sigh, I drew Mule and held her with two hands, pointed down and away.

The vents let loose with a sigh, steam rolling out as the slats rotated, allowing for a large gap between each of them. The Doctor ducked through easily in her sleek and slender armor, and Firebird slid gracefully after her. Regina and Ori had a more difficult time of it, their weapons catching on the slats and Regina's backpack barely letting her squeak through. After some prolific swearing, they finally managed it. The slats were just starting to swing closed when I bolted in. I wouldn't call it graceful, but I got the job done.

I rolled to a stop beside Regina's boot, Mule clutched to my chest. She hoisted me up like an afterthought, her gaze fixed to Dr. Ravin. I turned, and my heart sprang into my throat.

There were *people* here. Or rather, on the other side of a glass window, its surface strangely oily. They were working in a lab, wearing white coats and clear goggles, and they took no notice of us. The lab itself was white, with silver instruments and charts on the walls.

The vent we stood in had heat rolling off its black sides. If it weren't for the lab and the feeble light it let into the chamber, we would be in total darkness. With a deep breath, the Doctor waved for us to follow her.

"One-way glass?" Firebird asked, her visor catching blue light as she glanced over the lab.

"Dimmed," the Doctor corrected. "When the vents first engage, they burn orange. It's a spectacle, but would be distracting if seen with the naked eye. Andronicus had the engineers install this, instead. It gives the labs something like flare, and helps them keep an eye on the mechanics. You wouldn't want a rockslide blocking any of them, if there was an emergency."

"So, they *could* see us?" Regina asked, moving closer to the wall.

"You're all in dark armor. It's fine."

"You're wearing rusting *white*," Ori hissed. "And Jezi's *bright red*."

"*If* they were to notice me, I'm just a worker. You're overestimating their interest, and this mountain's security. Andronicus isn't worried about a couple of people wandering in his city. And it *is* a city."

"Then why didn't we come in the front door?" I asked.

"Because we don't want to go through security. *And*," she continued, when Ori started to disagree, "We're going to need a way out of here, once we've infiltrated the labs. The Mountain will go into lockdown. Now hurry. I'd rather not be in here when the vents release, it'll overheat our armor and make us rather conspicuous."

"Isn't that what they just did?" Firebird sounded more skeptical by the second.

"They were cooling, not engaging. The chamber heats to a high temperature, powering the outer labs, and then releases. It's like a digestive system, and the waste is the air that we just walked through. We don't want to be here when the *actual* digestion takes place."

"Gross," Ori muttered, glancing at her feet, armor clicking against black rock.

We fell quiet, following our specter of a Doctor. The vent continued well after the lab disappeared, and we had to turn on the small lights around the edge of our helmets. From what I could see, the vent seemed like a cave, twisting and wandering deeper into the mountain. And, as we walked, my sensors warned about the rising temperature.

The vent eventually forked. The left took a sharp downward turn, sloping into another series of ventilation slats, which were currently tightly closed. The right ended in a metal door with a glowing, yellow sensor over it. There was no latch, no handle, no way of opening it that I could see.

"Here we are," Dr. Ravin said, moving up to the door, pulling a delicate-looking instrument from one of her belt's pouches. "Let's see if Brute followed my instructions."

She touched the instrument to each of the door's four corners, rotating it slowly, her head cocked to the side. I heard small clicks as she did so. Then, with a nod, she pulled a heavier instrument from a large pouch, setting it slightly off-center on the door. A few buttons, and it snapped against the metal, clinging like a super magnet. Dr. Ravin backed away, nodding toward Regina.

The big woman stepped quickly forward, taking hold of the object. She glanced back toward the Doctor.

"Counter-clockwise," Dr. Ravin said, then she shook her head. "No, it would be backwards. Clockwise."

Regina nodded, throwing her weight against the object. With grinding slowness, she began working the magnet in a circle. Finally, there was a heavy click and the door released a slow breath. She tapped the magnet and it disengaged, falling into her hand before she tossed it back to the Doctor.

"And here," the Doctor said, clipping a small, round device to one of the walls, "is our homing beacon. We should be set."

"Wait," Firebird said, stepping around Regina and tipping her head toward the door.

I would have guessed she was listening, but for the telltale pressure against my third eye. I eased away from her as Firebird used her power, uncomfortable as always. My mother had been an Empathic BioMage, and a powerful one at that. But everything that she had done, everything that she had been, didn't scare me half so much as the idea of Firebird's Inceptive BioMagic.

Eventually, she nodded and pushed the heavy door outward. I could *taste* the iron, even through my helmet's filtration system.

Firebird went first, followed by Ori, then Regina. I nodded for the Doctor to go next. Last, I glanced once more down the left tunnel. The slats had slowly started to rotate, and somewhere in its deep, empty depths, an orange light had begun to glow.

Not wanting to find out what happened during the *digestion* until absolutely necessary, I stepped quickly up and through the door.

We were in a dark chamber with pale blue lights around its circumference. Uncertain, my group was clumped awkwardly around the door. I closed it with a heavy push. There was a circular valve, the one Regina must have turned with the magnet, and I rotated it closed with significantly less effort than it had taken for Regina to open.

"What's next?" I asked, glancing at Firebird.

"Do you sense any guards?" Regina asked.

She shook her head slowly.

"No," Firebird's voice was careful, like someone testing the surface of a freshly frozen lake. "It's...empty."

"Empty?" Regina asked, and I could hear her frown.

"It's the Mutes," the Doctor answered for her, starting toward the far side of the vacant chamber. "Come on. This way. Quickly."

"Mutes?" I glanced back in the direction of the lab, spying a locked door with a glowing panel.

"He prefers to employ them," Dr. Ravin said, as though it was the simplest thing in the world.

"What? Why?"

"More convenient when they discover a new procedure, I suppose," the Doctor said, sounding distant. "That, and they're more eager to discover a BioMagic if they're the ones who will be wielding it."

"So you're Mute, then?" I asked.

"Hush," the Doctor gestured sharply at me. "Let me concentrate."

We darted through the room, making our way to the far side. There was a simple, white door laid into dark rock, and it opened with a gentle nudge from Dr. Ravin. I blinked, eyes suddenly assaulted by light.

The chamber was white, with a vaulted ceiling and harsh illumination, like the bleached belly of a monster. There were people here, working at computer stations, and they wore the lab coats and clear goggles. I wondered if they were like uniforms, all starched and cleaned for a united purpose.

Besides the scientists, there were other people. People in plain clothes, people in dark suits, people from every walk of life. I saw food vendors—like I would expect to find in a shopping center on Earth—and at least two bars. The chamber was a hub, a bustling center of activity, and the only thing I could think of as I followed my crew into its midst was that this was one of the more surreal evenings of my life.

"They're ignoring us," I whispered through our com.

"Look at them," Regina nodded toward a table, which had men in similar suits of armor. "We're nothing special."

"This is the west wing," the Doctor said, leading us quickly through the center of the chamber. "It's the facility for Andronicus's armed forces. That's why I brought us through here. You could just be recruits in training, or prospective soldiers. Like I said, Olympus is a city. The wings each serve a different purpose, but all of those purposes are part of a larger community. Come on, through here."

We passed full units of soldiers, some doing drills in large, clear spaces, and others obviously just off duty, their fully charged weapons leaning against bar stools. I frowned at them, wondering what a Unity commander would have to say about her soldiers drinking while in uniform.

The chamber narrowed, the ceiling dropping to about ten meters, and the people funneled closer together. I could hear the distant roar of engines, and the occasional squeal of tires on a runway. Instead of soldiers, we were moving with small groups of people in armor like ours, mismatched and personal. One had a jetpack on her back, and I tried not to stare as she stood at a food vendor and began to rip the meat off of something that looked like a rat.

"It reminds me of the Space Station," Ori said, sounding somewhat relieved.

"That's essentially what it is," the Doctor said. "Olympus is a hub for this section of Mars. People in route to Shay's Country usually stop by here—especially bounty hunters. It's the fastest drop for Deimos."

"Deimos? The moon?" I asked, staring at the armored people with fresh suspicion.

"It's the prison," Firebird said. "Deimos is where convicts are sent."

"Shit," I breathed. "I didn't know that when I signed up to be an outlaw."

"It's actually brilliant," Dr. Ravin said, distracted. "Instead of putting a holding block in an ocean or a mountain, they put it in the most inaccessible place in the Worlds. Mars' smallest moon. Without a spaceship, it's impossible to escape. And if you think the Space Station on Phobos is well defended, you've never seen Deimos."

"I'm with the journalist on this one," Ori muttered, sliding between two large men in full armor. "Sounds like something that should be put in the job description."

"We're almost there," the Doctor said.

We followed her through several branching corridors, each smaller than the last. The left wall opened into a dark window, showcasing the landing pad for the West Wing of Olympus. There were space crafts and shuttle crafts and hover crafts, basically every design I'd seen so far on Mars. And, as we walked, the people became fewer and farther between. Food vendors and bars were exchanged for clerks and bank windows, heavily guarded and hidden behind a thick layer of impact-resistant glass. I began to feel more and more out of place, with Mule hanging heavily from my belt, and I noticed that the Doctor quickened our pace.

At last, we came to a set of double doors, with a blinking security camera over them. Dr. Ravin turned to us, her face pale within the helm.

"We bought ourselves a few extra minutes, coming in the side way. But now we're on camera. After we go through these doors, we'll be racing the clock. There's going to be a long hallway. Don't draw attention to yourselves, but keep a brisk pace. I'll lead you down a side passage, and at the end of it, there will be two guards. Take them out as quickly and quietly as you can. We'll need one of their security cards to get the elevators working. Everything that we do once in the Core will be illegal. Are you ready?"

Firebird gave a curt nod, and Regina twisted her forearm, putting her sword on standby. Ori smacked her lips.

"Born ready, Doc."

She gave Ori a skeptical look, but turned back to the doors nonetheless. With a deep breath, the Doctor pushed them open and marched through, her head high and back straight. We followed briskly, single file.

This corridor was darker, less welcoming. Instead of lab techs, there were armed guards at the entrances to the side rooms, and they watched us pass with guns held at attention.

"I can't believe they're just letting us walk in here," I whispered.

"Still public domain," Regina answered, equally softly. "This is the bounty drop."

"You seem pretty familiar with it," I said, avoiding a particularly interested guard's visor.

"I've dabbled," she said, and for the first time since Biggie's Chryse, she sounded like she was smiling.

The Doctor took a sudden turn down a left corridor, and I jogged to keep up. In fact, as we started down a gentle ramp, we were all running. I could hear the Doctor's strained breathing. It sounded very close to panic.

"Just a little farther," she whispered. "But they'll have noted us going down here. When we don't come back, they're going to investigate."

"Just waltzing in the front rusting door," Ori said.

"It's the most efficient entrance. And besides," the Doctor slowed. "There are no back doors. The experimental labs are all in the Core."

Another few meters, and we were in front of a set of double doors. There was a guard on either side. Before they could so much as speak, Ori and Firebird were on them.

I blinked, more than a little shocked at their speed and determination. Ori hit hers like a wrecking ball, her knees taking him in his chest. Even with the armor, I could tell that it winded him. Ori twisted, dropping him to his knees, and ripped his helmet off with a snarl. Then, her arm was around his neck, choking him and eventually rendering him unconscious.

Firebird had her guard pressed against the wall, his hands to either side, frozen. She didn't touch him, but I could feel the residual wave of her Magic. I swore that it made the air thicker.

"They're Mute," Dr. Ravin whispered, staring at Firebird with wide eyes.

"They are," she agreed, voice strained.

Still, the guard was silent. Still, he remained against the wall. Ori, finished with her own guard, moved to Firebird's and removed his helm. As with the first one, she put him in a chokehold. He never once struggled, merely stared at Firebird with wide, uncomprehending eyes.

The man dropped in silence.

"We," the Doctor wiped her forehead with the back of her sleeve. "We need a security card."

"Convenient for them to have stationed two such cards right by the door," Ori said, riffling through her victim's armor and coming up with a glowing data card. She slapped it against the security panel and the red light above it went suddenly green, the doors whisking open with a breath of air.

"Don't bother keeping it," the Doctor said, stepping into the elevator. "It'll only be good for one clearance. They'll be investigating why he ran the card. Hurry."

We piled into the elevator. With our armor, there was barely room for everyone, and we clicked and clacked together as the Doctor keyed in our destination. The doors shut, and we were going down.

The coms automatically toned down the sound of everyone's breathing, since it would be all but deafening within the confines of a helm, but some still managed to leak through. And at that moment, as we descended into Olympus Mons, it filled my head. I thought I could even make out the underlying heartbeats of my companions.

"I see what you mean about getting in being the easy part," Regina muttered, staring at the numbers over the door, watching them plunge into the negative. "How far down are we going?"

"As far as down goes," the Doctor whispered. "This is where I was stationed. Research and Biology. There will be...things here. Anyone who confronts us must be dispatched quickly and quietly. Their armor monitors vital signs, so once they die, security will be alerted. If you can, knock them out. But it doesn't really matter." She breathed deeply. "They'll be a step behind us, either way."

"When you say *things*?" Ori asked, checking her rifle's chamber.

"Creatures. Mutants. Andronicus works with accelerated evolution—he's created...space monsters."

I wet my lips, checking Mule's chamber. She only had six rounds, but they were enough to stop a charging rhino. Hopefully they'd be enough to stop whatever *monsters* Andronicus had managed to cook up in his lab.

The elevator stopped, the doors opened, and we were greeted by darkness.

15

MONSTER

———————————

Small red lights ran along the edges of the hallway. There were glass cases with dull, dark blue illumination laid into the walls on either side. As we stepped free of the elevator, I felt a tingling sense of apprehension. There was something unnatural about this place—something like a secret, something like a lie.

"Gods," Ori whispered, stepping closer to one of the glass panels. "What *is* that?"

My stomach curled in on itself as I moved next to her, peeking in the glass.

I wanted to say I saw a corpse, but if someone could decompose like this, it had to involve acid. It was a gelatinous red that pooled on the floor of the tank in the vague shape of a human body, with curls of black where the bones would have been. As I watched, a ripple passed through it, like wind touching water, and I felt an *awareness*.

"I told you, there are things here. Things that have no business existing in the natural world. Come on," the Doctor pleaded. "It's this way."

"Stay behind me," Firebird murmured, pulling her gaze away from the tank and taking the lead. "And keep quiet."

We continued down the corridor, with me still bringing up the rear. Dr. Ravin stayed in front of me, her slender form literally trembling, while Ori and Regina flanked Firebird, their rifles raised and pointed around her down the corridor.

Tanks dotted the hall, filled with dark, twisted things. I thought I saw a spider, but it was the size of a basketball and pulled itself back under a log when we passed. One tank had something like a starfish clinging to its side, but the arms were tipped by claws that tapped restlessly against the glass, as though searching for a weakness.

Firebird slowed, and I nearly walked into the Doctor. I blinked, focusing again on the end of the corridor. There was a door there, but it did not appear to have a lock. Firebird moved up next to it, cocking her head and using her power again.

I shifted, glancing at the tank beside me. It looked like something you would find at a nature exhibit, with foliage and a single log. I leaned closer, searching for the creature it contained. The floor of the tank was dark brown gravel, and my eyes couldn't quite focus on certain patterns there, something just enough off.

Suddenly, a tentacle slammed against the glass with a resounding *bang*.

I yelped, stumbling backwards and hitting the opposite tank with my back, Mule up and pointed at the tentacle. It seemed to be a mouth, with rows of razor-like teeth in soft, red flesh. It sucked at the glass, trying to chew something that wasn't there. I realized that the *log* was the creature's body, its camouflage shifting as it squirmed, trying to get at me.

Something scratched against the glass behind me and I scuttled back into the center of the room, embarrassed with my heart racing in my ears. Ori had twisted to look at me, and I could hear her throaty chuckle.

Firebird nodded.

"There are two men on the other side of this door," she said softy. "One beside it, the other in front. I think they're talking. Ori, I will take the one in front. Silence the other."

Ori nodded, crouching like a tiger preparing to pounce. Firebird breathed once, twice, and then kicked the door open.

She charged through, grabbing a white-coated lab tech by the face and hurling him to the ground. Even from back here, I could hear his skull crack. Ori, next through, caught an armored guard by the elbow and twisted him violently around, going again for the neck.

But this one was faster. He grabbed her free hand and jerked her forward, both of them going to the ground. Regina swore, charging into the room, sword materializing in her hand. With a single, precise gesture, she beheaded the guard.

Red vomited across Ori. She swore, kicking him off of her and scrambling to her feet. She wiped at her visor, now smeared with blood, but her armored fingers weren't designed for cleaning.

"Rusting Worlds," she swore, flicking blood on the floor. "Couldn't you have just stabbed him?"

"Couldn't chance him screaming," Regina reasoned, turning to the Doctor. "I'm assuming that thus far, they're suspecting an equipment malfunction."

"It's certainly possi—"

But she wasn't able to finish. From the deeper shadows of the room, there came a snarl. A rapid scrambling of claws on the floor, and some*thing* bolted toward us.

I'd guess it was a dog. At least, it had a very dog-like shape. But the fangs that sprouted from a black, rubbery muzzle were wicked and long. Its tail was twice the length of any big cat's and when it leapt at the Doctor, it reminded me of nothing so much as a striking serpent.

The Doctor screamed, throwing her arms over her head, and I reacted, jumping in front of her, taking the creature's attack. The weight of it slammed me to the floor, the metal of my armor squealing in protest as it raked me with wicked claws. Ori's voice

252

swore through the com and a second later, there was a flash of muzzle fire. The beast went limp on top of me.

"The hell is that?" Ori asked, grabbing the animal by its spiky collar and heaving it off of me.

My monitors were blinking warning lights all around my visor and as I stood, I realized that the bright red paint on my torso and legs had been deeply scored.

"It cut me," I breathed, mouth gaping. "It cut the armor."

My armor had taken rounds from machine guns. It had been blown up, thrown into space, and blasted by fire. I'd put myself through a giant blender once—*don't ask*—and had never gotten so much as a scratch.

"Monsters," Firebird said, turning to the Doctor. "Next?"

Dr. Ravin nodded and hurried to the dead lab tech, pulling a fresh security card from his pocket.

"This way," she said, scuttling across the lab's floor.

I ignored the tanks that we jogged past, ignored the creatures with too many eyes—or no eyes at all—that longingly pushed at the edges of their cages. The Doctor sprinted through rooms, using the security card with increasing urgency. There were fifteen guards, all told, and three more of the dog-like creatures. Firebird, Ori, and Regina dispatched them with the cool efficiency of a slaughterhouse.

All the while, we were descending. I could feel the slight tilt of the black floor under my boots, could see the way the walls twisted back and forth, a circular descent into the depths of the volcano.

Finally, Regina kicked a door open and bloody light flooded our dark hallway, revealing a long white table with a single woman sitting on the far side. She was short and blonde, and didn't look at all surprised when we stormed in, guns raised, bloodied and bruised.

The left wall was what could have been glass, except for the current of red magma it revealed. The river pushed from the far side toward us, the eerie red light coming from its startlingly vibrant eddies. It moved slowly against the wall, twisting and pulsing with a heat we could not feel.

There was a pause, and the woman regarded us coolly. She wore a white suit with a black tie, her mouth thin and her hands clasped on the table.

"Welcome," she said.

Regina hissed, starting toward her, but Firebird caught her arm. With casual grace, our commander stepped past us, striding toward the blonde, dropping her revolver on the white table.

"This is a surprise," Firebird said, voice robotic through her helm.

"Doubtlessly so," she said, her accent faintly of-then English. "For true,

Firebird, you did not have to go through so much trouble to reach us. My Lord would have been grateful for an audience. You are, after all, a natural wonder: the most powerful Inceptive BioMage in the Worlds."

"Perhaps," Firebird said, stopping just before the woman. "But it's not Andronicus that I'm here for."

"Oh?" The blonde blinked, a flash of surprise rippling an otherwise serene exterior. "He *will* be disappointed to hear that."

"Why in the rusting Worlds would we want to see him?" Ori snorted, flipping her gun up and onto her shoulder.

"He assumed, to kill him," the blonde said. "It's only logical, given the destruction of the *Ilena*. You've obviously sided with Mariana."

"So why would he want an audience?" Firebird asked, though it didn't sound much like a question.

"To change your mind, of course."

There was a pause. The red light slid across Firebird's black armor like ice on a warming pan. The floor was highly polished and, if I had to guess, something like obsidian. Uncomfortable, I glanced over my shoulder, down the hallway toward the dead guards.

Our commander's blank visor turned, pressing closer to the woman's face. There was a moment, fleeting as it was, when I thought she was going to simply kill her and be done with it. But then, she slowly reached up and undid the pressure clasps by her throat, pulling the helm off with practiced ease. Her black hair was pressed flat to her skull, her dark eyes catching red light as she looked at the woman.

"What are you—" Ori hissed.

"I didn't know," she said, raising a hand to stop Ori from coming closer, "that Andronicus hired Pawns."

The blonde's cheeks flushed.

"I have been trained in Suppression," she said, though a bead of sweat rolled down her hairline. "We have a working theory that anyone can be rendered Mute, with the proper discipline."

"Interesting," Firebird said, still holding her helm in her off hand. "And I assume that you're here to test that theory?"

"If it came to that, it is merely an additional benefit. I am here, truly, to offer...an alternative," she swallowed, eyes flicking to us. "Lord Andronicus is interested in your services."

"Why," Firebird said, easing even closer to the woman, almost close enough to kiss her. "When he has all of this, would he need someone like me?"

"He assumes that you work closely with his enemies, and could wield a scalpel where others would use hammers."

"I see."

Firebird's pupils pulsed wide, obscuring her irises, and the woman jerked back in the chair. I felt the pressure against my third eye, a small explosion of Will, and watched in silence as the woman began to tremble. Her hands flattened against the top of the table, pressed there as though to ground herself from being blown clean out of existence.

"It's important," she whispered, tears breaking free of her eyes, her gaze locked to Firebird's, "to maintain focus on what you know. It's important," and she squeezed her eyes shut, paling, "to remember your training and work through the pro—"

Silence.

The woman smiled.

"White snow is falling," she said. "It's cold outside."

Firebird's jaw tightened.

"Do we really need—" Dr. Ravin started.

"Quiet," Firebird snapped, brows furrowing. "I don't want to break her."

The room went still. For a moment, one that lasted far too long, there was only the sound of the magma, lazily pushing its way up the mountain.

"Val," the woman said, her smile widening. "My name is Val."

Firebird's frown deepened and she raised her free hand, twisting it slowly in front of Val's face, as though extracting something only she could see.

"There had to be thirteen," Val said. "It was the only way. After we got her subdued, the Muzzle contained her. The experiments weren't helping. We don't know what she is. She won't let us in. Our Empath...lost her mind," the woman laughed, tears breaking from the corners of her eyes. "She dreams about fire."

The muscles in Firebird's jaw bulged as she ground her teeth, murmuring: "Take us."

Val rose without hesitation.

"Now that he knows why we're here and who we are," Dr. Ravin said, hurrying to Firebird's side, "it's not going to be easy getting out of the holds. We have to be quick, or we're never getting back out of here."

Val turned, leading us toward the back of the room and a small, metal door. Ori glanced at me, murmuring:

"So much for the art of Suppression."

But I wasn't feeling humorous. As I moved at the back of the group, following Val and Firebird through the metal door, all I felt was sick. There had been a moment, when the woman offered the hope that Inceptive BioMagic wasn't all-powerful, that I felt... *relieved*.

Instead of cages, the deeper we went, there were shackles. We passed tables with amplifiers on them, tables with syringes and tables with clamps. I saw a white basin still splattered with blood. And, in a few places, I saw bits of bodies better left unseen.

There were no more guards, no more lab techs. For better or worse, Andronicus had pulled his people out. And the reasons *why* he would give us access to his laboratory flipped through my mind like pages of a grotesque storybook.

I suppose you want to know more. I suppose you're curious about the world under Olympus Mons, about the network that fuels the most powerful man in the Worlds. But the truth is, the things I saw in Andronicus's labs are things that no one should ever have to see. And so, you will have to make do with the knowledge that there is evil in this world—true evil—and if you ever have the misfortune to come in contact with it...

...Well, you'll understand my silence.

16

BRIMSTONE

———————————

At last, Val stopped. We were in the Twelfth
Hold. The woman hesitated beside the door,
her hand raised over the sensor that would
unlock it, and she began to tremble. Firebird,
immediately behind her, raised a hand, her
Will pressing against the woman.

"No," she whispered, voice
trembling. "Gods, please not again."

"Not again what?" Regina asked,
glancing back down the empty hallway.

"I don't know," Firebird muttered.

"Then just get her to do it," the
Doctor's hiss sent a chill up my spine, helmet
twisting back and forth as she scanned the
room, her figure slightly hunched. "We *can't*
get trapped down here. I'd sooner die."

I thought I heard Firebird's jaw pop
as she ground her teeth. There was a
pregnant pause. Then, Val sobbed and
pressed her hand against the sensor. A blink
of green, a release of air, and the door
whisked open.

I stood guard, still in the back, with
Mule aimed at the other side of the lab.

"There is something just so wrong
about this," Regina mumbled as Val stepped
first through the door, her limbs jerking

awkwardly, like her brain was screaming for them to be doing anything else. "I can't think of a good reason for Andronicus to let us..."

She trailed off. Our group paused. Back from the way we had come, I heard *something*. Something like a howl, something like a snarl. And claws. Too many claws, *clacking* on the tile floor.

"What is that?" I asked.

"Keep moving," Firebird said, following Val.

We each hurried through the door, moving with newfound enthusiasm. I looked over my shoulder as I went. There were shadows, shadows where there should have been light. I got in and the door flicked shut, the sensor turning dark.

The Thirteenth Hold was a cavern, maybe fifty meters wide and twenty high. The air was warmer, the floor was carved from black rock, and my heat sensors brightened under my feet. I glanced at Dr. Ravin. She was fumbling with the clasps of her helmet, clearly not used to wearing one, and when she finally managed to pull it off, it revealed a sweat-streaked face and haphazard bun.

The cavern was circular, with rows of little red lights around its circumference. Its ceiling was a dome, with a white light beaming down from its center.

And, in that pool of vicious white light, there was the woman we called Eve.

Her arms were chained at the wrists by thin, faintly glowing cords. The cords stretched to either side of the cavern, forcing her to her knees, and a metal cage wrapped around her torso, iron spikes against her spine. As I looked at the spikes, I felt a tingle of recognition. They were the same design that Spider had crippled me with, what he had called a Suppressor. But this woman had ten of them, each pressed against a vertebra.

She was muzzled, the metal mask snug against her mouth. Half of her head was shaved, the other half covered with lank, brownish-green hair. She was naked, revealing a red and black tattoo that wrapped around one of her shoulders and twisted down her body, like a serpent of flame.

Behind us, something howled.

"Hurry," Dr. Ravin urged, pointing across the room, where the cord met the wall. "You deactivate them there."

"And how do we do that, exactly?" Ori snapped, running to the other side and giving the cord a vicious jerk. "Seem pretty stuck."

I looked back at the door. Claws scraped against the other side, bringing to mind the deep scores in my armor. Raising Mule, I aimed at the door.

"Don't," Val sobbed. "Please, don't. You don't know what she is. You don't know what she's capable of."

"*Firebird*," Dr. Ravin fretted, wringing her hands. "Just *push* her. I don't care if she breaks. I don't care if she dies. We have to *hurry*."

I had seen Firebird *break* someone before, a Unity commander who had originally hired me to spy on Firebird and her crew. When he caught up to us, Firebird had quietly taken over his soldiers, killing all but him.

But when Dragons attacked us, when her focus waivered, something in the way she *pushed* her Will, something about the power, had...snapped him. Snapped something deep inside of him, something that bridged the delicate gap to insanity.

I don't know what became of that commander. I never asked. I truly never wanted to know.

Another push against my third eye, and Val was moving. She went to the place Dr. Ravin had indicated and, after another hesitation, pressed her hand against the sensor there.

The cuff on Eve's right arm fell from her wrist, clattering against the stone floor. The sudden slack let her collapse, the cage—like an external skeleton—clattering as she hit the floor. The Doctor sprinted forward, dropping to her knees in front of the woman's prone form. She disengaged something and the cage released, Eve's spine popping free of the Suppressors. Dr. Ravin examined her bruised back, each Suppressor leaving a vibrant, red, cup-like impression.

Movement caught my eye and I turned back to the door, only to find three black claws gouging through the metal and ripping violently down. The sound was hair-raising, a million times worse than nails on a chalk board, and I shouted, taking a step back and firing Mule.

"Jezi!" Regina shouted, grabbing my wrist.

I bit my lip, staring at the smoking mess I'd made of the already damaged door. There was a pause, then something came sprinting through the smoldering hole.

It wasn't a dog, not like the one that had attacked me. And it wasn't a cat, not like the lion Laurensen had tamed. This creature was more serpent than mammal, and it ran like a lizard on hot sand.

Again, I didn't think. I shot. Mule kicked in my hands, making my palms sting even through the armor, and the round caught the creature full in the chest. It exploded, purple lizard blood belching across the floor and onto my armor.

Then, they were *boiling* through the door. With a shout, I started firing. I lost count of them, all scuttling legs, teeth, and iguana-like tails. Too soon, I was clicking on empty, and I shoved Mule into my belt, struggling to get the assault rifle off of my back. It was stuck on something on my armor. A creature sprang forward, arms wide and claws exposed, rows of needle-like teeth flashing white in its black mouth.

I screamed, ducking down.

Regina leapt past me, sword held to the side. She twisted in a neat circle and cut the creature clean in half. Quick as I could blink, she was cleaving the next one's skull. The next, its throat. She ducked and wove and stabbed and slashed and *still* the monsters charged.

"Hurry up!" I shouted, turning from Regina to see Val deactivating the second shackle.

Eve laid on the floor, arms to either side as Dr. Ravin and Firebird tended to her. Her eyes remained closed, deep bruises circling them. The metal mask was buckled at the back of her skull and, when Firebird touched it, the lights around its edges went dark red.

"What's that thing even supposed to be?" I asked, creeping closer to them and farther from the door, where Regina continued to coolly dispatch monsters.

"I don't know," Dr. Ravin said, swatting Firebird's hands out of the way and fumbling with the clasp. "It's new tech to me. Seems to be some sort of," and she swore, finally managing to pop it free, "Suppressor."

"Yeah, great. Now for our glorious escape?" Ori asked, aiming past Regina at the doorway.

Regina killed the nearest one, then danced backwards, giving Ori room to open fire on the door. The chamber flared with the light of her muzzle, the sound deafening. Regina flipped the sword back into its place on her forearm and jogged toward us, unshouldering the backpack.

Dr. Ravin was frowning, checking Eve's pulse and taking a quick inventory of her injuries. She shook her head.

"This woman is dying," she said. "I need to get her into my lab. They've got her pumped so full of depressants, she's barely breathing. And *I*," she stressed, as though saying if anyone should know, it would be her, "don't know what the Suppressors did to her, mentally."

"Then we should probably quit gabbing and get to it," Regina said, dumping the spare suit of armor onto the floor.

Not knowing Eve's size, we'd brought one of Regina's old suits, hers being the largest. And as I helped fit her into it, I was surprised to find that it went on fairly well. She was as tall as Regina and heavily muscled, probably with a military background, judging by the crooked break in her nose. Her shoulders were not quite as broad, though, and I worried she'd flop around in the armor if I wasn't careful.

As I finished with the helmet, clicking it carefully into place and then double checking the clasps, Ori's gun went silent.

It was worse by far than a scream. We all jerked, hands darting for weapons, but when we spun to the door, we saw that Ori had simply stopped firing. The creatures were a smoking pile of ruin scattered around her, their blood dark purple and steaming. Ori turned toward us, shrugging slightly.

"Don't see any more."

"That's not good," Dr. Ravin muttered, standing and moving toward where she'd dropped her own helmet. "He's going to throw something else at us."

"You don't know that," I said, pulling Eve around and hoisting her into my arms. "Maybe he's going to surrender."

"Whatever would we do without our Fool?" Ori grinned, her teeth barely visible within the dark confines of her helm.

"One shudders at the thought," I replied sarcastically, shifting so that I could carry Eve over one of my shoulders.

It wasn't like carrying the hapless lab tech on the *Ilena*. Eve was larger than he had been, and her armor made her bulky. Even with my enhanced strength, my speed was dramatically reduced and when I moved, I did so with lurching overcompensation.

"We need to move farther down," Dr. Ravin had gone to the corpses, tentatively prodding them with the toe of her boot.

"I thought you said we should go back? That there would be less time in the heat?" Firebird's voice was strained. I glanced at her, and saw that she had Val standing at her side, a look of stark terror in the woman's eyes.

"I did, but I also don't know what's coming down from the upper holds right now," Dr. Ravin backed a step from the creatures as one trembled. "Deeper, and we won't have to worry about running into an ambush."

Firebird sighed, but she nodded. Gesturing to Val, she guided her to the only remaining door. The woman placed her hand on the sensor and it went green. Then, I watched as Firebird eased back on her Will, her pupils contracting to normal sizes as she turned her helmet over in her hands.

Val dropped abruptly to her knees, suddenly violently sick on the chamber floor. I grimaced, noticing the tightness around Firebird's eyes as she stepped back from her.

"You're a *monster!*" Val screamed at our commander's back, her blue eyes red.

Firebird quietly clicked her helm back in place, not turning to Val.

"You have no idea what you've done," Val continued to scream, even as we left her, starting through the door. "You'll burn for this! The *Worlds* will burn for this! That creature is a demon! She will kill you all! She will *burn* you *all!*"

"Someone's not so happy to see us anymore," Ori muttered, glancing back at her as we waited for the others to pass through the doorway.

"If you know anything about the Worlds, you'll shoot those *witches* before they kill you all!" Val started to get to her feet, trembling and weak, but she stopped when I pointed Mule at her with my free hand. Empty or not, it was an intimidating sight.

"You're lucky to be alive," I told her, anger curling in my belly. "Don't press it."

"Look at you," Ori said, elbowing me before she ducked through the door. "Firebird's avenging ankle-biter."

I made a face, following her through. When the door whisked shut and closed Val's sobs away, we breathed a collective sigh of relief.

The chamber was small and dark, reminding me of nothing so much as a maintenance room, and Dr. Ravin was already standing before what I was coming to quickly recognize as a maintenance shaft door. It had a red panel over it.

"You're sure the armor will withstand the heat?" Firebird asked, her voice dark. She glanced at me, at the deep scratches in my torso's plate.

"Pretty sure," Dr. Ravin said, pulling the same delicate instrument she'd used to unlock the first maintenance door from her belt. She waited, watching the warning light.

I shifted, adjusting Eve across my shoulder. I could see the strain on the edge of my armor's sensors, could see the energy it was taking to hold her. Martian Tech was as sophisticated as it comes, but even so, it wasn't invincible. I glanced back, toward the sealed door.

"We probably should have killed her," Regina said, giving voice to my own thoughts.

As a unit, we purposefully didn't look at Firebird. Our commander was silent, waiting by the maintenance shaft, her black armor seeming to suck the light from an already dim room.

"Ah," Dr. Ravin muttered to herself, as the sensor faded to orange.

She touched the instrument to each of the four corners, where a series of bolts were loosened. That done, she then grabbed the valve in the center and turned it in a counter-clockwise motion. It loosened with a heavy sigh, tendrils of heat whisking through.

"Sulfur?" Firebird asked, glancing at the monitor on her forearm.

"And carbon dioxide, and a plethora of other gasses," Dr. Ravin confirmed, slipping the instrument into a pocket, nodding toward us. "Toxic, to be sure. We have ten minutes before the chamber is flooded, less the closer we are to the core. So, I would suggest that we—"

"Boogie," Ori interrupted, springing through the doorway like a gazelle through a hoop.

"Yes, well, with care," Dr. Ravin muttered, handing Regina the heavy magnet before stepping next into the shaft.

Firebird followed, then me, and last Regina. She engaged the magnet and it snapped to the door, letting her pull it closed before she rotated it, securing the door with a heavy *clack* of locks. Two more buttons, and the magnet was fully engaged, locking the release valve in place.

"No one's coming through that way," she muttered, turning and following me.

The shaft was about half a meter too short for me to stand, and I awkwardly shifted Eve across my back, holding her arm and a leg to keep her in place. From the corner of my eye, I could see her head lolling crazily by my side.

It was dark. More than dark, it was pitch-black. The little lights around my face illuminated a grim procession, our crew stepping carefully into the bowels of the volcano. We soon met with an intersection, a larger tunnel traveling at a steeper angle. The right shaft shot down into darkness. The left, up into the same.

"Right," Dr. Ravin muttered, following Ori down a step and into the larger shaft, "We'll need to go faster, if we're going to clear."

"Of course we do," Regina muttered sarcastically, looking at me. "Do you need me to take her?"

"I've got her for now," I said, though sweat was beginning to run down the sides of my face. "I'd rather have you defending us from any creepy crawlies he sends in here."

"You don't think Dingus would do that?" Ori asked as we started up the chamber, moving at a trot.

"Dingus?" Dr. Ravin asked, glancing at Ori, her pale face illuminated by the white lights around her helm.

"Andronicus. Dingus. Seems to fit nicely," Ori flashed her grin.

"He's one of the Worlds' leading scientific minds," Dr. Ravin muttered.

"And a psychopath," Ori shrugged. "Being clever and being a Dingus aren't mutually exclusive."

"Focus," Firebird scolded, picking up our pace.

And so, we ran in silence. I watched the readouts around my view, watched as the toxins slowly began to rise. As my breathing increased, the filtration system began to hum in my armor, working harder, collecting the poison and storing it. Brute had explained the process, after our work in Southmarsh, but as with most things she was enthusiastic about, I hadn't understood half of it.

What I did understand was that when the filters were clogged, the armor would move to the reserves of stored air. And when that ran out, it would reboot to the original filtration systems, which would syphon out *most* of the toxins. Until they were filled too.

Through the coms, I could hear the group's muted heartbeats. They filled my head with wordless protest.

Occasionally, we would pass other maintenance entrances, always on the left. When we came across forks in the tunnel, Dr. Ravin would consult a readout on her forearm, following the homing beacon we had placed.

"It needs to push as much air through the propellers as possible," Dr. Ravin said, gesturing to one of the many tunnels in the ceiling, where I could occasionally see a turbine slowly twisting, "Powering the different branches of the mountain. "So there's an elaborate network of intersecting tunnels: a labyrinth, if you will. It's the most sophisticated example of thermodynamics, utilizing both heat and air."

"I wouldn't call it windy," Ori said.

"And you're not a scientist," Dr. Ravin chastised. "I don't expect to teach a pig to sing."

"Seems like a huge security risk," Regina pointed out. "Why didn't we just come in this way?"

"Do you not understand *labyrinth*?" Dr. Ravin's voice was becoming strained. "We didn't know which hold she was in. Firebird needed a Pawn to take us. That—and I can't stress this enough—we *don't* want to be in here when the volcano releases. Fumbling around in the shafts looking for the right hold would have been nothing better than suicide."

"Quiet," Firebird said. "Don't waste your air."

It was a fair point. Already, I could see the warning lights as my filters began to clog. The Doctor had said ten minutes, but I wasn't sure my armor had even that. I shifted Eve, wondering if she would be the last one alive, should things go badly. Unconscious, she was using the least air.

And the heat was rising. I could *feel it* through the scores in my armor, like tendrils of fire that occasionally touched my skin. Martian Tech had a thin membrane of bullet-resistant material as the inner layer of its armor. It was like medieval chainmail, Brute had told me. If something sharp penetrated my outer shell, the chainmail would hopefully catch it before my flesh did.

But, while it protected me from outward damage, it didn't handle the heat of the chamber as well as the full armor. And so, as I ran, I tried to keep my stomach sucked in, as far from the heating fabric as possible. My mind was quick to shove the image of my skin combusting within the armor before my eyes.

We ran. And, as we did, the tunnel continued to steepen. We needed to start using our hands more and more, pulling ourselves up. With the enhanced strength of our armor, we were inhumanly fast, like crickets bounding.

Regina eventually caught my arm, taking Eve from my back without a word. I was grateful, as the energy in my armor had rapidly started to drain. Without the extra weight, I was one of the fastest of the group, spurred by the sharpening heat near my torso. Glancing over my shoulder, I saw an orange glow emanating from the depths of the tunnel.

"Here," Dr. Ravin panted. "We're here."

It was a branch in the tunnel. Not just a fork, it split in five different directions, each tunnel wandering into darkness. I no longer needed the lights around my view to see my companions. The orange glow from the way we had come was radiating through the very rock beneath our feet, supercharging the fans and tubes of water, that the Doctor said were worked into the walls. The tunnel wasn't silent any longer. The whine of charging engines filled the air, trembled in the walls, and sighed through the passageways like a waking monster.

"Which way?" Regina asked. She had Eve over one shoulder and didn't seem worse for the wear of our sprint.

Dr. Ravin hesitated, moving first one way, then the other, twisting like a compass that couldn't quite find north. Finally, she nodded.

"This way."

The group hurried into the far-left tunnel. Regina nodded to me before following them, letting me take the rear guard. I breathed deep.

And blinked, when I realized how clearly I could hear that breath. It took a heartbeat for me to realize that it was because I could no longer hear everyone else's. My com had gone dead.

Panic tickled the back of my throat, a creeping realization. I started to follow them, tried to run down the tunnel.

But my armor didn't respond.

17

EVE

"Let's take a moment," she said, drawing a chair up to the table, "to talk about you."

I didn't want to talk about me. I was a writer, a person so content with silence, I spent my life creating new worlds in which to wander. And yet here I was, seated across from a reporter, staring just over her shoulder at the television displaying my mother.

"I'm nothing special," I said. "Just a cog in Unity's machine."

"But the way you write, the characters you build, they don't seem like Unity *material," she said, stressing the word.*

I shrugged.

"Who wants to read about something they already understand?"

* * *

I yelled, and the sound of it filled my helmet. Without the com, I was muted, a silent figure watching as her friends rounded a corner and disappeared. For a sweaty second, I was frozen in place, dripping inside my unresponsive armor.

Then, panicking, I searched the readouts with my eyes. The filters were clogged, and the fresh air reserves were already down by a quarter. I saw the heat warnings that I had thus been ignoring start to flash into blinding existence. I could feel thin bands of skin on my stomach begin to *blister*, pain pulsing through my core.

Desperate, I began to squirm inside of the suit, twisting my hands and arms, trying to work them up. If I could get some part of my body free, then I could pull the emergency latch by my hip. And while I didn't know how far I could make up the tunnel while holding my breath, it was far preferable to being burned alive.

Suddenly, the readouts blinked, going dead for a moment before coming back to flickering reality. It was like I was receiving a signal, mostly blocked by static. Another second passed, while I wondered if I'd triggered something with one of my squirming extremities.

Then, I was running. Or rather, my suit was. As realization dawned, I found myself sprinting in the wrong direction, springing through the far-right tunnel at break-neck speed. Someone was controlling my armor. Someone had broken the code.

I shouted again as my hands were thrust backwards, engaging the jets in my palms and feet and shooting me forward. It was haphazard even at the best of times, and drained my already dwindling power reserve, but it lent incredible speed to my sprint. Behind me, I could feel the temperature rising, could hear the subtle roar as fire brewed in the deep.

My controller overestimated the timing of a turn, and I went hurtling into the wall, warnings flaring across my screen as my helm cracked against the rock. I fell back, armor again unresponsive, and laid on the tunnel's floor. My head lolled to the side, stunned, and I saw the orange passageway begin to flicker with red, superheating even in the seconds it took for my controller to return.

I lurched to my feet. The glass of my helm was shattered, making a dizzying world beyond, and it seemed to be throwing off the puppeteer. I staggered forward, using the sensors on my hands to find the rock wall, following it like a drunk fumbling up a set of stairs. The rock beneath my fingers began to glow, heat rolling off of it in waves, and I choked, the first tendrils of sulfur finding their way through my cracked helm.

I was close to vomiting when my armor's jets engaged, thrusting me recklessly forward. I watched as the monitors around my viewscreen died, the power completely drained. For a moment, I was flying through empty space.

Then, light. White, clear light. I hit the ground in a clatter, armor and smoke twisting as I rolled to a stop. Through the helmet, the voices were muted, but I could still hear the panic in their voices. People ran around me, fleeting images through my shattered helm. I thought I heard the squeal of a valve engaging.

"Wait!" someone commanded, like a voice through deep water. The rest of it was lost to mumbled orders, blurred voices and heavy footsteps.

I counted my heartbeats. My head was spinning from the poison, my lungs burned. When I twisted inside the dead armor, I thought I could make out different shapes of people around me.

Then, someone disengaged the clasps at the base of my helm. There was no telltale breath as the helmet was released, no rush as the air inside my suit reacting with the room. Instead, there was only a sucking sound as someone peeled my helmet from my sweaty face.

I squeezed my eyes closed, gasping in a lungful of *beautiful*, crisp, fresh air. I very nearly choked myself and, while I tried to roll over, I found I couldn't lift the heavy deadweight that had once protected me. Instead, I was left to cough on my back, head to the side.

When I could breathe again, I took a moment. The room had quieted around me. I opened my eyes and found myself staring at a pair of heavy, metal-rimmed, black boots. I slowly raised my gaze, following the leather-clad legs of a woman squatting beside me, taking in her fingerless gloves, her long black trench coat, the collar that she had pulled up around her throat. She had a knife at her side, though I could find no other weapon. At last, I met her eyes.

They were light blue, almond-shaped and beautiful. She had a long nose, the bridge slightly bent, and metal piercings adorned her full, green eyebrows. I saw her head, one half shaved, the other sporting a thick mop of messy, bright green hair.

"Hello," she said, showing her teeth.

"You can't be," I replied, staring at her.

She gave me a tight-lipped grin, somehow making it sarcastic.

"Isn't it awful?" she asked.

She nodded at me and a man in a white technician's coat hurried to my side, working through the different manual clasps that held my armor in place. Another—a guard in the same white armor that Dr. Ravin had worn—pulled Mule from my belt, stuffing it into a black sack.

"Don't worry," the woman said, clapping her hands together, "we'll take good care of that. I believe your armor might be a shade past repair, but that's just an opportunity to make a better one for you, really. I'm trying to look at the bright side of things, these days."

"I don't understand," I said, finally able to sit up, watching as the tech continued peeling armor from my legs.

"Don't feel too bad about that, either," she shrugged. "It's confusing."

I looked at her.

"You're Eve," I said.

"And you're Jezi. Isn't it strange that we've both been briefed, but this is the first time we've met? Like stalking someone's social media and then having the uncomfortable situation of running into them."

"But if you're Eve, who did we just rescue?"

"Truth be told, I'm not sure *rescue* is the right word. The woman in the hold...well, she's not long for this world, anyway. Didn't take to the Adaptation. *Really* didn't take to the Evolution." Eve sighed, shrugging again. "But what can you do?"

I shook my head, trying to clear it. The tech pulled the last bit of armor from me, leaving me in my black leotard.

Eve stood, offering me a hand.

"Come on. We'll get a doctor to take a look at you. Sorry about the burns. We had to resist your little mission a bit, otherwise Firebird might have gotten suspicious."

"I'm still confused," I said, accepting her hand.

She easily pulled me to my feet. She had a similar stature to the woman in the hold, though there was a vibrancy to her that the other one had definitely lacked. She smirked at me.

"And people say you're bright."

Eve led me through a door and into a wide, brightly lit corridor. Everything had the too-clean feel of a laboratory, though the atmosphere was more of a...for lack of a better word, *pub*. There were people in plain clothes working in the rooms, cleaning and serving and—in general—going about their lives in the most ordinary way possible. We passed rooms with locked doors and small windows, where I could see technicians working at computers, but we also passed restaurants, bars, and—if the pulsing bass coming through the closed, double doors was any indicator—clubs.

"This is not clearing it up for me," I said, limping after her.

"Look," Eve said, rolling her eyes to me, not slowing her pace, "you've been working for Mariana. Of course, you're expecting Andronicus to be a scorpion with nine heads. But he wouldn't be an Overlord if all he did was terrorize the Worlds. He's a conqueror, but he's also a ruler. And rulers don't last long if their subjects hate them."

"No, I mean I don't understand why I'm here. Why you're here. Why this whole mission suddenly went..." and I frowned as we walked past what appeared to be a giant wolverine, who was laying on his back having his belly scratched by a little boy "...wrong."

"Wrong?" Eve snorted. "Did you really think that your little crew could infiltrate Andronicus's inner sanctum if he didn't *want* you to?"

"But we had," I hesitated, glancing at Eve. "Help."

"You mean Iona Ravin?" She laughed this time. "If you were to chalk up one character flaw for her, what would it be?"

I frowned.

"I really don't know."

"Take a guess."

"Arrogance?"

Eve tapped the side of her nose, winking.

"A little struggle, and she thinks she's rediscovering gravity. And Mariana," Eve turned, leading me up a set of wide, busy stairs, "she's got her head so far up the Oracle's ass, she doesn't even know what World she's on half the time. Andronicus knew you were coming before *you* knew you were coming."

"And he didn't want to stop us?"

"What would be the point in that?" Eve cocked a green brow. "We got what we wanted."

I swallowed. We came to a door, white and with twin green holograms floating where a security panel usually was. Eve put her hand within the circular hologram, and it rolled up her arm like a cuff. Then, sinking back, the doors disengaged and slipped silently into the wall.

"Me?" I asked, following her hesitantly into the room.

"You," she agreed.

It was a round chamber, white and very Unity-esque. Small, round robots flitted about, some with trays of food, others ushering tables of medical instruments. There were narrow, white beds around the circumference of the room. It seemed to be some sort of recovery ward.

In the middle of the room, there was a stark desk with a woman in a crisply folded hat sitting at it. She had dark hair, curled delicately around her sharp face, and she didn't glance up when we entered.

"Here," Eve said, shoving me down on the nearest bed. "I'll get a bot."

"A what?"

But she was already gone, striding toward the woman in the center desk, her trench coat billowing dramatically behind her.

Fear fluttered tremulously somewhere behind my heart. I felt it in the tightness of my throat and the dampness of my palms. But, if I'm being honest, I was not nearly as frightened as I had cause to be. I'm not sure that people can be truly afraid when they're as confused as I was at that moment.

Eve returned with one of the round robots hovering behind her, its center eye large and—for lack of a better word—cute.

"You have bots where you come from?" Eve asked, stepping aside and crossing her arms.

"I don't think so," I said, leaning back as the bot hovered uncomfortably close to my face.

Something inside the eye flickered and a moment later, I was being scanned with a thin, green light. It took in my body, then seemed to process data, humming with what could almost be considered contentment. I glanced to the side, at the bed next to me, and saw a sleepy-looking woman nursing an infant.

"They're handy," Eve said, picking at something in her teeth. "Frees up more of our doctors for Bio work."

"Medical doctors?" I flinched when the bot produced something like a syringe from an extending tray in its side.

"Sure. Andronicus isn't going to ignore the wellbeing of his assets, now is he? Hold still," she admonished when I batted the bot's syringe away from my arm. "You're compromising their efficiency."

"Look," and my tendril of fear abruptly electrified into something like anger, "I feel like you're glancing over the part where you kidnapped me. I'm not going to—"

I swore as the bot thrust a second syringe, produced from its other side, into my upper right bicep. Eve's smirk widened.

"They're used to dealing with children," she said. "Sneaky."

"What was that," I massaged my arm, panic setting in quickly.

"Just a pick-me-up. You're in perfect health. Let's go."

And Eve was making her way toward the exit. I glanced at the woman at the center desk—who seemed enthralled in some sort of video game on a data pad—and then at the bot who had administered my shot. It was now hovering beside the woman with the infant, scanning the newborn with the same indifference that it had me.

Still holding my arm, I hurried after Eve, who was already halfway down the stairs. Despite my fears, I did feel—if not better—less tired. When I caught up to her, we were once again making our way down the congested corridor.

"Where are you taking me?" I demanded, glowering as we passed a group of girls who pointed at Eve with wide-eyes.

"To meet your new boss," she said, rounding a corner and taking me down a narrower hallway.

"Excuse me?" I darted after her, only to be nearly run over by a palanquin being carried by what looked to me like giant emperor penguins. I stumbled out of their way, gaping as the creatures waddled on paddle-like feet.

"The hell," I whispered, turning back to Eve, who was waiting in front of an elevator.

"I call them Suits," she said, nodding toward them as I joined her. "Dumb as snot, and only good for lifting heavy things."

"What's the point?" I asked, momentarily sidetracked as a woman with what appeared to be a python joined us in waiting for the elevator. The serpent was looped carelessly around her neck, the massive, flat head resting on her upturned palm.

"Of Suits?" Eve shrugged. "Does there need to be a point?"

I hesitated as the elevator dinged, before saying, "Well, yes."

The doors whisked open to reveal a freakishly tall man with a leopard in a jeweled collar. I took an involuntary step back, but Eve ignored them as they stepped free. She moved into the elevator, narrowing her eyes when the woman with the python started to follow. The woman paled, ever so slightly, before backing a step away.

"Come on then," Eve prompted, holding the elevator door as I joined her. "And wipe that stupid look of your face. You're going to meet a king."

"Right," I muttered, scrubbing my sweaty hands against my thighs. "About that. What in the Worlds makes you think I'm just going to start working for you people?"

"Let's call it a hunch," she muttered, once again thrusting her fist into a series of spinning holograms. They twisted up her forearm, taking longer this time to register who she was. And then, without any other direction, we were shooting upwards.

"Then you're crazy. I'm not going to betray my people. I don't know who you think you are, but nothing would be worth that. And *why* are there animals running around all over the place? Isn't it dangerous?"

"I'm not crazy," Eve said, crossing her arms and staring at the rising numbers on the elevator's front. "We're not asking you to betray your people. And there are animals because that's where it's most convenient for them to be. We're accelerating Martian Adaptation. How else do you propose we go about it?"

"But isn't it dangerous," I asked, also glancing at the numbers. "Don't you worry about...I don't know, venomous lion attacks?"

Eve rolled her eyes down to me, somehow more cutting for their blueness. I think they reminded me of my mother's.

"Maybe you haven't heard of this thing called BioMagic."

"You're telling me that there are Bestial BioMages here?"

Eve cocked a brow at me.

"Really, they said you were bright," she muttered.

Before I could retort, the elevator dinged and the doors opened.

The first thing that I noticed was the smell. Warm air rushed past us, twisting the sweaty curls around my face, and carried with it the intoxicating aroma of old books, leather, and cinnamon. The second thing—though by a narrow margin—I noticed was the fireplace. It resided in the center of the room, a massive open fire with a copper dome hovering above it. Literally, hovering. The smoke twisted into it, but never emerged.

Eve motioned me into the room and I slowly obliged, eyes taking in every detail. The furniture was dark, deep reds and browns, and a low table covered most of the carpeted floor in front of me. There were fat pillows around it, and glowing styluses beside each seat, with data pads on standby, their shimmering fronts displaying Olympus's emblem—a simple outline of the volcano.

The far side of the room was cast in the pale, white light of a hundred small windows overlooking the snow-coated Quilt. There were window seats, their cushions the same dark red as those around the table, and a few had open books laying on them.

And sitting in a high-backed chair, with his feet propped up against the fireplace's edge, was Overlord Andronicus.

18

MOUNTAINS

———————————

There was a black cat sleeping across his knees, the unusually long tail twisting back and forth like a pendulum just over the floor. Its yellow eyes opened when I stepped into the room, slitted pupils fixed to me. Andronicus had a book resting on one arm of his archaic chair, though it was a data pad that he held in his hands.

He seemed absorbed. Eve shouldered past me, moving into the room with the air of someone returning from an errand. It wasn't until she'd seated herself on the edge of the table, in between two of the vacant data pads, that Andronicus looked up.

"Hey," he said, flicking the screen off and twisting in the chair, glancing over Eve. "How'd it go?"

"Clockwork," she said, twisting in her seat, her spine issuing several loud pops.

"Good," he said, gaze rising to me.

He smiled, and the first thing that I could think of—my natural reaction—was *friendly*. Andronicus had a thick beard, immaculately trimmed to the contour of his firm jaw, and he stared at me through a pair of black-rimmed glasses. He flicked a long-fingered hand at the cat on his knees and, with a resentful yowl, the creature sprang off of him, padding along the edge of the fire. It looked like a small housecat, though its hide was the same rubbery insulation as the lion's.

"I trust you've been to the infirmary," Andronicus said, rising from his chair.

He was taller than I would have thought, over two meters, and thin enough that the baggy shirt he wore seemed oversized. He had a mop of brown hair, wavy and perhaps not entirely clean. I scowled at him.

"I don't see why it's going to matter. I'm not betraying anyone to you, so you might as well get to torturing me."

Both of his bushy eyebrows shot up.

"Torture you? Why's that everyone's first reaction? Do I *look* like I torture people?"

"I think it comes with *Overlord*," Eve muttered, still working at picking something from between her teeth.

He gave her a look, one that I could imagine Harry giving Ori, and thought on that for a moment. Then, gaze returning to me, he spread his big hands wide.

"Well, I'm not going to torture you. Please, come," he beckoned toward me and— in the way that I had come to expect from arrogance and Will—turned and led the way without even checking to see if I would follow.

As it was, I hesitated. My eyes wandered to Eve. She wasn't doing anything, just sitting there, examining whatever she'd managed to extract from her teeth. Her mop of green hair hid a blue eye, but I could feel...*something*, something like attention, something like focus. I looked at the fire and suddenly, the room was too warm.

Twisting my thumbs against the pads of my fingers, I followed Andronicus. The far side of the room had a distinctly chilly atmosphere, particularly in comparison with the other half. Here, cold winter light seeped through short, wide windows. I noticed that the red cushions were not faded, despite the constant light, and a part of my mind wondered at that as I joined him.

We were overlooking the Quilt. From this height, its marbled expanse truly lived up to its namesake. There were pockets of snow in dips within the black rock, and there were streaks where the hovercrafts had sped. Far east, the sun was just rising, dipping the purple sky in shades of blue, yellow, and red.

"It's beautiful," I said.

"It is," he agreed, though some of the early warmth had already evaporated.

That was when my gaze fell to the long shadows to the south. The *Ilena* looked like...an *elephant* came to mind, its magnificent body fallen to cruelty. Anxiety sprang back into my blood.

There was a long silence. It stretched from the corners of the room, tangled in my hair. I could hear it in the weighty *snap* and *crackle* of the fire, feel it in the chilly stone beneath my feet. I wasn't wearing any shoes, I realized, and my insulated socks had been sweat-soaked within the armor. When I moved, I could catch a whiff of myself and— despite Maya's tech—I decidedly did *not* smell like roses.

He sighed.

"I suppose I should introduce myself," he said, turning to me, extending a hand. "Andronicus."

"Jezi," I said, automatically taking his hand. His fingers were surprisingly callused, nails trimmed painfully short.

"Jezi," he repeated, releasing me. "I've been reading your stories."

"You have?" and I was incredulous.

Here's the thing with writing. You know that people are going to read it. You know that they're either going to like it, or not. Maybe they'll hate it. Maybe they'll set it down and forget about it. But the idea of someone reading your work is abstract. You don't *think* about this person actually taking your words into their mind and following the pictures that, always before, only you could see.

Sharing imagination is something like magic, my husband had said. And he wasn't wrong. It is a strange, ancient, wandering kind of magic.

But when someone says they saw your magic, *read* your imagination, it's like getting suddenly slapped in the face by a fish's tail, all wet and surprising and unpleasant. It snaps the obvious into what you experience and no part of it feels right.

Or at least, that had always been my reaction. But now, standing before a man Firebird called our enemy, it was more than obvious. It was surreal. *Those stories aren't meant for you*, I wanted to tell him. *They're to inspire people, people who need to be inspired.*

"I like them," he continued, when I didn't say anything. "Laurensen is my favorite."

I gaped at Andronicus.

"Why?" and while I meant *why* as a larger question, I realized it could apply to any part of our conversation since I entered the room.

"I'm not sure," he shrugged, looking thoughtful. "She seems *real*, like someone I could meet. Of course," and he laughed. "I suppose I could, couldn't I?"

"You probably wouldn't like her quite so much, if you did," and it was the closest thing to a threat that I think I'd ever said.

"I suppose," and he sighed, heavier this time. "That brings us back to our original quandary."

"You mean the kidnapping?" I asked.

"Which one? The BioMage's? Or your own?"

"Either, I suppose," I glanced over my shoulder, toward where Eve lurked.

He drummed his hands against his thighs, a nervous habit, something people do to fill the longer silences.

"I'm a planner," he eventually said, shifting from one foot to the other. "I like strategy. I like setting the dominoes up. The great thing about plans is that if they're well-laid, all I have to do is tip a finger," his fingers twitched against his legs, a flicking gesture. "I like to see how little effort I can possibly make in order to achieve the desired result. Really the opposite of what Firebird does."

"So, you wanted her to break into Olympus," I said, frowning at him. "You know, if you would have asked to meet with me, you could have probably put in a lot less effort by just *asking*."

He gave me a disappointed look.

"I really thought you would be sharper," he said.

"That's what I said," Eve called from the other side of the room, now lounging on her back in the pillows.

"If the goal was to simply talk with you, Jezi, I would have emailed you. It's not that high of tech, been around for centuries," he gestured to the window seat nearest me. "Sit? Something to drink?"

"Water," I said, my head feeling light as I took the proffered seat. "What *did* you want?"

"Well, a number of things. That's the greatest part of strategy," and his eyes glinted as he took a seat on the cushion next to me. "You don't have to work toward one end," he flicked something on his wrist, and a green hologram appeared, "not when the greatest game is succeeding at several different branches of a larger one."

He tapped through the hologram before it whisked back into a small, black disc that looked like an old-fashioned watch. A moment more, and that too faded from existence. Noticing my gaze, he flicked his wrist out toward me.

"BioTech," he said, more than a little proudly. "My brain sends the technology simple commands, like desire, and the watch appears. Opens an algorithm that extends everything from my kitchen to my warzones."

"If you can do that, why not just order the water with your mind?" I asked, frowning at his wrist, trying to make out some kind of band.

"Good question. We're having some issues mapping the brain waves, to put it in layman's terms. Consider this: you find yourself thirsty, and you start to summon a beverage. But then you get a message that someone just blew up your fuel station. Now, you're angry and you've got the map open and five seconds later, there's a nuclear bomb on its way to the Chryse," he smiled an empty smile at me. "BioTech can be a little too receptive to nonverbal commands."

A small portal opened in the wall, its circular door rotating open and allowing a bot to enter. It reminded me of the infirmary's, though this one was a dusty pink color. It stopped in front of me, a glass of water hovering in a Grav-Field in front of it. I accepted the glass, though I spared Andronicus a glance before taking a sip. I couldn't think of any strategy where poisoning me would be beneficial, but still.

"Anyway," he continued. "We weren't talking shop. We were talking about why you are here. The simple answer, Jezi, is that I'm interested in helping you."

"Helping me," I said, a little more deadpan than I'd intended.

"Yes," he dipped his head sagely. "Of course, as the first of your kind, you interest me on multiple levels. But the fundamental purpose of my empire is to help people tap their true potential, unlock their hidden strength. Take Eve, for example. She came to us a Mute, a girl fresh off of the streets of the Chryse. For years, she worked with our labs, subjecting herself to a myriad of tests and brainwork. She cleaned the creatures' pens when she needed work, scrubbed the lab equipment when credits were tight. And then, one day, something just," and he *snapped* his long fingers. "Suddenly, she wasn't a Mute. Suddenly, she was one of the most unique people in all the Worlds."

"I created Olympus," Andronicus continued, his voice cracking slightly, as though he wasn't used to using it quite so much, "because I believe the Worlds are the same as Mutes. There's bottomless potential, just laying there, stagnant save for the energy to keep turning. But we all could be so much more. Think of this world, think of what it was a hundred years ago. A thousand. Think of the stories from of-then Earth, when the red planet was a place we could only send droids to, where no man could breathe the air. When there was no purple sky. Think of it."

"I *have* thought about it," I muttered, before taking a longer swallow of the cold water, savoring it as it rushed down my throat. I didn't know how long this hospitality would last, but I wasn't about to pass up a chance to quench my thirst.

"Then think *harder*. Where would we be today, if it weren't for people like me? *I* am not altering the future, Jezi, I'm *creating* it."

I paused, meeting his gaze. His eyes were green and gold, mostly hidden behind the thick lenses of his glasses. I wondered at that, as I wondered at the cushion I sat upon. Why would the ruler of a third of Mars and more of Earth choose to wear glasses? The tech existed in Unity for complete eye transplants, the new eyeball grown in a machine. If Unity had it, I could only imagine the sort of technology Andronicus had at his fingertips.

"You might be creating it, but it's with you at its center," I said. "If you read my stories, you know that everything you stand for is fundamentally opposed to what I am, what Firebird does. You are trying to rule the Worlds—we are striving to be free."

Andronicus stared at me, stared at me long enough that I began to feel the water in my gut twist with my every breath. I wanted to run. But my eyes flicked to Eve, and I could *feel* that same heat I had when the Oracle first showed her to me.

"Of-then Earth tried democracy once, you know," he said, standing. "Have you ever seen Earth from Mars? I would like for you to look at it, sometime. Look at Earth through one of our telescopes and tell me that humankind left to its own devices is what is best for humankind. Red planet, indeed."

He started for the door and I sprang to my feet, abruptly enough that the black cat—who had found her way closer to

Andronicus—arched her back and hissed at me.

"How do you think you're going to help me?" I asked. "I'm not going to betray Firebird. And I'm not going to be fooled into believing you're a gentle, misunderstood Overlord. If you mean to help, then let me go."

Andronicus paused, glancing over his shoulder at me. The light of the fire flashed across his glasses and, for the briefest of moments, I thought I saw an image within them.

"The first Inceptive BioMage killed her sister," he said. "Belial, they called her. She isolated herself for years, attempting to understand what she was, what she could do. Now, Inceptive BioMages learn from Empathic BioMages. If another Inceptive BioMage can be found—though they are rare—then they learn from them. Bestial BioMages as well. The BioMagic associated with biological creatures shares a common thread.

"But when Eve was changed, no BioMage alive could teach her what she needed to know. She does not alter a mind. Her magic shares no common threads with that of a BioMage.

"The same surely is true for you. MetalMage. And while I cannot offer the wisdom of another MetalMage, Eve *can* help you understand what it is to alter the physical world around us."

I frowned at him.

"If this is true, why would you want to give it to me? I'm your enemy, Andronicus. We're fighting on different sides."

"I am quite certain that a single Mage would prove wanting, should she attempt to overthrow my empire." He smiled, the corner of his mouth twisting. "But her insight into what it is to alter the minerals of the world around her? Invaluable. It is a worthy exchange, one," and his smile widened, "*side* to the other."

19

MAGIC

I woke in a bed soft as dreams, under a mountain of blankets in a room with a window the size of a small spaceship. My room had a fireplace, and the rippling flames cut the morning chill. I sat up, pushing my hair back from my eyes, and yawned.

It wasn't until this moment that I realized I hadn't been sleeping well on *Redwing*. The constant motion of the ship, the sweltering heat (Ori couldn't stand being cold), and the sudden interruption of inevitable trouble...I doubted that anyone on that ship had gotten a full night's rest in the past year.

But now, as I stretched and pulled myself from bed, I felt refreshed and revived, a little bear trundling out of its winter den.

I shouldn't have been happy. I knew that. I was a captive in a hostile Overlord's empire, a puppet to his whim. At any moment, Andronicus could decide to take me down to this subterranean laboratory and have my brain dissected. But if I had learned anything from my time in Unity as a spy, it was to enjoy the good moments while they lasted.

So, I stood by the fire, watched the glowing coals—heated from the mountain's own breath—and tapped an order into the small data pad Eve had given me the night before. A moment passed, and then one of the serving bots appeared from its small vent in my room, a steaming cup of coffee proffered before it.

"Thanks," I said, taking the mug.

The thing blinked green lights at me before whirring back into the wall. I moved around my room as I sipped my coffee, going from the windows—that overlooked the northern side of Olympus Mons, where the Quilt was devoured by ice—to the small bathroom. The floor was black stone, heated, and instead of a shower, I had an ornate bathtub. There were bottles—not bars—of soaps and lotions and other luxuries that I had gone a year without. On a space ship, every inch of space is important, every drop of water precious.

But Olympus Mons had access to water in the glaciers to the north, and all the heat Mars could offer. There were ships and traders moving to and from the mountain every day, bringing coffee and chocolate and spices that Andronicus couldn't make on his own. And—growing in the botanical gardens beneath us, with their artificial light and accelerated production—we had fresh vegetables, fruits and berries. I had eaten a platter of grapes and watermelon for dinner...*real* grapes and watermelon.

Even before Firebird, having fresh produce was an event. Unity used most of their greenhouses as designated O2 centers, pumping the oxygen into the world as quickly as they could produce it. Fresh vegetables took time and energy, time and energy that our dystopia couldn't afford. My mother grew strawberries in secret, maintaining her own little biosphere, but it was a practice that was frowned upon as an extravagance. Why should Unity's members waste their time growing vegetables, when every nutrient they needed could be synthesized at a fraction of the cost?

"Because it's good, that's why," I muttered to myself, setting my coffee on the sink and turning on the cold water.

I washed my face, scrubbing the water back through my aura of black, tangled hair. It had become less and less manageable, growing from the trim orb of curls that had been my style when I joined Firebird to the unruly halo that now snarked around my face. If I didn't pull it back in a bun, it floated around my cheeks like a dandelion's seeds. My eyes flicked to the mirror over the sink, and I ran my fingertips around the edges of my eyes, cleaning away the night's sleep.

I had never been considered a slender woman. My mother had been strong, with a sturdy kind of build, and I hadn't known my father. I wasn't particularly tall and while I had gained a deal of muscle in the last year, I'd also maintained a healthy appetite. My cheeks had never lost their roundness, and my dark complexion didn't conceal the splatter of freckles across the bridge of my short nose.

I pushed damp fingers through my hair again, scrunching. I didn't have a mirror in my room in *Redwing*. I wondered now why I hadn't asked for one. I supposed, with everything that I had been through since arriving on Mars, my appearance had been the least of my concerns.

A figure appeared over my shoulder, her green hair electric in the chill morning light.

"Enjoying yourself?" Eve asked dryly.

"Much as I can," I said, turning to her.

She still wore the black trench coat, though her boots were less—for lack of a better word—punkish. As her light blue eyes flicked over my body, I stood a little straighter. Dressed only in the pajamas left for me the night before, I was a distinctly less intimidating figure.

"You're going to want to put something on," she said.

"What would you suggest?" I asked in return, striding past her and back into my warmer bedroom.

In answer, Eve snapped her fingers. My bedroom door whisked open, allowing several men in dark suits entrance. At their sides, hovering racks of clothing whirred along. I gaped as they shuffled the wardrobe into an empty closet near the fire. None of the men so much as glanced at Eve and me. Their discipline was so absolute, I wondered if they might be androids.

When they had gone, Eve strode past me, saying before she left:

"Suit up, then meet me on the third floor. We're going to see what you're made of."

I stared at the door as it closed after her, softly chewing my lower lip. No part of this, clothes or no clothes, was going to work out well for me. Of that, and little else, I was sure.

* * *

"Magic," said the PyroMage, "is like pushing."

"Pushing," I repeated, unimpressed.

Eve cocked an eyebrow at me, piercings catching the light.

"Pushing, right," I shrugged, continuing. "I just thought it would be something…more…"

"Magical?" She filled in, and her look of disdain did little to bolster my enthusiasm. "You're not in a fairytale, in case you haven't noticed. Magic is science and science is logic in the world around us. It makes sense. It's not," and she made an extravagant gesture with her hand, like waving a wand, "*cute.*"

We stood in the center of a circular room. It was Level 3, a training floor, and I couldn't help but notice that the black floor had a glassy cast to it, like it had been tempered at high temperatures. Around us, veins of red heat pulsed toward their various purposes in maintaining Olympus Mons, and already sweat was beading along my hairline. There were white androids placed at various places in the room, their feet small wheels and their hands bearing something that looked like stun-guns.

"I just don't see how it's like *pushing,*" I said defensively, rolling my shoulders. "That makes me think of…childbirth."

"Well, maybe it is like childbirth," she said. "Or a child. You have to create it, nurture it, and when the time is right, expel it from your body before it destroys you from the inside out."

I made a face at her. Eve stood in front of me, her trench coat exchanged for a light set of workout clothes. Her white tank top was nearly transparent, and I could see the coils of a fire-like tattoo snaking around her body, identical to the one on the woman we had pulled from the Thirteenth Hold.

"So, show me," I said.

Eve didn't hesitate. There was no fanfare, no dramatic twist of her wrist. One moment, I was standing beside a white android. And the next, I was standing beside a pillar of flame.

I yelped, flinging myself away. I could smell burning hair, and I flopped on the floor, beating at my halo of hair. The charred fringe left black residue on my palms. I scrambled back from the burning android, gaping as fire belched from its hollow eyes and empty mouth, from the cracks where its fingers held the gun.

Just as quickly as it had appeared, the fire winked out, leaving in its wake the charred remains of a once-white android.

"Hell's bells," I breathed, clambering shakily to my feet. "You can burn metal?"

Eve rolled her eyes, striding to the android. She flicked its metal chest. There was a clang, and a shower of dust fell from the inside of the shell. The wheels turned to ash and the whole thing tipped over, hitting the floor with a *clang*.

"Not the metal, the inner workings. I've never made rock or metal burn. It's...difficult. There's nothing there *to* burn."

"So, you couldn't just...I don't know...make a jet of flame?"

"Depends on what's between us," she said, turning to me. "Combustible gas? Sure. But it would burn me every bit as much as it would burn you. I must have a target to maintain any kind of control. And I have to..." she paused, getting the same look that Laurensen did when I asked her to explain Bestial BioMagic "...understand it."

"But how do you understand combustible *gas*? It's not like it has a mind or emotion."

"If it did, I would be a BioMage," she snapped. "I don't have to read the android's mind—it doesn't have one."

"So then how do you understand it?"

"How do you understand that you have to breathe?" she arched that pesky eyebrow again, and I felt a flare of irritation. "Do you read your lungs' mind? Do you look into your stomach and realize it's *thirsty*? Or do you just understand it? There are things in the world that we understand less the more we try to figure them out. Instinct is what guides me."

"But you didn't always understand. You used to be a Mute."

"So did you. How's that working for you?"

I frowned at her. Eve shrugged. She turned to a stack of metal balls someone had placed toward the back of the room.

"Can you move those?"

"With my mind," I grumbled, "but only if they're actively threatening me."

"Believe me, that can be arranged." She made a clicking sound with her tongue. "But in all fairness, I had the same problem.

The issue wasn't that I needed to be afraid, but rather that I didn't understand Magic. My instincts knew how to wield fire—but the rest of my body needed to learn."

"So, you're saying that you could teach me the fundamentals?"

She shrugged.

"Probably not, but who knows. We're the only two non-BioMage Mages in the Worlds. It's more than likely that metal and fire aren't the only two non-biological elements humans can influence, but here we are. Maybe there are some similarities. And maybe you're wasting my time."

"Andronicus didn't seem to care."

"Andronicus isn't down here sweating with you."

I moved toward the metal balls, staring at them, wondering what fundamentals metal and I could possibly have in common. Eve lurked behind me.

"Why is it so hot down here?" I asked. "Couldn't we train somewhere cooler?"

"The heat helps me burn," she said, making it sound like she wanted to add a *duh* to the end of it. "What has helped you, in the past?"

"I'm not sure," I reached the metal balls and leaned over, picking one up. It was heavier than I'd expected. "Like I said, it helps if I'm being threatened. But even then, it doesn't always work. I've had guns to my head that I couldn't move an inch, but one morning I sent my fingernail clippers across the room when I cut myself. There's not much in between."

"What kind of metal?"

I frowned, thinking about it.

"Iron, sometimes. Titanium and nickel." I flinched, remembering: "A gold ring, once."

"What about raw metals? What about ore?"

"I guess I've never tried."

"Rocks?"

"Not that I can think of."

"Interesting," Eve stopped beside me, picking up another of the balls. "Each of these is composed of a different metal. Some are alloys. I'm curious to see if you can't move some of them."

"I really doubt I'm going to move *any* of them."

"Do you usually push the metal away from your person, or pull it towards you?"

"Push, I guess," I said slowly. "Although I think I pulled it a couple of times."

"Could be handy," she started backing away from me, tossing the ball up and catching it. "Let's test that."

Even though I'd been expecting it, when Eve threw the metal ball at my head, I made a small sound and flung myself to the side. The ball hit the wall behind me and rock cracked, chips of black stone trickling down

312

to the already charred floor. I scowled as she picked up another one.

"I feel like we could start by just rolling them," I said.

"And I feel like I want to leave you down here with a Gila monster," she said. "But it's a workday."

* * *

By the day's end, we were both sweat-soaked, bruised, and exhausted. I hadn't managed to move a single flake of metal, and Eve had set three more androids on fire in her frustration. I had a long gash in my cheek, from when I tried to tackle her to the floor and collided with one of her eyebrow studs, and the bottom of my white shirt was still smoking. We sat across from each other in a small room that smelled like grease, while a man behind a food counter burned a pair of burgers.

"What time is it?" I moaned, resting my forehead on the table.

"Don't know," she mumbled in return.

"I just want to sleep."

"Then sleep," she said, snatching her food from a bot and stuffing the still sizzling burger into her mouth. "You can die here, for all I care."

"Sweet of you," I mumbled.

Cattle were too costly for Unity to bother with. If it couldn't be grown in a petri dish, it wasn't worth the effort. When I came to Mars, a few months after our first mission, Ori introduced me to the reinvention of the cheeseburger.

There are a few things about Earth that I miss. The blue sky, the soft gray clouds, small furry animals that didn't surprise me with venom...but cheeseburgers, well, they could make up for most any longing.

With a grateful sigh, I followed Eve's example and attacked my burger. She was already half done with hers, and I had a feeling that she wouldn't be waiting for me to savor mine.

* * *

Night came and went. I quickly realized that having a soft bed just means that it's that much harder to crawl out of it in the morning. I had scarcely dragged my aching bones from the mattress before Eve was there, tossing a belt at my head.

"Today, we're going to try something different," she said.

The belt had loops and ties, and each of them contained a metal ball of different sizes. It was heavy and I had to cinch it around my waist instead of my hips, for fear of it sliding off and—if I was any judge of weight—drop straight through the floor.

We returned to the charred, over-heated room, and Eve produced an old-style pistol, powder-base and archaic.

"You're not going to shoot at me," I said, staring at her.

In answer, Eve angled her weapon, pointed it at my foot, and squeezed.

I spent two of the next five hours in the infirmary, having my muscles and flesh knitted back together by a surprisingly gentle bot. When Eve looked at me, something in my *veins* flinched. She said the weapon was a Glock and that her grandfather had brought it from of-then Earth. I told her what she could do with it, and I think it was the closest thing to a smile she had that day.

Or the next day.

Or the day after that.

Eve's training was to Firebird's as a candle to read by is to an inferno in a library. She was destructive, callused, and utterly without pity. On the fourth day, she strapped weights to her fists and had at me with them, neatly breaking one of my elbows and fracturing her own knee. We finished early that day, and I did not speak to her for half of the next.

In the evenings, I walked Andronicus's halls. He did not seem to care where I went or what questions were answered. I spoke with lab techs, software writers, geniuses who put Dr. Ravin to shame. I moved through the renovated corridors of the mountain, with their glass and their metal and their polish, and I poked around the timeless structures, built before Earthlings terraformed Mars.

One day, I wandered to the First Hold—in the basement substructures, it was the first on a descent toward the core—and found myself in what I pictured to be an archaeological dig. I stepped free of the elevator and was immediately in the way. There were people in sandy coats dusting along the floor, following thin rivulets of blue stone inlaid within the surprisingly red rock. I gaped at them, edging along one of the walls and trying to stay out of their way.

Here, unlike the panther lab I'd stumbled across yesterday, I didn't ask questions. Instead, I moved carefully through the labyrinth, following the brilliant blue mosaics. They flowed along the hallways, wrapping up the walls, across the ceiling, and down to the floor. My eidetic memory soaked it all in.

Later, I sat in my room and sketched what I had seen. I started finding patterns in the shapes I'd watched the areologists uncover, small figures that plucked at my finely-honed memory. Many of the designs were simple geometric figures, triangles and circles and squares. Some were wavy lines, corresponding in separate and distinct patterns.

316

They were strikingly similar to the Martian Tech that we had discovered last year. Except, of course, that had been an extremely advanced algorithm that even Brute hadn't managed to unravel and this...well, this reminded me of the ancient cave paintings in of-then Earth. Or...I paused, my pen hovering over paper, tracing and retracing the thin, wavy lines.

It reminded me more of hieroglyphics. It *was* a hieroglyph. It was the hieroglyph for water.

* * *

"Frankly, I'm disappointed," Eve told me on the morning of the fifth day.

"Not as much as I am," I snapped in return, wiping the blood from my eyebrow. The ball she'd thrown at me hadn't been heavy, but Eve had an arm on her. She prowled on the opposite side of the room, tossing a golf-ball sized bearing into the air and catching it.

"Not in your performance, though that certainly does leave something to be desired. No, I'm disappointed that you haven't tried to escape yet."

"Where exactly do you want me to escape to?" I asked, flinching when she paused.

"Back to your phoenix," she said.

"And how would I go about finding them? Even if they stayed where I left them— which, believe me, Harry wouldn't do if she thought I'd been taken captive—I have no way of navigating back without my armor. I suppose I could steal a ship and try to make it to the Chryse, but I don't know how to pilot it. I could pay a transporter, if I had any credits to my name, but I doubt they'd take me there on the promise of a good time."

"How do you not have any credits?" Eve cocked her blasted eyebrow, a habit that I found even more frustrating as it was a gesture that I could not replicate. "Don't you get paid?"

"I get my room and board, and an," I hedged from the word *allowance*. "A credit, of sorts. But even if I did have access to my account, I don't have my data pad. I've got nothing to transfer. As I'm sure you know."

"Andronicus probably knows," she shrugged. "But Andronicus also probably cares. I don't. The point is, you haven't even tried."

"I really don't have a reason to try," I argued. "They're going to come for me, eventually, and I'm gathering priceless intel from the inside of Andronicus's home. And you're trying to teach me how to use Magic. For the love of a purple sky, that's too cool to pass up."

Eve wrinkled her nose at me.

"I can't decide whether you're a genius, a traitor, or a coward."

"The same problem my mother always had with me," I flashed a smile at her.

"But what she never understood was that the three aren't mutually exclusive."

Eve stared at me for a moment before shrugging. She tipped her hand and let the ball roll from her palm to the floor.

"Regardless, this isn't working. I've shot you, punched you, thrown every metal thing I can get my hands on at you, and it's like I'm playing fetch with a well. I need something new."

"Like what," I asked, striding closer to her, to where our water bottles were stacked.

It started toward the back of my heart. It was a slow heat, like I'd eaten something spicy and it wasn't sitting quite right. But then the heat spread, touching my lungs with spider-silk fingers, tracing through my veins. My eyes widened. I dropped my water and staggered back from her, one of my hands darting to my throat.

"What are you doing?" I gasped, my eyes watering, the world around me blurring.

I've had fevers before. Who hasn't? It's a horrible kind of pain, the kind from which you have no escape.

When my gaze met Eve's, when I stared into her dilated pupils, I felt that same fear. When we are young, fevers can warp our minds. When we are old, fevers can bring us to our deathbeds.

I was neither young nor old, but suddenly I was both. I fell to my knees and I screamed. Sweat rolled out of my body. My heart raced, though it was the blind racing of the panicked, and when I collapsed, something in my brain shut down.

Dreams leapt at me, delirious and spinning, and when I finally opened my eyes again, I could not have told you my name. Eve stood over me, her eyes returned to normal, and she did not smirk. She stared at me, at my empty shell of a body, and she simply breathed.

"Why," I croaked, when I could speak again.

"Just curious," she said.

"You could have killed me," I sat up, seizing my fallen water and forcing it down my throat. "That's the worst thing I've ever felt in my life. What is *wrong* with you?"

"I've never tried to burn a Mage before," she said. "Since BioMages have no effect on other Mages, I wondered if the same could be true about me." She shrugged. "But there is no one like me."

Eve strode to the other side of the room, staring at the pulsing red veins within the room's stone walls. Not turning, she continued:

"Andronicus's theory that since we are not BioMages, we must have something in common, is inherently flawed. You can't say that the rock is like the bird because neither are water."

"What're you saying?" I pushed myself to my feet. I trembled, every fiber of my being begging to flee. "That this is a waste of time?"

Eve cocked her head back toward me.

"Fire isn't what I control," she said slowly. "You can't control fire. Fire is just what happens to the things I influence. I see your body, I see the combustible shape it holds, and I *change* it. I convince your flesh that it is something it is not, and your body *burns*."

"I can't convince a ball bearing that it's time to flee," I muttered.

"No," she said, turning toward me, raising a hand, her pupils expanding, "But maybe you don't have to."

I howled at her when I started to feel the tickling edges of heat around my fingers, around the thinner parts of my body. I smelled my hair begin to smoke and shrink back toward my skull, saw the edges of my shirt curl and blacken.

Panic is what I held, but rage is what controlled me. I snarled at Eve, and I *pushed*.

It was her turn to scream. The woman stumbled backwards, her hands flying to her face. My fists were clenched at my sides, my teeth bared, and even through my anger, I felt the *shift*, the subtle touch of Will. When Eve slowly lowered her hands, they were covered in blood.

The metal stud in her eyebrow had been torn away, as though someone had tied something heavy to it and then given it a heave. She looked at me, blinking red from the corner of an eye. Then, her gaze shifted past me, to where I heard something moving.

I turned. One of the metal balls was rolling lazily away.

"Oh," I breathed, understanding trilling across my tongue.

20

TITAN

———————————

"Sometimes, it's not that we can't understand the world, but rather that we're not quite looking at it in the right way. A poor-sighted woman could stare at a book for a thousand years, but if she did not have glasses, she would never read a page. No amount of turning and agonizing and pondering could change that."

I frowned at my husband.

"She could get someone to read it to her," I said. "Then they both would have read the book."

Jerry paused, his hands poised over my bare feet. I could feel the absence of his massage, the blood working its way from my arches. I prodded his chest with my big toe.

"But that wouldn't be the same as reading it herself. Would it?" he asked, genuinely derailed.

"Wouldn't it?"

We stared at each other, wondering about a nearsighted woman who couldn't see the world for want of a pair of glasses.

* * *

That was how I felt now, staring at Eve's bleeding face. I felt like a blind woman suddenly given the gift of sight. More than that, I felt like a child who finally understood that two plus two equals four.

"*I'm* not pushing the metal," I breathed. "I'm *connecting* the metal. Like how you convince matter it's on fire, I convince it that it's…it's…"

"A magnet," Eve finished, somewhat more glumly than I had. She dabbed at her torn eyebrow with the corner of a sleeve.

"Sweet purple skies, yes!" I clapped my hands together, ecstatic. "But I'm convincing them that they're like-poled."

"*Like*-poled?" Eve snorted. "Is that really what that's called?"

"And if opposites attract…" I continued, darting across the room, picking up two of the metal balls.

I held them out in front of myself, staring at first one, then the other. I licked my lips, excitement and fear trembling inside my chest. I frowned, moving them toward each other.

"Amazing," Eve said sarcastically, slow-clapping her bloodied hands.

"Shush," I hissed.

"Remember that you're not the one moving them," she said, walking cautiously around the edges of my vision. "You're making them something they're not."

My mind *shifted*. The only way I could possibly describe it would be the subtle *click* when you finally unravel a riddle, or see the world from another point of view. It just suddenly *made sense.*

The balls snapped together so quickly, I heard them give a sickening *crack.* Of course, now that I was no longer holding them, they dropped to the floor. I leapt backwards, narrowly avoiding them as they bounced off the stone floor and went flying. I looked at Eve.

A manic grin split my face and I leapt into the air, a victorious roar escaping my lungs.

"*YES!*" I shouted, searching for another pair. "YES!"

I ran to the middle of the room, holding my hands out to two separate chunks of metal, one iron and one gold. I made a stretching gesture with my fingers, like the flexes my mother had taught me when she showed me the piano, and the two chunks trembled. It was more difficult than the pure steel bearings had been, but after a few seconds of strain, the chunks rolled lazily away from each other.

"So the type of metal *does* matter," Eve murmured, crouching down, watching me over folded hands.

"Or maybe it's the gold," I said, turning, binding two chunks of gold together. They trembled, then flipped over the floor to connect. I giggled, clapping my hands.

Eve shook her head, the barest hint of a smile in her icy, blue eyes.

I ran. I bound the metals together, springing around the room, herding them toward the elevator. I held one chunk of iron in a hand, using it to shepherd the others. The one in my hand felt twice as heavy. After a while of watching me, Eve picked up one of the iron balls.

I grinned, binding the one in my hand to the one in hers. Eve immediately dropped it, the ball shooting out of her hand and toward me. I shouted as it connected with the one in my hand, pain shooting up my arm from the force of it. Dropping both, I turned and bound the ball between Eve and myself to one behind me.

The two rolled equally away from each other. Then, the one behind me hit the wall, making the other shoot backwards so fast, when it too hit the wall, it left a sizeable dent in the rock.

I don't know how many hours I spent in the training room, but when I finally was exhausted, Eve had left and I was drenched in sweat. The metal around me was crumbling, chipped and broken. I had made dents in the walls, broken the glass on one side of the elevator, and my lip was bloody from when I'd bound a ball to the ceiling light. I felt drained in a way I never had before, like cramming for a thousand exams in a single hour.

And, as I dropped down to sit on the floor, it was the best I had ever felt in my life.

* * *

I slept very little, dreaming of power in a thousand different forms. Excitement pumped through my blood in a way it hadn't since I was a child, the desperation for the next day to arrive overwhelming me. I felt alive. I felt...*real*.

Before the sun had risen, I was up, bathed and brushed. I fished through the closet gifted to me and found a black pair of pants and a dark shirt, with fingerless gloves and high boots. I'd always preferred black, though since arriving on *Redwing*, my style had been meshed with Maya's (and let me tell you, she wore far too much white). But suddenly, as I finished pushing up my sleeves, I felt like *me* again.

And while I'd never really cared about clothes, I think it was more than my ability to once again choose what I wore. It was more, even, than being out from under Firebird's watchful gaze. There was something about finally understanding my power that made me complete. I wasn't afraid.

Fear is like happiness in that it is not a passing emotion. There is excitement, and there is terror, but those are fleeting edges of a blade I cannot see. Fear sits in the back of your heart, much as happiness does. It's a state of mind and, unlike happiness, it is exhausting. I hadn't realized it, but I'd been afraid since Unity first rose. Since my home became Sector X, and all that I knew was boiled down to *of-then*.

I glanced at myself in the mirror, and I flashed a white grin.

Eve was already striding down my hallway when I exited my room. She'd made a trip to the infirmary, I saw, and I frowned when I caught a glimpse of the telltale glint in her eyebrow. She snorted.

"They're plastic," she said, giving her pierced ear a tug. "So rust off."

"To be fair," I said, falling in to stride with her as we started back toward the elevator, "you were starting to burn me alive."

The corner of her mouth twitched.

"Andronicus wouldn't be happy about that," she confided, shoving her fist toward the door's lock, letting the green hologram wrap around it. "It's been duly noted that I don't have the best control, when I start to burn someone."

I shot her a dirty look.

"*I'm* not happy about that."

"But you don't sign my credits," she said, stepping onto the elevator and flicking through another hologram. "Or have a lethal, ill-tempered bodyguard."

"Bodyguard?" I asked, watching as the numbers on the elevator began to drop. "I thought you were his bodyguard?"

She snorted again, louder this time.

"I'd rather rot in a coffin than spend my days following him around."

"Then who's his bodyguard? We were the only ones in his room, that day."

"Were we?" she asked, a little too mysteriously.

"Probably some kind of invisibility Mage," I grumbled.

"You should be so lucky."

"Nothing about an invisible bodyguard seems lucky."

"You only think that because you're not thinking like Andronicus. Sometimes, things are better off hiding in plain sight."

"You still didn't answer my question."

"And you're still an idiot, if you think I'm going to."

I shrugged, looking again at the plummeting numbers.

"We missed the training room," I pointed out, as we were now moving into the Holds.

"We did," she affirmed. "Andronicus wants you to meet someone."

"His invisible, ill-tempered bodyguard?"

She rolled her eyes to me.

"How do you know she isn't here right now?"

So, I was more than a little uncomfortable as the elevator stopped and the doors opened to a Hold simply labeled *ZERO*.

"Zero?" I asked, following her out.

The room was dark and small, reminding me more of an airlock than anything. There were no windows, only a single, red door on the far side. It was hot, much more so than our original training room had been, and smelled slightly of sulfur. I fidgeted with my gloves, tugging at the snug, leather hem around my wrist.

"Zero," she unhelpfully agreed.

"But why zero?" we were starting toward the door, and I felt something—some hidden, primal instinct—that made my hackles rise. "The numbers usually rise in the Holds. The Thirteenth Hold is deeper than the Twelfth. And we are much closer to the core than that."

"I got to name it," she said simply.

Eve wore leather gloves today, and she tugged one off before placing her palm against the center of the red door. It looked like polished marble, with the same blue inlays that I had seen at the areology dig. Instead of a green hologram, when she touched the door, the blue stones brightened, almost seeming to twist in the stone door. I took an uncertain step back.

The door shimmered. And then, it simply was not there. I stared past Eve into a dark chamber.

She looked over her shoulder at me, a gesture I was coming to associate with pain, and she said:

"There are some rules, in Hold Zero."

"Rules?" From what I had seen, there weren't many people who cared less for rules than Eve.

"You're familiar with the concept," she asked, dryly.

"I lived in Unity," my reply was equally dry. "If there's a regulation, I feel right at home."

"Good. Because your life depends on following these. One: no sudden movements. Two: stay behind me. Three: *no* Magic."

I frowned at that one. I had, after all, just discovered how to use it. That was like being given wings and then being told not to fly. But when I saw the look on Eve's face, I thought better of arguing. She didn't look irritated or angry...she looked...*calm*. And it made my skin crawl.

"Alright," I said.

She nodded and stepped through the door, her trench coat immediately swallowed by the black. I followed slowly, my gaze fixed to the outline of her pale head and green hair. It made her easy to track, even in the near-pitch darkness. When I cleared the doorway, the red stone reformed behind us, the faint blue etchings glowing slightly.

I turned to Eve and gasped. I was blind. Not *couldn't see*. I was *blind*. There was nothing. There was no world save the beating in my chest. It was the true darkness of a cave, a darkness that made my soul feel like it was floating in a pool of nothing. The air I pulled into my lungs was heavy.

"*Eve?*" I whispered, pushing my hands out, searching for her.

"Shush."

"*How can I stay behind you if I don't know where you are?*" I hissed.

She caught my searching arms by a wrist and gave a meaningful, painful, squeeze. I *shushed*, moving close enough to her that I could touch the back of her coat. I glanced over my shoulder and was relieved to find that the door was still glowing faintly.

We were silent, and as my senses sharpened, I became aware of the gentle *hum* of the volcano. We were close to the core, close enough that the ground beneath my feet was hot. I could feel it even through my boots. I thought I heard something moving, something heavy and deep, like magma through tunnels, and if I held my breath, I found that Eve was not the only other living thing in the room.

I couldn't be sure of size, but I knew from just the way the sound of my own body interacted with the air that this place was *immense*. I could feel it in my bones, in the very rock beneath my feet. And, sure as I was of my name, I knew something was *watching* me.

"Titan," Eve whispered, the name deep in her throat.

If it hadn't been so dark, I never would have noticed when the wall in front of us began to glow. It was a soft red color, and it traveled slowly up, narrowing as it went. I frowned, stretching my neck as I followed the glow up, and up. It made a serpentine turn and then split into vein-like contours. The glow seemed to be outlining something, something like a face.

"Eve," I said, not really meaning to, her name on an exhale.

That was when the wall moved.

It was a small adjustment, a shift in weight. The veined contour turned, angling toward us and offering a wider view of its many edges. I thought I saw a soft glint, a gleam that my instincts warned belonged to an *eye*.

"Eve," I whimpered, taking a step back.

The glow intensified, red air bleeding into the room, outlining Eve. She had her hands stretched wide, her head tipped back as she stared at the *thing*. The *gargantuan*.

The Titan.

Brighter still. I could make out its edges, the scaled arms, the long neck, the dark claws that *scratched* as it shifted, as it bobbed its massive head. There were horns, pale horns that twisted back from its brow. Something built in my chest. At first, I thought it was terror. But then I realized, it was *sound*. A guttural growl. And it was not mine.

Eve twisted her wrists, the soft popping of her tendons audible in the thick air, and the glow became a burn, light radiating from the chest, neck, and nostrils of the creature. It lowered its massive head, the size of *Redwing*'s cockpit, and turned. A vibrantly green, impossibly large eye fixed to us. It had a slit pupil and, even within the face of this beast, seemed oversized. It twitched, moving from Eve to me, and I saw the raw light of its own body reflected in it.

"Eve," I breathed. "Is that…"

"Burn," the PyroMage purred.

And there was fire. The beast threw back its head and sprayed it at the vaulted ceiling. Red flame, blue flame and yellow: it rolled in great waves around the dome. My eyes ached as they adjusted to the light, my scalp prickled as *heat* poured down on us, forced from the upper reaches by the sheer *power* of the beast's breath. It made a sound, a deep growl, and the geyser of flame dissipated, leaving the room's ceiling glowing with radiant heat.

I could see Titan, now. His scales were red and shining, each catching the light with its own fine edge. A tail wrapped around the chamber, yellow spikes dotting from its tip, all the way up the ridge of its crouched back, between the ivory horns and down its long face to the end of its nose. It twisted, and a pair of bat-like wings widened for balance. The massive, orb-like green eyes flicked around the room, like a predator that catches scent of prey, and when it flitted across me, I felt something in my stomach loosen.

"Eve," and this time, I barely found the breath to make the words, "is that a dragon?"

21

WEAPONS

"They want to use us," a reporter said, her face too clean.

Jerry looked at me, and we both knew what it meant. They want to use us.

My brother had always taken me seriously, but he'd never liked me. That's what I chose to believe. It made it easier than the alternative.

That we were destined to be enemies.

Jerry tried to take my hand, but I pulled back. It was just a reaction, as simple as moving from an open flame, but I felt something shift in my heart as I did it. I didn't want to be touched.

I stared at the screen, at the inferno that contained my brother, and felt the iron form behind my soul. Reports had dwindled after the initial crash, when a tan-skinned woman in a convict's suit emerged from the ship's twisted body. She had looked at the camera, the fire burning in her solid black eyes. Like a phoenix.

This changed nothing.

And yet, everything would be changed.

* * *

"They want to use us," I said, following Eve from my chambers the next morning.

"Who?" She didn't turn to look at me. She had exchanged her trench coat for a plain, white outfit—one devoid of metal.

"When Firebird took control of the Sector X ship and crashed into the hospital— the lab—the reporter said that *they want to use us*. She'd meant that the rebels were trying to influence Unity's population and that they should not allow themselves to be manipulated. But anyone who watched Firebird rise knew that *they* weren't the rebels."

"Why do I care?" Eve stepped into the elevator and keyed in our destination. "Unity is history."

"Well, we can learn from history," I said, feeling like I shouldn't have to. "But besides that, that's what I feel right now. They want to use us."

"The rebels," she cocked her infuriating eyebrow.

"*Andronicus*," I whispered. "He's making weapons. *We* are weapons."

"You can't tell me that you're just figuring that out," she snorted. "Why the rusting hell else would he pump trillions of credits into BioMagic research?"

"To further humanity's cause," I mumbled, though I'd certainly never believed that. "To make the worlds *have* magic. But I don't understand how you're okay with him manipulating you toward his conquest. You're from the Chryse—he's got his sights set on destroying it."

"He's got his sights set on destroying Biggie," she corrected. "But if he ordered me to burn every soul in the Chryse, I'd do it. What about my persona makes you think I'm a pacifist?"

"Pacifist," I shrugged, "no. But I also see you as an independent woman. How can you blindly follow a man set on destroying the Worlds?"

She frowned at me as the elevator came to a stop, the doors whirring open to reveal a cool room with high ceiling.

"Andronicus isn't destroying the Worlds—he's conquering them. I didn't see Unity doing your precious Earth any favors. He liberated them."

Eve stepped out of the elevator and into the room. I followed her, though more hesitantly than I had during the previous days. The floors, walls, and ceiling were a dull steel color, with heavy bolts. The room smelled of fresh work, and I saw metal flakes scattered around the bolts, as though they'd only just been laid.

"He destroyed them," I corrected. "And what was left of Earth burned. He's cruel and set on ruling an empire. I don't want to live in an empire, Eve, and I can't believe that you do."

"Where's all of this coming from?" she turned back to me, crossing her arms.

"Titan," my voice drifted off, my mind still struggling to comprehend the creature in Hold Zero. "He's magnificent. He has wings, but he's kept in the darkness of a cave. Andronicus has bred magic incarnate, and he has it locked in a dungeon."

Eve hesitated, staring hard at me. Her light blue eyes were even more vivid in the cool, ambient light of the metal room. She averted her gaze.

"Titan will have his day in the sky," she said simply. "If not for Andronicus, he wouldn't exist. And if not for Titan," she raised her hands, snapping her fingers and igniting a single wisp of flame between us, some speck of dust obliterated. "I would be nothing."

"You wouldn't be nothing," I mumbled. "You'd be a soul. He's using you, using Titan. He *bred* Titan, like he's his personal property. I was in the Holds, I saw the labs. I know what he does to creatures in order to create these...*monsters.*"

"Titan isn't a monster," Eve snapped, and I saw fire in her eyes. "And here, the ends *always* justify the means. Welcome to Olympus Mons, Jezi. It's about time you woke up."

I scowled at her, but acquiesced.

"Where are we?" I asked instead, glancing around the room. There were no metal balls today, though I supposed with the room being metal, that was probably safer for both Eve and myself.

"Same training quarters as before," she said, frowning at the room. "Andronicus had this put in last night, so that you could have a more compatible training environment."

"Interesting," I said, moving into the room, scanning the bolts and walls with skepticism. "I don't know what would happen if I tried to push here."

"Our technicians are assuming nothing would. You would create a magnetic field, but the walls cannot be pushed outward. They're laid within stone, within a volcano. However, I do feel the need to warn you against *pulling* the walls. If they should come unfastened, I'd imagine your soft body in the center would be..." and she finished with a clenched fist and a *squished* sound.

I grimaced.

"What's the point, then?"

Eve thrust her chin toward the elevator. I turned, and saw that I'd overlooked a suit of armor laying in the corner. It wasn't my Rose, as I'd come to calling Maya's armor, but it did have a dark red sheen to it. There were gray bands down the sides, arms, and legs with a bright silver streak emerging from the helm and running along my spine. I walked over, picking up the helm. It had a narrow band for my eyes, much thinner than what I was accustomed to. I glanced back at Eve.

"I don't get it."

"Suit up," she said, dropping to the floor and crossing her legs. "We want to see if you can fly."

I gaped at her, a chill running through my veins. Granted, I'd only just become acquainted with my Magic. But the thought of pushing *myself* had never occurred to me. I looked back down at the helmet. And then, I couldn't get the armor on fast enough, all moral questions suddenly thrust to the back of my mind.

While not Rose, the armor fit well— perhaps even better. It had obviously been custom-made with me in mind, the contours perfectly matching those of my body. It was easy to put on, with fewer buttons and wires than Rose. This was a simple suit, equipped with a well-calibrated assist and, as I finally pulled the helm on, a fantastic viewscreen.

The narrow band allowed in a natural frame of light, but the rest of the helm somehow transmitted a full view of the room around me, as though I was seeing everything with my natural eyes. I turned finding Eve.

"Is it transmitting the visual directly into my brain?" I asked, not sure I was comfortable with the thought of constant radiation within my skull.

"Into your retina," she corrected, rising and striding toward me. "Like the

Unity visors used to. Perfectly safe, or at least that's what the nerds told me. You've got Suppressor defense," she said, moving behind me and slapping my back, the impact registering on a separate column on the right side of my viewscreen. "The aluminum inlays help withstand some sort of beam or whatever. Your joints are reinforced," she plucked at my wrist, "so that they can withstand greater force as you propel yourself. Don't want you coming apart at the hinges, apparently."

She stopped in front of me.

"It's damn fine armor," she said. "Think of it as an exchange for that outdated Martian Tech that we captured you in."

"I don't want Andronicus's armor," I said, flexing my fingers, amazed with the response time in the power assist. Even Rose had lacked finesse when using power assist in delicate work.

"I don't care what you want," she stepped back from me. "Take it up with him."

I frowned, lowering my hand and staring at the floor. The metal under my feet had a stink to it, as all metal did to me, but it seemed more distant from within the security of my fancy new helm. It didn't seem *real*. I looked back at Eve.

"I'm not sure I can use it, from inside this. It's like...trying to see something through a sheet of metal. I can't push against the outside if I am on the inside."

"Sure you can," she flashed a grin as she stepped into the elevator. "I imagine it's just going to take forever for you to figure it out."

The doors closed, and I was alone.

* * *

Over the next countless hours, I frustrated myself from within my metal suit. I tried binding my hand to the wall, first. But moving my concentration past the metal in my fingers to the metal beyond them made my head pound. I took off the gauntlet and bound it to the wall separately, more to make sure that I hadn't suddenly lost my Magic. When it snapped away from me and against the wall, I felt a swell of relief.

But that was all I succeeded in. I tried binding the suit to the discarded gauntlet, but all that did was make it fall off of the wall. I tried taking my helmet off and binding myself to the ceiling, but even without the virtual relay, I couldn't get past the fact that *I* was inside the armor.

More than that, I couldn't figure out how to bind the armor as a unit, rather than a thousand different pieces of metal hooked together. Before, when I was pushing and pulling the bearings, I was focusing on a single unit. But the armor wasn't a single unit. And it wasn't a single mineral. The composite within my hands alone baffled and amazed.

I don't know how long I struggled with it. In the secure room, I could only guess at the passing of time, but it was long enough that when I finally sat in the center of the room and pulled my sweaty helm free, I was hungry, irritated, and thoroughly defeated.

Turning it in my hands, I eventually found my reflection in the bright silver streak down the back. I looked sweaty, my hair plastered against my scalp from sweat, and my face seemed so very lonely in this room of metal. I looked around, wondering if this was how those creatures in Andronicus's labs felt, their walls empty of possibility.

And, for the first time since I'd been captured, I felt alone.

I wondered about Firebird, about the crew and the ship that I had come to think of as home. My mind wandered to dangerous ideas, problems half-solved. A tendril of fear—like a flame flickering to life—trilled within my chest.

I thought about the woman we had pulled from the Thirteenth Hold, about her face and how Andronicus had given it to her. I thought about Regina. I wondered if she would ever get Zander back, since we wouldn't be able to deliver Eve. And, under it all, I feared what was to come for *me*, my role in all of this.

"Selfish," I whispered, dropping my helmet on the floor.

That was what my brother had called me. It was the last thing he'd said before he'd gotten on that helicopter with the woman I eventually would name Firebird. He said I was selfish. The worst part was, I couldn't even remember why.

The elevator doors opened behind me. I turned, expecting to see Eve. Instead, I watched as Andronicus stepped into the room.

He seemed taller here, though whether that was because I was on the floor or because we were alone, I wasn't sure. I twisted around, rising too quickly with my armor-assisted legs. The black cat padded out of the elevator behind him, slinking near his ankles. I watched it for a moment before raising my gaze to his.

"No luck?" he asked, taking in my disheveled state.

"Afraid not," I answered, turning my helmet over in my hands. "It's different than just shoving bearings around."

"I'm sure," he nodded, looking grave. "It's the difference between scribbling on paper and writing a sentence. It requires study and patience, and a profound desire to *learn*."

"I want to learn," I muttered, feeling—of all things—abashed. "I'm just not totally sure where to begin."

"At the beginning," he smiled. "Walk with me. You look like you could use a break."

I hesitated, but there didn't seem to be too many options. Gathering up and replacing my discarded gauntlet, I tucked my helm under my arm. I glanced again at the cat before I followed Andronicus into the elevator. The feline followed us.

"Her name is Ghini," he said. The cat sprang from the floor to his shoulder in a single, startling bound. Her tail was long enough to dangle to the small of Andronicus's back, small barbs down its length flexing and retracting.

"Cute," I said, feeling uncomfortable under the yellow gaze.

"I'm more of a dog person, really," he admitted. "But she plays her part. Eve tells me that she introduced you to Titan."

It wasn't a question, not really. I nodded, my mouth twisting.

"She also said that you were disturbed by his captivity," Andronicus didn't look at me as he spoke.

"I loath to see any creature in captivity," I replied, showing him a shade of my truth. "I'm sure you can understand, since you know about my time in Unity."

"Of course. And can you understand why his captivity is, at this time, necessary?"

"I'd imagine you are intending to use him as a weapon, when your war for Mars comes."

"The War for Mars," Andronicus smiled to himself, glasses flashing. The elevator was taking us up, though he had not keyed in a destination. "Is that what you're calling it?"

"It's honestly just something to say," I shrugged. "Wars are all the same. Everyone loses in the end."

"That's not entirely true, although I can appreciate your perspective. Unity was a failed idea. The Worlds I seek to create are *proven*. Empires have existed for thousands of years. People need order. But they also need freedom," he looked down at me as the elevator stopped. "I am not blind to that, Jezi. My empire will be more than great, it will be *good*. It will be just. I'm a guide, morally and rationally, but people are people and I encourage them to grow."

We stepped out of the elevator and into a long, glass hallway. It extended away from the mountain, floating some thirty meters off of the ground and running due north. I followed Andronicus as he strolled along it. As far as I could see, there was nothing around us save the rolling black rock and white snow. I was relieved that I didn't see any stray chunks of the *Ilena*.

"You've met Overlord Mariana," he said.

"Of course."

"Then tell me honestly, Jezi. Is she the woman you want leading the Worlds?"

I still carried my helm under an arm, and now I was twisting it back and forth against my hip. It made a dull scraping sound. My anxiety had flared, understandably, but now I could feel the sweat begin to roll down the back of my neck.

"No," I answered.

"So why do you fight for her?"

"Firebird fights for the people. It's why I follow her. Unity, Mariana, *you*...it doesn't matter. She answers to no one."

"So she's an anarchist. Are *you*?"

"I don't think that Firebird is an anarchist," though to be fair, I didn't know what she was. "She just doesn't want to see what happened to Earth happen to Mars. Why can't you just be happy with ruling your *third* of a planet? Why is it never enough for you people?"

"Mariana is unhappy with her portion of the Worlds as well," Andronicus reached up to his shoulder, subconsciously scratching behind Ghini's ear. "Why would you help her acquire what you deem is wrong for *me* to have?"

"She caught us in a bad lie," I said. "We didn't have a choice."

"And when she destroyed the *Ilena*?" He didn't look at me, and I pointedly refused to look at him.

"We didn't know that was her end game. We were just stealing the fuel schematics. Firebird wanted to keep the Overlords balanced. We are...*I* am ashamed. And I am deeply sorry for the loss of your people."

"Even if that's true," Andronicus stopped, turning to face me. "What makes Firebird the moral compass for your crew? What makes her values more right than my own? If given the opportunity, would she rule the Worlds?"

"I don't think she would," I looked again around us, thinking I heard something humming through the glass floor. "I could see her appointing someone she thought worthy to rule...a *republic*."

"Republics don't work any better than Unity," Andronicus said dismissively. "They're all destined for failure."

"And somehow empires aren't?"

"Oh, to be sure, my empire will undoubtedly fall. Most likely to someone like Firebird. But that's the beautiful thing about empires. I will shape the development of these Worlds for decades, perhaps even centuries. I will recreate them in my own image, and it will be that image that the next rebel must tear down. You seem to think that all I care for is to have my name at the top of the pyramid, to have power and rule. But what is my small life in the grand scheme of things? I'm a moment, a blip in the universe, here and then gone. But what I can *make*," he gestured at the barren landscape. "Well, that's an eternity to man."

He sighed.

"And war with Mariana is what that's going to take."

"I thought you were the domino emperor," I muttered. "Set up all your plans and then watch them fall. A frontal assault with a dragon doesn't seem very eloquent."

"Nor overly effective," he agreed. "Demons and dragons are impressive monuments at the head of any army, they're letting the Worlds see what the future looks like. But one thing has remained true for the history of man, and that is that wars are won with soldiers."

"I think you've got a long way to go, if you're going to make an army to take over Mars. You've not only got Mariana, you've got Overlord Shay. I don't see her helping you, not when your victory would eventually mean her defeat."

"Shay is no concern," he said, his hand falling from Ghini. "She's already sworn fealty to me."

I stared at him, my mouth turning to ash. He watched me, devoid of expression. Eventually, I managed to swallow.

"Why would she do that? You're no more likely to win Mars than Mariana is, at this point. Neither of you has an army, you've lost the *Ilena*, and what soldiers you did have were sent off to Earth to destroy what was left of Unity."

Andronicus smiled then, and it was a smile that will haunt me for the rest of my life.

"Shay has soldiers, but *I* have the army. Soldiers are only soldiers until they are organized. Then they're an army."

"I've lived in your Olympus for days now," I spread my hands. "I've seen maybe a hundred soldiers. Hardly enough to conquer the Worlds."

He continued to smile, staring north, down the glass hallway. It seemed to go on forever.

"Do you like your new armor?" He asked, throwing me off balance.

I shrugged, shifting my grip on the helm.

"It's impressive tech. But I don't accept it as *mine.*"

"It was mine to give and I gave it to you. I had it custom made, of course. Whatever you decide, you're too precious to risk losing. Even if you fight for Mariana, I'd hate to see something happen to our only living PolarMage."

I gave my head a brisk shake.

"First of all, I'm a MetalMage. You don't get to name what I am. And secondly, it might be yours to give, but if I don't accept it, it remains yours. Why would I ever trust your armor? Especially after what you did to mine, hacking into it and controlling me like a puppet."

He laughed, small and dry.

"*Maya's* armor, Jezi, could not be hacked. It's the finest Martian Tech, created by Mariana's own labs. You cannot break an unbreakable code."

"Then how—"

"And you don't influence the metal, you influence the poles. But we'll come back to that. Now, there is something I'd like for you to see."

"Why?"

"Because you aren't on my side yet. I'd like to convince you."

Andronicus raised his arm, and the small black wrist watch materialized. His eyes darkened behind his glasses.

Color.

It was the first thing that my brain computed. Before, where there was black rock and white snow, now there was *color*. It surrounded us, flew over us, moved under us, buzzed around us.

And after the color, I saw the machines that bore it.

A thousand. A hundred thousand. A million, maybe.

War vessels, tanks and hovercrafts. Razors and Ridgers, shuttles and transports. The world north of Olympus Mons was divided into neat edges, groups of barracks, soldiers doing drills. There were guns and creatures with too many legs that had long necks and massive, black eyes.

My knees weakened, and it took every bit of my will to not drop to the glass floor right then and there. As it was, I put a hand out, leaning against a wall for balance. It was impossible. My mind couldn't wrap around what my eyes told it was real.

What I saw under Andronicus's feet was the potential annihilation of my Worlds, Earth and Mars both. It was destruction given flesh, given metal and jaws. Something flew over us, and I looked up to see a flock of Avies, their great necks folded back as they hovered, like feathered bombers. I remembered how they'd torn through our camp a year ago.

"How can this be possible?" I whispered, my voice an empty husk.

"Reflectors," Andronicus said, very matter-of-fact. "I have a grid set up around the perimeter, rendering my army invisible. It's not foolproof, but more than sufficient in obscuring my true numbers."

"Why would you show me this?" I was fading, my disbelief warring with a healthy urge to don my helm and run.

"To convince you," he said, as though it was the most obvious thing in the world. "Join my ranks, PolarMage, and you will be one of the commanding officers of the army that unites the Worlds. *This* is the winning side, the *right* side. Together, we will fulfill both your purpose and mine."

"You cannot think that this...this...*display* could change my mind, my *morality*," I glared at him, heat rising. "I don't know what kind of weak-willed cowards you're used to dealing with, but your shiny toys are not enough to make me forget who you are, who *I* am. You take and you take and you think yourself a god. But no single soul can have this kind of power and still be a *soul*."

Andronicus sighed.

"Logically, a show of strength is a good start to winning a war. And, as far as convincing you goes, everyone has a price."

"Not me. Not *us*."

He smiled, glasses flashing.

"That's just not true, Jezi."

He nodded to something behind me. I turned, still shaky, following his gaze to the elevator.

Where, floating just outside the closing door, Brute was waiting.

22

LOYAL

_____

Of all the things I could have said, what I did say was nothing.

I don't know if I stared or if I looked away. I don't even know what I felt when Jiggy whirred closer to me, her lights close to black. I didn't look inside. I didn't find Brute within. I knew she was there. I could sense her. I could sense her shame.

I'd been here before, after all. It's just that the thing that had broken, the thing that had been the shell, wasn't Jiggy this time. And I wasn't the one who had done it.

"I'm so sorry," Brute whispered, her of-then Japanese accent thickening. "It was the only way."

"Brute," I whispered, my voice hoarse. "What are you doing?" Another thought floated to the surface. "Are you alright?"

"Of course. Jezi, I...I am so sorry. He can help me. He can help me be _Martian_. I couldn't say no...and I knew he wouldn't hurt you! It was the..."

"You came here on your own," I whispered, anger burning in the back of my throat.

"Jezi, you just have to listen to—"

"And you controlled my armor? Forced me to abandon Firebird? You knew that we weren't rescuing Eve?"

"I swear, Jezi, I made them promise that they wouldn't hurt you," I felt her Grav-Field touch my shoulders, felt the small pressure like an invisible embrace. "I thought that, since Eve wouldn't have gone with us, maybe Firebird could use the double to get Zander back. Everything would work out. Andronicus promised—"

"What about when our coms went dead in the Chryse? Were you working for Mariana, too?"

"I'm not *working* for anyone, Jezi. I'm still a part of Firebird's crew. It's just that," the lights went darker still, ebony, "I needed something. You don't understand what I've gone through, the pain that I have every day. They can *help* me here, Jezi."

"*Were you working for Mariana, too,*" I asked again, my voice a hiss like a tea kettle about to boil.

Jiggy twisted, a fidget that I'd come to recognize.

"Not Mariana. But at Andronicus's request. He needed you to meet the Oracle and—"

I looked at Andronicus.

"I want to leave," I said, my voice deep, my body rigid.

He met my gaze, though I don't think I was really seeing him. I don't remember what he said—or if he said anything at all. I just remember that he backed a step away and gestured toward the elevator.

I walked. I *marched*. Brute started toward me, Jiggy's small gears humming, but I *flexed* something in my mind and pushed her away, using the metal of my shoulder and the metal that was her shell as easily as exhaling. She made a small sound, a fearful sound, but it hadn't been a hard push. I felt the force of it in my own body, within my own shell, and some part of my mind computed the amount of force I could exert before I was shoved as well.

It wouldn't end well for either of us.

Blink. I was on the elevator. My arm was in the green hologram, that gauntlet off and in my other hand. I didn't remember doing it. But here I was.

Something was building inside of me, something behind my heart. I twisted my fingers, keying in my destination. The elevator complied. Part of me had expected it not to. Why would it, after all. I was the enemy. If not before, certainly now.

I forced air from my lungs. I could only remember being this angry a handful of times, something beyond fury, something sharper for the pain. If I wasn't careful, I would lose part of myself.

The doors opened and I strode through, my shoulders squared, my head down. I was pushing ahead, marching down my corridor, the plan unfurling in my mind. I opened my chamber door and entered. It was all the same, my closet of borrowed clothes, my borrowed bed and borrowed bathroom. I glanced out the wide window and saw the remains of the *Ilena*.

I moved with practiced efficiency. I had done this a thousand times since being captured. I'd gone over it in my mind, routing and rerouting, planning for contingencies. It was to the point where I could do this in my sleep.

In all the spare hours I had spent in my room, I had not been idle.

First, the armor. I slapped the helmet on the dresser, top down. I pulled a thin device from my hair, where I'd hidden it at the base of my skull days before. I'd stolen it from a lab, of course. But, of course, I'd stolen a lot of things.

I flipped a small toggle and turned it on, blue light radiating from its slender tip. It immediately resonated within the padding of the helm, highlighting the wiring and command centers. I twisted the helmet, following a particular line to the front dome.

"Got you," I whispered.

I opened one of the dresser's drawers, not looking, and removed a scalpel. It too had come from a lab, from a place where there were bits of claws and flecks of blood on the floor. I made the incision in the padding, exposing a cluster of command wires. With a slow breath, I clamped the mechanical fingers of my left hand around the wires and tugged. They popped free easily. Two more incisions and I had the small module cut loose.

I held it in front of me, narrowing my eyes at the tiny device. It had been designed with a single purpose in mind. To receive commands.

I tossed the module over a shoulder and shoved the helmet back onto my head, letting it seal around my collar. Then, I replaced my right gauntlet. A grid appeared on it, and I quickly keyed in the codes.

A second later, and there was a voice in my helmet:

"Already?" of-then Russia filled my ears.

"Too loud," I hissed, fumbling around the dials on my forearm until I turned Dr. Ravin down. "Okay. Yes, already. Something happened. We have to move now."

"Firebird won't like that," Dr. Ravin warned. " She hasn't managed to extract the data yet. Did you find Brute?"

I clenched my teeth.

"Yes."

"And you're ready?"

"Almost."

I moved efficiently around my room. I grabbed a packed bag from under my bed, slinging it over my shoulder. At the desk, I reached under it and fumbled with the gauntlet's fingers until I found the small bundle of papers taped there, against the underside of a drawer. I pulled them free and stuffed them into the bag as well.

The beauty in paper is that it cannot be hacked. I'd learned this a long time ago, when I was writing for Firebird from within Unity. Maybe even before that, when I wanted to keep secrets from my mother and brother, who—if I hid my journals well enough— couldn't spy on me as they did the rest of the world. And, in the end, I did it against Jerry, too. Let's just say that we fell out of love. Hard.

I turned to the door of my room, breathing heavily, anxiety warring with the overwhelming desire to simply drop my belongings and jump out the window. My new armor was shiny. It probably could withstand the impact.

"You removed the command cells?" Dr. Ravin asked.

"First thing," I mumbled in return, shooting a dirty look at the small nodule that I'd removed from the helm, now laying sullenly on my bedroom floor. "Not making that mistake again."

"We can only hope they had just the one," Dr. Ravin drew a deep breath. "The elevator is in motion. You should be gone before it arrives."

"Eve?" I asked, a deep kind of fear twisting inside me.

"Most likely. Exit your room and take a right. The hallway will lead to a viewing platform."

"Every hallway does," I agreed, pulling the gauntlet off again and striding to my door. I pushed my arm into the green hologram. It took longer than usual to open. When it did, I exhaled.

"Security is already tighter," Dr. Ravin informed me. "He knows you're running."

"There were only two options," I answered. "After he showed me."

I hesitated.

"There's something you should know," I said as I stepped out of my room.

"Later would be better," she warned. "The elevator is almost here. Run."

I didn't need to be told twice. While replacing the gauntlet, I ran down the hallway, my enhanced strength practically launching me down it. I reached the viewing platform and slid to a stop. To my left, there was a vent.

"I'm really sick of this," I told her as I knelt in front of it, jabbing my metal fingers into the rungs and clamping down.

"Running?"

"Vents."

"Naturally."

I heaved and the metal came free with a squeal. I had to step on the grate to pull it from my fingers. As I did, the elevator doors whisked open.

I glanced down the hallway, fear rising, and saw a trench coat begin to emerge from the door. I didn't wait to see the rest of her. Without a second thought, I sprang into the vent.

It went straight down. I freefell, the lights around the edge of my helm coming on automatically. Part of me had been concerned that I would have removed too much of the command center, would have ruined the helm's efficiency, but it seemed that I'd paid close attention to Brute's many lectures after all.

Brute. My heart twisted.

"Three, two...one, now!"

I shoved my hands out in front of me a second before I hit an angle in the vent, the trajectory flinging me sideways. Warning lights flared around my screen, red and blinking, and I twisted onto my back, sliding down the tunnel with startling speed.

"It's good armor," someone said in the background.

"Is that Ori?" I asked, trying to regulate my breathing as I shot downward, heat warnings and damage alerts coming on around the edges of my screen.

"In the flesh," she said, suddenly much louder. I thought I heard Dr. Ravin swear. A moment later, and she was back.

"You're coming to another grate," she said, though I could barely make out the words.

"You nervous, Doc?"

"Why?"

"Your accent gets thicker when you're nervous," I said, suddenly slamming into metal slats.

They had been closed, but the force of my impact broke straight through them, my heavy boots *clanging*. I exploded from the vent with a trail of black rock and smoking mars tumbling out after me. I rolled to the side, coming up on one knee with my hands outstretched.

There were three lab technicians, their white coats nearly blinding after my dark tunnel. I didn't hesitate. I bound the first one's metalic, Olympus insignia to the metal table beside me and *pushed*. He squealed as he flew backwards. The table shot in the opposite direction, colliding with the wall I had just broken out of. When it did, the insignia punched through his chest and he dropped like a sack of laundry.

I lurched to my feet, charging after the second one. She was quicker and was already making for the door. I grabbed her by the collar of her coat and heaved her backwards, my enhanced strength letting me throw her halfway across the room. She hit a tray of instruments and went tumbling to the floor. I ignored her scream.

The last technician was pointing a gun at my head. It was charged, an electric-base pistol, and if it hit me, it would render my metal armor useless. I bound it to my palm and made a grabbing motion with my fingers. The weapon shot into my palm as I was pulled sharply forward, the impact making even more warning lights appear. I was getting good at ignoring those.

"Where," I said, fumbling with the gun, tossing it into my dominant left hand and pointing it at the tech, "is Lab 1A?"

The technician was trembling, his red curls quivering around his blue eyes. I glowered at him.

"Jezi, are you sure you're broadcasting?" Dr. Ravin asked.

I swore, glancing down at my right forearm. I was still on com-only. I glanced at the tech, but he didn't seem to be going anywhere. I tucked the gun in my armpit and tapped a button on my forearm.

"Where is Lab 1A?" I repeated. "Can I reach it from here without the elevator?"

My voice was raw power. It was still mine, sure, but it was…enhanced, almost like it had been forced through some kind of robotic amplifier. I sounded, well, I sounded impressive.

"Y-you're in 1C," he managed, backing until he was pressed against the wall. "Please, I have a family. Please."

"I *told* you the schematic showed the labs," Harry's voice, this time. "They're just fuzzy because of the transmission barrier."

"It seems like stupid flaw," Dr. Ravin muttered, her accent thickening to the point that I was expecting her to be speaking of-then Russian before the day's end. "Get out of C and keep moving. They're locking down."

"Brilliant," I muttered sarcastically, slapping my new gun to my hip.

Instead of sticking there, like Mule had, it just clattered to the floor. I glanced at the tech.

"You didn't see that," I muttered, flexing my palm and making the gun jump back into it.

"Jezi, would you quit pissing our time away and move?" Ori cackled.

"Keep your pants on," I muttered, turning and jogging down the hallway.

"Did you leave the tech alive?" Dr. Ravin's voice.

"It's not like he's going to tell them anything they don't already know," I argued. "Where am I going?"

"Hold on," Dr. Ravin's voice tightened. "There's something ahead of you."

"I'm sure there is. It's Lab 1A. Are you sure I can't just take the bloody elevator out of here?"

"Andronicus could reroute you anywhere he wanted," Harry's voice. "Not a fantastic plan."

"You're not a fantastic plan," I grumbled, but knew she was right.

The Lab 1B was empty except for a growling little dog-like creature, and it was chained to the far table. I sprang through and into Lab 1A, where I was greeted by a startled technician with a cup of coffee in one hand. He flinched back as I ran past him, dousing his white coat and then shrieking some inventive curses after me.

His curses trailed quickly off when I pointed the pistol at his head.

"Let's do this nice and easy," I said, trying to put some of the *zing* that Ori did on her words.

Lab 1A was a BioLab. There were a multitude of cages around me, with small animals that cried out when I burst into the room. One of the technicians, a young girl with a thick braid and round eyes, screamed. I moved the gun to her, holding a finger to where my mouth would be, if I wasn't wearing this hell-suit.

I turned, taking the room in. There were only two doors, the one I had come through, and the elevator. I saw that the lights above it were green, not red, though I suspected Harry was right. Andronicus probably wanted me on that. I'd be like a mouse in the cat's paws.

"I don't see a vent," I said to them.

"You wouldn't," Harry's voice. "You're over the docking bay. The vents are in the walls, used to filter the exhaust back out of the mountain."

"So then if I can't take the elevator..." I trailed off.

"That's what we had you get the mines for," Dr. Ravin said. "Do you see the creature?"

Along one wall, there was a long, bright aquarium with some kind of spiny fish, its huge eyes glistening as it looked at the world beyond the glass. I turned. The techs were huddled against the far wall, the woman holding a small, furry spider in the bowl of her hands. I frowned at it, suddenly certain she intended to throw it at me.

"I don't see it," I said.

"He has to be there," Dr. Ravin argued. "We checked the schematics *exhaustively.*"

"I'll say," Ori muttered. "Try beating it out of the techs."

"It wouldn't be a spider, would it?" I asked, moving closer to the woman, who tucked the arachnid closer to her chest.

"I sincerely hope not," Harry said.

"You there," I boomed, pointing at the woman. "I'm looking for a—" I hesitated "—What's it called again?"

"You're looking for Fitz," Dr. Ravin groaned.

"Yes, well maybe they—like me— don't know what a bloody *Fitz* is, Ravin," Harry snapped, and I thought I heard a *slap.*

The doctor began swearing, and their argument filled my headset.

"Guys, I'm kind of on the clock here," I muttered, glancing at the elevator.

"Tell them you're looking for the— broadcast my voice," the Doctor said, suddenly excited.

"Why—"

"Just do it!"

I looked away from the techs to glower at my forearm, poking a series of commands that looked like they could— conceivably—have the desired result. A moment later, and the Doctor's voice filled the room. And I hadn't been wrong—she was now speaking of-then Russian.

When she fell silent, the two technicians stared at me blankly. Then, there was a shimmer in the woman's hands. She yelped as the spider leapt from her, flying toward me with startling dexterity. I flinched as it landed on my shoulder. But now, instead of being a spider, it was a small, furry creature with oversized ears and a tiny, pointed snout.

"Awww," I said, gently brushing back the little guy's ears. "You didn't tell me that he was cute."

"Enough chit chat," Ravin snapped, suddenly all business. "Put him in containment and get moving. The elevator is on its way."

I quickly pulled a round, glass-like ball from my bag, opening it and allowing Fitz to leap in, his long, furry tail twining comfortably around himself. I sealed it, then replaced him in my bag.

I went to the fish tank, pulling another device free. This one was black and spiny, and when I placed it against the wall beneath the tank, it shot several darts back into the wall.

"You should probably get away from it," Ori said.

I hurried back, turning and dropping to a crouch. The techs screamed and took off down the hallway. I waited one breath. Two.

BOOM.

The wall exploded. The fish's tank shattered, water spraying out into the room, and rock and dust peppered my metal back. Even through my helm, my ears were ringing. I waited a second, and then, I pushed myself off of the floor and ran to the wall.

"It's a really small hole," I informed Dr. Ravin.

The fish's tank had been laid into the wall, weakening the structural integrity. Even so, I'd managed to blast a hole less than half a meter wide in the thinner part of the wall directly under the tank. Waves of heat and smoke began to roll out of it, my monitors warning me of the rising toxicity in the room.

The elevator dinged.

I dropped to a knee, throwing my hands out, binding the doors together. They shuddered, fighting me. I could feel my heart throbbing in my chest. The doors were forced slightly farther apart.

Through the crack, I saw a single, blue eye.

Panic, crisp and clear as fire, flared through me. I snarled, struggling to keep the doors bound as I turned back to the tiny hole and tried to make it bigger, ripping and digging at the rock wall with my metal fingers. Sweat dampened my torso, stuck to my chest. I felt sick, not knowing if that was Eve, or the simple stress of my situation.

I'd managed to make a hole slightly smaller than my shoulders before my Will snapped and the elevator doors flew open. I swore, throwing myself in the toxic, make-shift vent. The force of my push allowed me to thrust one arm and my head through.

But then, I was stuck.

I swore again, louder this time, and reached out, toward a metal grate I could see some ten meters below me. With only my fear and my instincts to guide me, I bound the grate to the metal of my shoulder.

With a horrible *shriek* of metal on rock, I shot through the hole and down.

This fall was shorter, and I was moving faster. I hit the grate like an avalanche. It was laid into the ceiling. Between my feet, I could see the docking bay, vehicles moving under me, tiny, soft little bodies shuffling to-and-fro. I spotted a bright yellow shuttle. It had a skinny woman with her black hair tied into a bun in the passenger seat.

"Where are you?" Harry's voice. She stood outside of the vehicle, leaning against the door with her arms folded.

"On top of you," I said, running my fingers along the edges of the grate. "This is reinforced. I don't know if I can get through this way."

"Why don't you just Magic your way out, like you did with those nerds and save us the suspense?" Ori asked. Her mouth sounded full.

"If I do, it's going to make a scene," I warned. "Are you ready to get out of here?"

"Every second you waste is one more Andronicus has to realize why you're going to the docking bay," Harry said, looking up. I saw her eyes flash as they swung over me.

"Right," I breathed, searching the ground.

There was a transport lumbering toward the exit.

"Right," I repeated.

I focused binding the metal beneath my feet to the transport. Or, at least, tried to. Nothing happened.

"What are you waiting for," Dr. Ravin hissed. I thought I could hear shouting somewhere below me.

"Don't yell at me," I replied, the sound of my own breathing deafening within the helm.

"That wasn't yelling," she said, her voice like a teakettle about to burst. "If you don't get down here soon, I'll *show* you yelling."

Another sound from above me. I glanced up. A shadow fell across the vent's opening, blocking white light.

My eyes snapped back to the transport, terror boiling inside of me. I focused on a smaller piece of the ship, locking it to the grate.

To be honest, I don't know what happened next. There was a roar around me. The metal beneath my boots began to tremble. The transport continued inexorably on, the metal bar I'd bound the grate to bowing backwards. And then, there was fire.

I screamed as the tube around me belched flame. Heat monitors flared around my eyes, blocking some of my view as I looked up. I couldn't see Eve. She would be standing back from the vent, away from the heat.

I howled. The metal bar snapped clean off of the transport and came rocketing back up toward me. It hit my grate so hard, I thought that it might snap straight through and skewer me. I dropped my bond a moment later and the bar fell, spearing a small Ridger that was about to take off.

Eve was burning the exhaust from the docking bay. It was superheating my little tube, blistering the walls around me. I started reading the text flashing on the sides of my view, and I knew I was close to *melting*.

But if my armor was almost melting, the grate couldn't be faring any better.

I bound the metal of my cage to Harry's hovercraft.

"Punch it!" I screamed at her. "Fly!"

"Fly where?" She shouted back her eyes wide when she saw my fiery prison. She turned and leapt into the hovercraft.

"ANYWHERE!"

Harry flipped two switches and threw the craft in reverse. My ties instantly snagged, and she was brought to a stop, her engines groaning, the metal beneath me shrieking. I ducked my head lower, closer to the cooler air below, and grabbed the little orb that contained Fitz—my bag had long since disintegrated.

"COME ON!" I screamed at her.

Harry threw another lever and the engines went into overdrive. The machine started swinging back and forth, pulling against seemingly nothing. The metal beneath me was turning bright red, and my armor's warning lights suddenly shorted out.

There was a sound like no inanimate thing should capable of making. The grate gave way, showering red metal and rock on the world beneath me. I fell, my screen going black, all except for the narrow band of glass that was the natural viewfinder.

Through it, I watched the docking bay turn once. Twice. And then, I hit the stone floor and I didn't see anything at all.

23

CROWNED

I had always known that Brute was involved, of course.

My first day in captivity, I'd managed to pilfer a data pad from an unobservant tech. Three hours later, and I'd rerouted my signal to *Redwing*, using the data stream that Firebird had set up for us before we started our mission. She had assumed some—if not all—of us would be taken captive.

So, on the very same day, I'd contacted Firebird and been told that Brute was missing. Laurensen and Harry said that she had gone north, to where she would have better signal for her transmissions. We all had assumed that she had been taken captive.

In that, we had been wrong.

It made sense, looking back. The sudden loss of our communicators when we were in the Chryse, the way she'd acted while we prepped for our mission into Olympus Mons. In my heart, I'd known that there was something wrong. But, as with most things our hearts tell us, I hadn't listened until it was too late.

* * *

My eyes snapped open, and I was gasping. My screens were black. I was on my side, staring at chaos through a narrow band in my borrowed helmet. There was fire—but then, there always is. There were people running, hovercrafts shooting at each other. I thought, even through the confines of my dead helm, that I could hear the screams.

I shoved myself upright, still cradling Fitz against my chest. I looked down at him, bumping my head against the glass of his containment field. Within, he had his long tail wrapped around himself, his large black eyes fixed to me with concern. But the false Grav-Field of his shelter had protected him from the fall. I exhaled.

Without the assist online, I could barely move within the armor. Setting Fitz in my lap, I began to disrobe, pulling the helm off first, then each glove. A battle raged around me, but I controlled my breathing and calmly unfastened each of the latches within my suit, relieved despite the danger when I was able to peel the hot, sticky, Olympian Tech from my body.

"JEZI!"

I turned at my name, surprising myself with my calm. I briefly considered that I might have a concussion, but the thought drifted as I spotted Ori.

She hit an Olympian soldier with the butt of her rifle, sending him flying and twisting to me. Her black armor flickered *red* in the flames around us. She shouted my name again, her voice amplified through her helm, and I was briefly aware of how small and *squishable* I was, sitting with half of my armor removed in the middle of the docking bay.

Shaking my head, I set Fitz aside and began working down my legs, undoing each clamp, peeling each bit of armor from my black leggings underneath. The reinforced joints had been a good idea, though it took twice as long to manually remove them. By the time I was clear, Ori had managed to battle her way to my side.

"What's happening?" I asked, somewhat too carefree.

Ori glanced at me, the black glass of her helm catching some hovercraft's headlights.

"You crazy or something?" she asked.

"Maybe," I said elusively, scooping Fitz up from the ground and tucking him under an arm. "Where is everyone?"

"Apparently when you've got a hovercraft in overdrive and the 'brake' suddenly lets off," she jerked her chin toward the far wall, where the smashed, yellow hovercraft was currently sending up pillars of black smoke, "*even the best pilots can't avoid destruction.*"

She finished in a poor imitation of Harry's accent.

"Well I've got Ravin's thing," I hoisted Fitz up, so that Ori could see him. "Can we go now?"

"We're in the process of commandeering a new ship," Ori pointed with her rifle, indicating where I saw Harry exchanging fire with a bulky looking pilot in a black vessel. She hesitated. "Is that seriously all there is to Fitz?"

"Right?" I turned his little ball, watching as his tiny paws slid against the glass. "I'd thought he'd at least be a lizard."

"A lizard? What?"

"I suppose he did transform from a spider a few...minutes? Ago? How long have we been here?"

Ori stared at me for a second. Then she grabbed my shoulder and shoved me into a crouch beside her as a Ridger—with one jet failing—went spinning over us. It crashed into the wall beside our hovercraft, blasting my unprotected face with heat.

"Too long," she said. "Andronicus apparently doesn't want you skipping off into the purple sunset."

"Lying bastard," I muttered, tucking Fitz under my arm.

"Where's Brute?" Ori asked.

I flinched, glancing at Ori.

"You said you had her!" She shouted at me, grabbing my arm and dragging me away from the center of the docking bay. "I *knew* this was too fast. What happened? Where is she?"

"Ori..." I trailed off, blinking back the sudden tears. Maybe I did have a concussion.

"What is it?" Harry—having won her standoff with the other pilot—turned to us, dropping into a crouch beside Ori.

"She doesn't have Brute!" Ori snarled, raising her rifle and blasting a charging Olympian with fire.

"What?" Harry's eyes darkened.

She had her green armor on, the soft shades charred from her recent crash, but her helm was missing. A gash above her right eye had blood fanning down her cheek. It was the most intimidating I'd ever seen her look.

"She did it, Harry," I groaned, ducking as another ship went up in flames, the Ridger colliding with an evacuating Razor. "She *came to him.* He promised that he would help her be a real Martian, get her out of that drone. She betrayed us."

Harry stared at me, her mouth thinning. Ori, on the other hand, sprang to her feet and charged a pair of Olympians, ducking under the first blow and skewering the second with the jagged knife on the end of her rifle. I swallowed, my throat thick with smoke.

"You're sure?" Harry asked.

"I'm sure," I said.

The pilot searched my eyes. Finally, she nodded.

"Then we should get ready."

Harry stood, keeping her free hand on my head, forcing me low. She raised her pistol and shot the last Olympian fighting Ori, making the black-armored woman turn to her.

"We'll get the ship ready," Harry shouted. "Grab Ravin and let's run!"

Ori nodded, sprinting off in the direction of a heap of scrap metal, the abused sides of a hovercraft that had been in for repairs. A second later, and she'd hauled the unarmored doctor from her hiding place, half carrying her as she sprinted back toward us.

Harry grabbed my arm and heaved me into her stolen hovercraft. I tucked Fitz carefully down between my feet, wedged as tightly as I could beneath Harry's front seat. The doctor, despite being bodily thrown into the seat beside me, seemed the least disheveled of the group, her bun so severe, it had pulled her eyes to an angle. She looked at me from behind round spectacles—that I had never seen her wear before—and she smiled.

"Good to see you, Jezi."

I frowned at her, wondering if Harry had drugged her. With a breath, I reached down and pulled Fitz up, meaning to hand him to her. She didn't give me the chance.

"OH!" She exclaimed, practically springing across my lap in her hurry to collect the little creature.

Dr. Ravin cradled the clear ball to her chest, Fitz scampering in tight circles, his little black nose quivering as he strained to get closer to her. I gaped at her, hardly recognizing the cold, distant woman I'd come to know as our doctor. Harry threw the hovercraft into gear, the shielded top coming online as she engaged the engine.

"I wish these rusted things had guns," Ori growled, her own rifle still smoking as she propped it against a metal thigh.

"They're fast," Harry assured her. "And have the best armor rating for a craft of this size."

She punched a couple of levers and the craft swiveled, making something uncomfortable tug behind my navel. Around us, a set of soldiers opened fire. The bullets sparked and flashed against the vessel's shields, and I watched as a series of bars on Harry's control panel began to drain.

"Why are we still here, then?" I asked, trying to keep the fear from my voice. Slowly, my head was beginning to clear.

"Firebird and Laurensen are still in the labs," Harry said, heaving the levers and whipping us sideways, taking the legs out from under several soldiers.

"She's *here*?" my shriek was far too loud in the confines of the craft. "I told you to keep her away from here! Are you crazy?!"

Harry gave me a flat look in the rearview mirror, her face pale beneath the streaks of blood. There was an uncomfortable silence while my heart raced, hammering my ribs as the realization sank in. *The greatest game is succeeding at several different branches of a larger one*, Andronicus's voice echoed in my mind.

"That's what he wanted," I whimpered, dropping back against my seat. "I told you to keep her from this place."

"You ever try to tell Firebird what she can and cannot do?" Ori snapped, her voice fragile under the shield of anger. I saw something in the whites of her eyes, something as she twisted around to look at me. And, if I didn't know her better, I'd have said it was *fear*.

"We can't wait much longer," Harry muttered, her eyes dropping to the shield monitors, which were almost completely drained. Even with her maneuvers, the majority of the ammunition was finding its mark.

"There!" Dr. Ravin shouted, pointing out her window.

Two figures came sprinting into the docking bay. Firebird was on the left, her dark armor seeming dull and battered. Laurensen—free of armor—had her black handkerchief pulled up over the lower half of her face, a pistol held to the side as she ran with our commander. She raised the weapon and shot one of the soldiers firing at us without even breaking stride.

"Finally," Harry breathed, twisting our craft around.

She had barely started forward when she began to scream.

It was a scream like nothing that should ever come from a human being, a scream that slipped straight past a person's hearing and into a soul. Her hands jerked away from the controls and clamped against her skull, like she was trying to keep something from hitting her. And, as I watched in horror, I saw tendrils of smoke begin to rise from her hair.

I knew what I was looking for. And so, I was the first one to spot the woman in a long black coat, her green hair matted with sweat. She moved toward us, one hand extended toward our craft. I looked back at Harry, saw her face twist in agony, watched as her extremities began to char.

Without thinking, I threw myself between the front two seats and slapped my palm against the shield monitor. It disengaged the mechanics and released, the ceiling blinking out of existence. I sprang from the hovercraft, stumbling a little as I hit the floor running.

I didn't have a weapon, but the world around me was a shrieking chaos of twisting, broken metal. There were bullets on the floor, empty cartridges and dropped reloads alike, and I scooped one up as I ran. Extending my hand, I bound the cartridge to our hovercraft behind me.

It shot from my palm with a velocity that left a deep gouge in my own flesh. My aim was off. It caught the edge of Eve's coat before rocketing harmlessly into the wall behind her. But it had been enough.

The PyroMage dropped her hand, her black gaze shifting to me, her focus breaking and then reforming. I felt the heat in the pit of my stomach, like a sickness taking hold, but she was too late. Instead of using my magic, I hit her with my own body and we went down in a tangle of black cloth.

Eve was a soldier. I—well, despite my change in venue, I was a writer. She caught my arms as we fell and twisted, landing with me beneath her. She punched me in my short ribs before I had a second to grab a breath and I nearly vomited over myself. I wrenched one of my wrists free of her, but her second punch took me across my jaw and stars *popped.*

She wore no metal, she'd learned her lesson. But from the corner of my eye, I could see a ship, broken and bleeding fuel onto the floor. I bound it to something I couldn't see on my opposite side, a metal I *smelled.*

The ship didn't move. Instead, my discarded helmet came flying from the other side, hitting Eve in her ribs with a force that made bones audibly *crack.* She gasped, dropping my wrists, and I took the opportunity to twist out from under her, giving her a punch as I did so. It was clumsy and had little force behind it, but still. She hit the floor on her back, grasping her side where my helmet had hit her.

I released my bind on the helmet and turned back to where I'd last seen Firebird.

She and Laurensen had been split up. The assassin was behind her, taking down a soldier with a couple of shots. She dropped to her knee, twisted, and shot a third one as he ran up behind her, something like a saber raised and intended for her unguarded back. Instead, he fell with a bullet hole neatly carved through his forehead.

Firebird was almost to Harry's stolen hovercraft. Our pilot was unconscious, her head lolled to the side as Ori struggled to pull her from her chair, accidentally punching one of the controls as she did so and making the craft spin crazily. It nearly hit Firebird and she leapt backwards, catching sight of me as she did so.

Her head tilted to the side, looking past me. The narrow band of her visor caught a reflection of fire.

She jerked suddenly, like she'd been shot. She took a step back, gauntleted hand going to her side. Something bright and metallic was stuck there, about the size of a baseball. A green light flickered to life in its center.

The second one came flying past my head like a bullet, almost too fast to see. It hit her in the chest and Firebird went down, hitting the round on her back hard enough that her armor left a dent in the concrete floor. I screamed, scrambling to my feet, a third capsule nearly punching a hole in my chest as it zipped past me toward Firebird.

I turned and found myself facing a monster.

24

EMPEROR

His armor was an empty kind of black, dull and lifeless as the vacuum between stars.

He hovered a half meter from the ground, his already tall figure looming over me. Pale, razor-like plates flexed up from his shoulders, almost like wings if wings were made from knives. His helm was without a visor, made from that void-like metal, and it had been crafted to look like the head of a monster, its maw red and smiling. His gauntlets were also black, though there was a strange aura around his fingers. I could see the band of the watch popped up around his right wrist.

"Andronicus," I whispered.

A pair of metal arcs swiveled slowly around him, like they were fastened on an invisible, rotating circle. They were made from that same black material, with the pale, silvery capsules fastened to their outer edges. They were slightly longer than he was tall. When I looked at him, the arcs spun faster, blurring as they whirled around him.

"Jezi," he answered, his voice a baritone that resonated within my own chest.

A capsule shot free. I tried to push against it, but the first thing that I thought to bind it to was Andronicus himself. Instead of finding the metal of his armor, my focus was connected to the spinning arcs and it was like...*nothing.* I felt nothing, pushed against nothing, like in an airlock when I couldn't reach the far side. It was like he was a void.

The capsule whipped past my head and hit Firebird, even as she tried to stand. It bowled her over, making her twist and hit the ground facedown. The next capsule took her in her back.

"Leave her alone!" I howled, binding a fallen, metal container to a ship on the far side of the room.

It leapt away from me, but sailed harmlessly beneath Andronicus. He turned that red maw toward me.

"You should have left your armor on," he admonished.

He said it the way a father would tell his daughter that she shouldn't be outside without a coat on. His concern was real. It made me sick.

"Then you should quit trying to kill us," I snapped, grabbing a fallen pistol, pointing it at his empty eyes.

"I'm not trying to kill you," he said, another capsule flying from the arc. I didn't have to turn to know that it had found its mark.

I fired at his head, three rapid squeezes, but the bullets hit the metal arcs and ricocheted. I didn't see it, but a bright lash of pain split the top of my right ear.

"Careful," he said.

I snarled at him, spinning away and running to Firebird. Toward a far corner of the docking bay, I saw that Ori had finally managed to get Harry out from the pilot's seat and into the back. If I could mobilize Firebird, there was still a chance we could escape.

Her armor was coming apart. I slid to a stop beside her, fumbling desperately as I tried to keep her together, but the joints seemed to be dissolving, smoke curling from the intersecting pieces. She seemed dazed, sitting with her legs out in front of her, staring as her gauntlets began coming apart at the seams.

"Firebird?" I said, catching a piece of her chest plate before it could fall into her lap.

She looked at me, her pupils as small as I'd ever seen them, and blinked.

"What?" she whispered, her voice hollow.

"What are you doing to her?" I twisted back to Andronicus, fury lashing across my tongue.

That red maw smiled back at me.

"Jaimie," Firebird breathed.

I looked again at Firebird, and something very like terror twisted in the pit of my belly. She took my hand, her fingers rough and callused, but her touch was gentle, her eyes wide. A smile touched her thick lips. I felt like sobbing.

"Stop it," I shouted, grabbing Firebird, trying to drag her toward Ori, toward the craft, toward an escape. We had to turn our backs on Andronicus. I lifted her, almost got her standing.

Another capsule came flying off of the spinning arcs. This time, when it collided with her, she had no armor to protect her. It hit her in the back, in between her shoulder blades, and a spasm went through her body like she had just been struck by a lightning bolt. She was flung forward, away from me, and her body froze midair. Firebird's feet dangled a meter from the ground, her back arched and her arms spread, mouth open and eyes staring wide at the ceiling.

The next three capsules came in rapid succession, snapping into place along her spine, glowing green nodules turning slowly red as they buried themselves in the meat of her back. The air around her shimmered with energy, the voice in her throat frozen as surely as water turned to ice.

Panic took over. I stretched one hand toward the capsule and another toward a crashed Razor, binding them without thinking. I felt the strain begin behind my eyes as the metals magnetized, saw the air around Firebird electrify. The capsule started to vibrate, started to twist reluctantly back and forth. And then, with a horrible *pop*, it disengaged and went hurtling through space, toward the Razor.

That was when Firebird screamed.

"Leave her alone!" I shouted at no one in particular, binding the next capsule, watching as the Worlds' most powerful BioMage howled in agony.

Something hit me from behind. It was a sharp blow, not overly forceful but wickedly precise, connecting first between my shoulder blades, and next at the base of my skull. I dropped like a sack of stones.

Ears ringing, I found myself staring at the ceiling. I saw the hole where I'd forced the metal grate open, the crumbling stone around it. I saw how it was blackened and charred from the fire Eve had unleashed.

Blink. My hearing returned with a *pop*, bringing with it a splitting headache.

Blink. I gasped, dragging smoky air into my lungs.

"Firebird," I groaned, rolling to my hands and knees.

Eve was in front of me, standing at a painful angle, holding her side with one leather-gloved hand. She was raising the other, pointing toward a blood-sprayed woman with a handkerchief pulled up over the lower half of her face. She was almost to

Firebird. I saw Laurensen's mismatched eyes widen as she slid to a stop, her pistol raised toward Eve. Pain flashed across her body, a shock as sudden as being unexpectedly plunged into ice water. Or, in this case, a cauldron of fire.

"NO!" I lurched to my feet, meaning to tackle Eve from behind.

Before I could, I saw Laurensen's gaze tighten, her pupils expanding. And the next second, there was a snarl. It built behind my heart, like a lion's roar, and filled the already shrieking room with a feral howl.

An animal exploded from the shadows, a lithe creature with spotted sides and wicked white fangs. It was a leopard, her jeweled collar glinting, and she moved with a speed that would have put her Earth cousin to shame. In the space of a heartbeat, she had crossed the docking bay and collided with Eve, legs wrapping around her to sink black claws into her back, the leopard's head twisting while she clamped her teeth down on the place where Eve's neck met her shoulder.

She didn't have time to scream. There were limbs and blood and a struggle for life. I moved around her, not looking, not wanting to see.

Laurensen stumbled forward, seeming sick, her gaze still dilated. Together, we reached Firebird. There were five capsules against her spine, four of them with red lights and one with a flickering green.

She remained frozen in the air. And a horrible part of me thought she might already be dead.

Before I could bind the capsules, the red ones disengaged, dropping to the floor like discarded scales. They blinked their red lights at me like a riddle too grotesque. The last, I bound to a ship. Firebird's entire body started to move, the binding pulling her with the capsule, but Laurensen and I grabbed her and, with one last exertion of my Will, forced it from her. This time, she did not cry out. Instead, when the capsule was broken from her spine, she simply fell from the air and into Laurensen's arms, her body as limp and pale as a corpse dragged from a river.

Behind me, there was an animal scream, an agonized *yowl*. I glanced over my shoulder to see the leopard as a ball of flame, her body exploding with fire. Eve rolled to the side, her face a mask of blood, her shoulder pumping life onto the concrete floor.

Last, I saw Andronicus.

He hovered toward the back of the battle, watching from within his monster's helm. The arcs around him had slowed to a lazy turn, and all but three of the silver capsules had been used. I could feel him watching me, could sense his dark humor, and I was suddenly uncertain. He planned everything, allowed for every contingency. Why was he not intervening? Why was he letting his soldiers trickle in and die when he had an army just outside, one that could overwhelm us in a heartbeat?

I felt a wash of panic, of disorientation. But Laurensen shouted my name and I broke away from Andronicus's gaze, turning to find Ori's vessel beside us. She was pulling Firebird into the back, her enhanced strength making quick work of it. Laurensen was next, if shaky, and last Ori extended her hand toward me, black metal shining.

I looked over my shoulder, one last time. And, riding a hunch, I reached for one of the capsules. The closest to me was the flickering green one, the one I'd forced from Firebird, and it shot toward us with startling velocity, snapping against the side of our vessel. There was a shout, and immediately Andronicus's arcs began to spin faster, his hovering form tilting toward us.

I let the capsule drop into my hand and took Ori's with my other, letting her bodily heave me into the craft. Before I was seated, we shot off. She wasn't the pilot Harry was, but there isn't much to punching a couple of levers. So, with blinding speed, we shot from the docking bay and into the night.

I twisted around, sitting on my knees and looking out the back window. There, I could see Andronicus. He had stopped in the mouth of the bay, arcs blurring around him, fire and blood at his feet.

25

LOVE

"If not for love, who are we?"

I looked at Jerry, my own question cradled on my tongue, and had no answer worth giving. Instead, I worked the ring from my finger and dropped it beside his, two empty circles in an empty home.

* * *

Fitz sat on Dr. Ravin's shoulder. His ears were about the length of my finger and as wide as my palm where they met with his skull, tapered to fine points with little white hairs. He had actual fur, as opposed to the usual Martian rubber-like hide, and his tiny black nose trembled as he tested the air. His tail was long and a deep, auburn color, wrapped tidily around the Doctor's neck like a furry scarf.

"Is that his natural form?" I asked, nodding toward the little creature.

Dr. Ravin blinked, realizing that she wasn't alone. She was hovering by Firebird's bed, the Doctor's features skeletal in *Redwing*'s medical chamber. I sat in an uncomfortable chair at the end of the bed, my elbows resting on my knees, hands clasped between them. I'd been there for a long time, long enough for my silence to have grown stale on my tongue.

"Fitz doesn't have what you would call a *natural* form," she answered, a hint of a smile touching her lips as she raised a hand for him to snuffle, her long fingers tracing around the base of his ear. "When we first discovered him, we were accelerating chameleon DNA. It took weeks for him to solidify. Though it was in this form, when he did."

"I have to admit, Doctor," I said, offering her a tired smile, "when you named your price for infiltrating Olympus, I really didn't think it would be a pet."

"Fitz is more than a pet," she said. "He's my companion. Besides," and the Doctor tucked her chin, giving the little creature a quick peck on the top of his head, "he's invaluable for further research into amorphous DNA. Shapeshifting is an age-old Earth legend. Perhaps none of us are who we think we are."

While she sounded excited by the prospect, it made something uneasy squirm in the pit of my belly. I stood, stretching tired muscles, and walked to the far side of the room, where the capsule I'd stolen was sitting in one of the Doctor's many experiments. Currently, she had it wired inside a device that looked to me like a microwave. Data was streaming onto a monitor above it, though it was scrolling past too quickly for even my mind to remember.

"What do you think they are?" I asked, not turning.

"I'd guess some form of Suppressor," the Doctor said, confirming my fear. "Although if Andronicus was distressed by your taking one, I am concerned that they may hold...lingering effects."

I turned back to them, my eyes trailing over Firebird's prone form. She was under a white sheet and her normally tan, healthy face was almost equally pale. Her black hair clung lank to her scalp, her mouth slightly open. I would say that she was sleeping, save for the fact her eyes were open wide.

She had been like this since our escape, staring at nothing, saying nothing. The Doctor had several wires coming from her skull, connected to their own monitors, but so far, all that we had managed to conclude was that she was, indeed, alive. I watched her chest rise and fall with the shallow breath of the unconscious.

"When will she recover?"

The Doctor did not look at me. Instead, she fussed with tubes that emerged from Firebird's forearm, running to the IV bottle hanging by her bed.

"I don't know," her voice was almost too soft to distinguish amongst the gentle beeping of her machinery. "If she does, I'm concerned for the...integrity of her mind."

I watched Firebird, her eyes slowly blinking, like someone too tired to focus. She swallowed. She breathed. She *lived*, but there was something missing. I took a step closer, taking her hand in mine, giving it a quick squeeze.

"I need to go," I said, more to Firebird than the Doctor. "Let me know if anything changes."

"The very second," the Doctor agreed. Fitz chirruped, nose trembling, dark eyes wide and searching.

Clenching my jaw, I turned and strode from the room, my heart pushing sluggish blood through my leaden veins. *The integrity of her mind.*

We had returned to one of our camps outside of the Chryse, as far from Olympus Mons as we could get without encroaching on Overlord Shay's domain. Harry was in the cockpit, though the door was closed. There was a definite aura of solitude about the crew. I passed Brute's empty chamber, the door closed and the glass dark. There was the soft hum of the ship, of the life it contained, but otherwise I walked through silence.

It felt wrong, somehow. It was an ending, but not an ending anyone would want to hear, certainly not one I would want to write. Firebird had been broken, Brute had betrayed us, and we had ultimately failed in our mission to "rescue" the PyroMage. Empty, I put my head down, wondering how

I could tell this story. Wondering who would ever want to read it. Wondering if *I* would want to read it.

To my surprise, when I rounded the corner toward my room, I found Laurensen leaning against the wall just outside of it. Her arms were folded, her hair greasy and plastered to her skull from the hat that now dangled from one of her hands. She glanced up when she heard me.

"Any change?" she asked, sounding hoarse.

"None," I answered, slowing to a stop. "How are you feeling?"

Harry had taken two days to recover from Eve's attack. Her fingers were blistered and her voice was raw, but the Doctor had managed to ward off any permanent damage. Laurensen had refused any help. She rarely let the Doctor tend to her, save the occasional bullet wound.

"Tired," she said, pushing herself off of the wall and standing in front of me. She had a habit of looming, of pushing the boundary of people's personal space, but it was yet another thing I'd come to get used to. In fact, now I thought I'd find it odd if she *didn't* intimidate me.

"You should rest," I said, quirking half a smile.

"Planning on it," she said. "Wouldn't be much use to anyone in a fight, right now."

I raised my eyebrows.

"Really?"

"You seem surprised."

"Well, that you'd admit it, maybe..."

Laurensen narrowed her eyes at me and I widened my smile, spreading my hands defensively.

"What can I do for you, then?" I asked.

She stared at me for a moment longer, as though to make sure I wasn't mocking her, then sighed. Reaching to the back of her belt, Laurensen procured a heavy-looking package from one of the belt satchels she used for ammunition. Offering it to me, she said:

"Got something for you, when Firebird and I were in the Holds."

"The Holds?" I frowned, taking the package from her. It was, indeed, heavy, wrapped in a dark green oil cloth.

"Just so happened we were down there when you contacted Ravin for extraction," she said, crossing her arms, staring at the thing in my hands. "Had some unfinished business to attend to. This just happened to catch my eye."

I turned it over in my hands, unwrapping it carefully. When the red metal appeared, I laughed.

"I never thought I'd see her again," I said, hoisting Mule up and squinting down her barrel.

"It's good to have a weapon you're familiar with," Laurensen said, touching the butt of her Widow sniper rifle, which was—as usual—slung across her back. "Tend to get attached to them."

"She's saved my hide more than a few times," I agreed, lowering the weapon and smiling at Laurensen. "Thank you."

Instead of answering, the assassin shifted, frowning at the gun in my hands like a person with something difficult to say. She worked her jaw, chewing on the inside of her cheek, and raised her mismatched eyes to me.

"I like to keep a good weapon with me, always. You never know when you'll be in a fight. Or when," she paused, "a friend might need a hand."

I frowned at her, more confused than before.

"Do you need something? I'll help, if I can?"

Laurensen let out a puff of air, too irritated to be called a sigh. We stared at each other for a moment longer. Then, she slapped a hand down on my shoulder, moving to go around me. As she did, she said softly:

"I don't much know about being in love, don't much care for the irrationality of it."

And she was gone, limping around the corner toward the back of the ship and her chambers. I gaped after her, Mule heavy in my hands.

"What..." I muttered, turning and moving slowly into my chambers.

I'd barely entered my room when it clicked. It felt like my heart jumpstarted, a spike of adrenaline eager for action. I blinked, nearly dropping Mule.

Swearing, I charged forward, knocking over my nightstand in my hurry to reach my closet. I didn't have armor, but I did have one of the "chainmail" suits that we wore under them. I stripped out of my clothes so quickly, I think I ripped my shirt. Stumbling slightly as I struggled into the suit, I leaned one shoulder against the wall for balance, holding the hem in my teeth while pulling the zipper up my chest. It was a little too baggy, proving that Eve's training had indeed managed to slim me down, but there wasn't time to find a better fit.

I threw myself under my bed, tossing things to the side until I found a belt. It wasn't the one I'd worn over Rose, but when I cinched it around my waist, Mule snapped easily into the Grav-Holster. I wished that I had knives and grenades and the plethora of weaponry that the rest of the crew boasted, but it was likely safer for everyone involved if I limited my access to sharp, metal objects—at least until I had a better understanding of my Magic.

I found a pair of leather boots and I tugged them on while hopping toward the other side of my room. There I grabbed a watch-style communicator—in case things went badly—and a half-eaten snack bar, which I stuffed into my face. No point in charging into the mouth of hell on an empty stomach.

Last, I snatched a black hoodie from the floor of the closet, pulling it on and tugging the hood up and around my face. It too had been Maya's—of course—and I was grateful for what little anonymity it offered.

I poked my head out of my room, glanced both ways, then bolted for the door, my footfalls light with the leather boots. I was still chewing when I sprang through the airlock, making an uncomfortable half-swallow when the vacuum sucked at my face. I flew free and into the afternoon, damp forest air whirling around me as I landed outside of *Redwing* in a crouch, my hands sinking into the soft turf.

I paused, breathing deeply. Then, I was off, sprinting through the trees, wondering if I was already too late. I didn't know how to fly a hovercraft, after all, and the Globe-class vessels weren't something I could learn on the spot. Panic was just setting in when I burst out of the underbrush and collided with a fist.

For what felt like the thousandth time since the start of this mission, I saw stars. The world tipped and I was on my back, one leg slung across a fallen tree, the other caught awkwardly under me. Luckily the ground was soft, otherwise I probably would have found yet another concussion. Instead, I blinked up at the forest canopy, panting for breath and more than a little relieved.

Regina glowered down at me, her sword arm held threateningly to the side, blade silvery in the deep, forest light. Her off hand, still balled into a fist, had a smattering of blood sprinkled across it.

I touched my broken lip tenderly with the tip of my tongue, tasting blood, and smiled stupidly up at Regina.

"Hey," I said.

"Rusting skies," she swore, grabbing me by the front of my coat and heaving me upright. "I could have killed you. What are you doing, sneaking up on people like that?"

"I wouldn't call it sneaking," I said, dizzy as I regained my footing. "I'm pretty sure I was sprinting."

"Well, you startled me," she frowned at my smile, which was undoubtedly a bit red. "Are you alright?"

"I'll be fine," I said, dragging my sleeve across my mouth. "I was just worried I'd miss you."

"Miss me?" her frown deepened.

"Before you went to rescue Zander," I said, as though it was the most obvious thing in the world.

The muscles in the sides of Regina's face bulged as she clenched her teeth.

"You're not coming," she said, turning to go.

"If the point is to rescue him, then you'll need some backup," I rationalized, following her. "If the point is to get yourself captured and him killed, then by all means, leave me behind."

"You'd be more hindrance than help," she grunted, slapping her hand down on the data pad of *Galaxy 1*. It went green, the shuttle's roof rotating open.

"Well that's not quite fair," I made a face at her back. "I'm a MetalMage, after all. I could push people around and shoot them and stuff."

Regina paused, one foot already in the shuttle. She twisted, looking over her shoulder at me. Her eyes were an icy blue, and I realized that she was afraid.

"It will be dangerous, Jezi," she said softly. "I don't know if I'll be coming back. I can't ask you to—"

"You didn't ask me to do anything," I said, hoisting myself up the other side of *Galaxy 1*, moving toward the back of the shuttle. "I'm volunteering."

Still, Regina hesitated, one foot on the shuttle, the other on the ground. I sighed, leaning forward.

"You're my friend," I said. It was a simple thing, even ordinary. But in that moment, it changed the world around me. It was the first time I'd said it, the first time I'd really thought it. And, most extraordinary of all, it was true.

She stared at me for a moment. Then, she pulled herself into the shuttle and took a seat by the controls. I'd never seen Regina in the pilot's place before and she seemed comically huge, her shoulders hunched so that she could reach the controls by her knees. A few taps later and the shuttle door had swiveled closed.

"I don't suppose you know how to fly, then?" she asked, engaging the engines.

I gaped at her back.

"Don't you?"

Regina shrugged, poking a few more buttons.

"Of course I do. If Harry does it, how hard can it be?"

And we were vaulted into the air. I squeaked, grabbing the pillows around me helplessly, and Regina quickly stabbed a few more buttons. We rolled once, well over the trees, and then were hurtling forward. Regina swore, dragging the speed back down, and instead we plunged crazily to the side. Another roll and we were hovering a meter over the canopy.

Regina cleared her throat softly. She glanced over her shoulder at me.

"I admit, it's been a while," she said.

We were off again. *Galaxy 1* took out a few branches before Regina managed to pull us skyward. After that, she seemed to find her stride. Though the trip took twice as long as it did with Harry, eventually we made it to the Skyway, where the auto lanes took control.

I felt the bass begin to pulse through the floor, even before the first lights of Biggie's Chryse whirled beneath us. With a slow, steadying breath, I began checking Mule, making sure she was loaded and that I had her ammunition at hand. And, while Regina and I were quickly accelerated toward the Overlord's mansion, I tried not to think of a gap-toothed grin.

Still, the circle of fear that tightened around my heart had a name, and that name was Spider.

* * *

"So, how are we getting in?" I whispered, crouching beside Regina.

We had landed well back from the mansion and picked our way up the hillside on foot, moving in the shadows and avoiding the roadway. I had been unconscious for our approach the last time, and so I hadn't remembered all of the guards or the security net that Biggie engaged along her perimeter. Regina, however, had. And with an efficiency that startled even me, she had managed to work her way to the mansion itself without detection.

"The front rusting door," she growled, her eyes fixed to the gigantic, elegant entrance.

"Ah, yes, well," and I scanned the mansion, feeling small and pathetic before the hulking behemoth, "that's one way."

It was like a medieval Earth castle, with its stonework and towers. But there was a flare of Martian Tech, as well, small ribbons of metal that carried data, blinking red lights that signified lasers and shields. As I crouched beside Regina, I was fighting the pathetic part of me that carried the urge to flee.

"Before we go," Regina said, glancing at me, "there's something that you should know."

"That we'll be tortured and die horribly if we're caught?" I offered, sounding more dismissive of the idea than I actually was.

"That," she agreed grimly. "But also, there's Firebird."

"What about her?" I asked, suddenly subdued.

"If we're successful, if we retrieve Zander, and if she is...alright," Regina hesitated. "She won't be happy with what we're doing."

"Why? We're rescuing your husband," I frowned.

"What we're doing is breaking a contract," Regina's gaze was deadly serious. "To Firebird, that's unforgiveable."

"But it's *Biggie*. She had us tortured, forced Firebird into the mission."

"Doesn't matter. Firebird stakes everything on her reputation, on her code of honor, if you will. If we break that, we're breaking our vow to her as well as our contract."

"You mean that *none* of you have ever broken a contract before? I mean, some of these people are...impossible."

"Ori did, once," Regina looked back to the entrance. "I've never seen Firebird like that. The only reason she's still part of the crew is that it was her only offense. And, if we're being honest, because Firebird needs her. She's the best at what she does. But it was made clear to all of us that if she ever did something to break a contract again...well, being kicked off the crew would be the least of her trouble."

I fidgeted with Mule's holster, my gaze following Regina's to the mansion.

"I guess that explains why I'm sitting here instead of her," I eventually said. "So, in the front door?"

Regina glanced at me, but I avoided her gaze. The truth was, if I hesitated for much longer, I was going to lose my courage.

"Yes," she said.

"Right then."

And I was up and running. Regina shouted something after me, but I'd caught a tendril of adrenaline and by the purple sky, I wasn't going to let it go. Before either of the guards by the front gate could so much as unholster their weapons, I had them bound together by the metal, Unity-style visors they wore. Their heads audibly *cracked* when they flew together. I ignored the blood, sifting through one of their pockets and coming up with a key card. It was surprisingly similar to the ones we'd used in the Holds of Olympus Mons.

Regina came up at my side, still winded, and I nodded at her before waving the card across the lock.

Sometimes, the world just made sense. Something clicked into focus, and it was like I saw things clearly for the first time in years. That was how I felt as Regina and I strode into Biggie's mansion. I had this new, unbridled power. It was raw, it was wild, and I used it with a certainty that I'd never felt before. I bound the first guard by his shoulder plate to the metal lighting overhead, letting him drop back to the floor without ceremony. Regina's silver sword flashed, taking down a pair of startled guards, and I snapped a fourth's neck by binding the side of his visor to the bronze statue behind him.

It was as quick and efficient as a butcher laying out a corpse. And, so far, it was silent. Regina and I charged up the stairs, red carpet soft beneath my leather boots, and burst through the doors that led to a long corridor. Luckily, I had been awake for our departure from this place, and so with a quick cataloging of memory, I had us sprinting back the same route we'd used to leave.

Knowing that every second counted, Regina and I never hesitated. She took out guards even before they saw us. And I...well, I did my best. Some of the men I threw didn't die. Some broke bones, others simply slid against whatever bit of metal I'd managed to spot. Most of them screamed.

When we burst into the throne room, I was relieved to find Biggie where we had left her. Seated in the elevated chair, she seemed more intimidating, taller and stronger than I knew her to be. Still, Regina and I ran the length of that room without pausing for breath. The guard at her side shouted, raising his rifle and firing without warning. I bound the weapon to the light in the ceiling and the bullets went flying crazily. Something hit my side with a *pop* of white-hot pain, but I didn't slow. Instead, I bared my teeth and bound the guard to the other one on the far side of the throne, causing them both to shriek and flip crazily toward each other.

Regina was ahead of me. She leapt over the pair of guards as they flipped into her path and up the stairs to Biggie. The woman had her finger on an alarm and she managed to push it before Regina had her by her throat. She spun around, holding the Overlord out away from the throne and between herself and the room.

All around us, there were lights and whistles and shouts. More quickly than I would have thought possible, the room was flooded, armed guards pouring in through every door. I felt their guns train on me, on Regina, and I raised one hand over my head, the other pressed to my side. I glanced down, saw the blood welling between my fingers. It was hot and sticky, and I felt light headed. But, for some reason, there wasn't that much pain. I drew a sharp breath, steadying myself.

"They open fire," Regina said, holding Biggie by her throat, "and you're going to be just as dead."

Biggie was scratching at Regina's hand, which had nearly encircled her neck. Her feet kicked helplessly as she was lifted into the air.

"All of the guns and tech in the Worlds won't save you," Regina continued, surprisingly calm despite panting for breath. "And I'd gladly die with the knowledge that I took you down with me. But, there's the matter of my husband. My *Zander*," she lowered the Overlord slightly, grabbing the front of her shirt so that less pressure was on her throat.

"He's safe," Biggie choked. "I swear—"

"Then send for him," Regina growled, giving her a shake.

I glanced around myself, counting guns. For a moment, no one moved. Then,

Biggie nodded, one of her hands making a shooing gesture, and a guard with a red cape nearest the throne turned and hurried off, the others moving to make room for her departure.

A guard at my side made a move closer to me and I narrowed my eyes, binding his gun to the fallen guards at Biggie's throne. It was ripped from his hand so abruptly, he screamed. The men around me shifted, anxiously glancing toward Biggie.

"Be still, you fools!" She shrieked.

The ensuing stillness was one of the longer silences I've ever endured. Regina seemed content with scowling at Biggie, but I kept taking inventory on the shifting guards around us, on the likelihood of one of them being a bit too trigger-happy. All that it would take would be one bullet and our little mission would be over.

Finally, a door opened and the red-caped guard returned, a slender, dark haired man in tow. He had rectangular glasses, one of the lenses broken, and a deep, purpling bruise on that side of his jaw. He wore a white, button-down shirt that was stained with blood and dirt. His dark blue pants were dirty and torn and he walked with a limp.

When Regina saw him, her face went ghostly white.

"You said he was unharmed," she snarled, her grip on the Overlord tightening.

"I said," Biggie choked, clawing at Regina's hand, "that he was safe."

Regina bared her teeth, a snarl building in the back of her throat. The guards moved their guns from me to her. I stepped forward.

"Regina," I whispered.

A heartbeat. Then, Regina swore, setting Biggie down and pulling a knife from her belt. She held the Overlord's thick, luxurious braid in one hand and held the knife to her throat with the other, nodding toward Zander.

"You're going to escort us out," she told the Overlord. "The guards stay here. When we're outside, I'm going to let you go. And unless you want me breaking down your door, you're going to forget this ever happened."

Biggie said nothing. Regina couldn't see her expression, but I got the whole blast of it. I felt that same twisting fear deep inside of me, the helplessness I'd felt when Spider tortured me. I knew, beyond a shadow of a doubt, that this woman would be forgetting nothing.

And so, Regina started walking, forcing Biggie along in front of her. She had to crouch to do it, being that she was a whole person taller than Biggie, but she managed. I reached for Zander with my free hand and the red-caped guard gave him a push toward me, making him stumble to his knees. I scowled at her, but hurried to help Zander up, letting go of my side as I did so. Blood ran hot down my ribs, clinging to the inside of my thin armor.

His arms were emaciated, his face gaunt. Whatever Biggie said, this man had not been fed properly in weeks. He was almost too weak to stand and, when he did, he proved to be a good head taller than I was. I took most of his weight across my shoulders and, together, we limped after Regina.

Sweat prickled at my scalp. I expected after every step to be shot. It would have almost been a relief, to stop anticipating the bullet. But the guards kept their distance, held their fire. I struggled to keep up with Regina.

We had to pick our way around the fallen guards. When, at last, we managed to make it outside, Regina turned back to the mansion, Biggie still held in front of her. She scowled at Zander, her gaze sweeping over his beaten form. Slowly, he shook his head.

"No, Gina," he whispered, his voice close to a plea.

The blade at Biggie's throat trembled for a moment. Then, Regina scooped her up and over a shoulder. The Overlord shrieked indignantly, but we collectively ignored her. I could feel the lasers trained on our backs as we started to run back down the hill toward *Galaxy 1*, could feel my heartbeat in the pain of my side.

And so, with slightly less finesse than we had entered with, Regina and I fled Biggie's mansion.

When we reached the shuttle, Regina wasted no time. She threw the Overlord unceremoniously into the alley where we had hidden the shuttle. Slapping her hand against the data pad, Regina glanced back the way we had come. Already, guards were streaming out of the mansion, keeping cautious distance.

The pad went green—much to my relief—and the door whisked open. Regina reached to help Zander, but he was a step quicker. Grabbing Regina's hand, he pulled her toward him, kissing her with a desperation that made the world—if only for a moment—fade away. When they broke apart, he clasped her face between his hands and whispered:

"I knew you'd come."

"Then you're more of a fool than I gave you credit for," she answered, her tender voice betraying her words.

Biggie began to choke, clutching her throat in a bejeweled hand, and one of her dark eyes was fixed on us with a godlike fury. Zander took Regina's arm and let her help him into the shuttle. I glanced over my shoulder, at the search lights that were already beginning to light up the sky, and felt a wave of nausea rake through me. I stumbled sideways and would have fallen if not for Regina.

She caught me around my waist and swept me up and into the shuttle, barely pausing before flipping herself in after me. Clutching my side with one hand, I crawled toward the back, tipping into the pillows when Regina thrust us into the air. Whatever reason I hadn't been in pain before was quickly fleeing. Agony pulsed across my ribs with every breath. I clenched my teeth as the shuttle jolted, Regina hurtling over the buildings, avoiding the Skyway.

Zander crawled to my side, gentle hands pulling my arm out of the way so that he could look at my wound.

"How bad is she?" Regina asked without turning, her voice sounding strained as she concentrated on not killing us all.

"Difficult to say," he answered, surprisingly calm. "Do you have a med kit?"

"Under the left cushion," Regina twisted the shuttle sideways, zipping between a pair of slow-moving transports and then pushing full power toward our base.

Zander moved with quiet certainty, pulling the med kit free and then opening it to reveal a plethora of bandages, syringes, and bottles. He extracted a few, shuffling back to my side. He used a pair of scissors to expose the wound, and I cringed when I saw

416

the neat bullet hole, blood drooling lazily out of the opening.

"Doesn't look critical," he murmured, cocking his head as his fingers prodded at my ribs. "The suit slowed the bullet enough that it didn't cause too much damage. But it's still in there," he glanced at me. "Might need to wait for a more stable environment."

"You're a doctor?" I asked, watching as he filled one of the syringes with clear liquid.

"BioTech Surgeon, actually," he answered, smiling as he gave the syringe a practiced flick. "But they do make us go to medical school, if that's what you mean."

"BioTech," I breathed, looking quickly away before he administered the syringe, the sharp stab making something in the pit of my stomach turn restless.

"Alright?" he asked, noticing as I paled.

"Needles," I said, as though that was more problematic than the fact I had a high-velocity bullet hanging out in my gut.

He nodded, pressing a bandage to my side.

"Hold that there, if you can," he advised.

Already, the pain killer was doing its work. I pressed the bandage tight to my ribs, leaning my head back against the pillows and breathing deeply. Zander shifted closer to Regina, quickly scanning the rearview.

"They don't seem to be following us," he said after a while.

"It won't take long. She'll have them searching for our bases, if she doesn't already know where they are. We've got to get back and move the ship."

Zander chuckled, resting his hand on his wife's shoulder, kissing the back of her neck softly.

"What's funny?" she asked, glancing back at him.

"My dear, you just abducted a Martian Overlord as easily as raiding a pantry," he said, kissing her again. "I love you."

"Well, she's not going to make that mistake again," Regina muttered. "Arrogant bastards never adequately guard the front door. But she's going to have an army out looking for us. We're probably going to have to lay low for a few months, maybe get into Shay's Country. Ditch the Tech."

Zander went deathly still.

"You don't know?" He asked.

"Don't know what?" Regina fumbled with a series of corrections, our ship dipping dramatically before resuming our heading.

"Gina," and he leaned back, his hands going to his lap. "Overlord Shay is dead."

"Dead?" Regina twisted to look at him, her eyes swinging down to me. "When? How?"

"Assassinated," he said. "I thought the Worlds knew by now—it was a couple days ago."

"We've been rather busy," she said. "If Shay's dead, who's controlling the Country?"

Zander hesitated.

"They say she's taken an old Earth name," he began.

"And? What is it?"

He drew a deep breath.

"Sun Tzu."

ACKNOWLEDGEMENTS

I'd like to first thank Adam Holden of adamholdenphotography.com. His expertise and generosity allowed me to have an actual, professional author picture, instead of a grainy selfie of myself and a—while delicious—unnecessary beer.

As always, my undying gratitude goes out to my beta readers.

To Chris, who as a naturalist and my mother, respectively keeps my science and my person honest.

To Matthew, who manages to find even the sneakiest of flaws.

To Taylor, who has professionally edited over 1,089,000 of my words (yes, I keep count).

To Becca, who not only shares my love for Ori, but who inspires her badassery.

To Joseph, who rescued me from several spectacularly horrifying blunders.

And, lastly, I want to thank Don, my father who—while not a beta reader—brightened the light by which I see. Both literally and figuratively.

Without you, these books would not exist. And I likely would have already pole-vaulted into madness.

CPSIA information can be obtained
at www.ICGtesting.com
Printed in the USA
FSHW012326220919
62273FS